ALSO BY GEORGE PACKER

Nonfiction

Last Best Hope: America in Crisis and Renewal
Our Man: Richard Holbrooke and the End of the American Century
The Unwinding: An Inner History of the New America
Interesting Times: Writings from a Turbulent Decade
The Assassins' Gate: America in Iraq
Blood of the Liberals
The Village of Waiting

Fiction

Central Square
The Half Man

Plays

Betrayed

As Editor

All Art Is Propaganda: Critical Essays by George Orwell
Facing Unpleasant Facts: Narrative Essays by George Orwell
The Fight Is for Democracy: Winning the War of Ideas in America and the World

The Emergency

The Emergency

A NOVEL

George Packer

FARRAR, STRAUS AND GIROUX

NEW YORK

Farrar, Straus and Giroux
120 Broadway, New York 10271

EU Representative: Macmillan Publishers Ireland Ltd, 1st Floor, The Liffey Trust Centre, 117–126 Sheriff Street Upper, Dublin 1, DO1 YC43

Copyright © 2025 by George Packer
All rights reserved
Printed in the United States of America
First edition, 2025

Library of Congress Cataloging-in-Publication Data
Names: Packer, George, 1960– author
Title: The emergency : a novel / George Packer.
Description: First edition. | New York : Farrar, Straus and Giroux, 2025.
Identifiers: LCCN 2025026684 | ISBN 9780374614720 hardcover
Subjects: LCGFT: Novels | Fiction
Classification: LCC PS3566.A317 E44 2025 | DDC 813/.54—dc23/
   eng/20250625
LC record available at https://lccn.loc.gov/2025026684

The publisher of this book does not authorize the use or reproduction of any part of this book in any manner for the purpose of training artificial intelligence technologies or systems. The publisher of this book expressly reserves this book from the Text and Data Mining exception in accordance with Article 4(3) of the European Union Digital Single Market Directive 2019/790.

Our books may be purchased in bulk for specialty retail/wholesale, literacy, corporate/premium, educational, and subscription box use. Please contact MacmillanSpecialMarkets@macmillan.com.

www.fsgbooks.com
Follow us on social media at @fsgbooks

10 9 8 7 6 5 4 3 2 1

This is a work of fiction. Names, characters, places, organizations, and incidents either are products of the author's imagination or are used fictitiously. Any resemblance to actual events, places, organizations, or persons, living or dead, is entirely coincidental.

for David Becker

and

Daniel Bergner

with thanks for miles gone and still to come

PART I

1

Looking back, Doctor Rustin realized that the Emergency had been a long time coming. This was how empires of old that he had learned about in school fell: imperceptibly, then shockingly. Even with an enemy army gathering outside the walls, no one can believe that a way of life is about to end or imagine the strange new life that will replace it.

Reports of an impasse at the top of government reached the provinces like word of some far-off, slow-moving threat, an outbreak of a new disease halfway around the world. The standoff dragged on for weeks, paralyzing imperial functions; but even news of street fighting in the capital between mobs armed with nail-studded clubs and iron bars made little impression on Burghers in the city by the river amid the high drama of exams week. Selva, the older Rustin child, was sitting for hers, and the family was much too distracted to notice that the empire was collapsing.

And then, one day in late spring, a week after exam results were announced across the empire, the ruling elite fled the capital. In the city by the river local officials abandoned their posts, police disappeared from the streets, communications across the region went down, and the *Evening Verity* never arrived. It was the start of the Emergency.

That night at dinner, sitting at the head of the table, Doctor Rustin informed his family of the situation. Annabelle gave her husband the satisfaction of bringing the news and pretended that she didn't already know. "We'll go about our normal lives," he said. "These things never last."

"Is there going to be a war?" Pan, their eight-year-old son, asked.

His father laughed. "Are you thinking of enlisting?"

"What if they cancel the next round of exams?" Selva asked. "I've been working so hard."

"You've done so well," Rustin said. "Don't worry, just keep studying."

"Are you sure this won't last, Hugo?" Annabelle asked.

Rustin reached across the table for his wife's slender hand. "Doesn't everything turn out okay for us?"

The next morning, he left for the Imperial College Hospital as usual—not out of personal courage or civic duty, but because he was too rational to imagine all that could go wrong. The streets were nearly empty and the tram wasn't running. The few people he met avoided eye contact, and as Rustin walked along the silent tracks he suddenly understood in his central nervous system that only the threat of consequences from higher authority had allowed him to share a street or tram without fear of violent death. Now anyone could do anything. All that mattered was whether this person approaching intended to kill him.

The director, the chief of personnel, and most of the junior staff were missing, and the hospital was down to a skeleton crew. The two dozen who had shown up gathered in the meeting room—still configured in the old way, with a podium at the front facing rows of chairs. As chief surgeon Rustin was the senior medical officer present, and he stood at the podium and thanked everyone for coming to work amid such uncertainty. He asked for volunteers to take on the basic duties of patient care, admittance, security, and cleaning. He said that he himself would begin the day emptying bed bottles.

His colleagues refused no task, however lowly. They were not acting on orders but of their own free will, out of concern for the good of the hospital, the patients, and one another. Rustin had never felt before that they were his brothers and sisters, but he felt it now. He could almost hear the heartbeat of everyone in the room. The meeting, which lasted just ten minutes, left him transformed. They all went out in a kind of delirium. No one used the word or spelled out the principles, but on that first day of the Emergency the spirit of Together came to the hospital.

The looting started that night. Most of the looters were teenagers, and they went street by street through the Market District shouting, "Our city!" and hurling loose cobblestones at shop windows. They were followed through the shattered glass by big-eyed children and a few stray adults picking over the remaining goods. The city by the river was an orderly, judgmental place where Burghers kept an eye on their neighbors' property and loud noises were discouraged. This wild energy must have been lying there all along, held down by custom and censure, now exploding in the streets.

By the third day most shops had been cleaned out and the looters went searching for other targets. A rowdy group of a dozen headed uphill along the tram tracks, passing the Warehouse District—where they would have had a tough fight on their hands—toward the hospital. It held a commanding view of the city, and through the canteen windows Rustin saw them coming from a quarter mile off. He had expected the looting to stop on the first night, and even when it continued for a second and third day, he never thought it would reach the hospital. He rushed to the main entrance.

The heavy-faced guard in blue overalls had procured an iron rod, but Rustin told him that it would be foolish to use force against the looters. Suzana, his deputy, offered to summon the police, then cut herself short with a dry laugh. There was no way to summon them, and there were no police. It was the director's first day back, and he stood helplessly with his hands stuck deep in the pockets of his white coat. "This is unprecedented," he kept repeating, as if the insight might solve their problem. The title "Director," stitched in red thread on his coat, was so familiar that Rustin had never been aware of its reassuring power until now, when the power was gone.

The looters appeared outside the double doors and banged on the glass and shouted "Our city!" They could have shattered the doors and stormed the lobby, but something kept them back, as if their desire was waning but they didn't know how to stop. A sinewy boy with an intelligent face scarred by acne pushed in front of the others. He squished his open mouth against the crossed rifle and book of the imperial seal that was etched into the glass, and from deep in his throat came a howling noise—a human sound that Rustin had never heard before.

The director opened the doors a few inches. "This is a hospital. You have no right to do this."

"We'll do whatever we fucking want!" The boy, who seemed to be the leader, looked around for support, and shouting rose from the others: "Our city! Freedom!" The director made an ineffectual attempt to close the doors, which only goaded the looters into shoving back. Rustin pushed the director out of the way and opened the doors wide.

Stumbling inside, surprised to find themselves in the lobby, the looters gazed at the instructional signs, the white lights overhead, the long corridors. Rustin addressed the leader.

"What do you want? Medicine?"

"Where is it?"

Standing just behind the leader was a younger boy, maybe fourteen but small for his age, with dirty hair and an injured look on his face. Rustin thought he'd seen him before.

"Were you in Selva Rustin's class this year?"

Startled, the boy half-nodded.

"What's your name?"

The boy glanced at the leader. "Iver."

"Iver, right. You sat next to my daughter."

The leader stepped forward, puckering the corners of his mouth in a sarcastic grin. "Yeah, Iver here tried to diddle your daughter. Where are the fucking pills?"

Rustin took a breath and kept his voice steady. "Tell me what you need."

The leader hesitated, and his grin dissolved. He leaned forward and said in a low voice, "It's my mama."

"Really? What's wrong with her?"

"It hurts here."

The leader tapped his chest. His mother's pains had started just before the Emergency, during exams week. "Was this your year?" Rustin asked, keeping eye contact. He liked to think that one of his talents was staying calm in tense situations. "She must have been anxious for you. We certainly were for Selva. How did you do?"

For an answer the leader snorted derisively. He seemed like the kind of boy who would slack off all year and then cram for a few nights and do well enough to pass.

Rustin persisted: "What's your father's guild?"

"My papa? The Guild of Dickless Assholes. Heard of it?"

"I know a few members." This was meant to be a friendly joke, but the leader's scarred face went a deeper color. "Of course, Selva's headed for medicine. Does that interest you?"

"Fuck medicine! I'm joining the Guild of Excess Burghers."

The term was considered improper, but everyone used it. Rustin realized that these boys would enter no guild. They had failed their exams, their hopes were over. They were newly minted Excess Burghers.

"Iver, too—right, Iver? All of us are. We're taking over the city. *Ex-cess Bur-ghers! Ex-cess Bur-ghers!*"

There was a round of mirthless chanting.

"I can give you something for your mother," Rustin said. "When the streets are safe, bring her in for an examination."

The looters made a show of rifling through closets, but their spirit was spent. On the way out, in a last act of self-assertion, the leader grabbed the guard's iron rod and delivered a blow to the front door's imperial seal that spread a thousand tiny fractures across the glass.

When the looters were gone, the director offered Rustin a grateful smile. Suzana patted his shoulder: "Well done, doctor." He waved them off to conceal his pleasure. He had relied on a belief that all people, young and old, Burghers and Yeomen alike, could be brought to reason if he addressed them with respect—not necessarily as his equal, but as fellow human creatures. He tried to treat his patients this way, train his staff, raise his children. This was his creed, and it had a private name that was too grand to share with anyone but Annabelle: humanism. It had worked with the looters.

In that first week of the Emergency everyone Rustin knew asked the same question: *What can I do?* Doing nothing was inconceivable. Some of his neighbors organized an anti-looting platoon, arming themselves with fireplace pokers and garden tools, and dragging out trash barrels to barricade their street. Annabelle knocked on doors where elderly shut-ins were known to live and took down requests for food and medicine—the demand for pet food was especially heavy—then organized her reading circle into a delivery service. Selva and her school friends went to the Market District with brooms and bags to help sweep up the littered shops. When the schools reopened, Pan brought his collection of dead caterpillars to class in case anyone wanted them, though no one did.

Even with the loss of public services and basic goods, those were magical days, set apart from normal life. Self-reliance and solidarity, opposites in ordinary times, joined together in the vacuum left by the Emergency. No one seemed to mourn the empire much, as if it had been an abstraction, but a fierce attachment to the city by the river stirred the hearts of its Burghers. They didn't wait to be told what to do, for there was no one to tell them. They just moved, and because they did it freely, there was a pinch of heroism in every act, love in every face. Throughout the week Rustin ached with anticipatory nostalgia.

2

For as long as anyone could remember, the empire had been governed by two factions that took turns in power. Though their programs differed, they both enjoyed the legitimacy of the imperial seal. In the marble halls of the capital, political conflicts seemed like death matches for the largest stakes; but in the provinces, including the city by the river, these dramas went barely noticed by the empire's ordinary citizens, its Burghers and Yeomen. Even higher-status Burghers like Doctor Rustin had trouble keeping the factions in the capital straight. Over the years nothing much changed as people went about their lives. The children of Burghers sat for comprehensive exams at age fourteen that placed them on tracks to positions in their family guilds. The children of Yeomen inherited their parents' farmland and artisanal skills. The age-old harmony between Burghers and Yeomen rested on the three pillars of the imperial system, known as Good Development: patriotism, mutual obligation, all in their place.

Perhaps the predictability and comfort of empire contributed to its collapse, bringing on a cognitive decline in the form of thick-brained boredom. Much later, Rustin would try to retrace the warning signs. There were the frequent manias that swept through the imperial ruling elite, such as the obsession with a new cheese produced by Yeomen sheep farmers in the capital region. This cheese, called Venus, soft-ripened in buttery wheels, with a thin blue line of mold and a satiny rind, was so delectable that it soon appeared in every shop window and on the dinner table of every ambitious host. Eating Venus became a competitive activity, driven less by its taste than by the display of wealth—for the price of the cheese soared, though the rain of money never seemed to descend as far as the Yeomen producers. Waistlines in imperial offices widened, and a syndrome called "Venus Goo" left avid eaters sluggish and unmotivated.

The cheese bubble burst one summer week when Venus lost all its prestige. The wheels in shop windows went unsold, and the price dropped by three-quarters, ruining the sheep farmers who had committed a whole season's milk to making Venus. The ruling elite returned to the sober business of running the empire, until the next mania took hold.

And perhaps boredom even led to the Little Border War that broke out the winter before the Emergency. The strange thing was the uncertainty of why it started at all. There was no territorial dispute, no quarrel over fertile land or mineral deposits. There wasn't even an ideological conflict. Good Development created the best possible life within the empire, but this system could never be imposed on other lands where relations between citizens were less friendly and more fraught.

Yet war came. In one of their usual power struggles, the two factions in the capital tried to outdo each other in hurling charges against the empire's western neighbor. One faction accused the neighbor of massing troops in the forests along the border; the other faction raised an alarm that the neighbor was sending hordes of semi-nomadic plains people, called Strangers, across the mountains to infiltrate the capital for some purpose of sabotage. Neither charge could ever be proved (in fact there was no truth to them at all), but the same impulse that had created a frenzy for Venus cheese now drove the empire into an ill-advised, three-week war.

After early battlefield success, overconfidence in the imperial officer corps produced a series of tactical mistakes. A regiment of mostly Yeomen troops was caught in an enemy trap that led to terrible casualties. Whole units dissolved in chaotic retreat or surrendered en masse. The empire was forced to sue for a peace that imposed humiliating payments, and the slump that followed lasted several months. The war became so unpopular that each faction tried to blame the other for starting it.

The Little Border War hardly touched the city by the river. Some Burgher families with special ties to the ruling elite were able to buy their sons out of fighting. As for the Rustins, their two children were under the age of military service. Spring arrived, the school year neared an end, and Selva sat for her exams. Then came the Emergency.

As a boy Rustin had been taught that empires fell after catastrophic events—foreign conquest, earthquake, plague, revolution. The empire in which he had lived all his life died of boredom and loss of faith in itself.

3

After the upheavals of the first week, Rustin waited for everything to settle back into the old ways. But when the anesthesia of the magical time wore off, he became aware of constant discomforts. Life before the Emergency had been relatively frictionless; he often told Annabelle that he could not imagine a better one for himself and their family. But now even small pleasures began to elude him. The cigars that he enjoyed on evening walks by the river with Zeus left dry tobacco flakes clinging to his tongue. The right shoe of his favorite leather pair now squeezed as if the shoe had shrunk or the foot had grown. He associated these petty new irritations with the Emergency.

Every community of the late empire had to find a way to govern itself. It was impossible to know what was happening out in the countryside. Tales reached the city by the river of unspeakably cruel rites with farm animals, of whole villages swallowed up by forest, but it all sounded like nonsense to Rustin. He was certain that Yeomen would fall back on sturdy traditions. As for the city, he expected a group of respected Burghers from his generation to assume control of civic affairs until the establishment of a new regime, or else the restoration of imperial rule with necessary reforms to the system of Good Development. But nothing like that occurred.

Instead, the informal groups of the early days turned into self-organized committees that took over the running of everything in the city, from the transport system to the schools. How these committees got started was something of a mystery. They seemed to be leaderless and open to anyone who wanted to participate, regardless of background, age, or skills. Excess Burghers not only were allowed to take part but assumed important roles. The committees followed the looters' cry of independence and ownership: "Our city!"

"Self-org," as it was soon called, didn't strike Rustin as a durable model. It had the strengths of spontaneity and fluidity, but before long Burghers would want the return of duly constituted authority. He believed in the dignity of all human beings, but he didn't intend to waste his years of expertise emptying bed bottles. Nor did he see why it was necessary to close down every guild club in the city, including the Physicians Social Club. Rustin hardly had time to use his membership, but several evenings a month he stopped by after work to sink into a leather armchair and sip grain whiskey with the director and their senior colleagues. It was important to be seen at the club, since he was regarded as the leading candidate to take over the hospital when the director retired. After two decades in medicine, individual patients no longer held much interest for Rustin—the same injuries and illnesses, even some of the same names—and he turned more and more responsibility over to his deputy. At the club he relished high-level talk about health systems and policies affecting large numbers of people—that, not patient care, would be his future. Also, not every doctor in the city by the river was a member of the Physicians Social Club; it was an honor to be invited.

Suddenly the guild clubs were considered discredited relics of the empire—even a little shameful. A word you began to hear around the city was "irrelevant." First the bankers club shut down, then administration and law, and finally medicine. The windowless stone mausoleum on Gold Street in the Market District was converted to the use of several self-org committees, though just how this happened was one of the mysteries of the Emergency.

As a professional Rustin believed in getting rid of practices that had become medically outmoded, and he intended to reform some of the hospital's systems once he took over as director. So he didn't object when the traditional scrubs that had been color coded by position were discarded, and everyone in the hospital was issued identical yellow tops and purple pants. Still, it was jarring to be called "Hugo" by the junior staff and not "Doctor Rustin." Every time a nurse assistant or surgery resident used his given name in the operating room, his skin prickled, and he had to suppress a rebuke. Suzana—who was cynical about everything—assured him they'd soon forget this new fad and revert out of sheer habit, but she was wrong: first names became standard usage. It was strange how easily people stopped doing what they'd done for years and replaced it with something new that only yesterday would have been unthinkable—as if a world that had always seemed carved from marble turned out to be made of wax.

For example, there was the new language that some of the younger staff began to use. An unfamiliar phrase that Rustin heard in the street or on the tram, such as "mobilize for self-org," would migrate within a few days to the hospital and soon infect the speech of everyone who worked there. Some of the new vocabulary came from within the hospital itself. You weren't supposed to say "nurse" anymore, or "nurse assistant," "orderly," or "housekeeper." The general term for lower-status positions was now "Healing Associate," shortened to "H.A." Also, "patient" became "Healing Recipient," or "H.R." The idea was to get rid of any suggestion of rank and convey a feeling of general improvement. Rustin never learned where this new language originated, and no policy guidance was ever issued—that would have gone against the spirit of self-org. A word simply appeared one day as if it had always been in use, and after that "nurse assistant" would draw a sharp look, like saying something incredibly rude.

Rustin seemed to find it harder than most of his colleagues to adapt. He would catch himself mid-word before rerouting his sentence in the right direction. He tried to draw the line at "Healing Technician"—"H.T."—but soon even "doctor" sounded vaguely offensive.

Rustin never understood where Together came from, or even what exactly it meant. A few weeks into the Emergency the word began to appear on posters glued to the walls of public buildings and on banners strung from lampposts along the central avenues. The signs that went up in the main square were large enough to include each of the six principles. He wondered if Together had somehow been passed by a citywide vote that he'd missed. It soon became as ubiquitous as air.

Together was clearer to Rustin as a passion than a philosophy or program, like the emotion that had briefly come over him in the meeting room at the start of the Emergency. But rather than dissipating, Together's energy pulsed in the streets where everyone spoke louder, made larger gestures, laughed more often, and seemed happier. People chatted with strangers on the tram, something that wasn't done under the empire. Hospital staff now arrived early and worked late, and the canteen was alive with voices instead of the noise of mechanical eating. Teenagers who had failed their exams, and might have ended up drinking on benches in the main square with the older Excess Burghers, became local heroes for their work on self-org committees. Selva heard that her former classmate Iver was active with both Animal Care and Safety. The old imperial system of Good Development had been imposed from above, but Burghers could claim Together as their own creation. The city by the river had always been known for its vanity; this was real pride.

But Together squeezed tight around Rustin's foot and put unwanted words in his mouth and dark pictures in his head. He felt excluded from its happiness—nowhere more than in his own home.

4

Two months into the Emergency, on a summer morning walk with Zeus, Rustin encountered a makeshift shack of rotten plywood and rusted sheet metal. It had gone up overnight in an alley of the Rowhouse District, the neighborhood along the river where the Rustins lived. From inside the shack came the sound of a baby crying and a woman singing a lullaby in a language he didn't recognize. A Stranger family.

In the following days groups of Strangers arrived in the Rowhouse District: single men, with their short, taut bodies and long hair and tattooed faces, trudging on the riverbank carrying burlap sacks over their shoulders; whole families, the older children uncannily quiet, with wide staring eyes and dirty noses, the mothers with braided hair and faces tattooed less prominently than the men's, carrying small children or pulling them by the wrist, scolding, soothing, in a tongue that sounded to Rustin like nasal singing in a minor key. Their bleeding feet and flaxen clothes that appeared to have been devoured by hordes of locusts told the story of the Strangers' two-week journey on foot over the mountains and through Yeoman land to the city by the river. The heads and hands of some of the men and older boys bore angry lacerations that looked to be from a sharp instrument, though Rustin didn't believe the theory that they'd been attacked by Yeoman farmers on the way.

Over the years a few solitary Strangers had appeared in

the city by the river, but never in anything like these numbers. Little was known about them, except that they lived on the plains beyond the mountains where they built seasonal dwellings and grazed their herds. A prolonged drought had driven Strangers into camps along the empire's mountain border. When the Emergency came, and imperial border guards shed their uniforms and abandoned their forts, the camps began to empty out. Small groups of Strangers ventured over the border into the mountains, down through the foothills where Yeoman farmers plowed the land, across the switchgrass plains and along the river that led them to the city. Now they were fanning out across the Rowhouse District, building shelters from material that they scavenged in piles of garbage left uncollected by the irregular service of the self-org Sanitation Committee.

One night at the dinner table, Annabelle announced that in the morning she had cooked a meal of chicken, rice, and beans, and brought it in a covered pot to the family in the alley around the corner. The father had put his hand on his chest and shook his bowed head. Then one of his children—the oldest of three, a girl of about ten—tugged on his sleeve and pointed at the youngest child, a boy not more than three, with a waxen face and bony arms. The father bowed again, and this time he accepted the pot, quickly handing it off to the girl. Then, from somewhere in the looped rags of his clothing, he produced a metal disc, copper-colored and the size of a gold coin, with an engraving of a tobacco leaf. When he offered it to Annabelle, she imitated his gesture of refusal. But the father insisted.

Rustin examined the disc and tried to picture his wife, in her tailored Burgher dress, conversing with this Stranger family outside their shack. Annabelle was fine-boned, with large, luminous eyes in a small face, an anxious mouth, and a manner that refused lavish gestures. She held her body still while her eyes roved around her field of vision as if preparing to ward off some not altogether pleasant surprise. Everyone assumed that she was just shy, but Rustin long since understood her reserve as a determination to be true to herself, to keep her integrity safe from the world's predations. Her encounter with the Strangers amazed him.

"I don't know how they're going to survive here," she said. "But I saw something burning in his eyes." In Annabelle's eyes Rustin saw excitement burning.

"Strangers are the best people," Selva said. "Much better than Burghers and Yeomen."

"How do you know?" her father asked. "You don't speak their language."

"By observing them," Selva said sharply. "Language is just an artificial barrier we've created. Like Mama says, look into their souls."

"Language is what makes us human," Rustin said, but Selva rolled her eyes in a way that warned him not to continue, as she did these days whenever her father upset her sense that she was helping to make the world new.

Strangers had always been too far off and weak to matter in the city by the river. When they began to appear, Rustin noticed that they quickly assumed a place of honor in Together. They were regarded a little like saints or small children, as if their simplicity and pain offered a model of goodness, a promise of renewal. Mutual incomprehension left a blank space in which Burghers could believe that the Stranger way of life had already achieved Together's highest goals. To Rustin they were simply desperate people with immense needs that his wife and daughter and city would never be able to meet without the aid of a functioning empire.

When Annabelle mentioned that she'd heard of neighbors temporarily lodging Strangers, Selva jumped up from her chair. "Let's host Mama's family!" she cried, clapping her hands. "We'll learn so much from them!" Annabelle smiled at Rustin to say, "Why not?" and Pan, who followed his big sister's lead in almost everything, said, "I'll teach the girl magic tricks," and in a giddy rush of goodwill a thing that none of them had ever imagined doing seemed about to happen. So Rustin raised the obvious objections. The house was already too small—now five kids? Where would the family sleep? How long would they stay? What if the Strangers were disgusted by the Rustins' habit of feeding Zeus at the table, allowing him on the furniture, and generally making him an object of worship? And what of the Strangers? They must have unpleasant customs of their own.

He knew that all these practical questions could be worked out. Something deeper troubled him. The Emergency was creating hairline fractures in his family. The Rustins were no longer the tight foursome that played word games at dinner and took family camping trips to a lakeside clearing in the woods a couple of hours outside the city that they called the Place.

Selva no longer returned on the tram after school, but instead she disappeared into the city, attending the daily gathering in the main square called We Are One, staying out for hours. She seemed to have joined a group of slightly older kids who were involved in some form of self-org that would be ruined by the slightest contact with adults.

A colleague at the hospital once told Rustin that he'd noticed Selva at the Suicide Spot. This was a patch of sidewalk in the Market District, in front of a dissolute old tavern called the Sodden Spot, where teenagers in the Mind Committee built a gallows—a real wooden gallows, with a rope noose and a trapdoor. The purpose was to give confused young people a way to free themselves from the time before the Emergency, especially from their parents, and become unconflicted, pure agents of Together. They would climb the ladder to the platform and stand on the joint between the flaps of the trapdoor and drape the noose around their neck. They would tell their story, thoughts focused on the final moment, while two of their peers—specially trained Guardians—stood beside them and, using the message of Together, talked them out of the idea of hanging themselves.

The Suicide Spot instantly became popular. Night and day there was always a line of kids at the ladder, and a crowd of onlookers on the sidewalk below the gallows calling out encouragement, then cheering when the noose was finally removed and the boy or girl climbed down. The job of Guardians was so draining that they rotated in forty-five-minute shifts. To avoid inadvertent hangings the Suicide Spot was never left unattended, not even overnight, and no child had yet been lost.

The colleague had seen Selva one afternoon in a group of Guardians on the platform. But when Rustin asked her about it, she said, "That's confidential."

Selva's secret life left her short-tempered around the house. Her parents'—especially her father's—every remark became a spur to resentment. She rejected any evidence that Together wasn't making the city better and better. If he said, "The tram was bad today," she answered, "Whose fault is that?" and he knew whose fault, for wasn't the generational failure that had produced the Emergency his gift to his children?

A change had come over Annabelle, too. The first days of the Emergency plunged her into a mood where she was unreachable. Rustin once caught her standing in the middle of the kitchen staring into space as if she had forgotten what she was supposed to be doing. When she noticed him watching, she said, "How did I become such a useless person?" and her eyes wandered around the room as if the answer lay in embroidered dishcloths and canisters of grain. She was the least useless person he knew. Every minute of every day was taken with some task—her children, her household, her small group of friends, and her widowed father, who lived in an old people's home near the hospital and whose mind was slipping away. He had served in imperial administration and expected Annabelle to enter his guild at a time when it was still unusual for girls to follow their fathers. Instead, she had met a young surgeon, married, and given up the guild path. Rustin became the family's public face, its connection to the city and empire. Annabelle never suggested that the arrangement suited her any less than him.

After two decades together he took their alignment so much for granted that he thought her sudden remoteness reflected unease with the Emergency. But when he asked, "What is it?" she smiled and shook her head and disappeared into a book or a chore in another room.

The idea of bringing Strangers into this disturbed life was alarming. So Rustin overruled his family: "I don't want Strangers living in our house." Annabelle argued, at first gently, and then with an intensity that surprised him. Not only were they able to shelter Strangers, she said, but they had a duty as Burghers during a crisis in their city. "If we believe in Together, this is something we have to do."

He had never said that he believed in Together, or that

he didn't. He had assumed she shared his feeling that the fever dream passing through their city and their children would dissipate with time, and then the Rustin family would return to its own togetherness. But perhaps he'd been wrong about Annabelle.

He made a show of hearing her out, pursed his lips thoughtfully, nodded once or twice, but didn't yield. Pan grabbed a cooking pot and wooden spoon from the kitchen and marched around the house, banging away, chanting "No one is a Stranger"—which was one of the six principles of Together. As for Selva, she spent the evening mute with rage.

There was something unhealthy about the whole idea, as if Selva wanted to drive a wedge straight into the heart of the family and Annabelle failed to see it. He was right to say no, but they didn't let him forget.

5

The next morning, Annabelle went door to door on their block and enlisted neighbors to collect food and clothes for Strangers in the Rowhouse District. By the end of the day the Rustins' front room had become a storage depot for piles of bags and boxes overflowing with coats, clothes, shoes, toys, and bottles of milk, baskets of fruit, wheels of cheese, and strings of sausage. The work of sorting donations kept Annabelle up past midnight for an entire week. She soon realized that the task of feeding and housing hundreds of Strangers, clothing them, caring for their chronic illnesses and festering wounds and throbbing teeth, entertaining and educating their children, was more than her little group could manage. The task was monumental and had to be coordinated. With a few friends she decided to form a self-org Stranger Committee. She doubted her competence to lead (technically there were no leaders in self-org), but she soon became indispensable.

Annabelle was the one who came up with the idea of hostels. All around the city, offices of the old municipal government sat empty, their occupants having fled to the capital or simply vanished. Why shouldn't those buildings, with their ample, high-ceilinged meeting rooms and functional kitchens, be converted into temporary shelters where Strangers could sleep and eat until they were able to participate in the life of the city?

It was one of those ideas that made perfect sense once

someone thought of it. Annabelle threw herself into the project with an energy that her husband had never seen. She began spending longer hours away from the house than he, and when she came home all she wanted to talk about was her work, every detail of which obsessed her—the cots donated by one of the furniture depots in the Warehouse District, the cooking rotations divided between self-org Burghers and Stranger women who insisted on sharing duties.

One morning—it was late summer, the Emergency was three months old—Rustin came home exhausted from overnight surgery at the hospital. An obscure grievance was bothering him like an itch he couldn't find—wherever he scratched, the itch moved somewhere else. He felt that no one was paying attention to him, though he knew this was untrue and, anyway, an ignoble feeling.

He seldom talked about his patients to Annabelle anymore, but now, to satisfy his need for consolation, he told her the story of his night: a boy about Selva's age had been brought in with bullet wounds. Annabelle looked up from her paperwork, startled. Some Burghers (though not the Rustins) kept a grandfather's hunting rifle or antique pistol locked away in a closet, but gunfire was never heard in the city by the river. He didn't tell her that the boy had come from a Yeoman village, which would have spoiled the effect a little.

"He was in bad shape, but we managed to save him," Rustin said.

"Thank goodness." The tender smile he'd craved rose to her eyes. "But that's frightening."

Encouraged, he continued the story—and this was where it veered away from complete accuracy. He said that during the operation, which had lasted four or five hours, one of the young nurse assistants had left the room without asking permission. She was gone for at least fifteen minutes, an eternity during a critical case, and she returned with no apology or explanation—didn't even look at the chief surgeon, as if they happened to be passengers in the same tram car.

"What did you do?"

"Well, I asked where she'd gone. She said the bathroom. I reminded her to scrub again—which she hadn't."

Annabelle glanced at her inventory records. The story was starting to lose her.

"There were other things, too," Rustin insisted. "It's a bad sign. Things at the hospital are starting to slip."

"A young nurse goes to the bathroom and takes longer than usual? Maybe she was menstruating."

Annoyed, he muttered, "I thought she was unprofessional."

Annabelle looked up and met his eyes. Hers were worryingly cool. "Hugo, not everything is to my liking, either, but I don't want to go back to the way things were. Try to accept. You'll be happier."

She returned to her paperwork. Rustin said nothing more, while the itch flared, intolerable. They'd always had an understanding that she would stroke his hair and take his side whenever he returned wounded from the battlefield. Now she'd broken it.

He watched Together possess his wife. He didn't know if it promised a new way of being human to her as it did to Selva, but it gave an outlet to energies that must have been stifled for years. That he must have stifled. He wondered if some inner dullness, some loss of spark from decades practicing his profession, kept him from feeling what they felt. Why didn't he see Together as a way to move beyond the routine of patient care and imagine a better form of medicine for the whole city? But he knew why: because it refused to grant him the place he had worked for and deserved. He told Annabelle and others and even, at times, himself that he was proud of the Stranger Committee, but something kept getting in the way. The endless intrigues bored him, and when she relayed the latest gossip about Strangers who had become Rustin household names, he wanted to tell her for God's sake to stop. He imagined taking a hammer and smashing each letter in a set of wooden blocks that spelled out TOGETHER.

The Emergency is over, he kept thinking, and he tried to live as if it had never begun. But that turned out to be impossible.

6

One afternoon in early autumn, during the fourth month of the Emergency, Rustin was invited to join the hospital's self-org committee in the meeting room where he'd spoken from the podium on the first day. When he arrived, he was surprised to find the podium gone and the chairs arranged in a circle. A group of his colleagues was already seated, waiting. The circle worried him, and his left eyelid jumped, a tic that had recently developed.

"The last one's for you, Hugo," the director said. Rustin sat down in the empty chair. The room was chilly because of the conservation regime and smelled of disinfectant.

A vestigial instinct made him look around for who was in charge. Officially, no one—that was the meaning of the circle, and why it left him uneasy. But there were always subtle clues and it was important to read them.

At twelve o'clock sat the director. In his late fifties he was a decade older than Rustin, with a patchy beard that failed to conceal his fallen chin, and a satisfied face of professional success. His posture suggested softness, slackness, a leader no longer strung tight for leading. To his left floated the long, domed head and tight, bloodless lips, almost a Burgher caricature, of the chief of personnel, who was watching Rustin with grim anticipation. It was an open secret that this bureaucrat was angling to elbow him out as the next director, and even on a good day Rustin disliked him. On the director's other side sat Suzana, Rustin's deputy surgeon, her skeptical eyes avoiding his.

"Can this really be your first self-org meeting?" the director asked.

"I was at the all-hands right after the Emergency was declared," Rustin said. Skipping self-org meetings had obviously hurt his standing. "It's been pretty busy since then."

"We've missed your presence."

The younger staff were grouped in a tense cluster around three o'clock. These days Rustin was always one of the oldest people in any room. When had that happened? A man of twenty-five or -six was staring at him with unconcealed contempt. He was a resident in medicine—Rustin recognized him from surgery rounds: square glasses, dark beard trimmed to a pointed goatee, neatly shaved jaws that clenched and unclenched with the pressure of some restless, straining energy. His name was Saron, and he fascinated Rustin, even frightened him a little: the shirts that flattered his build, the woody smell of his fragrance, the refusal to ingratiate himself with the hospital's chief surgeon. An image flashed in Rustin's mind: Saron, stripped to the waist, coming at him with a raised fist.

"There's something I want you to understand, Hugo," the director said. "We are not only your colleagues but your friends. We're not here to harm anyone. We're here to repair harm."

The director held out his arms, palms upward, and closed his eyes. Everyone in the circle did the same, with Rustin last. The sound of humming traveled around the circle and arrived at him, and he began to hum with the others.

"*Everyone belongs,*" the director's suave voice intoned over the humming.

"*I am no better and neither are you.*" That was Suzana.

"*No Burghers are Excess Burghers.*" It sounded like the chief of personnel.

"*No one is a Stranger.*"

"*Listen to the young.*"

"*You shall be as gods.*" That might have been Saron.

The humming stopped. Rustin opened his eyes and found himself looking at a girl seated in the youth cluster next to Saron. She was barely out of her teens, with a wide, sensitive mouth and hair tied back in a ponytail. She was one of the nurse assistants—he'd forgotten her name. He wondered what someone from nursing assistance was doing here. The purpose of the meeting, he'd been told, was to discuss the "management" of his surgery team. Her head was turned in his direction, but it was impossible to know where she was looking, for a set of large white goggles was strapped across her upper face, covering everything from the part at the middle of her hairline down to the mole on the bridge of her nose. The eyepieces were made of a hard, dark material that concealed the eyes behind them and reflected whatever they faced. The goggles were a new invention of the Emergency; Rustin had never seen them worn at the hospital.

Posted on the wall behind her was the familiar sign: a purple-and-yellow background, a chain of cutout silhouettes holding hands, and, in a child's stylized scrawl, the single word

TOGETHER

The trouble was going to come from three o'clock.

"Saron, will you guide this Restoration Ring?" the director said.

"I will." The resident lifted his chin toward Rustin. "You've heard of a Restoration Ring, Hugo? Even if you've been too busy to attend meetings?"

Rustin admitted that he hadn't heard of a Restoration Ring.

"It's the only way to deal with disruptions to self-org. If there's been a break in the circle we have to close it before the hospital can do its work."

Rustin was certain that the girl was looking at him from behind her goggles. *Lyra*—that was her name. She was the nurse assistant he'd told Annabelle about.

"Three weeks ago you had a young male Yeoman with multiple gunshot wounds," the resident said, as if he'd memorized the words. "Do you remember, Hugo?"

"Of course."

The boy was fifteen, skinny, almost malnourished, so that the hip bones and coccyx stood out sharply. The bullets had entered through the shoulder and lower back, and parts of the skeleton were blasted into fragments. His parents—anxious, crushed-looking people—had brought him to the hospital from their rural settlement on a grain truck. They'd had a very hard time getting in—something about checkpoints on the road, lengthy searches, disabled trucks blocking the way—and the boy had lost a large amount of blood. The father was polite in the way of a Yeoman dealing with Burghers in the city, but the mother wailed unceasingly despite her husband's efforts to get her to stop. The shots had been fired during "games"—that was all the father would say.

Rustin caught sight of the boy's face just before it disappeared behind the mask. The expression was uncomplaining and passive, like a wounded animal's, except for the appeal in the wide, glassy eyes: *Don't lose me*. Rustin's patients no longer made much impression on him—he rarely remembered what they looked like—but this boy's face stayed with him, and throughout the surgery he was in the grip of an urgency as if his own happiness depended on the outcome, as if the life in his bloody, gloved hands were his own child's. He couldn't explain this feeling, and he had left it out of the story he told Annabelle, along with the other thing.

The operation stretched from midnight until shortly before dawn. When the patient was finally wheeled into recovery, and Rustin stumbled out into the gray light of morning, he still saw the boy's eyes: *Don't lose me.*

"Fortunately, we were able to save him." But as he described the case he knew that this wasn't what the Restoration Ring wanted to hear.

"Lyra was with you," the resident said, leaning forward, holding Rustin's gaze.

"Yes."

"Do you remember what you said to her?"

The girl in goggles lowered her head.

"She made some mistakes. It's possible I corrected her."

"'Corrected' her?" Saron flexed his jaws. "What kind of word is that?"

As far as Rustin was concerned, she should never have been in the room and wouldn't have if the hospital hadn't lost a third of its staff in the past four months. The first thing he noticed was that she failed to follow the scrubbing protocol, hurrying over her fingers and nails, finishing in a minute when everyone else took at least three. True, some of the younger doctors found the ritual archaic, but to Rustin scrubbing was more than a matter of hygiene—it established the mood and rhythm of the whole operation, like a vestigial notation on a piece of music. Then she failed to gown her chief surgeon, and he had to do it himself. As they stood over the Yeoman boy on the operating table, she offered a number eleven blade when he'd asked for a number fifteen. Once, she handed him the hemostat by the rings, not the clamp, so that he briefly lost his concentration. More seriously, she allowed the gauze to run out in the third hour, costing time when the boy was bleeding heavily.

None of these mistakes was a firing offense (if such a thing still existed). But what made it all intolerable was her manner. She was *familiar*. There was no deference in her tone or body language. She didn't apologize for her mistakes or reply to his corrections, only gave a look that struck him as defiant. Then, in the fifth hour, when he was preparing to sew up the last incision and they were all fading on their feet, she had said—

"Lyra," the resident asked, "do you feel able to be here with the goggles off?"

She lifted her head. Hesitating, she pulled the goggles away from her face and let them settle over her forehead. Rustin expected to be met by that defiant look; but her eyes were shining with what seemed like fear.

—she had said, "Hugo, I think you left a sponge in the incision."

At the sound of his name a red wave of rage had drowned his vision. His blood pressure rose and his hand trembled so that he almost let the hemostat fall to the floor. He felt that a maddening finger was poking him in the side, had been poking there for a long time while he tried to ignore it, and that the only way to make it stop was by plunging the hemostat in the nurse assistant's slender neck.

He forced himself to focus on his patient and saw a bit of blood-soaked sponge lying next to the exposed scapula.

The room was called the operating theater. It was *his* theater—he was its director, and it contained all the drama of life. He had been trained to assume responsibility for everything that happened there. The difference between a good surgeon and a master was self-knowledge, and after two decades he knew everything about his performance, including his weakness: a tendency to be unforgiving, to demand almost as much of everyone else in the room as of himself. If this made him a bit authoritarian, he knew no other way to save a life. But he was not a tyrant like some surgeons. He never abused, he tried not to raise his voice. If someone pointed out a mistake—for he was human—he thanked them. That was part of his creed.

But he had not thanked the nurse assistant. Her offense was unforgivable: she had saved him from a calamity. She had shown that he was wrong about her. The least significant person in his theater, she had undermined him with a few words.

"Can you tell us what Hugo said?" Saron asked gently.

"He said, 'Who do you think is in charge here?' And he said, 'You don't belong in this room.'"

The circle gasped in unison.

"What else did he say?"

"He called me 'child.' He said, 'You're a *child*, Selva.'"

"'Selva'? Hugo called you 'Selva'?"

The nurse assistant nodded. "He must have been confused. I don't know a Selva."

"Anything else?"

"He said, 'Give me any Stranger in a hostel over this child.'"

From the chief of personnel came a disgusted expulsion of air.

"What was his voice like?" the resident asked.

"He was screaming at me."

"What did you do?"

"What could I do? I kept working."

Saron sat back and watched his examination take effect around the circle. Everyone was looking at the culprit, the younger staff in shock, his peers with shades of anger, Saron faintly smiling, barbarous with his own power. Rustin's face was hot, his heart racing. His words had exploded in the room like little bombs. He *had* said all those things (he didn't remember using his daughter's name), had felt justified in saying them, and had quickly forgotten them as the gravity of his surgical error had sunk in. He tried to recall the atmosphere that night, the boy's eyes, the intensity and exhaustion, the finger poking him. He'd called her "child" to keep from killing her.

A week ago, the director had stopped Rustin in the hallway and mentioned a complaint—something about words in the operating theater. Then he patted Rustin on the back: "We're all figuring out this new world." But apparently that had not been the end of it. The director must have come under pressure—first from junior staff led by the resident, Rustin guessed, then the chief of personnel.

He turned to face the nurse assistant, who was staring at her goggles. "I'm sorry, Lyra. I deeply regret what I said to you."

"That's it?" the chief of personnel broke in. "Nothing else to say, Hugo?"

"It was a difficult surgery that night, and she—I—I'm making no excuse. I'm sorry," he said again. "It was wrong of me."

The chief of personnel made a dissatisfied clicking noise in the back of his throat. "I hope I won't offend if I say that the purpose of this Restoration Ring was never to air your code of ethics."

"What else do I have?"

"*What else do you have?*" the resident shouted, a blue artery bulging in his neck. "That's the wrong way to think! Self-org, that's what! It's not about you anymore, Hugo. This city isn't going to get through a collective trauma with your code of ethics. You have Together! Do you even know the principles?"

How could he not? They were scrawled across sidewalks, proclaimed on banners, repeated on the street and the tram, spoken at the hospital, at home, by his wife, by his children. And he believed in them. At the beginning, anyway.

"*Everyone belongs . . .*" In a low monotone Rustin recited the six principles of Together. When he finished, the resident shook his head in wonder.

"You needed thirty seconds in that room to defile every single one of them. You almost had to be trying."

"*Were* you trying?" the chief of personnel asked.

Together was a creation of the young, with their devastating and unanswerable insight: "You're leaving—we're coming." Youth gave Saron his power, and not just physical—moral power. But the bald, humorless chief of personnel was in his late forties like Rustin, and next to Rustin's silver-and-black thicket of hair and long jaw with its easy underslung smile, he looked a decade older, and Rustin wasn't going to take this from him.

"You're a bureaucrat, Stefan. You've never been in that room. Every minute, I have to make eight decisions. Incompetence gets patients killed. Together didn't save that boy. It was years of experience."

He glanced at Suzana for affirmation. She had been silent throughout, the trace of an enigmatic smile on her lips. He had trained her at the Imperial Medical College, hired her at the hospital, promoted her to succeed him as chief surgeon in anticipation of the day when he would take over as director.

If he had a friend here, she was his friend. Over lunch in the canteen they shared war stories and gossip, and from her quietly cutting asides he knew that she could be a tart critic of Together. She pulled off wicked imitations of the sudden fervor of their senior colleagues, the excessive confidence of the junior staff. She scoffed at the disrupted working systems, how patient charts were left unfilled and washrooms began to smell while everyone's time was consumed with meetings and reports on meetings. But she was more careful than he. She always made sure no one was listening.

"*I* was in the room," Suzana said. "It wasn't incompetence that set you off, Hugo. It was lack of respect." Her eyebrows rose as if challenging him to deny it. "She didn't treat you like the great surgeon. And why should she? That's not what saves patients either. Leaving that sponge in could have killed the boy."

"It doesn't matter what 'set me off.' I've apologized."

"But it *does* matter, Hugo," Suzana said, and the resident vigorously nodded. "I know you, and your dignity is still offended. That's going to be a problem for you."

"I'm not here to be diagnosed." Rustin turned to the director. "Are we finished?"

The director shrugged as if to say it wasn't up to him.

"We're not finished," Saron said. "Your 'apology' and 'code of ethics' don't repair the harm you've done to us."

"What the hell do you want from me?"

"You have to change, man! Together has driven you so crazy, you made a medical college mistake!"

"Together has transformed us all in different ways," the chief of personnel said gravely, "but not you, Hugo. Why do you think that is?"

Rustin was about to take things on a course that would

hurt him. He would probably never become director. But they had connected him to a current of fury, and the urge to yowl for justice or revenge flooded his throat. "Because Together is going to get people killed."

"You're mocking us," Saron said. "Mocking Together."

"It was a beautiful idea but it isn't working," Rustin said. "Meat trucks aren't reaching the city. Why are we getting so many trauma patients here? Why is everyone always about to blow a fuse—why am *I*?"

The resident glowered. "We have too many Yeomen in the city."

"So Together doesn't include them?"

Saron flexed his jaws. "Yeomen are incompatible with Together. They don't think like us. They believe in hierarchy, dominance. They think more like you, Hugo."

"How I think is none of your business."

"*Wrong!*" Saron was jiggling a thigh as if he felt an overwhelming impulse to leap out of his chair. "I've watched you in that room. You scrub your nails like you're polishing the family silver. You people hoarded up your status like pigs— now we have to deal with the shitshow you left behind. Sure, Hugo, you're a good Burgher, man of science, but your bones are dried up." He sat back and let out a giggle. "You're irrelevant, old man!"

Rustin was forty-eight. Though his lower back never stopped aching from thousands of hours bent over the operating table, and his sexual appetite was a bit diminished (*Did Saron say "bones" or "balls"?*), he had never thought of himself as old—and irrelevance was an alien concept. But this young man had struck him a blow below the sternum that drove out all the compressed air along with the fury, and Rustin could barely breathe.

The director cleared his throat as if embarrassed by the direction things had taken. "I disagree with Saron. It remains to be seen whether Hugo is able to complete the restoration. We bear you no malice, my friend. This incident could have been easily resolved, but your statements today have not served you well. I'm afraid you've lost the hospital."

Rustin didn't know what this meant, but he wanted to ask: *How do I get it back?*

"If you'd joined self-org from the start, there would be a stronger basis of trust." The director's face was a mask of pained purpose. "I told you we're not here to punish. We have no such power or desire. My advice is a period of reflection—though no one can keep you from coming in tomorrow if you like."

Rustin would have to use the freight entrance to avoid the guard's embarrassment at the front doors. The surgery team would not be waiting in the prep room with expectant looks and his favorite music playing. Suzana would hand him the schedule and turn away before he could begin their roundup. There would be no private jokes that set them off from a clueless world. He realized that these rituals, long since taken for granted, were the heartbeat of his life, and now that they were going to disappear—were already gone—he felt that physical punishment, a kick in the knee from the guard's boot heel, would be better than this expulsion. The pain under his rib cage where Saron had landed a blow hardened into a knot of sadness, and Rustin thought of the boy on the operating table, and then he thought of his daughter.

"I can stay home for a day or two and think things over."

The director laughed gently. "Self-reflection can be a lengthy process."

"What about my patients? My team?"

"They'll manage without you, Hugo. That's something I've had to discover. '*Everyone belongs*' has a corollary: no one is indispensable. Not me, not you."

His voice was soothing; he had always been a reasonable boss. Rustin thought: *They'll come for you, too.*

"You told me Annabelle started a Stranger Committee," the director went on. "Wonderful. Go around with her for a month, see what's happening in our city. Then come back, we'll gather again, and you'll tell us what you learned."

The circle disintegrated. The sun was setting earlier, and no one wanted to be on the street after dark. The director went out with his hand on the chief of personnel's back. The junior staff left as a group, buzzing excitedly around the resident, and Rustin suddenly realized that young Saron, bursting with angry sap, and not the dry, jealous chief of personnel, would be running the hospital, maybe soon. The nurse assistant, forgotten by the others, trailed behind, the goggles back over her eyes. In the doorway she brushed against Rustin—distracted, or hurrying to get home, but he allowed himself to believe that she intended some kind of forgiveness.

In the hallway he felt a tap on his shoulder. "Still friends," Suzana whispered as she glided past. "But we must bend with the times."

7

The tram was crowded and smelled of a sour, end-of-day fatigue. Rustin was wedged at the back of the car, between a window that looked out on darkening streets and a group of teenagers, boys and girls, seventeen or eighteen—a few years older and more confident than Selva—all wearing goggles.

Were the kids looking at him? He couldn't tell. If so, he was a public embarrassment—the source of the unpleasant smell. If not, he was irrelevant. His eyelid jumped. He turned to the window and saw, in the reflection cast by the tram's ceiling light, his faceless head with the outline of his jaw.

A team of self-org inventors introduced the goggles a few weeks into the Emergency, after all public communications had gone down and the region outside the city walls had fallen into darkness and silence. The goggles didn't solve this problem so much as distract from it, for they immersed people in a continuous stream of images that seemed to leave them smiling and optimistic. At first you never saw goggles outdoors, only in the privacy of people's homes and offices, as if it would violate the principles of Together to walk down the street or ride the tram with reflective eyepieces between you and the world. They made the wearer look like a giant, grinning insect, with swollen black eyes and a blank, blind gaze, always at risk of bumping into some object or person.

Rustin never wore them himself—they offended his dignity, as Suzana would have said—except once, when he asked his daughter what the goggles were like, and she took off her set and handed them to him. To his surprise he could see perfectly well through them. Selva explained that the goggles allowed the movement of your pupils to shift the view instantly between the world beyond the eyepieces and whatever vision they had called up. Rustin's eyes flickered from his daughter's face watching his own to images of cell division, and at once he was enveloped in a separate underwater world of such depth, such dazzling colors and vivid shapes, that he was afraid of losing Selva forever. His pupils flickered back to the room. Her mouth was open in a delighted smile. But he longed to be in the other world, to drown in huge, coral-red blobs of mitosis.

"See?" Selva said. "Admit you were wrong."

He returned the goggles to her and never put them on again.

Lately, he'd noticed more and more goggle wearers around the city—most of them young, of course, but others too. He started to keep a mental list of sightings as the number grew week by week: a sign hanger taking a break from stringing Together banners on the lampposts along the river, a pair of middle-aged women in the yellow jumpsuits of the Cleaning Committee sweeping out the gutters of a downtown street, even a bicyclist in the park. The list, which remained his secret, was a piece of data that exposed the gap between what people said, or what they thought they were supposed to think, or even what they believed, and how they truly felt. It became a way to measure happiness under the Emergency. If power in your neighborhood kept going out, or the supply of painkillers in your storeroom ran low, or your teacher stopped coming to class, you could always withdraw into the goggles on your face.

He learned all this from observing Selva, to whom he paid more attention than to anyone else in his life.

The tram rattled downhill from the hospital, past warehouses and traffic circles, across the wide, shop-lined streets at the edge of the Market District, toward the clock tower and then the wooden rowhouses that huddled along the river. In one of them, his family would be going about their evening, awaiting his arrival to sit down for dinner.

The tram jolted to a stop, throwing a large teenage body against him. At the same instant, the lights cut out. Silence followed, broken by groans, curses, nervous laughter. This had been happening almost every evening, and it might take half an hour for the power to come back on and the tram to start moving.

One of the first committees to self-organize had been the Energy Committee, and for months the members had worked feverishly to find new sources of power. Some of their achievements were ingenious. A derelict watermill where the river plunged down a chute of granite boulders was brought back to life and now illuminated the Rowhouse District where Rustin lived. But it was impossible to make up the entire loss of the Imperial Power Authority. Shortages plagued the city, and lately they'd grown worse as Burghers found ways to siphon electricity to their houses using private lines. Everyone knew this rise in theft was the main cause of recent brownouts, though people tried not to say it publicly, for the same reason they didn't talk about uncollected trash piling up: belief had to be sustained.

Rustin leaned against the window. With the tram lights out, he could see shadows moving in the darkened street—a mother holding a child's hand as they scurried across the tracks and disappeared down a side street. The tram had stopped in a neighborhood that was becoming notorious for nighttime break-ins, assaults, and the power outages that made them more likely. He imagined the alarm in the woman's face, the hard grip of her hand on the child's.

No one said what they meant anymore. Falseness reacted instantly with thought, hardening inside people's heads, impossible to break up because they were unaware of it. You told a lie until you forgot it was a lie. This process, he felt, was more effective than anything done by command under the empire, because shame turned out to be stronger than fear. A list of banned words and forbidden ideas posted next to a TOGETHER sign would seem clumsy, harsh, and people might openly flout it. Much better if the ban lived only in the eyes of others.

For example, just now at the hospital they had all been lying to one another, and probably to themselves. If they had told the truth, the director would have said, "This hospital is rotten at the top, the young colleagues despise us, but you've made a problem for me, and I'll be next if I don't get rid of you." The chief of personnel would have said, "Fool, you've handed me the hospital." His deputy surgeon would have said, "Why be such a martyr?" The nurse assistant would have said, "Maybe we were both wrong." And he would have said, "The name is *Doctor Rustin*." Only the resident had said what he thought: "You're irrelevant, old man!"

In the silent tram the teenagers began muttering, a low, atonal chorus repeated like a kind of chant. Rustin imagined he heard "*You've—lost—the—hos—pital. You've—lost—the—hos—pital.*" The voices rose together and filled the car. They were chanting, "*What have you done for us today, what have you done for us.*" The teenagers were exciting themselves into higher and higher spirits, and they began moving as a bloc through the dark car, dim figures in goggles, stomping their feet in time to the chant as passengers tried to move out of their way. A boy in the rear of the group looked like the leader of the looting gang, the one with acne scars. Perhaps he was an important member of some self-org committee. Together had abolished the category of Excess Burghers.

"*What have you done for us today, what have you done for us.*"

The stomping came to a halt.

An old woman's shaky voice: "Raised hens for the school."

"*Together!*" came the cry of the teenagers. They were advancing deeper through the car, stomping, chanting, "*What have you done for us today, what have you done for us.*"

The chant ended, the stomp stopped. A man cleared his throat. "I'm on six self-org committees."

A murmur of laughter rippled through the car.

"*Together!*"

The teenagers made their way to the end of the car, then turned back. The chant and stomp grew louder as they came closer to Rustin. He looked out the window. In the distance, at the top of the hill, he could see the lights of the hospital still burning, casting a yellow glow across the brick façade and the double doors where red letters said EMERGENCY.

"*What have you done for us today, what have you done for us.*"

They were back where they'd started, right in front of him. He continued to stare out the window. He was trying to get away from the feeling that had come over him at the sight of the hospital: that he didn't belong there and never had, that he was a stranger, even to himself. The teenagers, the other passengers, the dark street, the lit-up façade, the city: these were all real. Only he wasn't.

"*What have you done for us today, what have you done for us.*"

They wanted an answer. There was no avoiding it. He turned from the window and faced a battery of goggles.

"I've—" *Done nothing for you. Lost the hospital. Fucked up.* Then the car burst into light and shuddered with the rumble of electric power, the passengers cheered, the teenagers shouted "*Together!*" and the tram jerked into motion, carrying Rustin home.

8

His footstep at the front door set off a scrabble of scratching and whining inside. He paused with his key and listened as Zeus's desperation built. All the way from the riverfront tram stop to his rowhouse, Rustin had been preparing a face of mild contentment that would hide the disgrace stamped on his features. But for Zeus, and Zeus alone, Together didn't exist. He was the same dog as before the Emergency, frantic to greet the same man whose return at this hour every evening made life whole. When Rustin opened the door, Zeus didn't pause to question him with a suspicious sniff but rose on his hind legs and flung himself at his master's face, spinning, tail thumping, careless of his shaved left rib cage with its bandaged sutures where the stick had lashed him. Rustin crouched to Zeus's level and cupped the velvety black ears and held the head still while utter joy thrashed the muscular body. Wet brown eyes gazed into Rustin's with such feeling that Zeus seemed on the verge of saying something. Instead, he jabbed his pointer snout at Rustin's nose and licked it.

As Rustin closed the door, he noticed a tiny hole just above eye level, the diameter of a six-penny nail. It gave him an unsettling jolt, like a portrait from which the face had been wiped out.

During all the years they'd lived here, the nail had held up a piece of red cedar, cut in the shape of a shield and divided into quadrants, each quadrant engraved with an image. In the upper left there was a caduceus—the pair of snakes coiled around a winged staff that symbolized medicine, the family guild—along with his carved initials, *HR*; to its right, a medallion with the crossed rifle and book of the old imperial seal; below the caduceus, the famous clock tower that was a visitor's first view of the city by the river; and below the medallion, the silhouette of a dog in full sprint. At the bottom of the shield, undulating across a carved banner, were the words of his personal motto: HUMAN FIRST.

A coat of arms was handed down through the male line of every Burgher family. Most of the images remained constant for decades—the caduceus was a Rustin fixture going back more than a hundred years—but at least one symbol changed with the choice of each new generation. When the Rustins moved into the rowhouse, and he commissioned a woodworker in the Warehouse District to make a coat of arms for the front door, he chose the dog, with its optimism, its loyalty, its unconditional love, to represent his own family.

By then, Burgher coats of arms were considered old-fashioned, even a little embarrassing. They were still a common sight on doors in the older districts, but it was impossible to mention them without an ironic smile, like a traditional song that sounded comically stilted but people still sang at holidays. Rustin accepted his family's—mostly his daughter's—teasing ("Papa wants to use pig lard for lighting"), and they tempered their mockery because they knew that the shield was not just a display of family pride but also, in a slightly silly way, an embodiment of what bound them together, an emblem of love.

In the early days of the Emergency, coats of arms disappeared from front doors all over the city. No one ordered this to be done, since orders were now noxious and archaic, but a feeling took hold that the symbols belonged to a discredited time—the past. This feeling was stronger than any mandate or vote because, without a procedure or tally, it seemed to be unanimous and threatened a consequence more dire than any punishment for the violation of an order: the disapproval of neighbors, friends, even family members. Who could live with that?

Reluctantly, Rustin took down his coat of arms. As he pulled out the nail, he thought of his father, a small, bearded, laconic man who had died when Hugo was just ten. The piece of red cedar in his hands connected him to that remote figure, and to a history that went back centuries: to its famous personages, its books, its food, its language, legends, prejudices, scandals. Some Burghers made a show of bringing their shields to the main square where a bonfire was burning, and throwing them on top to whoops of delight. Rustin told his family that he had "disposed" of theirs, but he couldn't bring himself to get rid of it. Instead, he buried it at the bottom of a chest in the storage closet, under a pile of moldy medical texts. Now all that remained to remind him of the sober, accomplished, complacent lineage of the Rustins was a nail hole in the front door.

Rowhouses had been fashionable a generation ago, but more prosperous Burghers now considered them cramped and shabby. The Rustin house, like most in the district, was a century old, wood-framed, with wide hemlock floorboards. Every square foot of flooring uttered a distinct cry when stepped on, and Rustin knew them all. The rooms were high-ceilinged and narrow, with door openings out of level and cozy furniture out of date. Tonight the warm smell of beef stew from the kitchen filled the front room.

Upstairs, Pan was singing, or attempting to sing, the

new Together song that the primary schools were teaching. It was a sort of ballad, with a slow, repetitive melody, called "Brave Bella." It told the story of a girl who ventures outside her town's walls to collect mushrooms in the woods, where she meets a bear. The bear warns Bella that a gang of trolls with torches, jealous of the beautiful town and its peaceful, happy people, are planning to storm the gates and burn down a wooden mural that townspeople have just finished painting, an image of the town itself in all its splendor—buildings, streets, parks, people, sky—a mural so grand that the trolls in the woods see it rising above the town walls, and are tormented by it. Bella runs back to alert the adults of the coming raid, but they refuse to believe her—they can't imagine simple-minded trolls doing such a thing. So she gathers her friends, and together the children lock the town's gates just in time to keep the marauders out. Bella has saved the mural, and no one is hurt, not even a troll.

Rustin hated the song. He hated the mix of smugness and suspicion that had set in with the Emergency. But he had learned not to quarrel with his children over the trivia of Together, and tonight he had nowhere to stand. He paused in the entryway and closed his eyes and let his son's high, off-key voice fill his mind with sweetness. Pan didn't know most of the words, so he kept repeating the refrain: "Oh, ho! Brave Bella!"

In the front room Selva was sitting cross-legged on the sofa where she always did her homework. She was wearing a yellowish-gray cotton tunic that hung loose off her shoulders, and yellowish-gray drawstring pants that ballooned around her bare feet. This was the unofficial uniform—as colorless and shapeless and charmless as clothing could be—of Together youth. The design imitated the simple flaxen clothes in which most Strangers arrived in the city. Over her face, extinguishing the glow of her eyes, was a pair of goggles, and for a moment Rustin was back in the circle, stabbed by regret.

After Annabelle had brought a set home, Rustin asked Selva to take them off at least when the family was eating, talking, being together. She refused—"I can see you, I can hear you"—until finally she wore him down and he stopped asking and decided to work around this new barrier between them. Even with her eyes hidden, Rustin could still read her mood, which often determined his own. From the upward tilt of her chin and the muscle strain in her neck, he knew that tonight would be difficult.

"Sel, my love!"

"Hi, Papa." Behind her goggles she was also studying him.

"How was your day?"

"Fine."

"Did you go to school?"

"No. I told you about the teacher."

Selva's teacher lived in a new settlement outside the city walls where young Burghers, just entering lower-status guilds like education, and unable to afford lodging inside the crowded city, bought smaller, cheaper houses. Before the Emergency, no one gave a thought to a settlement that put Burghers within a dozen miles of Yeoman villages. But after the regional guard disbanded, two groups of Yeoman smugglers began fighting to control the traffic of goods on the road to the city that passed through the Burgher settlement. Several days ago, a truckload of timber went up in flames, and there were reports of gunfire in the surrounding woods. The Safety Committee decided to close the North Gate temporarily. The teacher might have found another way to reach the school, but instead she had stopped showing up, and Selva had spent the past few days at home.

"Did you at least go outside?" He knew from her slumped shoulders and dull cheeks that she had been sitting begoggled on the sofa all day. An expulsion of breath registered her displeasure with the question.

"I had Student Committee work. What's so magical about walking out the door?"

"That's where the world is."

"Going outside" had come to stand for all his worries about Selva. First: that she would never get past the attack on Zeus in the park, which was the last night she had left the house and the real reason she had stopped going to school. That she was withdrawing into her goggles as life in the city deteriorated. That she couldn't admit or even see this because, with no new round of exams to look forward to, she had placed all her hope in the promise of Together. That she blamed him for her disappointment, knowing that, whatever his well-meant halftruths, he didn't share her hope. That the breach opened by his failure was a betrayal of the closeness he'd always cherished.

"Papa, just say it."

"Say what?"

She lowered her voice to a melodramatic whisper. "*I don't want to lose you to the goggles.*"

This was so painfully apt that a laugh escaped from the pressure in his chest. "Well, I don't. So take them off and tell me about your day."

The frames left deep grooves across Selva's forehead and cheeks. And here were her eyes: almond-shaped, keenly focused, without an instant of aimlessness. She told her father that a few members of the Student Committee had met today at the Rustin house, and one girl had raised a hypothetical question. If there wasn't enough food in the city to feed everyone, who should get to eat first? Some students said the hungriest should eat first; some said the youngest; some said the Strangers, who had arrived from across the mountains with little or nothing of their own. One boy said everyone should eat less and stop eating meat altogether because the Yeomen were keeping it for themselves. Selva alone said that the first to eat should be those who worked hardest for Together, since the city wouldn't survive without them.

The discussion had excited her, and as her narrative raced on, her eyes widened with simple joy just the way, five or six years ago, she would have told him about catching a carp with the rod he'd made for her, or feeding sheep at a farm near the Place where the family went camping.

"How would you measure it?" he asked when she paused for breath.

"Measure what?"

"Who works hardest for Together. On the tram a man said he belongs to six committees. Should he get to eat first?"

"It's not just about committees. It's how you treat people."

"That's very hard to judge. Who would decide?"

"I don't know! It was just a question someone asked." She glanced down and fiddled with the goggles.

"And it was a good question." He should go into the kitchen and see Annabelle, but something was still unresolved with Selva—and now he felt her slipping away again. "But don't the answers go against Together principles?"

"What do you mean?"

"Except the answer about everyone eating less."

"How does *my* answer go against the principles?"

"*I am no better and neither are you.*"

She stared at him as the light faded from her eyes.

"Maybe Together makes some people better," he said, and immediately regretted it.

"Those are—" She struggled for the word. "They're *ideals*! You can't expect—" Her face reddened and twisted violently and she burst into tears. "What's wrong with you? What do you hate so much about being a good person? Why do you have to ruin it for me?"

Exactly what Rustin did not want to do he had just done. Until this moment he had not known whether to tell Selva about the Restoration Ring. Now he never would—not Selva, not even Annabelle. His standing was far too shaky. His wife would eventually put it behind them, but even if he waited out his volatile daughter's shock and anger, he risked whatever ties still connected them. She would certainly identify with the nurse assistant. The goggles were already back on her face.

THE FAMILY SAT AROUND THE WALNUT TABLE WITH FOUR BOWLS of stew. Meat had been hard to find for several weeks, after a livestock truck was stopped by unknown men at the last Yeoman village before the South Gate, and the driver led away into the woods. At least that was the story that spread among Burghers in the city by the river—it was impossible to know for sure. Rustin doubted the bit about the driver. It smacked of the hyperbole that infected every mention of the area of darkness where Yeomen lived out there beyond the city's flickering lights. Their familiar, almost quaint old name suddenly inspired grisly fantasies—blood sports at midnight. But why would Yeomen try to starve their Burgher neighbors? Even forgetting the second principle of Good Development—

mutual obligation—which was officially defunct along with the empire, their mutual *dependence* remained real. No one had a good explanation for the incident with the livestock truck, but the Transport Committee announced a temporary ban on Yeoman traffic through the South Gate. A few trucks still got through—security remained chaotic—and Burghers willing to pay a premium could find their favorite cuts of meat on certain days in certain markets. Annabelle, with her excellent connections to various self-org committees, must have heard this morning where to buy beef for stew.

Pan kept slipping wet hunks of meat to Zeus under the table. Selva, in sacking and goggles, had fallen into a deep well of silence as she chewed.

"Mind if I go to the hostel with you tomorrow?" Rustin asked his wife.

"Don't you have work?"

"I've been given the rest of the week off."

She tilted her head in confusion. "Why?"

"Gratitude for my years of devoted service."

"Something happened," Selva broke in. "I can tell. Your eye is doing that thing."

"What thing is my eye doing?"

"What happened, Papa?" Pan asked. "Did somebody die?"

"Nobody died. The hospital thinks I've been working too hard since the Emergency. You'll have to put up with me for a few days."

He suddenly remembered that Annabelle and the director's wife had a mutual friend. The chance that she would learn the truth worried him less than the risk of telling her.

"So can I go with you?"

"But what for?" she asked, still skeptical.

"To see what you're doing."

"Really? You haven't shown the slightest interest in what I'm doing."

"I thought you hated Strangers," Selva said with malice in her smile.

"I never said that. I just didn't think we had room here."

Later, with his hands in sink water as he washed dishes, he asked again.

"You've always been welcome to come." Annabelle searched his face. Hers had the concerned look that Pan called her "rain face." "You seem sad tonight."

"I'm worried about Sel."

In his ears his voice sounded strangled. Annabelle reached and touched his shoulder in the place where Suzana had tapped him on their way out of the meeting room. The feel of his wife's warm hand where the other had left a cold fact increased the pressure in his chest until it was about to spring open, and he had to fight down unshed tears.

"Let her do this her way," Annabelle said. "She'll be living with it longer than us."

9

The hostel, a twenty-minute walk from the Rustin rowhouse, occupied an old, three-story building of sun-faded brick and chipped slate roof tiles that loomed over the river, backing directly onto a water-worn stone wall. Before the Emergency, it had been the regional headquarters of the Imperial Water Authority; the name was still spelled out in bronze letters across the façade. Now, thanks to Annabelle's efforts, the building housed around two hundred Strangers. Though the windows were closed against the cool autumn air, voices inside were audible as Annabelle led Rustin from the riverfront boulevard up the path through a garden of lilac trees to the main doors.

The front hall was two stories high, and the hum of aspiration and need rose to the vaulted ceiling. Across the floor, long tables were set up in a horseshoe, and in front of the tables signboards in the child's crayon writing of Together, on purple-and-yellow backgrounds, said: REGISTRATION, KIDS' SUPPLIES, WOMEN'S SUPPLIES, CLOTHES, HOUSEHOLD, MEDICAL, FOOD, CLASSES AND ACTIVITIES. Strangers—mostly men, a few women with children—pressed against the tables, pointing, gesturing, hands together in prayer or palms out in distress, trying to make themselves understood to young Stranger Committee members, who leaned forward from behind the tables with kind smiles and anxious eyes. No one was shouting; the Strangers spoke and moved as if it would be uncouth and perhaps unwise to attract attention, as if they possessed a sharp sense of both decorum and danger. They weren't all small and wiry as Rustin imagined the Stranger type—some were rather tall, others stocky and pigeon-chested. A few were dressed in the donations of city Burghers, but most still wore the woolen cloaks and flaxen tunics in which they'd made the journey. Under the arch that led to a grand staircase a few Strangers were sleeping on the stone floor, heads resting on burlap sacks—the newest arrivals. The hall smelled of musty clothes and dried sweat and porridge being boiled in another room.

As Rustin followed Annabelle through the crowd, a burst of clapping and cheers rang out from the tables. She drew his attention to the doors behind them. A family of Strangers had just walked in, ragged and dazed.

"We applaud to make them feel more welcome," she said.

"And that works?"

Annabelle frowned. "Irony isn't helpful here."

She was stopped at every step by committee members and Strangers to receive an update or hear out a problem that she tried to solve on the spot. She was in charge, her words crisp and gestures efficient, and he was reminded of the early months of their children's lives, when the family's most important business fell to her and he watched from the sidelines, awed and unimportant. He had often wondered what the true meaning of Together was. Perhaps it was right here, in this overwhelming hall.

"Where do the Strangers live?" he asked.

She leaned toward him. "We've stopped using that name at the hostels. I should have told you."

Even his children, the first Rustins to pick up any new usage, still called them "Strangers." "What are they now?"

"Friends." Her tone warned him against amusement.

"Whose idea was that?"

"Not mine if that's what you're asking. Anyway, they don't call *themselves* 'Strangers.'"

"Did a Stranger complain?"

"Of course not. They have much bigger worries." She tugged him away from the registration table. "It was the younger members."

"Because 'Stranger' is—"

"Unfriendly. Or so they think."

"What do you think?"

"What I think doesn't matter. I think if we keep using a new word, it can become the thing."

Rustin had never heard anyone express this idea. He'd become obsessed with words and phrases because the constant invention of new ones—Therapeutic Recipient, Restoration Ring, Friends—seemed designed to blur out the failures of Together. Every time another old word disappeared, Rustin's heart sank, for it had just gotten harder to talk about something unpleasant but important: the maggoty trash piling up in the park, the frequent brownouts in the Warehouse District, the gunshot victim on his operating table, the unknown people arriving in the city. Together language tried to make everything ugly vanish by fiat, which meant the ugliness would persist—for nothing could be changed if it couldn't be faced, and nothing could be faced if it couldn't be named.

But Annabelle was saying that the opposite was true. A word changed the way people felt, and a better feeling would lead to better action. If you called fat people "pigs," rolls of flesh would gather around their necks, their bellies would sag, their eyes would narrow into greedy slits, and you would avoid them or insult them. But if you called fat people something different—if you called them "bigs"—their bellies would swell with the grandeur of well-fed chieftains, their lavish flesh would seem magnificent, and their presence would honor you. This was how Strangers would become Friends.

"Come on, the families live upstairs," she said. "I want you to meet Mr. Monge."

He couldn't help asking, "A Friend?"

"Yes. A Friend."

On the third floor, children were racing up and down a long hallway, letting out screams of delight and pretend-terror. The hallway was lined with dozens of opposing doors, and behind the doors—most of them open—were small offices that had been converted into dormitory rooms, with cots and bunks pushed up against the walls, and a strong odor of tobacco smoke and soiled rags. Clothes and bedding hung from lines of golden jute, and plates with scraps of food lay scattered on the floors. Rustin caught glimpses of families going about their lives, and quickly looked away. This floor, he sensed, belonged to the Strangers. They seemed more at ease here than in the presence of city people in the main hall or out in the streets.

Annabelle gently knocked on an open door and motioned her husband to enter. A man was sitting alone on an upper bunk, his legs dangling over the side. He climbed stiffly to the floor and made a little bow. "Mrs. Annabelle," he said.

He looked around forty-five, though Strangers often turned out to be a decade younger than Burghers' first guess from the hard work of herding and the heavy smoking of homegrown tobacco. The man was short and sinewy, with the blue dots and dashes of manhood tattooed across his cheekbones. His eyes shone bright as if they harbored a secret.

"Mr. Monge, this is my husband, Doctor Rustin," Annabelle said. "Mr. Monge speaks our language very well. He had a chance to learn at a border school near his family's grazing land."

"*Doctor* Rustin!" Mr. Monge's eyebrows flickered up and he smiled, revealing a row of upper front teeth stained brown. "Very good."

"How are you, Mr. Monge?"

"The pain is in my knees," Mr. Monge said. "Sit, please. Mrs. Annabelle helps me with everything."

Mr. Monge remained standing, and Rustin and Annabelle did the same. "Mr. Monge has registered for job training," she said. "We hope to enroll him in the new program for community gardeners."

"Why not bookkeeping?" Mr. Monge addressed the question to Rustin. "This was my work before."

"Of course!" Annabelle said. "We'll keep that in mind for later. First things first."

"Why not bookkeeping first?"

Again Mr. Monge spoke to Rustin, as if he had already run out of patience with Annabelle.

"I didn't know there were bookkeepers in your land," Rustin said.

"We are not always chasing animals. We have our money and we must count it. We have many things," Mr. Monge added, opening his eyes wider, making the secret more interesting. "Doctor, you have visited our Stranger land?" he asked. "No? Why not? It is very beautiful. We have too many kinds of food. And—I cannot remember the word—sunsets! Everything is beautiful. Sit, please."

Rustin and Annabelle sat on a neatly made bunk, and Mr. Monge sat opposite them. There was no sign that anyone else was lodged in the room.

"Doctor, I cannot offer you to eat. This is a big shame for me. You are my guests today. In our Stranger land where I was a bookkeeper, we always gave too much food to our guests—the lamb, grains, fruits, nuts. Here I have nothing, not even a table!" The bright eyes suddenly filled with tears. "Mrs. Annabelle, I do not feel happy in your city."

"I don't blame you," Rustin said. "No one wants to leave their homeland behind."

Annabelle glanced at him with irritation. "You've only been here a few days, Mr. Monge. I'm working on finding a place for you to live. Then my husband and I would love to be your guests."

"For example, Mrs. Annabelle, I asked you for the goggles," Mr. Monge said, ignoring her hopeful forecast. "I see them on my walks and they are very interesting. But you never give them to me. Why not?"

"As I told you, Mr. Monge, goggles are expensive and hard to find. They're something the city invented for people here because of the Emergency."

"Burghers have the goggles. Why not Strangers?"

"I'm honestly not sure why you would need them."

Rustin cut in. "You say your knees hurt?"

"This is very important, doctor," Mr. Monge said. "They are hurting from my journey."

"And I set up an appointment for you, Mr. Monge," Annabelle said. When she was unhappy, her eyebrows dove sharply down. "I am trying to solve these problems."

"I am very thankful for you, Mrs. Annabelle. But that doctor did not help me. The pain is still in my knees."

"Knees can be stubborn," Rustin said. He was experiencing a perverse sympathy for Mr. Monge—for his tiresome complaints and unreasonable demands, his refusal to accept the new life these well-meaning Burghers were offering. He felt that he knew how to talk to this man better than his wife, who was devoting all her time to Strangers. "Sometimes you have to wait for them to heal."

"You are a doctor. I respect you." Mr. Monge gestured at the window by his bunk, which looked out at an empty courtyard. "But we were hearing that the city by the river is rich. That Burghers can do everything. Now I am here and I see that children lead your city."

For a moment neither Rustin nor Annabelle answered.

"Children?" she said.

"Children sit at your HELP tables, children wear the goggles on your streets, children speak loud things in your square. Children lead your city—but children cannot do anything." The eyes fixed a look of mysterious satisfaction on Rustin. "You have children?"

Rustin nodded. "And I wouldn't trust them with the city."

"I have a boy," Mr. Monge said.

"But you told me you have no family," Annabelle said.

"I have no family *with* me."

"You left them behind when you came here?" Rustin asked.

"If I tell you more, the pain in my knees will go into my head. The boy's mother has died."

"I'm sorry." After a pause: "How old is the boy?"

Mr. Monge thought for a moment. "Perhaps he is thirteen years old."

"Excuse me for asking, but why didn't you bring him with you?"

"I was bringing him."

"I don't understand. Where is he?"

"In the forest!"

Mr. Monge stood up. From a trouser pocket he pulled out a wooden object about eight inches long, shiny and nutmeg-colored. It was a small pipe with a thin, curved stem; its bowl, half full of tobacco, was intricately carved into the face of a bearded old man. He felt around his disheveled bunk and came up with a circular flint, struck it on a metal upright, and held it to the pipe until he was drawing a smoky flame. He paced the few steps between the window wall and door and smoked as he told the story to Rustin, not looking at Annabelle.

On the tenth day of the journey Mr. Monge had been separated from his son, somewhere in wooded hills near a lake that fed the river flowing to the city. The boy had hurt his foot—Mr. Monge did not say how—and was unable to keep up with the others in their group. Mr. Monge had left his son propped against a tree and gone to seek help. After a futile hour Mr. Monge returned and found the boy was no longer there. Soon darkness fell.

"Did you look for him in the morning?"

"Until the next sunset. I was alone, and my situation was very bad with food. I had to follow the river to your city."

"You never told me this," Annabelle said. They'd been talking as if she wasn't there, and Rustin knew that she was wounded.

"Can I tell Mrs. Annabelle that I lost my son?" Behind a cloud of pipe smoke Mr. Monge's eyes were shining. "This is a big shame for me—for any Stranger. Any father."

"You were in the woods?" Rustin asked. "Near a lake?" Mr. Monge nodded. "Did you see any buildings?"

"Yes, but serpents were hiding them."

"Serpents? What do you mean?"

"All the serpents around trees and buildings in those woods."

Rustin had no idea what Mr. Monge meant by serpents.

"Was the lake surrounded by pine trees?" He tried to simulate pine needles growing from his arm. Mr. Monge gave an uncertain nod. "And a tower near it, an old tower built of wooden boards, and a metal water tank on top, shaped like this?" On his palm Rustin traced a cylinder with a conical roof. The nod began to carry conviction. "Did you see a pig farm? A lot of pigs behind a fence, and old farm buildings painted red?"

"I saw the pigs!" Mr. Monge jerked the pipe out of his mouth and thrust it rapidly back and forth to indicate a profusion of pigs. "I did not go near the farm because of Yeomen. They are dangerous."

"Who told you that?"

"My people, in our group."

"A few Yeomen are dangerous," Rustin said. "Most of them are good." He turned to Annabelle. "I think he lost the boy near the Place."

"Most of them?" she asked with uncharacteristic sarcasm.

He didn't want to argue about Yeomen. He turned back to Mr. Monge.

"We used to go camping there. The pig farmers are friends. I think"—Rustin wasn't sure of what he was about to say—"you'll see your son again."

Mr. Monge tucked his pipe in his mouth, straightened his arms at his sides, and bowed.

"DID YOU HAVE TO ENJOY THAT QUITE SO MUCH?" ANNABELLE asked in the hallway.

"What do you mean?"

"You hope things won't work, and that didn't work. Not for me anyway."

"I don't hope things won't work." He thought about mounting a defense—*I just refuse to pretend when they don't*—but Mr. Monge had spoiled her guided tour in front of her husband and left her depressed. "Love, it's hard, what you're doing. They've lost everything. We can't expect them to be grateful."

"I don't expect him to be grateful, but he's never been like that. He was doing it for you—'*doctor.*'" They were descending the staircase into the noisy brew of the main hall. She stopped to face him and her mouth tightened. "Did you come here so you could take it from me?"

"Take it?"

She poked his chest with her index finger. He couldn't remember her ever doing that in their lives. "You never wanted anything to change. You had the hospital—you still do. What did I have? Nothing. Do you understand what this means to me?"

"Annabelle, I've come here to try."

"And why did you tell him that? About his son. The chances are close to zero."

"To give him something. Imagine if Selva was out there, or Pan."

"What you gave him was false hope."

In the hall he lost her. Standing by the table of women's supplies, a little dizzy with Mr. Monge's pipe smoke, the Place in the woods, an injured boy propped against a tree, he heard a voice murmur in his ear: "What are you doing here, doctor?"

He found himself looking upward at the face of an unusually tall, long-necked, serpentine woman. Her mouth was pressed into a sour smile that scrunched up her nose and flattened her eyes. She was a Stranger Committee colleague of Annabelle's, around thirty, her name was Noa, or Noe, she always seemed to disapprove of him—and that was all he knew of her.

"I'm here with my wife." He looked around, but Annabelle had disappeared.

"Why don't you spare your wife and stay home?"

"Stay home?" he said stupidly.

"Come on, doctor. You touched, the girl declined, you humiliated, the hospital gave you the boot."

He started to walk away.

"If I already know, think who else knows. Half the people in this room know."

He didn't try to find Annabelle but left the hostel alone. He avoided the main riverfront boulevard and took a meandering route home, down side streets, through the yards of empty buildings. He was aware of every flicker of a human figure and tried to cross paths with no one he knew and no one he didn't know, but the city was full of faces with eyes. He imagined a group of boys and girls Selva's age following him, laughing, pointing, pinching their noses, calling others to join them—Selva herself.

Soon he forgot to stay alert and became distracted by the struggle to hold on to a specific thought: that he had not touched the nurse assistant. To prove it, he imagined himself walking into the meeting room and encountering the circle of chairs with one empty. He imagined taking his seat and looking at three o'clock where she sat hidden behind her goggles. At that moment a shadow of anxiety had passed over his mind. But not because he had touched her. This meant, must mean, that the serpent woman had put the idea in his head—it had not been there before. But whenever he tried to grasp this certainty, it kept vanishing like a perch that floated in the murky green light one moment and was gone. He went through the proof several times, always with the same successful result, and still he couldn't make himself believe it. The proof was in his own mind, where he might be tricking himself or missing some logical step, because outside the walls of his head, in the main hall of the Stranger hostel, at least a hundred people thought that he had touched the nurse assistant. They wouldn't recognize him by name or face, they had nothing against him personally, yet the immense power of their suspicion bore down on him and crushed his little proof like a matchstick house.

Hadn't he endangered the Yeoman boy without even knowing? If you were the only one who believed yourself innocent, then you were certainly guilty and probably insane. *They can't all be wrong. I must have done something terrible.*

And Annabelle: What if she knew? He ached to have her back.

He was walking through an alley when an upper-story window flew open and a hand tossed out a small bag. It sailed down and landed two steps in front of him and exploded across the cobblestones into a wet mess of torn paper and thick greenish liquid in which lumps of unrecognizable food floated. He just had time to jump back so that only the tips of his leather shoes were splashed. He looked up and saw someone close the window.

He had never set foot in this alley, didn't know anyone in the district, but he spent the rest of the walk home convinced that he was the bag's target, that the mess was a judgment on him, legal punishment.

Or something even worse. For the law's sanction was logical, finite, and, in a sense, contained within a crime, the way a shout contained its echo. Rustin had always understood power as the inescapable weight of the empire—the police patrols, the ancient, oak-paneled courtroom next to the clock tower, the dank masonry prison near the Warehouse District. He never really feared these things, for they were reactions included in an action, and he could avoid them by what he did or didn't do. He disliked the weight of this power but it made sense to him, and if he ever came under its hand he would submit to it like a painful treatment that would restore him to his prior health.

With the Emergency the police patrols had disappeared, the courthouse had closed, and the jail had released its prisoners through some extended process that hadn't much interested him but that sounded like a version of the Restoration Ring. Together principles meant the end of the old system of laws, which had relied on coercion—punishment. What replaced it? This, too, wasn't something Rustin had given much thought, since it didn't touch him as he made his surgery rounds. Now he understood. What replaced the judgment of law was the judgment of colleagues, friends, strangers in the street, his wife's acquaintances, and finally his own family—all except Zeus. The whole population of the city was deputized to render a verdict on him. Unlike the law's verdict this one was personal, even intimate, and therefore truer and more just. It fell on him as a doctor, neighbor, husband, father. It was delivered by the scrunched-up nose of a gossip he barely knew who now had more power over him than any policeman or judge—the power to say *"You're disgusting."* This verdict nullified a talent that he cherished as much as medicine itself: his ability to meet others of all kinds on common ground as fellow human beings.

He would go on living as a Burgher in the city by the river. He might venture out of the house in the early mornings or at dusk to walk Zeus in the park—might even be allowed to return to the hospital. But the verdict would be written on his face, stuck to the sole of his shoe, he would carry it everywhere like a dog that scrapes and drags but can never get rid of the string of shit dangling from its hindquarters.

What everyone else knew him to be he would finally know himself. And the word would become the thing.

10

From the window blinds stripes of light came streaking across his eyes. The sun was high, the bed empty.

Normally he rose before dawn, the first one up. He would dress noiselessly in the gray bedroom while Annabelle tossed and resisted consciousness. He would lay out pastries, fruit, and coffee on the kitchen table, every move watched with keen interest by Zeus, who waited for his cue. Then they would head off to the park in a ritual they both knew by heart, the simplest happiness of the day. For an hour the agenda belonged to Zeus: scour the patch of dirt around the riverfront plane tree, squat by the park's entry gate, trot along the path to the meadow, greet the old man with a cane and his dyspeptic mutt, race—off leash at last—to chase ducks into the willow pond. By the time they returned home, the rest of the family would be stumbling through preparations—brushing hair, scarfing breakfast, frantic search for some vital lost object, gloves or house keys lying in plain sight. With her usual precision Selva would organize the color-coded notebooks in her schoolbag according to the day's classes.

Every morning the same routine—orderly, banal, satisfying. *Human things*, he called them. Now apparently worthless.

Today was Tuesday, he remembered. Annabelle had her citywide self-org meeting, and then her weekly visit to her father at the old people's home. Pan would be at school, but had Selva gone to class? How long had he slept? His limbs felt leaden from lack of use. Demoralized by oversleeping, he searched for something to wear and found a pair of corduroy trousers and a flannel shirt folded on his dresser. Annabelle must have laid them out—weekend clothes, for home repair projects or gardening. But today was a weekday, and he had nothing to do.

It had been a week since he and Annabelle had stumbled onto fraught ground at the hostel. But instead of exploring it, they had retreated into the illusion of harmony by avoiding each other's irritabilities. Every time he imagined telling her about the hospital, he saw her eyebrows knitting downward, a rain face that would be permanent. Before the hostel he might have told her, but not now. So Annabelle and Pan maintained a Rustin presence in the city while he stayed home every day without giving a reason, sharing the house but little else with Selva, who had gone out only two or three times, and never to school, since the incident with Zeus.

That evening she had taken him on his usual walk to the park, where he loved to snuffle through piles of leaves and chase small rodents. The park was a green gem, one hundred acres shaped like a diamond in the heart of the city, a place of ancient civic pride. It was laid out like an artificial wilderness of surprises, with rolling meadows that curved out of sight behind tree lines, winding footpaths that happened on ponds shaded by weeping willows and fed by quiet streams, a place where you could get lost even though the city was always close. Selva was walking on one of the paths—this was how she later told the story—and Zeus was not far ahead, but hidden around a bend. Suddenly he began to bark in a way she'd never heard before, frightened and fierce, as if he'd come across some wild animal. Selva ran toward the noise, and when she rounded the bend a tall figure was standing in the middle of the path.

The sun had set, the last of the light was failing, and she could see only a faceless outline. The figure wore a dark hooded cape and clutched a long stick—she called it a "staff." With a swift motion the figure raised the staff and whipped it across the left side of Zeus's body. The blow fell so hard that it sent Zeus flying off the path into the bushes with a howl of pain. He began whimpering, and Selva ran to him and held him where he lay. It was too dark to see the wound in his black fur, but her hands came away wet.

When she looked up, the hooded figure was gone.

Zeus was lean from exercise but muscular and hard to carry any distance. Selva managed to bear him out of the park, and then, with the help of a woman walking her dog, down to the river. By the time she reached the rowhouse Zeus's blood was all over her tunic and pants. The laceration across his ribs was so deep that, when the family gathered around Zeus on the kitchen floor and Rustin parted the fur, there was a collective gasp, and Selva began to cry, which started Pan crying. Rustin clipped and shaved the fur, then cleansed the wound with boiled salt water and sutured it as well as possible with instruments he had at home, while Zeus lay silently breathing and watched him work with dim, accepting eyes.

Rustin asked Selva if she wanted to report the incident to the Safety Committee. She said that it wouldn't do any good: she hadn't seen the face, and anyway, with Zeus's barking it might have been a case of self-defense.

When the family recalled that terrible night, their talk always went back to Selva's heroism, Zeus's courage, their relief that he was still with them. The hooded figure on the path disappeared—but Rustin knew that his staff had struck such a blow at Selva's cherished Together that she couldn't speak of it. That night began her retreat into home and goggles.

When she was around four, she had once asked him, in all innocence and profundity, "Do mice love other mice?" His answer—that animals remained a mystery to us, that some were no doubt capable of affection, but probably not love in the human sense of wanting another's happiness more than one's own—was met with tears that showed how desperately she'd wanted it to be true of mice. This long-ago disappointment rose up from the forgotten past early in the Emergency, when Selva—who still needed to know her father's view at fourteen as much as she had at four—said to him, "I think people are naturally good, don't you? We just had to get rid of all the social fluff that came with the empire. That's what Together is about." And he had replied, "I think people can be good or bad. A lot depends on what's around them—customs, laws. Is that what you mean by 'social fluff'?" He always tried to stay close to her by being honest, but this answer had made her no happier than the earlier one about mouse love.

The attack on Zeus did not come as a shock to Rustin. In a way he'd expected it. From the day the empire fell, that hooded figure had been lurking in his mind, a shadow on the city, a mad spell released with the wild new energy and hope that made his daughter's world so beautiful and fragile that just one moment at twilight in the park was enough to shatter it.

In the room below him the floor creaked. He recognized Selva's tread. She was moving around with swift, purposeful steps. Then the front door opened and closed.

He went to the window. Between the blinds he saw her gray-clad form walking quickly, head down, goggles strapped on, schoolbag slung over her shoulder, free arm swinging with her stride as she crossed the street toward the riverfront tram stop, hours late for school.

Rustin finished dressing and went downstairs. Zeus, stretched out on the sofa in the front room, gave his tail a flurry of thumps. One thump would have been a simple greeting, but several meant higher hopes, a late walk in the park. Zeus didn't question his master's presence close to noon on a workday. Rustin sat on the edge of the sofa and inspected the wound: a raised pinkish line crisscrossed with sutures on the smooth gray oval of shaved skin, surrounded by black fur. It was healing well; he could take the sutures out. That would give him something to do.

"Later today," he said, scratching Zeus's neck. Rustin suddenly wanted to leave the house. He took his canvas fishing jacket from the coat stand by the front door. Zeus jumped off the sofa and followed. Then, as it dawned on him that he would be left behind, he sat in his good-boy position and his eyes clouded over, as if to say: "What do you have that's more important?"

"I want to be sure she's okay," Rustin explained, but it wasn't true. He knew only that he wanted to follow Selva, and that it was one of those inexplicable impulses to be obeyed.

The morning was overcast and warm for mid-autumn. She was standing alone next to the tracks that ran along the riverfront boulevard. A tram was pulling up, its bell ringing. The sign on the lead car said MARKET DISTRICT. Rustin stopped a hundred feet away. He could have made the tram by running, but he stood still and watched her get on. Along with the impulse to follow was the desire for Selva not to know. He wanted to trail her, not accompany her—yes, to spy on her. Another tram was coming right behind the first.

Years ago, when Annabelle was home sick one day, he had left the hospital early and gone to pick Selva up. On the street outside the schoolyard he waited for the sound of the bell that would release a river of small bodies in plaid through the high double doors, and something made him hide behind a lamppost as he waited. He wanted to see her before she saw him. He wanted to observe the thrill of freedom in those keen almond eyes, memorize her way of running on tiptoe in her school jumper, savor the anticipation of her hitch-skip of surprise at the sight of him, the light that would suffuse her face—to preserve the image of this unknowing little girl and hold it forever.

He knew what this meant: she must never change. And wasn't it wrong to want that? Wasn't it a kind of death wish?

He boarded the second tram and stood behind the motorman, keeping an eye through the window on the other tram just ahead. When it pulled up in the middle of the main square, Selva got off. We Are One took place here, but it was too early, the gathering would happen after school let out, around three. So she'd told him—he'd never seen it himself. The broad expanse of red-brick pavement was sparsely occupied with people who had nothing to do in the middle of the day: old men feeding pigeons, mothers pushing strollers, sunburned Excess Burghers lying on benches in disheveled heaps of clothing. Not the young looters now absorbed in self-orgs, but fixtures of the main square, too old to join Together.

With the same decisively swinging arm Selva crossed the square, a solitary goggled gray figure on a parched plain. She passed under the clock tower and vanished into a side street that was like a tunnel carved through the high limestone wall of one of the buildings that bordered the square.

The Market District, the heart of the old city, was full of blind alleys and twisted lanes in which he could easily lose her. His tram crept across the square. When the folding doors finally opened, Rustin jumped off and, feeling conspicuously like a fool, ran in the direction where his daughter had disappeared. The side street was an arched passage known as Jewelers' Row. She was nowhere to be seen. As he hurried past glittering shop windows he noticed advertisements that had not been there a few months before. *"Tell her Together means forever,"* said one, the words set inside the sparkling circle of a jeweled ring. Selva would have torn it down. She hated anything commercial that exploited Together, especially luxury goods.

Jewelers' Row came out onto a street of cheesemongers and butcher shops. He looked to the right and caught sight of a gray figure two blocks away as it rounded a corner. There was no capturing her now, no indulging the sweet pain of trying to hold on to what could never be held. He just wanted to keep up, but the streets where she led him seemed hardly solid enough to support his steps, the cobblestones were rolling underfoot, cornices came melting off roofs, ham hocks and cheese wheels danced in shop windows, the whole city was turning liquid.

He ran the two blocks and flattened himself against the wall and stuck his head out to see if she might be looking back. But she was gone again, and there was no sign of her in the alley where they sold leather goods. Shoppers were congregating, making it hard to pick anyone out. Rustin broke into an aimless run and reached a broader street of new stores that seemed to lead out of the Market District toward the central avenue and the tram line that went uphill toward the hospital. He stopped to catch his breath. He turned around and went back inside the labyrinth of older lanes. He had lost her.

He was about to retrace his steps to the main square and start looking again when he realized that he was on a street of liquor shops. The cobblestones smelled of red wine and urine. Around the next corner he would see the awning of the Sodden Spot. Rustin hadn't set foot inside since the age of twenty-five, on the night when he celebrated his diploma from the Imperial Medical College, which was also the last occasion on which he'd thrown up from too much grain whiskey. In recent years the tavern's reputation had deteriorated. The Sodden Spot had become notorious for a clientele of Excess Burghers who went there to watch fights or start them.

And on the sidewalk outside stood a gallows.

11

When it came into view, Rustin was struck by its size. The platform rose on six-by-six wooden posts at least twelve feet off the ground, with enough room up top for a small deck party, and the staircase from the sidewalk was a steeply pitched ladder. This gallows was raised to last—built not only by children but for them, since few adults would have the agility and daring to reach the top. Its height and solidity gave the sense of a play structure, the crossbar that loomed above the platform a climbing feature for the truly fearless, and the rope noose perfect for swinging and letting fly if only the gallows had been built over water.

A drop by the neck from twelve feet into midair would not be play. The designers of the Suicide Spot had been impressively serious. Rustin ran his hand over his own neck and forgot his mission.

About thirty people were gathered around the base, spilling from the sidewalk into the street. Most were teenagers skipping school, though there was a scattering of grown-ups and a couple of families with younger children. High up on the platform, two girls in yellowish-gray clothes stood on either side of a boy. He looked a year or two older than Selva, with a wild thicket of hair and a tough face. He was tugging at the rope as if to test its strength, eyes narrowed, lower lip jutting out in a kind of defiance, while the Guardians leaned close and spoke to him in voices so quiet that Rustin, keeping back and half-concealed under the tavern's red awning, couldn't make them out.

In front of him a middle-aged couple was carrying on a conversation—under an umbrella, though it wasn't raining—that made it even harder to hear.

"You didn't have to come," the woman said. "I could have come by myself."

"You were afraid to. 'What if one of them really does it?'" the man said, mimicking her panic.

"I never said that."

"Shh!" Rustin hissed. The Suicide Spot belonged to the young, and he didn't want to be associated with the disrespect of the middle-aged.

The boy's shoulders rose and fell. He looked down to check the position of his feet over the trapdoor, then draped the noose around his neck. A murmur, almost of satisfaction, passed through the audience.

A Guardian placed her hand on the lever connected to the trapdoor. In a voice clear enough to carry over the crowd, she asked: "Do you want to leave this world?"

The boy's face tightened. His eyes twitched in rapid blinks, his lips disappeared as if cold fury were coursing through his body. Then his features crumpled and he exploded in tears. He sobbed openly, without shame, like a little child, his whole body shaking. Several times he tried to master himself, but he couldn't stop.

Keeping a hand on the lever, the Guardian reached with her other and touched the boy's heaving shoulder. "Hey—we're here with you. We're suffering with you. We love you."

The boy buried his face in his hands, and the thick nest of hair trembled as if in a wind, and the sobs, though muffled, grew louder. Sighs of pity rose around the gallows.

"What do you want to say to your parents?" the other Guardian asked.

The boy looked up mid-sob, startled. "My—I—"

"If they were here, what would you say to them?"

He opened his mouth but no words came out, only a stuttering sob.

"This is pointless," the woman under the umbrella said.

"You were the one that wanted to come," the man said.

"Why don't you both leave?" Rustin asked. They turned around to glare, but their talking stopped.

"Mama!" the boy suddenly cried out. "I'm sorry!"

"You have nothing to apologize for," said the Guardian, her hand still gripping the lever.

"Do it!" the boy wailed.

The Guardian didn't move.

"Talk to us," the other Guardian said. "We don't want to lose you."

"Shut up and do it!"

"Talk to your parents. Why are you sorry? *They* should be sorry."

"Mama will be when I do it!"

The Guardian on the lever, who seemed to be leading the session, nodded. "Oh, *Mama* will be sorry. But what about us? You're gone, and we needed you. Do you know what's on the other side of that door?"

The boy looked down at his feet. He shook his head.

"A great big empty hole. When you went through that door, the hole got bigger than you can imagine. That hole is bigger than this city."

The crowd drew in its breath as if the boy was already dangling broken-necked from the noose.

Rustin tried to imagine this girl and boy talking in someone's bedroom, which was where teenagers used to have difficult conversations. Talking in private was supposed to allow you to open up, but maybe it wasn't true. If Rustin and the nurse assistant had sat down together in the director's office instead of the Restoration Ring, maybe she would have been too nervous to speak to him. Maybe it was easier to say everything like this, with a crowd at your feet and a rope around your neck.

"Please just do it," the boy said in a voice strained from sobbing, but softer, losing conviction.

"And we were about to try something that never happened before," the Guardian went on. "We were going to make a new city! Make ourselves new, too! We were young and dumb enough to think we could do it. How can we now without you?"

The boy murmured something Rustin couldn't hear.

"And what about your Better Human? All that work you did. What's going to happen to *him* now that you're gone?"

The woman under the umbrella tugged at the man's coat sleeve. "What did she say? Better what?"

"How the hell do I know?"

Rustin hadn't understood either.

The Guardian went on talking while the boy listened. He began to nod, and after a few more minutes he lifted the noose off his neck. She let go of the lever, and the crowd, as if its team had scored a winning goal, broke out in cheers and applause. Startled, the boy looked down at his new fans. There was no adolescent defiance or child's anguish in his face now. Wide-eyed, grinning, he climbed down the ladder like a boy who never in his life expected to win first prize.

And again the ground was undulating under Rustin's feet, the tavern awning about to collapse on his head, the gallows the only fixed thing in sight. He had seen enough.

As he turned to go, a girl began to mount the scaffold. She wore the same clothes as the Guardians, with a bag slung over her shoulder and goggles dangling from her neck.

Found you! was his first thought, and then: *She's going to replace a Guardian. That's how it works—short shifts.* He watched her come out onto the platform. She carefully removed her goggles and set them down with her bag. She took her place between the two girls and planted her feet apart. Then, with the same decisiveness he'd seen from the moment she left the house, Selva reached for the noose and draped it over her head.

His stomach dropped as the trapdoor opened beneath his own feet, plunging him into a void of air. *No!* He must have said it aloud, because the couple under the umbrella turned on him: *"Shh!"* His neck was tingling, his knees barely held him upright.

"Do you want to leave this world?" the Guardian asked.

No! This time a silent cry. He would run to catch her legs before the rope went taut, but she would be just out of reach, her head listing forward in the choke hold of the noose.

"Possibly," Selva said.

"What do you want to say to your—"

"Listen, Papa," Selva said before the Guardian could finish. "The other night you asked why I'm angry."

She was speaking in her debate voice—quick, strong, a little tremulous with effort. He knew that she had carefully prepared what she was going to say, and from his hiding place under the awning, he was listening. He had never listened so closely to anyone.

"As usual, I didn't think of an answer fast enough. Well, here's my answer, Papa: because you never believed the world could be better or worse than the one you gave me. And that breaks my heart."

A rumble of approval from the crowd. "Oh, this one's good," the woman under the umbrella said to the man.

That's my girl up there, Rustin wanted to tell her. *Our pride and joy.* It had been a favorite phrase of his, until Pan came along and Annabelle asked him to stop using it, but sometimes he couldn't help himself, because even Selva with the noose around her neck was exactly that. Those eyes! Their intelligence shone all the way from the gallows. And didn't she have a point? Even here at the Suicide Spot he couldn't imagine any life for his daughter other than the one that had always awaited her under the empire.

"The world was worse than you ever knew, Papa. Remember the exams?"

He would never forget them. Every year in May the whole empire came to a stop for three days while fourteen-year-old Burgher kids sat for their comprehensive exams. In the city by the river the authorities raised banners across buildings and lampposts to proclaim pride in their children and wish them luck. The rituals were ancient and unchanged since Rustin had sat for his. The night before, Annabelle made the traditional meal of baked rabbit, asparagus, and custard. Rustin drilled Selva one last time on complex equations and imperial history. Pan touched his sister's forehead with a frond of rosemary, and the family held hands around the table and solemnly recited the Prayer for Wisdom and Success: "If it cannot be me, then let it not be me. But let it be me."

The next morning, Burgher parents—oblivious to the fighting that had broken out in the capital—lined the walkways and cheered as their children filed into schools with pencils and notebooks and tense faces, some bravely managing a smile, others rigid with fear. A few of Rustin's colleagues were on hand in their professional capacity in case a child fainted. As Selva walked past her parents, she kept her eyes fixed straight ahead. "Look at her," Rustin whispered to Annabelle. "She's going to murder it."

"I had to place in the top five percent," Selva went on from the gallows. "Not just to qualify for provincials and have a shot at the Imperial Medical College. But for you to still love me."

Someone in the crowd loudly booed.

Selva, no! Not true!

"I didn't look at you, because I was afraid I'd see it in your eyes. Being your daughter, I did what I had to."

As always, the results were announced in the main square two days after the last exam, with practically the entire city in attendance. It was a gorgeous spring day, dry and fragrant, lilac and chestnut trees coming into bloom. One of the old councilors mounted a temporary stage erected in the middle of the square, next to the statue of a historic Burgher that stood on a pedestal surrounded by a gushing granite fountain, and for an hour he read from a long scroll of paper, while the children who had taken the exams lined up at the foot of the stage facing out toward the crowd. When they heard their name called, they stepped forward and shouted, "Here for city and empire!"

The names were read out in order from first rank to last. The family of Selva Rustin did not have long to wait. Out of 179 children, she was third.

"You beat your papa and your grandpa," Rustin had said that night over the most expensive bottle of wine he owned. "What a day for the Rustins." On the coat of arms, in the quadrant with the caduceus, next to his own initials he carved *SR*, welcoming his daughter into the family guild. She was set for life. And as he stood now in the shadow of the gallows, he thought: *We sat around the kitchen table and sang our favorite songs. You pretended Zeus was your patient. Was that world so bad?*

"The next day, the boy who sat next to me in class wasn't there," Selva continued. "We all knew why. He was down around 170."

Everyone in the square had been keeping a rough count as the councilor approached the bottom of the list. Burghers with no family interest in the results were there just to see who had fallen into the bottom ten percent—that was a bigger draw than honoring the top five percent, who would sit the following month for the provincial round. Even if you lost track of the count, the cutoff point became clear as soon as the shouts of "Here for city and empire!" started to come out weak and choked. A few children didn't even answer when their names were called.

"Iver was an Excess Burgher."

Everyone knew what future lay in store for the bottom ten percent. They, too, were set for life. No prohibition was announced, but they would never be allowed to join a guild. They would finish the school year and then look for work. The lucky ones would find a job in one of the markets, or learn a trade in the Warehouse District, or, with the right family connections, go to work for the city as a street sweeper or trash collector. Some of the girls were hired as servants in the homes of higher-status Burghers, though Rustin refused on principle to consider it. A few sank into the underworld of prostitution. But the great majority of Excess Burghers would end up like the ones who drank and fought all night at the Sodden Spot, lay around the main square asleep at midday, and spent most of their foreshortened adulthood in the city prison. Rustin's next-door neighbor thought they should be sent directly from school to compulsory work gangs. Some disappeared from the city and were swallowed up in the Yeoman hinterland. Most Burghers considered it more respectable, more in the natural order of things, to be a Yeoman than an Excess Burgher.

When Rustin was a boy there had been no such people as Excess Burghers. Every child in the city was admitted into a guild—of course, some at lower status than others. But around the time he was studying at the Imperial Medical College, he heard that children who had not done well on their exams were leaving school and falling out of view. No ordinance was passed that declared the bottom five percent of Burgher children (later raised to ten) superfluous, but this was the beginning of a long period of economic contraction throughout the empire, and competition for a dwindling supply of guild positions became intense. That was when the practice began of parents withholding food from children who performed badly on their pre-exams as an incentive to study harder (Rustin personally thought this was taking things too far, though he kept the opinion to himself). So did the first accounts of cheating and payoffs during exam week—a blow to the belief in fairness on which the whole system of guilds depended. Excess Burghers became a fixture of imperial life, the answer to a chronic social problem, the unfortunate result of simple arithmetic.

"Do you remember what you said that night?" The tremble in Selva's voice was thickening; she was coming to her purpose. "I told you about Iver, and you said—"

That's just the way it has to be, Sel. She had come home from school troubled, and he'd wanted to comfort her. He hadn't wanted poor Iver's fate to take away from her magnificent achievement. She hadn't replied, but a cloud had passed over her face.

"'That's just—the way—it has—to be.'" Selva raised her chin, causing the length of rope above the noose to go slightly slack. She closed her eyes and shook her head from side to side and stamped her foot on the platform just as if she'd reached the end of endurance during one of their arguments that had escalated far beyond his wishes. When she opened her eyes, they pierced his chest. "Why?" she cried. "Why was that just the way it had to be? Why in the world did you ever think that was just the way it had to be?"

More approval from her audience, shouts of "Why? Why?"

"Here's what you *should* have said, Papa: 'I'm sorry, sweetheart, but our whole life is a stinking pile of shit, that's how it is, we live on it, we eat it, we fuck on it, we'll be buried in it, but I love you so let's not talk about it anymore.'"

The shouting grew wild. Even the two Guardians were shouting—they had become part of Selva's audience. Her color rose and her throat quivered inside the noose and her lips tightened in expectation of a response that he wasn't there to give. He felt as if he were letting her down by not standing beside her on the platform to receive the full force of her indignation, to coax the last glimmer of her brilliance. One word of his and she'd finish him off, cut him to pieces. He was witnessing one of the greatest moments of her life, as great as that morning in the main square. *That's my girl*, he thought again—but also: *It wasn't just me! Everyone believed it. In the old days beggars were drawn and quartered in that square. It sounds terrible now, but four months ago it was normal. You'd be surprised what people can get used to.*

"If you'd said that, it would have helped me. But you didn't have the courage." Selva dropped her chin and lowered her voice. "So I kept going. I started cramming for provincials. My dream was to reach the imperial round. Instead, we had an Emergency."

A cheer rose, half-heartedly—they weren't sure where she was headed.

"That was the end of exams. To be honest, it felt like the end of me. I actually, literally, didn't know who I was. Without the next round, why get up in the morning?" She gave a hollow laugh. "Then Together came, and I thought: Okay, I'll do that. I'll join a self-org committee. I'll be the best damn Together girl in the city."

Someone laughed too loud. Rustin knew from the tremolo in Selva's voice that things were going wrong.

"Except Together wasn't about that—it was the opposite of that. *I am no better and neither are you.*" Selva brought her hands to her forehead and squeezed her eyes shut as if a massive headache had just come on. "So here I am. I don't have the right thoughts, I keep thinking things I don't want to think, they go around and around and I can't make them stop. I can't stop being your girl!"

The woman punched the air with her umbrella. "Oh my God, she's great!"

The Guardians spoke to Selva as they'd spoken to the boy, telling her what it would mean to leave the world, reminding her to think of her Better Human, but none of it worked, her silence was too strong for them. She stood there in the grip of unuttered answers that would have defeated their philosophy, and her father knew that she was struggling with the decision. When the Guardian released the lever and the second Guardian embraced Selva, she removed the noose from her own neck and descended the ladder into a swarm of cheers with failure in her eyes.

12

As Rustin followed Selva back through the labyrinth of the Market District, the sound of voices from the main square grew louder. They drifted on the warm, moist air over shop rooftops, rising and falling in rhythmic unison like a toneless choir, or the sound of waves on a beach approaching, breaking, receding. The voices carried themes with variations, separate patterns of conversation that came together in pitch and rhythm, higher, lower, as if guided by a single mechanism. A clock in a window on Jewelers' Row read just past three. It was the hour of We Are One.

The meetings had begun as a way to deal with the lack of communications across the city. They'd quickly grown popular—the best self-government was face to face, people said—and became a daily forum for essential decisions about the city. Selva used to go every day after school, until the incident in the park with Zeus. Rustin had never attended; he was always busy at the hospital. She told her father that if he saw We Are One in action just once, he would understand Together. But the process she described was hard to follow, its terminology confusing, and, nodding all the while, he had stopped listening.

The square rolled out before him. Selva disappeared into the voices. He guessed that a thousand people were gathered in a wide circle around the granite fountain and pedestal. But the fountain was dry, part of the water conservation regime, and the pedestal was empty. The bronze statue of a porky Burgher, notorious for gluttony and corruption, provincial governor in a long-dead era, had been pulled down in the first fevered days of the Emergency. Selva told her father that, at an early meeting of We Are One, descendants of the Burgher governor had considered possible replacements for the statue and come up with the perfect idea of having none.

The air was thickening into mist. Rustin stopped on the outer fringe and kept watch for anyone who might recognize him. The gatherers were overwhelmingly young, teens and twenties, many wearing tunics and drawstring pants, a few with goggles strapped over their faces. They all looked toward the middle of the circle until a wave reached them, then they turned around and passed it along to those behind. What had sounded like the crash and ebb of the sea was actually their collective voice, emanating from the center outward in stages, growing louder as it approached the circumference where the gatherers were most numerous, pausing before it returned, growing softer, to the still center.

There was no chatter or laughter, as if they were there for a speech of great importance. But no one was giving a speech. They were saying something in unison, and he strained to hear actual words in the pattern of voices expanding and contracting in concentric circles.

Beside him, a small woman in a purple raincoat kept standing on tiptoe to see better. When a voice-wave reached her, and she turned around to pass it on, he saw that she was older than most of the others: perhaps thirty, eager eyes under bangs cut low, narrow aquiline nose, scarlet mouth in an expectant half-smile. Rustin made out her words as they broke with the same words of other people around him:

"Are Yeomen friends or enemies?"

This was followed by a few seconds' silence—the pause that he'd heard earlier. People around him exchanged looks. He remembered Selva's explanation that meetings of We Are One answered questions too fundamental to be left to the self-org committees. The right to decide belonged to all the gatherers; whoever came to the square that day was given a voice.

But who asked the questions? No one knew for sure. In theory anyone could offer one. When he had asked Selva what happened in the event of a disagreement, her answer became hard to follow and, sensing the onset of annoyance, he didn't press it.

In a loud voice, almost shouting, the woman in the purple raincoat said:

"*Yeomen are enemies.*"

In nearly the same moment others around them were yelling, "*Yeomen are enemies,*" and the voice-wave quickly made its way from the edge of the circle toward the center.

Had she started it? Rustin wasn't sure. Perhaps he'd heard her first because she was closest to him. Someone else might have spoken up just before her. Perhaps everyone around them had said it at once. But that seemed impossible, unless they were all given a script and a cue. No—he had the impression that the question wasn't known in advance; the pause was for thinking; the answers were spontaneous. Then how could they have also been simultaneous? And unanimous?

The mystery seemed important. It wasn't conceivable that everyone could independently arrive at the same answer at the same second. Was the right answer somehow communicated in advance to the crowd? No one appeared to be giving orders or passing out instructions. Selva had insisted that no one was in charge of a We Are One meeting—that was the whole point. The pedestal at the center was empty.

Perhaps the answers had come in a kind of lightning chain reaction, like a chemistry experiment. Wouldn't that mean something different—that they were all waiting for someone else to go first before joining? Perhaps it was enough for five other people to say it first. Perhaps just one. His strongest feeling was that the woman in the purple raincoat had said what was already in the others' heads, poised to be released through their larynxes into the air, the way one person's laughter gave others permission to laugh, or someone's sneeze tickled an urge already fizzing in another person's sinuses, transmitting a virus from face to face until it infected an entire crowd. But someone had to sneeze first.

Another mystery troubled him even more: Why did everyone need to sneeze? How did they all get the same idea in their heads? Unless the collective voice spoke for a collective brain.

Rustin edged closer until he was standing next to the woman. He caught her eye.

"Did you know what everyone was going to say?" he asked as casually as possible, not wanting to seem an obvious first-timer.

She laughed and shook her head. "How could I?"

"I guess they all agreed with you. But I believe you were first."

"Was I? Someone had to be. I just said what I think. Like everyone else."

"Of course."

"That's the beauty of We Are One, isn't it?" She held his gaze as if to make sure he understood. "We're all free to say what we think. Everyone gets an equal chance. No one tells us what to say. We take different paths to the same place." Her eyes widened with surprise and pleasure, as if she'd just solved a problem. "That's it! That's what Together means, personally."

Something about her face appealed to him. It was a face he associated with the early time of the Emergency—open to the world, hopeful, but with a kind of vulnerability, as if the world might return bad news. Before the Emergency, Burghers had avoided making eye contact on the tram, all hiding something shameful, and if you happened to get caught looking, the other pair of eyes would harden: *Who are you to judge? You're no innocent either.*

"To be honest, I was about to stop coming," the woman went on. "The questions were getting so boring. 'Should we use bicycles to power streetlights?' Do I know, do I care? Last Friday it was so empty here, they didn't even need to use Together messaging. I thought, that's it, We Are One is dead. But a friend told me to hang on, the questions were about to get interesting. There's a *much* bigger turnout today."

"Do they ever disagree?"

"Of course!" She seemed to find him amusing. "You've never heard one?"

"Not the times I've been here," he lied.

"But you know how the system works." He nodded. She looked away and then back, as if she registered something wrong about him. "By the way, I didn't hear *you* say anything."

"I was thinking."

"How long do you need?" She made a show of looking at an imaginary watch on her wrist. "So—are they?"

"Are they what?"

"Enemies."

It was such a satisfying word. The question had contained

this answer before the woman in the purple raincoat said anything. The chain reaction began the moment the question was asked. The wave out and the wave back, the question and answer, were the same.

Rustin tried to imagine a lone voice calling out: "*I think Yeomen are friends.*" It would have taken more courage than pulling the lever at the Suicide Spot. It would have brought worse than disapproval—ridicule. Or it would have been futile, gone unheard, disappeared under a receding wave. Which again raised the mystery of how to disagree.

"I guess it depends which Yeomen you mean," Rustin said. "I know a pig farmer. He's a friend of mine." He hesitated before adding, "The answer's complicated."

"You're *making* it complicated," she said. "Some of them aren't bad as individuals, but the Yeomen *people*, of course they're against us. They want to start a war. There's no way we can live with them, in my opinion." The eagerness faded from her eyes, replaced by a staring insistence that fastened on to his so that he almost had to agree or take a step away.

A noise rose from the interior of the circle. The rumble of another voice-wave was approaching. The woman turned from him and stood on tiptoe. Around them people fell silent and listened. The question grew more distinct as it neared the outer edge.

"*Can we live with Yeomen?*"

"Ha! That's a first." The woman rapped Rustin's shoulder with the back of her hand—she had anticipated the question.

This time it was impossible to tell who answered first. The voices came together at a single instant in a single word: "*No,*" and again, "*No, no,*" and that syllable was so majestic and triumphant that if the solitary voice hadn't come from just a few yards away he never would have heard it say, "*Yes.*"

The chorus of *no*'s grew louder as it moved toward the center, but in the area around Rustin and the woman in the purple raincoat the *no*'s began to ebb. Then they were drowned out by a rhythmic clapping, which quickly spread across all the gatherers so that everyone who a moment before had been chanting *no* stopped chanting and began beating hands together in time with everyone else. Then the clapping stopped.

Another backhand from the woman in the purple raincoat. "Told you. Now watch."

The damp afternoon light was beginning to die, and it was hard to see who had said yes. Fifteen or twenty feet to Rustin's left, people were backing up, making room for someone. In the clearing stood a girl with a ponytail and goggles over her face. She was dressed in a loose tunic and pants, but not the Together uniform. She was wearing hospital scrubs. Rustin knew her at once. It was the girl from the Restoration Ring—the nurse assistant, Lyra.

"Goggles off, goggles off!" a male voice chanted.

She raised a hand to her face and lifted the goggles from her eyes in the same tentative way Rustin had seen at the hospital. She appeared startled to find herself isolated in this huge crowd and the focus of all its attention, as if she hadn't meant for her answer to be overheard.

"Speak, speak!" the male voice commanded.

"I"—she hesitated and gestured at her clothes—"work at a hospital." She spoke so softly that it would be impossible for anyone farther away than Rustin to hear.

Before she could go on, voices around her called out in unison: "*I work at a hospital.*" Voices farther off repeated the words, and the words echoed like an unwilling body tossed from hands to hands across the crowd until it reached the pedestal, where it lay naked in a sudden silence. Everyone waited for the girl to continue.

Rustin's heart had gone cold. She was going to announce his offense—expose him to a thousand inflamed Burghers, an enemy in their midst, and their chant would carry his words across the square: *Who do you think is in charge here? You child!* He looked around for a way to escape, but he didn't move. Everything was following a dreamlike logic that required his participation.

"We had to operate on a Yeoman boy."

"*We had to operate on a Yeoman boy.*"

"I was having a bad day. I'm not going to tell you why—that's private."

But nothing was private any more. Every word from her solitary voice was taken and lifted to the chorus of We Are One. She told the story in short bursts: how she had checked on the boy in the recovery room after surgery. How she was there when he woke up. How the first face he saw was hers. They were both having a bad day, but she smiled at him and he smiled at her. She left the room feeling that she had done one good thing for one person that day. She had been about to quit nursing, but the moment with the boy changed her mind. And that was the story. That was why she had answered yes. They could live with Yeomen.

As soon as her last words died at the pedestal, the brick pavement began to tremble under Rustin's feet. People were stomping in a rapid march-in-place and chanting in time: "*Yes, yes, yes!*" But the stomping and chanting were quickly overwhelmed by a stranger and far louder noise. It started in the area around the nurse assistant, and at first it sounded like wails of pain, but as it spread he identified a trilling of tongues and throats, high-pitched, ever rising. Hundreds of people were ululating, "*No no no no no no!*" The noise was thrilling and horrifying, as if a flock of furious birds had suddenly alighted and begun to peck Lyra to death. The whole square, even the yeses of a moment ago, was making the same sound.

The woman in the purple raincoat came close to Rustin. She raised her face to his ear and opened her scarlet lips. Her tongue fluttered, a pink blur inside her mouth, driving the sound deep into his brain.

"That's how we disagree."

Rustin turned away and looked for Lyra. He wanted to tell her something, he didn't know what—"You're here and I'm here"—but she was gone. And Selva, too, had vanished in the anonymous crowd as a light rain began to fall.

13

At dinner Pan recited the first half of "Brave Bella," Annabelle discussed the aspirations and aspersions of Mr. Monge, and Selva reported important decisions made at We Are One. Rustin was silent. But after the plates were cleared and everyone had returned to the table for tea and fruit, he said, as if he were announcing that he would go to bed early:

"I think I'll look for the boy."

"What?" Annabelle said at once.

"What boy?" Pan asked.

Rustin glanced at Annabelle. "A Stranger boy who's lost in the woods near the Place."

Annabelle shook her head. Selva took off her goggles and laid them on the kitchen table, and Pan grabbed them. She was looking at her father with new interest. "What are you talking about?"

"Mr. Monge was separated from his son on the way here," he said. "I'm going to take an extra day off work and find him."

"For God's sake, Hugo," Annabelle said. "That's a crazy idea. You don't know where he is. He could be dead. It's far too dangerous."

"How did the boy get lost?" Pan asked.

The fantasy had been playing over Rustin's thoughts all the way home from We Are One and throughout dinner. Nothing more than an image of himself walking through woods with a pack on his back, the sun warm on his head, the smell of pine needles, a boy tied to a tree, bloodied clothes—but he felt the pressure in his chest ease, the knot of grief under his sternum come loose. To be away from the eyes of the city, alone, longing for his wife and children, missed by them, to do something simple and good and then return home with the boy to the love in their eyes. Testing the fantasy, saying it aloud, was confirmation: this was the thing for him to do.

"I don't want you to go," Selva said. "Yeomen are man-eaters."

"Don't call them that."

The slur was becoming popular. Rustin had heard it from a table of orderlies in the canteen. He'd wanted to go over and remind them of certain Together principles, but he'd thought better of it.

"Everyone at We Are One agreed," Selva said. "Yeomen are enemies."

"Everyone?"

"Papa, they're eating each other out there. The Safety Committee made a presentation to our class."

"And what do you suppose they're saying about *us*? We know Yeomen—the Cronks," he went on. "Last year Pan wanted to see their piglets. We still speak the same language, we belong to the same empire—the same land. They're still human. They're not eating each other."

Annabelle leaned toward her husband and spoke quickly in a low, firm voice. "It's not the same now. We don't hear much, but what we hear is all bad. They killed that poor man from the Water Committee who went out there to discuss the river level. They're blocking trucks we depend on."

"How do you know they killed him?"

"Did he ever come back? Hugo, even before the Emergency Yeomen didn't like Burghers, they just kept it to themselves. You've always had a romantic idea about them. They hate us."

"I don't believe it," he said. "They're still living by the old code out there. They haven't burned it all up in a bonfire and called it 'Together.' This Burgher preciousness—I'm sick of it. We think we're better because we say 'Friends.' Are Yeomen killing dogs?"

The whole family looked at the sofa where Zeus lay sprawled asleep in flying frog position, his long black muzzle nestled between his front paws.

"It doesn't matter if Yeomen aren't killing dogs," Annabelle said. "They want to kill Burghers."

Selva sided with her mother, but she was looking at her father in a way he remembered from early colloquies, with a hundred questions in her eyes. Now that he had no answers for her, his mind was made up.

"Let me do this," Rustin said. "Mr. Monge can show me where he lost the boy. And I'll take Zeus—he loves those woods. We'll camp overnight at the Place. I might even be back in a day."

"But Hugo, why?"

He slapped his palm on the walnut tabletop, surprising himself more than anyone. "I have to do *something*!"

He went to bed and dreamed of the Yeoman boy with the gunshot wounds. The boy was on the operating table wide awake with eyes that said *Don't lose me* while Rustin dug deep in his chest with forceps for the bullet, but the boy sat up and wrapped his arms around the surgeon's neck, and blood was getting everywhere, on his gown and neck and face, and with all the blood leaking from the wound the forceps kept slipping and couldn't grasp the bullet, but when he tried to make the boy lie still the boy rose again with those skeletal arms reaching for him, *Don't lose me*.

14

Suzana lived in the Heights, a hilltop district near the hospital that was coveted for spectacular views of the park and the river. Its residents took pains to keep their gardens tidy and their façades fresh, aware that neighbors would notice any dead leaves collecting in tulip beds or paint peeling off brightly colored front doors, and then neighbors would talk, and a cloud of disapproval would settle over an offending house. Every year on the summer solstice—it was called Visiting Day—people in the Heights opened their homes, and Burghers from other districts were allowed to wander through rooms and gardens, oozing with compliments while trying to hide their envy or disdain. The whole district became a hive of comparative gossip, and though no prizes were given out, by the end of the day everyone in the Heights knew the winners.

Before the Emergency, the district was governed by a council notorious for the strict tests it applied to newcomers, who had to present paint samples and interior decorating plans as well as brief life histories and testimonials from longtime Heights Burghers in order to be considered for residency. Suzana once told Rustin that she received her permit only because the council chairman's gallbladder had been removed on their operating table.

With the Emergency, of course, the Heights District council, like all the others in the city, was disbanded. The chairman, a hostile old man who kept an eye on his domain from his front-porch rocking chair, died soon after of heart failure. The new Heights self-org committee abolished Visiting Day and replaced it with Belonging Week. For seven summer days Heights residents left their homes at dawn and descended on the Warehouse District and other disfavored neighborhoods with hammers, handsaws, shovels, seed bags, and worked late into the long evenings. Despite their ineptitude at manual labor, these Burghers brought the same competitive intensity with which they'd once perfected their homes in preparation for Visiting Day to repairing the broken cabinets of homebound pensioners and planting lilac saplings in trash-strewn lots. Heights children gave an impromptu performance of "Brave Bella" for the residents of the old people's home where Annabelle's father was ending his days, while he muttered from his chair, "Who needs it?" On the morning after Belonging Week, Suzana returned to the hospital with gashed fingertips, her eyes sunk deep in darkened sockets. "The price of living in the Heights has gone up," she told Rustin as they scrubbed before surgery.

He had visited Suzana several times at home, where she lived alone. But he hadn't been to the Heights since it became a hotbed of Together zeal, and now he was having trouble finding her house. Street signs with the names of ancient district councilors had been replaced by BELONGING ROAD and THE WAY OF THE YOUNG. Placards with slogans were planted in gardens, and entire blocks of front doors, once painted in sober grays, were immaculately purple and yellow.

The morning was overcast and warm for mid-autumn. Rustin turned into a steep side street that looked vaguely familiar. In the middle of the block there was a big tree. He began to climb toward it. He remembered that her house was the smallest on its street, with most of its façade hidden by a chestnut tree, and when he came to the tree he caught his breath and tried to figure out if the yellowing leaves were those of a chestnut. A sign was planted in the mulch: I AM NO BETTER AND NEITHER ARE YOU.

"What are you doing here?"

Fifteen feet away, the purple-and-yellow door was open just enough to reveal Suzana's narrow, tense face.

"Exploring the city," he said. "At the director's suggestion."

She glanced up and down the street. "This is not a good idea. Stefan lives right around the corner. Oh"—she waved him forward—"hurry up, just for a minute."

She let him in the door and quickly shut it. They faced each other, Suzana in a blue silk robe as if she'd just gotten out of bed. The entry smelled of fresh-cut flowers. A dark hall led to a bright overhead light illuminating a table neatly set for two—but the doorway was as far as he would be admitted.

"You don't want to be seen with me?" She didn't answer. "You've repainted your door."

"Just tell me why you've come."

"I don't want to make trouble for you. I need a favor."

"I already did you a favor."

"When was that?"

"In the Restoration Ring, when I didn't tell them what it's like working for you."

Rustin had made up his mind not to take offense to anything she said. "What's it like?"

"Nothing criminal, just a lot of criticism and arrogance."

"Our colleagues have decided I'm a bad person. My daughter thinks so, too—possibly my wife. Am I?"

"'Bad' according to whose standard?"

"Yours!"

"Is that what you came for?" Her eyes shifted away as if the question embarrassed her. "Why ask me?"

"Your opinion matters to me."

"Then let me add 'getting dimmer with age.' Didn't that unpleasant experience at the hospital teach you our opinions don't matter, yours and mine? I've always liked you well enough, Hugo, but the standard changed. That's all that matters—not what I think."

Rustin searched her eyes for a flash of irony, but there was only the annoyance of a teacher faced with a slow student just before the bell.

"A week ago you were chief surgeon," Suzana went on. "What are you now? I have no confidence that my thought of the moment won't be obliterated tomorrow. We live in this city with other people—ask yourself what *they* think. What if your children grow up and decide that everything about us, clothes, houses, food, words, all of it makes us the worst people who ever lived? Would you be able to stand up to them?"

His plan had put him in a practical mood, and this mood had brought him to Suzana for a favor, but now that he was here he wanted to talk with her in the old, intimate way. Worse, he wanted her approval. "I didn't take the Emergency seriously enough."

"You took it *too* seriously!" Her voice rose before she caught herself. "Why couldn't you just keep your head down and wait it out? This isn't going to go on forever. But damn you, Hugo, you wanted to be the Last Honest Burgher, and now I'm stuck with those fools because of your vanity."

They fell silent. Eyebrows arched, she waited for him to leave. Instead, he asked about the hospital. She told him that in the days since his departure things had changed dramatically. Saron, flush with his triumph in the Restoration Ring, and without going through any of the senior people, had formed a new self-org committee entirely of younger staff called Wake Up the City. Its first decision was to stop admitting patients from outside the city—to stop treating Yeomen.

"They can't do that!"

Suzana put a finger to her lips and shushed him. "But they did."

He lowered his voice. "They took an oath when they entered the guild."

"They think Together is higher than their oath."

"The director's allowing this?" She didn't answer. "How can they justify refusing Yeomen?"

Suzana explained: according to the new committee, the disruption of livestock trucks and other sources of essential goods proved that Yeomen in the region were trying to strangle the city, and Burghers losing faith in Together were letting them do it. The others—the "wide-awake ones," Saron called them—needed to retaliate by blockading goods from the city that Yeomen depended on: not fuel or food, but medicine and education. Saron was talking to the School Committee about joining Wake Up the City's new policy.

Rustin had trouble understanding what she was saying. None of it made sense; everyone was falling into a fever dream. He stood in a stupor of his own, until Suzana put her hand on the doorknob and he recalled the purpose that had brought him here.

"One thing—the favor. That cousin of yours who works in the vehicle trade. Where can I find him?"

She wasn't sure of the address, but she suggested a backstreet in the Warehouse District. "Why?" But he only shook his head.

She opened the door, and from somewhere deep within

the house a man's voice called: "My love, did you desert me?" The voice was the director's—self-amused, complacent with sleep and pleasure. As the freshly painted door closed in Rustin's face, he remembered something that Annabelle's demented father had recently muttered, in a moment of characteristic vulgarity and sudden clarity: "When empires fall there's a lot more fucking."

15

The Warehouse District looked no different from before the Emergency. There were the same brick façades with broken windows and cavernous bays, the same lumber racked to the rafters and shelves cluttered with machine tools, metal vats filled with grain, stacks of bed frames and chairs blocking sidewalks, chickens hung from their shanks in slaughterhouse doorways, narrow tenement dwellings, puddles of gray water in cobblestone streets, the cold smell of grease and dust, the angry whine of electric tools and men. The city's dirty work still had to be done somewhere. Most Burghers never set foot in the Warehouse District, but Rustin sometimes came to buy cheap camping gear at a junk dealer's shop—less to save money than for the pleasure of getting lost in the district's decayed vitality. As he searched for the street Suzana had mentioned, he noticed that there were no colorful slogans scrawled on walls, no changed street names. The higher spirit of Together seemed to be incompatible with earthly odors and harsh noise.

In the area of the district given to used vehicles, a narrow street crowded with mounds of tires and mufflers and engine blocks matched the name. Outside a shop that echoed with the din of metal grinding and banging on metal, a man in a filthy blue jumpsuit and blue watch cap was kneeling on the cobblestones, hammering away at a piece of tubing.

Rustin stood by and waited until he glanced up.

"I'm looking for a Mr. Kask."

"You found him." The man wore an expression of friendly, dough-faced puzzlement. Rustin saw no resemblance of any kind to Suzana.

"I'm a colleague of your cousin Suzana, and—" Rustin was suddenly stymied by the unlikeliness of his mission.

"Yes, sir?"

"I need a vehicle."

The man set his hammer down and rose painfully to his feet, wiping his hands on the thighs of his jumpsuit. He was tall and pear-shaped, with a meaty neck into which his chin nearly disappeared. "Vehicle?"

"For just a couple of days. An errand in the foothills."

"What do you want to go out there for?" Kask's expression grew more puzzled, though no less friendly.

"I know the area. I've gone plenty of times."

"But when was the last time you went?"

Rustin answered vaguely and tried to return to the subject of a vehicle, but Kask persisted.

"It's a little different now, sir, with the Emergency and all. You have to be a little careful."

"Yeomen are eating people?"

"I'm not saying that," Kask said quickly.

"Oh, my daughter's convinced. Knives and forks."

Kask frowned and took off his watch cap and studied it. "That whole 'man-eaters' thing is overblown. Folks out there are afraid, just like here."

Rustin thought of the Yeoman boy on his operating table. His father had said something about "games." "Afraid of what?"

"No one knows what's going to happen next. They start seeing things different. They get ideas."

"What kind of ideas?"

Kask squinted, as if weighing Rustin's ability to take in what he was about to say. "Ever heard of Dirt Thought?"

Rustin pictured a circle of earnest pigs seated in a muddy pen. "What is it?"

"I can't explain it myself," Kask went on, "but it's getting pretty big with young folks out there. Something to do with the old Yeoman ways coming back. Ancient games—animals and such."

"Dirt Thought. I'm always the last to hear about anything new." Rustin wasn't certain what to make of it. "You've gone out there lately?"

"I get news. I know people in the country." A smile dimpled Kask's soft, heavy jowls. He had a surprise for Rustin. "I'm a Yeoman myself, sir."

Rustin felt his face go warm. He hadn't said anything outright insulting, but he'd been too knowing, too easy with his judgments. There was always an awkwardness with Yeomen, both sides stiffened by the effort to show goodwill and hide distrust, and it set in now with Kask.

"But you live in the city?"

"Came here for work when I was fifteen. Thirty-six now." His eyes brightened and the dimples deepened. "*She* brought me."

"Suzana?"

"You said cousin—that's not really true, sir. She was just a Burgher lady on a country drive who felt sorry for a dumb Yeoman boy because she ran over his dog after stopping for too much millet beer."

Kask watched with enjoyment as Rustin took this in.

"She set me up here in the district. All these folks around here are Yeomen." He waved at the shop where the clamor of metal was incessant. "Burghers can't do this work."

"Don't twenty years here make you a Burgher?"

"Like they say, born a Yeoman, die a Yeoman. Dirt to dirt." Kask laughed a little too hard and then stroked his neck and gazed down the street. Of course he was a Yeoman! All you had to do was look at the big-boned shoulders, the fleshy, leathered face, the eyes at once guileless and hard. Kask gave Rustin the sense that a whiff of pretense would be smelled and scorned—that any use of the new language would end their conversation, not violently but with a scoff. Rustin now understood why, in all the city, the Warehouse District alone had no self-org committee.

"A vehicle won't be easy, sir," Kask said. "There aren't many left."

"I know."

The Energy Committee distributed fuel through a system of ration coupons, but the shortage raised the question why anyone would want a vehicle anyway, as if going outside the walls would be an act of disloyalty. The vision of a city without vehicles captured Burgher imaginations, and owners made a show of bringing theirs to repairmen like Kask, who went into a new business as choppers, selling pieces of rubber, metal, and glass for other uses. Vehicles all but disappeared from the streets.

But Kask knew a man who wanted to sell him a small hauler with a wooden bed that ran on switchgrass fuel. That would be an advantage in the country, he said, since switchgrass and soy had just about replaced regular fuel. But the hauler was ancient, the engine badly maintained, and if Rustin ran into difficulty he would have to know a thing or two about repair work in case he couldn't find a Yeoman willing to help. Rustin said something reassuring and flatly untrue about his mechanical skills. An unexpected twinge of fear made his eyelid twitch.

They agreed on a price. Given the scarcity of intact vehicles, Kask could have asked for more. Rustin recognized the Yeoman's code of honest dealing. He was getting to like this ungainly and humorless man in a jumpsuit who seemed to take people as he found them. With a trace of old-fashioned manners, he still used "sir," a word that was now discouraged. Maybe he'd never heard of Together. Kask belonged to two worlds, and that appealed to Rustin, who was beginning to feel as if he belonged to none.

He remembered his last conversation with Cronk, the pig farmer, a year ago. They had discussed the rising price of barley—a subject that meant very little to Rustin but a great deal to Cronk—and they talked for over an hour, the farmer giving details of markets and deliveries, Rustin pretending to understand more than he did. If Cronk noticed, he didn't seem to care. Relations with Yeomen were like that: incuriosity made them openhearted as well as dull, and if you ignored the difference in status and didn't expect them to show any interest in the city world, a warm familiarity was possible, with none of the tensions and rivalries that beset relations among Burghers. Now Rustin wanted to hear the whole story of Suzana's role in Kask's young life, what he missed from the country, what he thought of Together, what the Emergency meant to the Yeomen out there who had raised him.

Before Rustin could ask anything, Kask leaned over and picked up his hammer. But he didn't get back to work; he wasn't yet willing to let Rustin go.

"No offense, sir, but you're a Burgher," Kask said. "I'm

sure you know what you're doing, but they don't see too many of you anymore. They might jump to conclusions."

"What conclusions?"

"They might not think you are who you think you are."

This brought Rustin up short. Not who he was, but who he *thought* he was.

"I'm pretty good at talking to different kinds of people."

Kask knelt down on the cobblestones and lifted his hammer over the piece of tubing. "Like I said, it's different now."

RUSTIN FOUND THE OLD JUNK DEALER ON ONE OF THE SIDE streets that was nothing but battered little shops, all huddled together and barely surviving. Most of Rustin's camping gear was misplaced or in doubtful condition, and he picked up a secondhand tent and pack, a torch, paraffin lamp, flint and steel, camp stove, canteen, antique brass compass, folding knife, and bedroll, while the dealer—a frail, dusty old man in oversized glasses and a leather apron, who appeared not to have seen sunlight in years—tried to interest him in teacups and snow globes. Rustin stuffed the gear in the pack, strapped on the bedroll, and carried everything out on his back. The unaccustomed weight felt like a promise of something new—something that was not the hospital or the city.

At the end of the street stood a sidewalk market. Rustin's mental list included fruit, bread, cheese, potatoes, a sack of green beans, a small bag of bulgur, canned meat. But as he made his way under the canopies, the baskets of produce looked almost empty. A few lonely pieces of meat that might have been lamb cuts and chicken parts lay on long sheets of bloody paper.

"Right here, love!" A wide-cheeked, boisterous woman seated on a stool waved Rustin over with a beefy arm. "What do you need, my dear?"

Her wooden boxes contained meager amounts of vegetables and grain. "You're almost sold out," Rustin said.

She rummaged in one of the boxes. "What about these gorgeous tomatoes?"

"Where are your goods?"

"Not sold out, love—can't get them. The wholesale men either."

"Why can't you get them?"

"The farm trucks aren't showing up like they're supposed to. Some nice carrots?"

She grabbed a handful and brandished them by their tops. She was the hard type of produce woman who would shift in an instant from sweet talk to invective if she didn't make a sale. Before the Emergency she would have held no interest for him, and he would have kept their talk to a minimum. Now he bought her carrots just to ask more questions.

"How long has it been?"

"Since the trucks stopped?" She thought about it for a moment, then shouted to a neighbor: "Rose, when did those dirty Yeomen stop coming?"

Rose, who had lank gray hair and a mournful face, counted on her fingers. "Six days ago."

"Six days ago, love," the produce woman repeated to Rustin. "They're trying to starve us to death. Hurting themselves, too."

"Why would they do that? I'll take the rest of those green beans and potatoes."

Smiling broadly, she emptied the boxes into a couple of

burlap sacks and handed them to Rustin. "They hate us, dear. They're not educated. My daughter, she's eleven, and she reads a book every week."

Rustin wondered if these market women might be from Yeoman land like Kask. "Did they always hate us?"

"Those truckers? We got along fine before the Emergency. That's when it started." A thought occurred to her. "You heard about Brave Bella? If that little girl hadn't thought fast, they would've burned the city down."

Was she recounting the song, or did she believe Brave Bella to be real? "You mean the trolls?"

"Trolls?" Her face lit up. "Never heard that one. Rose, listen to this—mister here calls those Yeomen 'trolls'!" He had put her in a fine mood. "I've heard 'man-eaters'—never heard 'trolls.'"

"But Bella is a girl in a song the schools are teaching."

"That's right," the woman said, "and where do you think they got the song, love? They didn't just make it up."

"You know that for sure?"

She was slightly offended. "Does Rose look like a liar to you? Of course I'm sure. Everyone knows it."

Brave Bella was real for the produce woman, and probably half the city. Torch-bearing Yeomen had tried to burn it down. He would never convince her otherwise.

16

It was after Rustin left the sidewalk market, and was walking on a path of slimy cobblestones along the waste canal toward the tram tracks, the straps of his crammed pack digging into his shoulders, that he saw, ten feet away in the open bay of a warehouse whose brick façade bore the faded letters ELECTRICAL AND PLUMBING SUPPLY, a room full of bodies.

They were laid out neatly in rows across a dirt floor, side by side on their backs, fully clothed, faces up, still as death. He flinched and looked away, thinking, *They moved the morgue.* It used to be in a windowless, cube-shaped building down the street from the hospital. As a medical student he'd spent many hours there. He looked again.

He had no fear of corpses, but he'd never seen anything like the ones lying before him. There must have been a hundred, squeezed together in identical positions without benefit of mortuary sheets, as if they'd been freshly massacred. Their postures were stiffer than ordinary rigor mortis, and they gave off no smell other than the oily fume that pervaded the Warehouse District. Their faces had none of the sunken solemnity that made the corpses he'd seen so remote, so inhuman. These possessed color and feeling, and their eyes were open. They gave the impression of being alive. The really terrible thing was that they were all young—children, teenagers, wearing fanciful garments in bright colors. Pinned to every chest there was a scrap of paper with handwriting on it.

A body lying in the first row was dressed in the blue blouse and plaid skirt and knee socks of a schoolgirl. The paper pinned to her blouse said MAYA. Rustin noticed that some sort of dull greenish, metallic sheathing, like antique armor, covered the girl's thighs below her skirt, and also her wrists and hands. There were pieces of metal on the corpses around her, too, over necks, collarbones, ankles—wherever missing clothes would have exposed flesh. And not just armor: bits of machinery, gears, dials, copper wiring, rivets, ratchets, rods where shoulders and knees and fingers should have been.

The thought shuddered through his limbs like a fever coming on: *They're not human.* These bodies were clothed machines. But the faces—they had the texture of human skin, and individual features. Maya, who looked about twelve, with a pretty upturned nose and pointed chin, was smiling expectantly as if she were opening a birthday present.

"No, no, no! Absolutely not!"

From the shadows in the rear of the bay a man was hurrying toward Rustin between two rows of bodies, making crisp waving gestures as if shooing away hens.

"We're not open to the public. By appointment only."

The man was maybe twenty-five but prematurely balding, with round glasses, a tight face above a pencil neck, and an air of superb self-assurance. His shirt and belt and shoes were too formal for a storage depot in the Warehouse District. As he approached, still shooing, Rustin didn't move.

"Appointment only," the man repeated. "Please leave."

"I was passing by. I didn't mean to intrude."

"But evidently you are." The man lifted his meager chin toward Rustin's overstuffed pack and bedroll. "Don't you have somewhere to be?"

"Not really." He heard himself add: "I just got to the city an hour ago."

"From?"

Rustin mentioned a smaller city thirty-five miles down the river.

"And you're on some kind of post-imperial grand tour?"

The tone was nearly offensive, but Rustin didn't care. Sarcasm directed at a clueless traveler from elsewhere had nothing to do with him. He was going to find out what this superior person—he thought of him as the Manager—was up to.

"Our governing council lost control," Rustin said. "Breadlines, street fights. I caught the last ferry out."

"And decided to add yourself to our burdens."

"We heard things were good here."

"Be more specific. What did you hear?" With finicky precision the Manager folded his arms across his white button-down shirt, as if even contact with himself was vaguely unpleasant.

"You never elected a council. Everyone organized themselves. It's called Together. And it's working."

This account seemed to please the Manager. "The whole city is a laboratory. We're experimenting with the last mile to utopia." He reviewed the flannel shirt and corduroy trousers that Rustin had been wearing for two days. "What was your guild?"

"It—engineering."

"Ah." This was obviously the right answer. "*Futurum condimus.*"

"Exactly." Rustin had no idea what it meant. He recognized the Manager as the type of Burgher who would be a snob under any form of social organization. "That's why your—your lab caught my eye."

"My workshop."

Trying not to be obvious, Rustin stole a glance at some of the nearby faces. They were uncannily lifelike: this short-haired, melancholy girl with flared nostrils; this boy with a droll expression and wisp of mustache who any moment was going to crack a joke. The Manager noticed, and his lips twitched in an effort to suppress the pleasure that was welling behind his round lenses.

"Really remarkable," Rustin said, engineer to engineer. "What—" He didn't know how to go on.

"What are they?" Self-restraint disintegrated on the Manager's mouth, but even his smile was sour. He turned and pointed at a high wall where a purple-and-yellow banner hung. But instead of TOGETHER it said:

BETTER HUMANS

Below, in smaller letters, the sixth principle of Together was written out: YOU SHALL BE AS GODS.

The words had a strange effect on Rustin. They took him back to the first days of the Emergency, that improvised morning at the hospital, the emptying of bed bottles in a warm, communal glow. Yes, that was it—to be better! It was what everyone in all times wanted, even if the wish lay buried for years under layers of quotidian debris. But the effort needed was immense, the human stuff so flawed—indifference, indolence, fear. Within a week of the Emergency he had found himself annoyed by his new brothers and sisters, and now they were all gone, as if he'd been offered a view of a stunning landscape and barely taken time to notice.

Rustin removed his pack and set it at his feet. "How do you do it?"

"The more interesting question is *why*." The Manager held

up a finger. "Understand something: we wouldn't be having this conversation if you were a native Burgher here. Everything in my workshop stays under the seal. You'll be on your way, am I right?"

Rustin nodded. The Manager took off his glasses and wiped them delicately with a handkerchief that he pulled from his trouser pocket.

"How do I do it? By the way, others toil here with me." The Manager waved at the crowded floor. "This is my workshop, but I certainly do not work alone. That would be impossible." He had a way of saying something and then holding Rustin's gaze as if every statement was a point won and he was waiting for the other to concede. "The faces impress you? They're the easy part—primitive. Form a life mask with sculptural plaster, fill with modeling clay, build out the head, decorate, cast in fire, horsehair wig and eyebrows. Our ancestors had all the tools. But during the interview we observe closely. We're after a characteristic expression. The human essence."

"What interview?"

The Manager closed his eyes and sighed extravagantly at the difficulty of explanation. "First, we don't recruit. They hear of Better Humans through friends or self-orgs, at We Are One, at the Suicide—never mind the local details. The point is they find their own way to my workshop. They all arrive in extremis. Nervous exhaustion. Many visibly underweight, those horrible gray costumes hanging off them like death shrouds." His thin upper lip curled. "Facial tics, permanent goggle marks. Some can't stop crying, some can't stop talking, and some can't say a word."

"What's wrong with them?"

"What's wrong with them?" The Manager gave a harsh laugh. "What's wrong with *you*? The pain of being human!"

His tone seemed to add, *you idiot*. "Most of them barely knew they existed. They burrowed their way like naked mole rats through the only possible world. Flash! The Emergency turns on the lights. Freedom! The city belongs to the young! *Futurum condimus!* They should feel euphoric, right? But consciousness turns out to be a form of torture. Have you ever tried really thinking for yourself?" He touched his own forehead at the thinned hairline and made a show of wincing. "Every neural pulse is an electric shock. There's a cactus in your prefrontal cortex. Outside your skull are these creatures called other people, all enduring the same thing. You made Together sound easy; I can assure you it's not. It takes work, and a lot of the time it doesn't work. People quarrel, there's a meat shortage. Not what they were told! And their cactuses are still growing! You have children?"

After a moment Rustin said that he didn't.

"Try to imagine. The past, the *human* past, is of no use to them now. What fool said making the world new would take four months? After blaming everyone else, they turn the torch flame on themselves. And then they come to us."

Rustin imagined a torchlight parade of shrouded youthful figures lurching single file along the canal amid a chorus of metallic groans, free arms swinging from shoulder gears on pulleys, faces fixed in fired clay.

"And you interview them?"

"We *prompt* them. 'If you could change one thing about yourself.' 'If you could live in a myth.' 'Your dream costume.' (Please, not the gray sack.) 'Imagine this city in five years.' 'Describe the perfect world.' We give them back the sense of possibility, and for fifteen minutes they forget the pain." The Manager registered these marvels with detached satisfaction. "While they answer, our artists sketch. What they sketch is not the face as it is, but the face we intuit the subject wants to have, without the hive of jabs and jolts behind the brow. That first interview gives us the key to the whole person. By the end we already have their Better Human essence."

While the Manager was talking, Rustin studied the bodies around the floor. They were no longer corpses, but young people, beautiful young people, resting from their labors, musing, dreaming.

"Now I come to the most important step—my modest contribution to the process—without which these assemblies would stay inert. While they talk, a little device of my invention inscribes their voice on a wax cylinder. When the subject comes back for the beginning of fabrication, we create more cylinders. Every time they return, more wax, more words, preserved in perpetuum. By now we have a dozen cylinders for each Better Human. Hundreds in all. Soon, thousands."

Eight or ten bodies away lay a boy who might have been the leader of the looting gang. No acne scars, but the same pursed, sarcastic mouth.

"Can you guess where we keep them?"

Half-listening, Rustin realized that the Manager was waiting for him to answer. He shook his head. The Manager tapped on his own chest.

"The Better Humans are *learning to speak*." The Manager narrowed his eyes to assess whether Rustin grasped the momentousness of this statement. "What do I mean? It would be boringly easy to have a voice box inside each assembly that repeats word for word what we capture on wax. The subjects don't come to us so they can hear how they already sound. They want to hear how their Better Human *could* sound. We train them to experiment with their cylinders, combine material, erase it and reshape it, manufacture new sentences, whole paragraphs, new forms of expression and thought—almost a new mind. What is it?"

Lying in one of the rows of bodies, next to a round-faced boy in a sort of jester's costume, Rustin had spotted a girl with keen almond eyes, a half-open smile with a slight overbite, an expression of eager readiness. He looked away.

"Go on."

"Now we come to why. This part requires your full attention, and even that might not be adequate." The Manager waited until Rustin nodded. "Why a new mind? Because our purpose is not therapeutic. We don't much care if the young people who come here *feel* better. Our goal is to *make* them better. See that?" He nodded at the banner on the far wall. "The last and highest principle. But is anyone else in this city trying to achieve it? Oh, no! Too hard!" The Manager's voice filled with agitated mockery. "They've all settled for '*Everyone belongs*,' which makes the children even unhappier because they know they were promised more. '*You shall be as gods.*' They can only get it here."

Struggling to pay attention, Rustin again peered at the figure of the girl. Her skin was painted Selva's olive color. Whoever molded the features had created the face that Rustin pictured whenever he thought of her. This was his ideal daughter lying twenty feet away, with the face of one of the goddesses she used to love hearing him read about when she was a little girl. Or the face Pan conjured when he sang the song. Brave Selva.

"The ridges carved on wax will gradually replace their own words—we call it the Crossover. At that point Better Humans will begin teaching subjects, not the other way around. The boys and girls we've interviewed several times are already thinking more clearly—logically."

He hadn't seen this face for a long time, not since before the Emergency, during exams week, and he wanted to cry: *It's you!*

"Then comes the process of inter-wiring. This will interest you as an engineer." The Manager's voice grew more resonant, as if he feared losing his audience at the crucial point. "We're not there yet, but connecting the assemblies and splicing their cylinders together will realize a combined cerebral power that we don't even know how to measure. Errors of fact—even of thought—will disappear. Dialogue will produce amelioration, not conflict. Don't let our name deceive you: the human individual is not our concern. The goal of Better Humans is to dismantle and rebuild the individual in a way that allows for the perpetual improvement of human society. And yes, I mean Burgher society. Imagine if we wired together a bunch of 'Better Yeomen.' What a horror! Short circuits, explosions, chaos! Or 'Better Strangers'—unknowable, we'd never get past the language problem."

The dress belonged to Annabelle, tailored from lambswool and dyed pomegranate, form-fitting through the bust and waist, ruffled at the neck and wrists. She had stopped wearing it after giving birth to Pan but kept it hanging in the same closet where Rustin later stowed the coat of arms. Of all things, Selva had chosen to wear this antiquated ex-dress of her mother's. When had she started coming? Why? He could imagine why.

"But when every young Burgher in this city has a Better Human, and all these Better Humans are inter-wired, then everything can be known, every question answered, every decision made, every difference resolved. Together will become a living reality, We Are One will be superfluous, self-orgs will disappear. *We will have perfected our humanity.* And then"—in the moment after striking this resounding major chord, the Manager's voice suddenly dropped to a quiet, almost melancholy minor note—"the place of the human individual will be uncertain."

Rustin was hardly listening. He was waiting for the girl to notice him, sit up, open her mouth, and cry, "Papa! You're here!"

"Am I wasting my time with you?" the Manager demanded.

Rustin turned away from the sight of his daughter. "Can I hear one of them speak?"

The Manager detached his scrutiny from Rustin and let it roam across the Better Humans. He seemed to be making some calculation, adding up figures in his brain to be sure that he would come out victorious.

"One and done. Your time appears limitless—mine is not."

"What about that one. That girl in the red dress."

There was just enough room between rows for the Manager to walk on tiptoe without stepping on his assemblies. He lifted Selva by the wrists and casually draped her over his shoulder. This person who put so much effort into human perfectibility was plainly repelled by actual people—he seemed to prefer them embodied in metal. Selva's hair fell forward from her scalp. The dress left uncovered her smooth, gleaming calves and neck and hands. Rustin sensed how light she was—how lifeless.

The Manager set her down at Rustin's feet, legs straight and flat on the floor, head and torso somehow propped up without support. Rustin knelt down to the level of her eyes.

They stared back at her father's with no recognition. His gaze fell to the scrap of paper pinned to her dress.

"Her real name is Hebe?"

"Of course not. They all take a new one."

"What was hers before?"

"Look around," the Manager said, exasperated. "We've created eighty-three Better Humans. You expect me to remember them all?"

I expect you to remember this one. What did she want to change about herself? Describe her perfect city, you supercilious ass. Rustin had repeated the story of Athena at countless bedtimes when Selva was five and six. Pallas had been her idol. Why had she named herself after a minor goddess? The little shit of a Manager must know why. Rustin felt a jealous rage boil up. This complete stranger had heard and forgotten intimacies that her father was denied.

"This one isn't finished. She came every day for a week and then stopped."

With a practiced hand the Manager reached for Selva's neckline and pulled it down to her chest. Rustin was about to protest when he saw exposed at the base of her throat a bronze knob with a serrated circumference. The Manager cranked it clockwise three full turns while hidden gears purred.

From somewhere within the assembly came a noise, whirring and scratchy. Then a voice.

"*Father, drink from my golden cup.*"

Selva's. Clear, dramatic. Her reciting voice.

"*Honeyed wine, sweet and pure. Drink and grow young through me.*"

Rustin, clutching at every word, understood nothing.

"*Mother, eat from my silver plate and I will fasten this yoke to your horses. Brother, I will bathe you and dress you for battle.*"

Rustin looked up for an explanation, but the Manager only raised his eyebrows as if registering another win.

"*Father, your fair-ankled daughter attends you. Eternal unaging, no loss or decay. Drink from my golden cup and grow young through me.*"

With a final scratch the noise stopped. The knob clicked off.

"There's a lot more," the Manager said. "This one wouldn't shut up."

"Can I hear it?" Rustin asked, subduing his desperation.

"We're done."

Rustin crouched at Selva's level and willed her to speak. Her almond eyes looked back, sightless.

"Out, out." The Manager was shooing again. "Come back in a month. Things are changing so fast, you won't recognize her."

17

Before dinner Pan sang the whole of "Brave Bella" for his father. It wasn't a long ballad, but halfway through Rustin forgot to keep listening—a habit with his younger child—and the end caught him by surprise. Pan glowed in the applause his father bestowed to make up for his inattention. He thought of telling a joke about the misinformed produce woman, but that would have spoiled his son's accomplishment. Instead, he wrapped his arms around Pan and pressed his shoulder bones and felt the small hands clutch his back, kissed the top of his head, breathed his clean child smell. With a parent's yearning for eternity, Rustin held on a few seconds longer than necessary as a familiar pang reminded him that the tightest hug did not stop time, that every throb of love was an intimation of grief. Not eternal unaging, but ceaseless change. Perhaps this was what made the Emergency his mortal enemy. In another minute his son would be on to a new game, a plan, a step farther away. Already Pan was wriggling out of his arms.

At dinner Rustin tried to raise spirits with selected tales of his day in the city. He left out the Better Humans workshop, which was dissolving into a realm of lucid dream. But a leaden mood had settled over the table. He found it hard to meet Selva's eyes, imagining the mechanical girl seated upright with her luminous clay face. When he looked, she was watching him with the same worried interest of the night before. Annabelle's gaze was downcast, and her full mouth was half-open with some pressure he knew to be sadness, which he was loath to take away because it made her beautiful.

All at once somewhere in the city the bells of clock towers and schools and temples of worship began ringing in unison. They didn't chime a musical melody, or toll the routine gong of the hour, but rang an insistent *clang-clang* like a collective firebell, an alarm sounding from nowhere and everywhere, *clang-clang* for a full minute, so loud that Zeus hid under the table and howled in reply, and Pan rolled his head and banged a fist on the table to the rhythm of the bells. Then sudden silence, broken by Pan falling into hysterics.

"What was that?" Rustin asked.

"The Wide Awakes," Selva said. The name made Pan laugh harder.

"Who are the Wide Awakes?" Annabelle asked.

"A new group."

"A self-org committee?"

"More like a super-committee."

"What do they do?"

"They wake up the city!" Selva said, as if the answer was obvious.

"The city isn't awake?"

"The city's half-asleep. The enemies of Together are already here, outside and inside."

Annabelle did not look pleased with this judgment. "And who are the enemies of Together?"

"Yeomen!" Pan cried.

"Not all of them," Rustin said.

"Some of them," Selva said. She added, "Some Burghers, too."

This came close enough to the family that it briefly silenced the conversation. Rustin remembered what Suzana had told him about the resident, Saron. "There's a Wide Awake at the hospital. One of the young doctors seems to be in charge."

"They're going to save us." Selva nodded with assurance, but her eyes flickered between her parents for their response.

"Do we need saving?" Annabelle asked. "Aren't we doing our best?"

"Look around, Mama! Do you think everything is wonderful?"

"I think we should look for friends, not enemies."

"No one my age thinks that way," Selva said. "We have to do better. *I* have to do better."

Rustin washed the dishes while Annabelle put away canisters of grain. "Poor Mr. Monge," she said. "He just arrived and now he has to go out there again."

"Mr. Monge declined to accompany me."

On his last errand of the day Rustin had stopped by the hostel and found Mr. Monge sitting on his bunk in a cloud of smoke as if he'd been waiting the whole time for the doctor's return.

"You are bringing good news to me, I think?" Mr. Monge lowered himself to the floor and took Rustin's hands in his own, which felt dry and cracked like tree bark. "A bookkeeper job?"

"I thought you were asking about your son."

"My son!" Mr. Monge gave a startled laugh.

Rustin noticed they weren't alone. On the opposite top bunk a figure lay under a cloak, back to the room, long hair in a tangle, shoulders hunched as if asleep.

"He is Mr. Camba," Mr. Monge said, following Rustin's gaze. "He came last night. He is very tired. But he does not have my problems. In our Stranger land he was a shoemaker for horses."

"Ah. A blacksmith."

"As you say. Mr. Camba is lucky. He will find a job easily. I am not lucky." Mr. Monge returned the pipe to his mouth, bent over, and tapped his legs. "Doctor, the pain is in my knees."

"Mr. Monge, I came here to ask if you will help me find your son."

"My son!" Mr. Monge straightened up and stared at Rustin for what seemed half a minute as the smoke grew denser until only the eyes with their secrets were left. He finally said, "My son is in the hands of our Stranger god."

"Come with me to the woods and show me where you lost him."

Mr. Monge looked away and shook his head. It was not possible—there were too many reasons why—the Stranger Committee's rules, the pain in his knees and in his head, the wild animals, the hostile Yeomen, the urgent need to start over from nothing in this new city. His son belonged to a world of loss that left Mr. Monge with the thinnest wisp of a self. If he went backward it would disappear.

By Rustin's standards—the sentimental standards of a Burgher father whose pride in life and place in the city had been to secure his children on a path of success in an empire that no longer existed—this refusal wasn't just wrong, it was incomprehensible. But he didn't blame Mr. Monge. He realized that he'd expected it.

HE SPENT THE REST OF THE EVENING PACKING. THE ROUTINE was familiar from camping trips to the Place: the supplies he'd picked up in town, two days of clothes, and from the kitchen a jar of coffee, a bottle of whiskey, metal cookware, water in the new canteen, and a bag of Zeus food. The boy, if he found him, was going to need first aid, and Rustin assembled a kit with what he had at home: soap, gauze, tape, ointment, medicine, tourniquets, sutures, and a few instruments. The whole time he was packing, Annabelle busied herself with dishes and committee work.

After twenty years, Rustin was certain that he knew the meaning of every quiver in his wife's face. He knew that when she was exasperated her hands flew up like startled birds. That she always yielded him the last meatball and on bad days quickly changed the subject from herself. He knew from the special pitch of laughter that she was with Pan in another room. That she loved the darkest chocolate and hated being left to wait for him in public. That she stopped speaking at the first hint she'd lost his attention, and placed her hands on his chest when he raged about some incident at the hospital. He knew that she spilled water on the floor when she drained noodles, and the irritated grunt when he accidentally woke her, and the taste of her neck, and the rhythm of her breathing when she was ten seconds from climax. He knew the care with which she instructed Zeus like a teacher who couldn't help loving her slowest student. That she said Pan-Pan and Sel-Sel when she was happy. The bend in the last joint of her right pinkie.

That night they made love with a passion that caught them both by surprise. When their bodies lay apart in the darkness, she asked, "What happened at the hospital?"

He brooded on what to say. Her hand found his, and her fingers stroked his palm.

"I'll tell you when I get back."

"Does it have something to do with this?" she said. "This trip?"

"It seemed small at the time, but it keeps getting bigger." Like a faint crack in the dirt that kept growing until it became a fissure in the earth large enough to swallow a whole life.

"So you'll go find this Stranger boy and that will make everything better?"

"Friend," he corrected.

"Why are you going?" she said. "You don't have to. Not for me."

In the middle of the night he woke up from not enough sleep to a violent *clang-clang*. Someone was standing over him in the dark.

"I'm coming with you," Selva whispered beneath the noise of bells.

PART II

1

She saw the objects in the road first and warned her father to slow down. On the approach to the high brick arch lay pieces of metal that looked like sections of railroad track, and behind them stood a couple of beer casks. At the North Gate itself, an iron rod was balanced between two trash barrels. It was all arranged so that a driver had to slow down, weave around the first obstacles, and then come to a halt at the barrier.

There was hardly room on the hauler's bench for the three of them: her father driving, Zeus squeezed in the middle—sitting up alert, paws on the gearshift, eyes fixed ahead like a navigator—and Selva with her left hand stroking Zeus's shaved fur and her right arm pressed so tight against the door that it was already beginning to ache. Her schoolbag, hurriedly stuffed with overnight clothes, bounced on the hauler's wooden bed along with her father's pack and bedroll. The vehicle smelled of burnt grease and old dirt, and the engine coughed a constant death rattle.

As they rolled toward the arch, two figures came out from behind the brick abutments on either side.

"Full stop!"

A girl was approaching the driver's door with her hand raised. She was about eighteen, hair tied back flat against her scalp, with an expression that stayed resolutely blank as she took in the sight of man, dog, and girl jammed together in an ancient vehicle. She was wearing a sort of uniform: matching pants, jacket, and forage cap in green serge cloth. The boy who appeared on Selva's side was closer to her own age, wearing the same uniform except his jacket was misbuttoned.

In the morning Selva had put on her tunic and drawstring pants in honor of the boy they were going to find, but her father had said that the outfit might attract negative attention from Yeomen, maybe even Strangers. Because he had leverage—he could always refuse to bring her—she'd agreed to dress like a normal Burgher girl, checkered jumper over long-sleeve top. Now she felt ashamed of her clothes, like a five-year-old being escorted by her papa to her first day of school.

"Papers, please," the girl said.

Her father laughed incredulously. "I need papers to leave the city?"

The guard gave a curt nod. She wasn't armed, and her uniform carried no insignia, but she had the bearing of a soldier or policewoman. Selva had never seen anyone this young with this much authority.

"My certificate of citizenship and guild member card are defunct, as you're probably aware," her father said in his I-know-better voice. He reached in his jacket pocket, took out his leather billfold, and produced a wrinkled piece of paper. "Will this do? It's a letter of appreciation from my hospital, for twenty years of service."

The guard unfolded the paper and studied it for a long time, though it contained just two sentences. On her forage cap, stitched to either side of the front, Selva noticed a pair of ovals in the form of eyes. They made the cap look like some solemn, big-nosed creature, a tapir or a sea bream. She fought down an urge to laugh, because she knew what the eyes meant.

"You're a doctor?" the guard finally asked.

"It says so right there."

She looked up sharply from the letter. He was using the wrong tone, showing that he didn't believe in any of it—the checkpoint, the demands. "What's your reason for exiting the city?"

"Travel."

"Humanitarian mission," Selva broke in, speaking from her chest to sound as official as possible. She described the injured Stranger boy, taking care to use the word "Friend," but the story didn't interest the guard, who withdrew deeper into blankness.

"You'll find my medical kit if you search our bags," her father added.

The guard glanced at the bed of the hauler, then at the letter again. She and her colleague seemed uncertain of protocol.

"Who do you intend to meet outside?"

"As few people as possible," he said.

"Names?"

"I don't know the boy's name. He's a Stranger. His father's name is Monge. Shall I spell it? M-O-N-G-E."

"Do you intend to meet any Yeomen?"

He hesitated before saying, "No."

"When will you reenter?"

"Tomorrow afternoon, I hope."

It was already noon. They were starting late because of Selva's last-minute decision, the argument it provoked with her parents, and the trip to the Warehouse District to pick up the hauler. More likely they would be gone two nights.

"Come with me," the guard said.

Her father sighed ostentatiously, got out, and followed her behind the abutment. Selva turned to the boy on her side, wanting to make up for any offense her father might have given. "We really appreciate what you're doing." She gestured at the cap pulled down over his brow. "The city needs to wake up."

He was doing his best to stand at attention, staring at some fixed point with his hands at his sides, then behind his back. His eyes shifted to hers, and he gave a slight nod while the pair on his forage cap seemed to mock his expression.

"Iver!" Selva cried. "It's you!"

Her former classmate looked stricken. He was obviously hoping not to be recognized.

"I heard you were doing lots of self-org work—that's so great! I'm on the Student Committee. Did you volunteer for Safety? And now you're a Wide Awake—that's so great!" she babbled, while Iver's Adam's apple rose and fell and he looked everywhere but at Selva. Her arrival evoked no pride in his new station, only the shame of past failure and the terror of imposture.

The female guard returned with Selva's father trailing behind, holding a piece of paper. In block letters it listed all their names, including Zeus's; the family's address; her father's occupation; point of exit, time of departure, and time of expected return; and the words "Humanitarian Mission." At the bottom was an illegible signature, and a blotchy stamp of an open eye above a child's scrawl that said SAFER TOGETHER.

"Don't lose your pass," the guard said. "You'll need it for reentry. Approach the gate with caution."

Her father got in the driver's seat with an affronted look that Selva hated.

"Is all this really necessary?" he asked.

The guard stiffened. "We're advising Burghers to stay inside the city. You're heading into a gray area."

"A Stranger boy needs our help," Selva said. "We're bringing him back here to save his life."

"Why are *you* going?" These words, directed at her, were the guard's first that sounded natural.

The night before, Selva had been unable to sleep, her nerves twitching with sparks of unspent energy, smoldering in a frustration that was almost physically unbearable. She lay awake on her back whispering the Together principles like a prayer again and again, trying to feel the happiness of hearing them for the first time and the many times after that, but now it was out of reach. Her father thought that Together had let her down because someone hurt Zeus—because the city was having problems. As usual, he didn't understand. She had let herself down, with her distractions and irritations, her cowardice, her selfishness. Her body had let her down by growing in ways that made her conspicuous and ugly. She thought of the Better Human lying in this very position in her mother's red dress somewhere in the Warehouse District, but made of imperishable stuff, thinking perfect thoughts, speaking words that glowed like gold. Eventually, she would become her Better Human—that was the point of all the work—but as she lay in the dark trying to imagine devoting her life to a city where everyone was happy because everyone belonged, unwanted thoughts kept pulling her mind away. She kept returning to the moment when the old councilor up on the stage had called "Selva Rustin!" and she had been so stunned—the ceremony had hardly begun—that she didn't understand it was her name. The kid standing next to her had to give her a little shove before she stepped forward and shouted, "Here for city and empire!" When the Emergency was declared right afterward, the transporting shock of that morning in the main square still hadn't worn off, and the name she didn't recognize echoed on in her head. She had been absent at her life's greatest moment—which was now a dead moment, almost shameful. It was the beginning of not knowing who she was.

She had left her bed and gone into the room where her parents were sleeping to keep from losing her mind. But already an idea was offering relief. Not really an idea, but an image: she was standing with an old hunting rifle in her hands, taking aim at a shaggy-bearded man who was about to set a lit torch to a pyramid of sticks stacked at the feet of a Stranger boy lashed to a tree. It was not herself but Selva in metal and clay and her mother's red dress whose finger touched the trigger. She hadn't yet squeezed it and didn't know if she could, feeling that not just the boy's life but her own depended on the answer.

It was in the grip of this image that she heard herself say to her sleeping father, "I'm coming with you," just as the bells began to ring.

When they were all awake, her mother interrogated her about man-eaters and other dangers while Selva paced beside their bed. "Papa's doing something right," she said, not adding *finally*. "He shouldn't have to do it alone." Then, without knowing why, she felt tears come on. "Please let me go with him," she sobbed, and she fell on the bed in a heap of weakness that bore no resemblance to the metal-and-clay Selva with the rifle. "I'm so unhappy!"

"But why?" her mother asked.

A wave of desolation had come and knocked her down. All the others—the girls in her self-org, the Wide Awakes, a tall, quiet boy she'd met at the Better Humans workshop and immediately fallen for—were purer than she was. They didn't still daydream about winning an Imperial Honors First Class. They didn't start stupid fights with their parents as a way to coerce approval. If she'd had any courage, she would have gone through with it at the Suicide Spot. The only thought that made her like herself even a little was of coming back to the city with Mr. Monge's son and seeing the admiration in those boys' and girls' eyes.

As Selva wept, she caught a glimpse of her parents through wet lashes. Her mother's expression was pained, wary, but softening; her father was looking away. He could have said no, the way he'd refused to open their house to Strangers, but he was almost smiling. Finally her mother gave up, with orders to be gone just one night and stay clear of unknown Yeomen.

But now Selva found herself unable to answer the guard. Why *was* she going? The reasons didn't add up, there were too many, she couldn't remember them.

"A doctor needs a nurse," her father said.

A shadow of skepticism passed over the guard's face. Selva glanced at Iver to see if he was a little impressed, but Iver was fiddling with the jacket button that he'd put through the wrong slit. The girl walked to the gate and lifted the barrier. Selva's father started the engine and guided the hauler through the arch and outside the city walls.

"I can speak for myself," Selva said.

"But you didn't."

She was looking back at the guards. "Did you see their hats? They're Wide Awakes."

"Did you see her gun?"

"What gun?"

"There was a pistol on the guard table."

Selva's notion of Wake Up the City hadn't advanced beyond alarms and uniforms and a sense of higher purpose that made her want to stand at attention. A gun was more serious than anything she'd contemplated.

"Well, what do you expect? They have to be ready."

"For what?" her father shot back.

"You know. For enemies."

"What if there are no enemies? What if being ready is what makes enemies?"

Selva didn't want to think about these things, because she was managing—just barely—to persist in the face of a glaring contradiction that the encounter with the guards had intensified. First, there was the thought that she was heading into something dark, frightening, possibly evil. And then there was the thought that she would be okay. She needed both to be true if she was going to answer the question that had come to her in the vision of stake-burning (*why hadn't she told that to the guard?*), and her father's questions threatened to upset her balance.

Instead of getting into one of their arguments, she said, "Oh, look!"

The land opened before them: the new outer settlements, the river marshes, the switchgrass country, the wooded foothills, the sawtooth mountain ridge that was the border of the old empire. And above everything the sun's watchful eye at its zenith.

She had forgotten about the sky. The Emergency had pulled her vision downward and inward, and for weeks nothing had existed except the city and its people; a self-org could contain a world. She knew that the sky today was beautiful, pale blue suffused with golden autumn light, but its presence frightened her.

"Could you stop for a minute?"

Her father steered the hauler off the hard road onto a patch of grass. Selva jumped out, grabbed her overnight bag from the bed, and fumbled inside until she found the goggles.

"You brought them?" her father said with a hint of accusation. "I thought you left them for Pan."

"I want to see if they work out here."

She strapped on the goggles and let out a little cry. She had hoped for new imagery, new visions, but the eyepieces were blanks.

"Maybe the range doesn't exceed the city limits," her father said.

"I'll try again in a few minutes."

But each time she strapped them on they were blank. Putting them on and taking them off and seeing the same sky was making her anxious. The sky was empty like the goggles; there was no escape.

She stuffed the goggles between her thigh and Zeus's rump. With two fingers of her right hand she felt for the pulse in her left wrist. She began to count.

Selva's pulse gauged the state of her mind and the level of meaning in the universe, *which were the same thing*. She never let anyone in her family witness this new habit of hers. Before the Emergency she had never needed to check her mood—had hardly been aware of having moods. But now she reached for her wrist almost daily, and on bad days—after the incident with Zeus in the park—she checked at least every hour. A rapid pulse meant that she was spiraling into a void, and knowing this only made the beats come faster. When consciousness became unbearable and the passage of time was an instrument of torture, she would put her head down and try to fall asleep. A few mornings ago, she had left the house and climbed the ladder and stood on the trapdoor hoping that the gallows would set her free one way or another. But when she removed the noose, nothing had changed. She was still herself.

She multiplied 26 by 4: 104 beats per minute. Not the worst, but not good. And they were just starting out. Her father glanced from the road and gave her a puzzled look. Selva ignored him—she wasn't going to explain. To distract herself from the sky she concentrated on the passing landscape.

The road ran north along the river, wide and sluggish as it flowed toward the city. They passed the newer brick settlements; her teacher lived in one of them. The sameness of family trips to the Place—this split oak tree, this beaver lodge midstream on a rocky bar of sediment—had always let her measure the changes in herself. Now there were changes outside, too—perhaps she hadn't known how to look for them. On weekends young Burgher families usually congregated in their gardens, but today no one was outside. The settlements seemed deserted, as if the life that spread incrementally outward beyond the city in all directions had come to a stop and begun to withdraw like a tide reversing course.

They left behind the last Burgher settlements. The river narrowed, and they crossed over a wooden bridge into a lush meadow fed by marshes and lined with giant hardwood trees. As the road diverged from the river, the green of the land began to fade and they entered the open country. The switchgrass was now tall and dry, fields of plumes swayed and shone golden in the early afternoon light. This had always been the boring part of the drive, the monotonous land endured with rounds of road songs while the foothills never seemed to get closer. The smell of dry grass entered the hauler's open windows on thin autumn air. After the past humid days, it had turned cooler; the night would be chilly. Zeus lay curled asleep with his chin on the gearshift while Selva stroked his tail.

"*I'm sailing across the deep blue sea.*" Her father waited for her to pick up the next line. When she didn't, he said, "Almost like old times."

"Not really. Where are all the trucks?"

Produce trucks usually passed them heading south in such numbers that she and Pan competed to identify all the major vegetables and grains, and their parents secretly tipped off her brother to give him an even chance. But today their hauler was the only vehicle on the road.

"I meant this. Our little adventure."

"Oh, like a fishing trip or something? With your coat of arms back up on the door?"

He laughed. "I'm learning to live without a coat of arms."

"It's not the same anymore."

She disliked the testiness in her voice but couldn't help it, so she gazed out her window in silence.

"One reason I'm glad you came," her father said, "is we never get a chance to talk much these days."

"We talk all the time."

"Am I right that you've been going out again? Self-org? We Are One?"

Selva groaned. "Papa, is it going to be like this the whole way?"

"Like what?"

"'*I'll show you my soul and you show me yours*'?"

"God, no. That would be disgusting."

A hundred yards up the road a clay-brick house came into view on the left, with several outbuildings around a dirt yard. A family of switchgrass farmers lived here, with a clutch of kids that seemed to grow bigger every summer. It was the first Yeoman settlement on the road north. The Rustins never stopped here, it was too early in the drive, but Selva and Pan always opened their windows and leaned out to wave and shout, "Hello!" and the switchgrass children raced from the doorway to the roadside and waved back, "Hello, hello!" since a vehicle passing with city children inside wasn't a common sight. After years of this brief annual exchange, the two families had come to recognize each other.

Children were playing in the dirt. Selva waved tentatively out the window. An older girl and a boy stopped what they were doing and watched the hauler pass. One of the little children started wobbling toward the road on undersized legs, but his big sister caught him by the wrist and yanked him into the air.

A tremendous noise exploded in the back of the hauler. It sounded like a bullet slamming against the metal gate. Zeus scrambled to his feet. Her father jerked the wheel right and nearly drove into the switchgrass before he was able to straighten out. Selva turned around to look.

A rock the size of a lemon was rolling to a stop in the middle of the road. Farther back, the girl had the toddler in her arms and the boy was waving a slingshot.

"Burghers!"

His call was neither a greeting nor a curse. It expressed no malice and no warmth. It was a loud statement of fact, a blunt identifier—yet it carried a message that struck even harder than the rock that accompanied it. The Rustins were no longer city people on their annual pilgrimage, known to the switchgrass family from past years. They were members of an alien tribe who had wandered onto terrain where their welfare was a matter of complete indifference. The boy had yelled "Burghers!" the way, momentarily interested in a flock of migrating geese, he might have yelled "Birds!" and fired off a spray of lead shot.

Selva exchanged a glance with her father and opened her eyes and mouth wide. Their little adventure. "*Someday, darling, I will return*," she sang out, leaving her panic behind, and they both burst into laughter.

2

At a wooden watchtower from some bygone era the hard road ended and turned to washboard dirt. This was the sign that they were leaving the open country, the golden grass and dry earth giving way to brown soil, the land gently rising into rolling hills, cultivated fields and pastures, evergreen tree lines along hidden streams, and Yeoman villages.

They had been driving over an hour and were more than halfway to the Place. Selva thought of the boy's father walking in the opposite direction, walking in a group of Strangers from the other side of the sawtooth mountains, possessions and children on their backs, heads down, past wild animals and Yeomen, day after day, step by step all the way to the city and an unknown life. Their courage awed her, and she wondered what misery had compelled them to endure such a journey. She refused to believe her father's story, that Mr. Monge had left his son for dead. She imagined a different one: Yeomen had kidnapped the boy and were holding him in a dank root cellar.

A couple of miles beyond the end of the hard road they came to the first village in this part of the foothills. It was relatively prosperous, known for its fruit trees, with a pretty house of worship in the middle of the village that also served as a meeting hall, a communal tractor that ran on switchgrass fuel, and a large stable of draft horses that belonged to the village council. Houses were clustered on either side of the road, flower beds and vegetable gardens and pieces of farm equipment in the front yards, green woods behind.

The Rustins always stopped here for refreshments at a roadside stand before driving the last leg to the Place. The stand was owned by an old village councilor and his wife whose house, built in the wood-frame Yeoman style, with a pitched cedar-shingle roof and vertical pine siding, was set back from the road in a fruit orchard. Whenever the Rustins pulled over, one or the other of the couple would emerge from the house and amble over to the stand and pour drinks and exchange small talk about the weather, the harvest, Selva and Pan's schooling. Her father would always intend to stick to persimmon juice, then give in to temptation and down a cup of plum wine.

One year, they happened to pass through the village on the day of a midsummer festival celebrating the fruit harvest. The road was crowded with food stands, choruses of villagers singing traditional Yeoman songs, children throwing horseshoes and jumping rope, horse carts giving hay rides, auctioneers selling off farm animals and equipment, men betting on cockfights while guzzling jugs of millet beer. In a field a game of kickball was being played with a goat's head. When the Rustins stopped, children gathered around to admire their vehicle, and a girl invited Pan and Selva to join a potato-sack race that was about to start, and peach pies were thrust on the parents. The Rustins had talked about that day for months afterward—one of their best family memories, brief admission into a different life. "That's why it's called Good Development," her father had said.

They waited in the hauler while Zeus relieved himself on the leg of the juice stand and picked up the scent of a rabbit or chicken. Selva noticed that the stand was empty—the usual jugs and jars and cups were missing. When no one came out of the house, she wondered if the old couple had died.

"Maybe they're inside," she said. "I'll go see."

Selva was out of the hauler before her father could stop her. She followed a stone path to the front porch, hardly more than a covered step, and put her ear to the door. Just above her head hung something white. She stepped back and took in the bleached bones and skull of a small creature—a bird, with a thin, rusty wire wrapped around its spine and looped to a nail in the door.

There was a soft noise on the other side, like wheezing. She knocked once, and the door immediately opened.

The old man stood staring at Selva as if he'd been listening at the door. His lips quivered over nearly toothless gums in an effort to form a sentence, but astonishment defeated him. His white beard was chopped straight across the middle of his chest, his features were knobby, his dim eyes moist. An unraveling cotton nightdress exposed the sagging muscle and bony flesh of his shoulders and calves. From within the house came a stale smell of unwashed bedding.

"I'm sorry to disturb you." She didn't know the old man's name. He seemed to have aged years since their last visit. "We usually stop for your delicious juice."

Alarm was clearing away the filmy web from his eyes. "We've got no juice, young miss. Trees didn't produce this year." He glanced over her shoulder to the street. "We weren't expecting anyone."

"What happened to your fruit?"

"Well—" The old man lifted a sinewy arm and scratched the back of his head. "Everything went wrong with the Conspiracy and all. The vines got so bad—you can see for yourself, miss, out back." He jerked a thumb over his shoulder.

"I'm too old to fight 'em. Took most of the whole orchard. My plum trees are just about killed."

"Did you say 'Conspiracy'?"

"You know. When they had that trouble in the capital."

"You mean the Emergency."

The old man's mouth fell open, and out of the dark cavity came a high, sharp laugh. "That's not what we call it here, miss."

"You call it the Conspiracy?"

"We like to give things their rightful name."

You, we, here. The conversation had already shifted from vines and fruit trees to the fraught topic of Burghers and Yeomen. She felt that her presence was unwelcome, but the old man was too polite to say so. He kept looking at the street, and when Selva turned around to see what might be there, her father gave the hauler's horn an anemic toot.

The old man withdrew a step into the house and laid a hand on the door. "If that'll be all, miss—"

"Hey!"

On the porch of the house next door a man was pointing at the hauler.

"Did you just honk?"

He put two fingers in his mouth and produced a whistle that was much louder than the horn. Within half a minute two men with swelling bellies appeared from nearby houses. They converged on the road and walked quickly three across toward the drink stand. They were wearing different kinds of farm clothes—overalls on the man who'd whistled, shapeless canvas jackets and laceless boots on the other two. All three were trailing long objects in hand.

Zeus, sitting beside a front tire and already agitated by animal scents, got to his feet and barked to warn off the men.

Her father shushed him and motioned Selva to hurry back to the hauler. She saw him grab the goggles and stash them under the bench. When the farmers were twenty feet off, he started to say, "Good afternoon—"

"You don't honk in this village." It was the farmer who had whistled. "There's rules." The men were about her father's age, shorter but powerful, even the two fat ones, with thick beards and hard faces. They were all holding machetes. "What are you doing here?" The first man pointed his machete at her father. "You from the city?"

"I was just talking to your neighbor about his fruit trees," Selva said, and she looked toward the house for confirmation, but the door with the tiny bird skeleton was closed. From behind a window curtain two faces, the old man's and his wife's, were peering out.

"Yes, from the city," her father said. "I'm Doctor Hugo Rustin."

That morning, after telling Selva not to wear her Stranger outfit, he added that he'd chosen clothing based on what would have been least acceptable at the Physicians Social Club—trousers losing their hems, an oversized flannel shirt, his canvas fishing jacket. She thought he looked just like a Burgher on a dubious trip to the country. And here he was, already putting on the air of a guild member.

The farmer again extended his machete. "Who gave you permission to come here?"

"What permission? We come every year."

The farmer spat out a harsh laugh that the other two joined. "Not this year."

"We're passing through. We stopped for something to drink."

The farmer extended his free hand palm up. The ring

finger was missing its top joint; the wound was ragged and blackened. "Let me see your hand."

"What?"

The farmer grabbed her father's hand with his damaged one and rubbed a thumb over the palm and fingers. He looked at the other two men and nodded. "You can always tell. Like a baby's bottom." There was more laughter at the Burgher's expense.

"Actually, I work with my hands," her father said. "I'm a surgeon, and I'd like to take a look at that finger."

"It doesn't want to look at you." The farmer ordered him out of the hauler and pointed his machete down the road. "Let's go."

She saw her father stiffen at the pressure of a hand between his shoulder blades and realized she'd never seen anyone use force on him. The hand gave a shove. "What is this?" he asked dismissively, the way he'd asked the guard at the North Gate whether the barrier, the questions, the pass were all necessary. As if the existence of two mutually suspicious, possibly armed camps was a misunderstanding that could be cleared up if they all just returned to their senses. This was her father's way of dealing with people of a different, usually lower, station, and what she knew and he didn't was that it enraged them.

As he was taken away Selva started to follow.

"You stay here, little girl," the farmer said.

"I'm going with him."

The men exchanged amused looks at the little girl's boldness. "Suit yourself." When Zeus started to follow, the man brandished his weapon. "Not the dog."

"Zeus, you stay," her father commanded, and Zeus sat by the hauler in his good-boy position with anxious eyes.

They led father and daughter down the road through the middle of the village. It was strange how few people were out—on previous visits the place always hummed with life, human and animal. Other than a woman kneeling in her vegetable patch, half-hidden under a headscarf, and a boy leading his donkey by a rope, the village appeared deserted. But Selva felt unseen eyes watching from houses, like the old man and woman at their window. She passed familiar landmarks—a hexagonal wooden well, a burial ground of tilted headstones—and they were like images in a dream, as if a curse had been laid on the village.

The meeting hall stood behind a row of sumacs. The sentry-like trees and the bright white of the horizontal siding told you that this was the most important building in the village. By now the slender leaves would have turned deep vermilion—but the sumacs had become stumps, except for two whose tortured branches had no leaves at all. The lower courses of the siding were stained green with mold spreading up from the dirt. As the group approached the tall double doors, Selva saw that the two wooden plaques, the traditional symbols of empire, temporal and spiritual—crossed rifle and book on the left door, raised hand with a spiral in its palm on the right—were gone. In their place was a pair of animal heads mounted on cedar boards: a black bear and a tawny fox, wide-eyed and snarling.

Inside, the hall was dark, with only two windows, and smelled of rotting wood. The men led Selva and her father to a front-row bench, then climbed a platform, took their chairs, and laid their machetes on the table in front of them: rough-bearded, sun-darkened farmers where the robed temple priest and village councilors would have once presided. The man who had whistled sat in the middle.

"This is Brother Baard here on my right and Brother Zorigt on my left," he said. "I'm Leader Gandorig. The committee will begin the proceeding. State your names."

Selva noticed that her father's eyelid was twitching. "Doctor Hugo Rustin," he said again, and added, "chief surgeon, Imperial College Hospital. This is my—"

"Selva Rustin," she announced, in a voice that she hoped was loud enough to conceal her fear.

Leader Gandorig looked at his hands. They were splayed flat on the table with the mutilated stub of a finger sticking out. He wrote nothing down, having nothing to write with or on. There was a long pause while he consulted in whispers with Brothers Baard and Zorigt. The strength of his whistle and machete was already ebbing in the dark hush of the hall. These farmers were like the Wide Awake guards at the North Gate, making up new procedures on the spot. The Leader's face was changing, too, filling in Selva's first impression of a standard Yeoman farmer with the features of a distinct person: beard growing far up his cheeks to just below the eyes, deep furrows between the eyebrows, tight lips, a face of laconic worry. Gandorig looked like a responsible man, and it was easy to see why he'd become the Leader. He would think before using his machete on another person, then bring it down decisively. Baard and Zorigt, with their wide, froglike faces emerging from rolls of neck fat, were more like the caricature of slow-witted Yeomen.

"State your purpose in trespassing on Yeoman land."

"Don't we all still live in the same land?" her father asked.

Baard slammed his fist on the table and muttered something vehement to Gandorig, who said, "Brother Baard here is recognized."

"Hell, no!" Baard stood up and jabbed a finger at the man

seated below him. "You Burghers come here and ruin everything. You ruined all our crops—fruit, grain. You killed our livestock. Now you say this is your land? We don't want you here! Get out!"

"Not my land. Our land."

Gandorig placed a hand on Baard's arm and eased him back into his chair. He turned to Selva's father. "You and your little girl wander into our village looking for plum wine like nothing's happened? Are you some kind of fool?"

"We've received very little information from your region since the Emergency." Her father lowered his voice as if he could settle the Yeomen down with his tone. "My daughter and I came here in good faith."

Selva leaned toward him and whispered, "They call it 'the Conspiracy.'"

Her father shook his head as if to tell her to keep out, but Gandorig had heard. "That's right. Smart little girl. 'Emergency' is one of your weasel words to let you people off the hook."

"Frankly, I don't believe in conspiracies," her father said. "Bad things don't happen because hidden powers cook up secret plots. They happen because people of every kind can be selfish and short-sighted—my people and your people."

Anger flamed in Gandorig's eyes. "No speeches!" He seized the machete and shook it at his prisoner. "Here's some news for you. Last year the vines came to our village. No one ever saw them before—I asked the old councilors. The vines weren't too bad, and we let them be. Seemed like winter killed them off. This spring, after what happened in the capital, we were too busy getting the village organized to notice at first. The vines came back alive. They started growing everywhere there was sunlight and a tree. Grew faster and thicker than we could keep up. Big as my arm." Gandorig grabbed his wrist. "Cut 'em back, they keep coming. Wrapping around the trunks and branches, strangling the trees like giant constrictor snakes, pulling them down, killing all the fruit that keeps us alive. We spent so much time fighting the vines, we couldn't take good care of our crops, and most of them failed."

"If these vines—"

"If? You damn Burgher." Gandorig displayed his injured hand. "Why the hell do you think I was chopping so hard I took off my own finger?"

Baard and Zorigt raised machetes and hands in solidarity with the Leader, though all their fingers seemed to be present.

"You talk as if it's our fault," Selva's father said.

Gandorig sucked air from his nostrils into his chest, and his lips disappeared into his mouth. He looked from Baard to Zorigt.

"Guess he is a fool," Zorigt said.

"Let's get to the thing," Baard said. "The punishment."

Gandorig let out the breath. "First we need to know why they trespassed."

"Leader Gandorig, please explain how the vines are our fault."

"Funny how they think they're so much smarter than us," Baard said to the other two, "and he couldn't find his ass in broad daylight."

"He's lying," Zorigt said. "He knows all about the vines."

"We never heard of them till now," her father said. "Lots of things have happened in the city that you probably never heard of. Do you know about Better Humans?"

Selva felt a shock pass up her spine. She had never told her parents about Better Humans. She was willing for them to know about every other new thing that got her out of bed and filled her days so that she didn't have to check her pulse every hour: self-orgs, We Are One, the Wide Awakes—even the Suicide Spot. But her Better Human was her private business, the secret poised between her deepest shame and wildest hope.

"We know about *worse* humans," Baard said. "Know all about lying, cheating, stealing humans. They're called Burghers."

"Our communities no longer trust each other," her father went on. "You've stopped selling us your goods, and we've stopped taking your sick and wounded. At my hospital a few weeks ago I operated on a Yeoman boy—that couldn't happen today. It's hurting everyone."

"Whose fault is that?" Gandorig shot back.

"It's an unfortunate result of the Emergency. We have to find a way to communicate again."

"You must think we're dumber than farm animals."

"Tell us what we did to you."

Eyes fixed on his prisoner, the Leader explained how, several years ago, Burghers had imported vines from overseas to plant in their little city gardens; how Burghers prized the vines for their pretty autumn berries, yellow and red; how migrating birds ate the berries and then flew over the countryside, spreading the seeds; how the seeds found perfect soil in the farmland of the foothills, and the vines found perfect hosts in the region's forests and fruit orchards.

As the Leader talked, Selva stole glances at her father: the thick, graying hair; the bland, handsome face; lips slightly parted in a reflexive smile; bright, straight teeth; hand cupping chin in attentive listening. This was her father and always had been, but she felt as if she was seeing him for the first time and through Yeomen's eyes: he was a disembodied head, refined and calm, all mind. Yet inside the head, she knew he was laboring to make sense of it, to think at all.

"Just try to deny it." The story had filled the Leader with fresh outrage.

"Then it's the birds' fault," her father said. "And some ignorant city people. I plant my backyard with native shrubs and flowers."

"You *planned* it," Gandorig said, jabbing the air with his machete. The other two made loud noises of agreement and hit the table with their fists. "Burghers could never beat Yeomen in a fair fight, so you found a coward's way. And you timed it for when the trouble started. Every Yeoman knows this."

Selva, thinking of the empty road behind them and the city's half-empty markets, asked, "Is that why you stopped your trucks?" The farmers didn't answer—she was too unimportant—so she insisted: "Did you stop your trucks because you didn't have enough food for yourselves?"

"That was at first." Gandorig still addressed her father, as if Selva hadn't spoken. "We had to hold back some meat and produce, and there was no fruit to ship. Then we put two and two together. Why go on feeding people that are trying to kill us off?"

She said, "People in our city think *you're* trying to kill *us* off."

Gandorig gave a disgusted laugh. "Burghers mean nothing to us. We do all the work in this empire. We grow the food, we fight the wars. We don't need you people. You're like those vines, choking us. You're—Brother, what's the word you said the other day?"

Gandorig looked at Baard, but Baard was unable to help. Then Gandorig had it.

"Parasites." His voice made the same noise over and over, hammering like a machine tool, driving its object to submission.

"This is the Conspiracy?" her father asked. Gandorig gave a firm nod. "But why?"

"You hate our way of life. You don't even think we're human. You want to starve us into slavery and live on the fruits of our labor and take over the empire. But you don't know what you've started."

Her father slumped in his seat as if he was succumbing to the gloomy light, the moldy smell, the hardness of the bench, the Leader's voice, the new reality too fantastical to resist.

"Moving on to the punishment," Gandorig said.

From outside the hall came the sound of voices, low murmurs with jags of cursing or laughter. It was the noise of an excited crowd trying to keep quiet, like in the main square on the morning of exam results. Selva turned around and saw, pressed up against the windows on either side of the entrance doors, a mass of faces—open mouths of eager children, blank stares of grown men.

"Lucky for you they respect our authority," Gandorig said, "or there's no telling what they'd do."

Selva cleared her throat. "I wish to inform the committee that you still don't know why we came here. Without a motive, how can you determine our punishment?"

Her father pressed his thigh against hers—a caution. She moved her leg away. The men on the platform were looking at one another with shades of humor and confusion.

"The little girl is smarter than her papa," Gandorig said. "All right, then. Tell us why you came here."

"To spy on us," Baard said.

"And laugh at us," Zorigt said.

"We came here because of what my father said." The story emerged all at once, clear and logical. "A Yeoman boy was brought to the hospital with gunshot wounds. My father saved his life. Now the boy is back in his village, and he needs follow-up care. One of the bullets is still in him, right, Papa?" Her father was slow to nod. "The hospital changed its policy because of anti-Yeoman sentiment, and now they won't take the boy. My father disagrees with that. He came out here to fulfill his professional duty, and he brought me along as his nurse. It's a humanitarian mission. Show them our pass, Papa."

From his leather billfold her father pulled out the hospital's letter of appreciation.

"The other one, Papa." When he produced the right document, Selva took it from him and stood up. "Request permission to approach the committee." Without waiting for permission she marched up to the platform and unfolded the document on the table before the Leader. She tapped a finger on the bottom of the page. "See? 'Humanitarian mission.'"

The men leaned together over the paper while Selva stood by. Something in the room had shifted. She hadn't softened them with her tale of this doctor's goodness, but her confidence had taken away a little of their power.

"What's this?" Gandorig held up the paper and pointed at the image of hand-holding, cutout silhouettes.

"That, Mr. Leader, is the symbol of self-government in our city. It stands for togetherness."

"Looks like something a child drew."

"'*Listen to the young*'—that's one of our principles. It's a symbol of the common bond between all human beings."

"Let's get on with the punishment," Baard said. Her words seemed to anger him.

"Just wait a minute, Brother Baard." Gandorig turned

back to Selva, who stood before the platform with her hands clasped behind her back like a student facing her guild examination board. "You're a smart girl"—she was no longer little—"so tell me how this works. We're all human beings, but a Yeoman boy can't go to your hospital?"

"That's the tragedy of this situation," Selva said solemnly. "We're torn between our principles and our safety."

Gandorig chuckled, and the furrows between his eyebrows faded. "That's a shame. Around here we're not torn up at all. You know why? Our principles *is* our safety."

"That's interesting, Mr. Leader. I was just wondering how you decided your form of self-government after the Emergency."

"Conspiracy," Baard growled.

"The councilors were all too old," Gandorig said, warming to their exchange. "We called the village together right in this hall, and they chose us three as having the deepest roots here. My family goes back seven generations."

"What about your ideas? Your governing values?"

"Same as before. Hard work, honesty, respect for the way things were always done. We're not going to start the world over like some farm boys around here think they can do." A thought made him frown, deepening the furrows. "Survival. That's our number-one value."

"I noticed you took down the imperial plaques outside, and replaced them with animal heads."

"That was just something a few young folks did." The subject seemed to make Gandorig uneasy. Selva stood before the platform until, with a gesture, he sent her back to the bench.

Zorigt was starting to look bored. Baard, his jowly face sunk unhappily into his neck, aimed a question at Selva's father. "What's the boy's name?"

"The boy?"

"With the gunshots."

He hesitated. "Kask."

"Kask? What Kask?"

"I don't know his other name."

"Half the people around here are named Kask. Brother Zorigt's sister is married to a Kask. What village did you say he's in?"

Selva didn't wait for her father to answer. She named the settlement, a mile or two from the Place, near where Mr. Monge's son had last been seen, and where the family of pig farmers named Cronk lived. She wasn't sure if she'd come up with a brilliant ruse or set herself an idiotic trap, but she felt certain that she was thinking faster than her father.

The three men conferred in low voices. Baard did most of the talking, and as he talked his flat face with wide-set eyes turned the color of a local plum. Gandorig replied in terse phrases. Finally he picked up his machete and sliced the air to end the discussion.

This old tool cut vines and fingers and maybe heads, but at least it contained the Leader's authority, like a judge's gavel or emperor's scepter. That was better than the faces at the windows. Selva thought of We Are One: how in the main square no one was in charge, everyone got a say, and the final decision was not only the right one but the one that left everyone happy. That was the best way to run things—far better than this committee of farmers about to deliver a verdict based on rumor and fantasy. But she would rather face Gandorig than a Yeoman We Are One.

"We've reached our decision," the Leader announced. The committee had heard the news of a boy with gunshot wounds. It was an unfortunate example of the youthful wildness that was all too common in the region as a result of the Conspiracy—though not in this village, where the adults were still in charge and the rules were strict. By unanimous verdict, the father and daughter would be allowed to continue their humanitarian mission (Brother Baard was glaring at a point above their heads), but being Burghers, they would need a special pass to travel safely through Yeoman land. Their city pass would remain in the committee's hands. It would be returned on completion of their mission, when they passed through the village on their way home.

What Gandorig handed over was not a document but a bone almost a foot long, jagged at either end, part of a large animal's leg or even a human femur. Along one side was a carved image of what appeared to be the blade and handle of a machete.

"Show this at checkpoints—they'll know," Gandorig said. "If you lose it, you're on your own." He remained seated, as if he were reluctant to let them go. "Don't try to fool us. We'll find you. All of us look out for each other."

The crowd out front had grown large and restless. The farmers hustled Selva and her father behind the platform through a small rear door, so low they had to duck. They came out onto a patch of overgrown grass. Beyond it stood the forest, as gloomy as the hall, green density receding into denser darkness. The trees were the height of mature cedars, but it was impossible to tell what kind of trees they were, for their shapes were lumpy and all flowed together. As Selva's eye followed them upward she realized that she was seeing not the trees themselves but swarming masses of shiny oval leaves, thickening as they climbed trunks and branches, luxuriating like plush velvet drapery. Most of the trees had disappeared inside their stranglers and only poked out at the top as bare, dead wood. Near a relatively free evergreen, a ropy vine grew out of the dirt unsupported through midair thirty feet up on a straight path to seize the nearest branch. Next to it, an oak was collapsing like an elephant pulled to the ground by lines and nets.

"You see?" Gandorig said.

Zeus was waiting where they had left him. His tail raised a greeting of dust. Selva had been fighting off a vision of his head hanging from a door, eyes wide in soulful surprise.

3

"*I'm sailing across the deep blue sea,*" she sang as they drove out of the village. She sang because she felt giddy with triumph, until a strange choking sound—part laugh, part gasp—exploded from her chest. "That was crazy! I can't believe they let us go."

"It wasn't a good idea to lie to them, Selva. Spies lie. We might not be so lucky at the next village."

"We weren't lucky." She was annoyed not to be profusely thanked. If her father had been on his own, right now he'd be locked in a wooden cage in the middle of the village, hogtied and flogged, mauled by trained wolves. He appeared to be less equipped for their mission than his fourteen-year-old child. Inside the hall he'd fallen into a daze from which she'd had to save them both. "You were going to let them punish us."

"No."

"Then what?"

His hands tightened on the wheel. "I was going to tell them about Mr. Monge's son. I was going to appeal to them as fathers."

She laughed again, but this was false laughter, tight and forced. "Oh, a Stranger—that would have worked! The farmer who was about to have a stroke? I don't think so."

The road dipped and climbed and wound uphill, past a half-mown hayfield and a bitten-down pasture where a dozen sheep grazed behind a broken split-rail fence. Her father's window filled with the western glare. The sun of late afternoon didn't frighten her; it wasn't the indifferent eye of midday; its melting light spread over her like a soft embrace. They had lost more than an hour, and it would soon be getting dark. Normally a prudent driver, her father accelerated into bends, spinning up dirt, making the hauler cough and shudder. Selva leaned out her window and breathed the rich smell of soil and manure.

Now she saw the vines everywhere. Some trees were healthy on one side and sick on the other. Some evergreens had lost all their needles and stood dead in the clutch of a rope curtain that was also dying. The vines had an appetite for anything vertical, even human structures. A grain silo was completely wrapped in greenery, and a barn stood abandoned in a sunlit field while vines crept up the sides and entered hollow windows, ran along the eaves, climbed the roof, punched through its shingles, and ate the exposed rafters, so that the entire barn was collapsing in on itself.

"*Serpents*," her father muttered. A minute later: "Do they really think we did this to them?"

She had never heard him sound so dispirited, and it made her nervous. "I tried to tell you. Man-eaters."

"They're not man-eaters," he said. "They're deluded. Which is worse."

"Why?"

"You can reason with man-eaters when they're full. Those farmers want revenge. They'll never get enough."

The road straightened and flattened as it passed between ragged hedgerows of yew and hawthorn. Selva always thought of this stretch as the beginning of the end of the trip.

"What's our plan, Papa?"

He took a breath to gather himself. "Camp at the Place, then go to the pig farm in the morning, see if the Cronks can give us any information. It'll be different talking to them. They know us, they won't—"

He hit the brake hard. Selva, gazing out her window at the dappled light through the hedgerow, was thrown forward. She looked up and saw what her father had seen.

Twenty feet ahead, a dead tree limb the thickness of a man's thigh lay across the road. On Selva's side, half-hidden by the hedge, a figure was sitting in a chair and pointing a rifle at the hauler. It was impossible to tell if the figure was old or young, male or female, or even fully human, because it had the shape of a bull. Black horns grew from a furred scalp. Severed ears and hooves dangled at its sides. The body was wrapped in a shawl of brown hide, and the face aiming the gun had the inflamed eyes and flared, gold-ringed nostrils of a bull mask of painted wood.

The bull struggled to get up on its hind legs. It was naked below the waist, displaying a young man's loins and a plainly human penis. Standing, the bull wobbled, knocking over the chair and spilling liquid from a clay pot, toppled backward to the ground, and fired a single shot straight up into the sky.

"*Yeeeaaarrrg!*"

The noise came from the far hedgerow. Another lavish figure ran out to the road. It was a wolf—a very tall one—also armed, also half-naked. The wolf dashed across the road in front of the hauler and stood over the fallen bull and jammed the stock of its rifle into the other's belly.

"Get up! Damn fool! *Burghburghkillems!*"

While the bull groaned and tried to get to its feet, the wolf ran to the hauler, waving the gun overhead. Selva's father wrapped an arm around her shoulders and with his other hand made an effort to cover her eyes. She pushed his hand off her face.

Just before reaching her door the wolf tripped, nearly fell, and righted itself. "*Fuck!*" It lurched toward Selva's open window, and she recoiled from the sour stink of millet beer and human sweat.

The wolf's face was not a carved wooden mask but the furry features of the animal itself, with pointed ears and open predator jaws and cutouts that revealed bloodshot eyes. The eyes roved over Selva and her father and Zeus, who was baring teeth and barking louder than he had that night in the park with the hooded figure. "Come on, *Burghburghkillems!*" the wolf yelled. "Gimme gimme give!"

"What do you want?" her father asked.

"Pay toll."

"How much?"

The wolf quoted a fee that was equal to half a chief surgeon's annual salary. It was drunk, Selva realized—too drunk to notice the bags in the hauler's bed.

Her father leaned under his seat and pulled out the carved bone. "We have this." He drew his finger along the machete engraving. "See? We're approved."

The wolf reached through the window across Selva, brushing her chest with a hairy forearm. Zeus growled as the arm withdrew with the bone. The wolf made a show of studying it. "No good."

"It's from Leader Gandorig. Safe conduct through Yeoman land."

"Gandorig! *Yeeeaaarrrg!*" The wolf tipped its head back and let out a howl of rage that set Zeus barking again. "*We* control here."

At that moment the bull arrived by the wolf's side, and

they fought over the bone. Both were standing too close to Selva's door for her to see more than heads and torsos, but she couldn't help thinking of what was down below. It wasn't their nakedness that horrified her but the fact that neither the wolf nor the bull seemed to care, or even know. They were beyond human reach.

The wolf regained possession of the bone, took it between its teeth, and shook it like rodent prey, then hurled the bone high over the hauler into the far hedge, prompting a squeal of laughter from the bull.

"Hey!" her father cried. "We need that!"

He was doing everything wrong again—talking, engaging. She knew they had to get free of these two right now, their breath and bodies smelling like death. On impulse she pulled the goggles from under the seat and waved them in front of the wolf and the bull. "Look! They're magic!" She tossed the goggles into the hedge and watched the two scramble after them, the wolf in front, the bull stumbling and thrusting its horns at the other's hairless buttocks.

Selva leaned across Zeus. "*Go!*"

The tree limb jolted all four wheels front and back but wasn't big enough to stop the hauler. In half a minute they were out of range. Selva waited for the sound of gunshots, but none came, and no village appeared—only road and fields and strangled trees in the setting sun. The wolf and the bull had set up their checkpoint in the middle of nowhere.

"Highwaymen," her father said.

"Highway animals," Selva said. "Happy? I got rid of them."

"We'll get another set."

She had meant the wolf and the bull, not the goggles. "I don't want another set."

"Bones and masks," her father said. "Animal worship.

Kask had a name for it—I can't remember." He pulled off the road and came to an abrupt stop on a narrow grass shoulder. In the woods below there was a stream. By now it was too dark to see, but they could hear water running over rocks. Selva gave her father a quizzical look. "Call of nature," he said.

When he returned, he sat with his hands on the wheel and stared through the windshield.

"What's wrong?" she asked.

He took his hands off the wheel and pressed them to his eye sockets. "Mama was right. I made a mistake, Sel, a big mistake."

In the dying light she saw on his face a look of defeat that she'd never seen. What she had always taken for a deep, quiet knowing of things she didn't yet know but would learn from him turned out to be mere comfort in the surfaces of a vanished life—table talk about school and work, a city without Strangers, plum wine. Take those away and he was lost. The realization terrified and thrilled her.

"What mistake?"

"I thought there'd be someone in charge that we could deal with out here. Every checkpoint is going to have its own boss." He began to hit his eyes with the heels of his hands.

"Papa, please stop."

"I'm sorry, I should have listened, why don't I listen to you?" Selva understood that he was talking to her mother. Then he looked up as if seized with a new idea. "We have to go home."

"What?"

"At first light. We'll find a back road."

"I refuse. We came all this way. We're doing fine."

"Sel, maybe you're too—"

"Just drive."

4

They left the hauler where they always parked, at a bend in the road, below a derelict water tower whose wooden supports were smothered in vines that climbed as high as the metal tank. But along the trail into the forest where sunlight didn't penetrate, the hardwoods were still visible. Zeus, liberated from his daylong confinement, galloped ahead, nose to the ground, sprinting after a scent and then returning to the trail. Selva followed behind her father, who pointed his torch at roots and rocks and a trickle of muddy stream. It was almost full night, and the path took so many turns that they would have gotten hopelessly lost if not for Zeus's memory of earlier visits. She knew the lake was near by the sound of the river running, the rising noise of frogs, glimpses of stars.

The Place was a flat clearing covered in pine needles between the woods and the ground's slope to the water's edge. They had happened on it one summer when she was eight or nine, during a family hike (Pan was still riding in the homemade carrier on their father's shoulders, constantly pulling off his hat). Selva, the dauntless pathfinder forging ahead, had been the first to see the lake. It wasn't very big—if you yelled loud enough you could almost talk with someone on the far side—but the tall pines ringing it all around were reflected on the sunlit surface, and its silver blue was the color of deep water, and the sight had brought her up short. She had stood in silence and held her breath, feeling that she had come upon an unknown land. She named it the Place because any other name would have diminished the sense of magnificent isolation, which not even the discovery on a subsequent trip of an abandoned hunting cabin in the nearby woods could take away.

Her father set his pack on the ground and pulled out the contents. He lit the paraffin lamp, and Selva poured a bowl of food for Zeus. They went through the procedure that he'd taught her years ago and she knew by heart: spread the canvas tent flat with its opening turned so that on waking they would see the lake, hammer the metal stakes all the way down with rocks, assemble the bamboo poles and thread them through the loops (when she was little she always got this part wrong), raise the structure so that tension on all sides kept the tent standing. While he hunted in the woods for dead branches and stones, she walked down to the dark water and filled the cooking pot. Then she crawled inside the tent and laid out the bedroll for herself and a blanket for him. She lay in the bedroll and watched her father make the campfire and chop potatoes and beans.

She should be helping, but it was so pleasant to lie here in the shelter of the tent with her face by the opening. The moon was a diminishing sliver above the lake, the stars profuse, and as she looked for the constellations he'd taught her to see she found herself slipping into a trance from the smell of cooking oil over the fire and the long drive and the strange encounters on the way. Her father was working in his fishing jacket, the rapid precision of his pocketknife, the stiffness in his lower back, shoulders a little hunched as he once said hers would also be after years in the medicine guild. He was humming tunelessly to himself, a habit when he didn't think anyone was paying attention.

All day she had found him annoying, as if he were a helpless child and she the parent. But now, watching him by the firelight, she was eight years old again and hungry from a hike and her father was cooking dinner for them. In a few minutes they would be sitting together with the crackle of the fire and forks scraping tin plates. If he was no longer the most perfect man in the world, she loved him all the more. And when he called her to eat, she knelt beside him and wrapped her arms around his neck.

"Oh, Papa."

By the time they had finished and washed up at the lake, the night was cold. He took the blanket from the tent, and they sat with it wrapped around their shoulders by the embers glowing in a ring of stones. He poured a cup of grain whiskey and speared a coal with his knife to light a cigar, while Zeus lay snoring at his feet. The familiar smells made Selva sleepy. She fought it off.

"What do you know about Better Humans?" she asked.

He drew on his cigar. "Not much," he said into a cloud of smoke. "Almost nothing."

"But what?"

"I saw a sign in the Warehouse District and asked a man about it."

"Who was he?"

"The type of odd character you find there."

"What did he tell you?"

"Something about being like gods. Perfecting our humanity. I didn't press him."

He waited, but Selva said nothing. Leave Better Humans alone. Talking about it would ruin it, the way her family had come up behind her after she'd discovered the lake and made banal comments about the pretty view.

"Where's my Sel tonight?" her father asked.

She stared into the campfire's orange glow. "Your Sel wishes she could light a match and burn the past. Just burn it all up."

After a silence he said, "Why would you want to do that?"

She wanted to destroy this mood that she had allowed to wrap her in its arms, the comfort of firelight and Zeus asleep and her father's soft voice in the dark. "To feel like I did today, with the Yeomen."

"How did you feel with the Yeomen?"

"Like I knew what I was doing." She didn't say: *Like I didn't need you.*

He took a sip of whiskey and set his cup on the ground. "If you set fire to the past, I'd lose a few things that are very valuable to me."

"Name one."

"The bones museum."

She had been nine years old the summer he took her by riverboat to visit the capital. Just the two of them—her mother was caring for her grandfather after his stroke, and Pan was too young for such a journey. Three days of sunning in her father's full attention, the trip planned to her wishes: a guided tour of public rooms in the old imperial palace; cheese and tea in a famous girls' clothing store; an outdoor performance, with music, of the folktale every child of the empire knew—the story of a Burgher girl who loses her way in the woods and meets a Yeoman boy watering his goat by a stream. Adventures with witches and wildcats follow, and along the way each saves the other's life. The tale ends in a meadow outside the walls of the girl's hometown, where a bullfrog jumps out from under a log and instructs the children to hold hands and repeat an oath (the more poignant for their imminent parting and the inevitable divergence of their lives) that the whole audience, including Selva, recited with the performers: "Let man nor beast come between us two, let Burgher nor Yeoman divide us. Friends today, friends for all days." This founding story of the empire made Selva and her father cry.

But the surprising highlight of the trip was the bones museum—the name she gave to the Imperial Museum of Man and Life. It had been her father's idea, on their last day in the capital, and to make him happy she'd feigned eagerness, expecting to be bored. But years later she still remembered the museum's smell of old cedar cabinetry, and the long dark hallways of the ground floor lined with glass cases that contained mounted animals, all amazingly lifelike—horses, wolves, falcons—and the assembled bones of giant mammals that no longer existed, skeletal birds suspended from great wingspans. The second floor held the human collection: an ancient skull fractured by some blunt weapon; the complete skeleton of a five-thousand-year-old child. There were scenes of early inhabitants of the region, with one family of clay models dressed in sheepswool and leather sandals. The papa stood facing the back of the case, legs apart, aiming a primitive rifle at a fleeing stag, and the mama squatted amid gourds of millet. In the foreground a boy of about Selva's age, nine or ten, sat cross-legged on the dirt, his close-cropped head bent over something in his lap—a wrinkled sheet of yellow goatskin, covered in writing that looked like rows of tiny pictures. On the boy's face was an expression of deep concentration, and Selva had assumed the same look as she tried to make sense of what he was reading. The brass label fixed to the bottom of the case said EARLY BURGHER FAMILY.

"How do we know they're Burghers?" she had asked her father.

"We don't," he had said. "There were no Burghers then, or Yeomen. Those groups came later. It might just be the museum's way of getting us to see the connection to ourselves."

"But what if we were Yeomen?"

He gave her hand an affectionate squeeze. "Good question! I imagine the museum gets very few Yeoman visitors."

That day there were few visitors of any kind. They had the hallways almost to themselves, and her father turned those two hours into an education in nature and man, explaining about the structure of bones, the classification of species, the rise of civilization, the principles of scientific inquiry, the values of curiosity and objectivity and common humanity. The museum described the establishment of the empire and its most successful creations: the imperial palace and its guards, the system of Good Development, the trade routes, cities, guilds, comprehensive exams. It was a story of gradual, continuous progress, and Selva imagined the city by the river and her own family as the pinnacle in the final room. She found herself thinking for the first time about the world as not simply there, something given, but as a subject for study and appreciation that could bring purpose to a whole lifetime.

As they walked out into the park by the river, her father—his voice breaking with emotion—said, "There's nothing higher than what is human, Sel."

"Why, Papa?" At that moment she'd been picturing the fractured skull.

"We build museums, we collect relics, we study and order and name them. What other creatures do this? Everything we saw in there is a tribute to the human spirit. Without it the world is just killing and eating."

As they had strolled along the river, she had become aware of a secret he was passing on to her and her alone: *This is how to live.* And now, remembering by the campfire, she again felt the wonder of that gift, bound up with a father's love.

"You'd burn the bones museum?" he asked.

"Yes."

"Why?"

"Because it was a *lie*."

"What do you mean?"

"All the things you were talking about that day. Progress and the glory of man. Life isn't a museum."

"Of course it isn't."

"But you still want me to live like you, when there's so much wrong with the world."

"Live like me how?"

"Like everything is the way it should be. Like if there's vines, we can't do anything about them."

"The vines aren't anyone's fault. There's no Conspiracy. The Yeomen didn't get organized, they didn't have the right tools."

"But the vines are *unfair*. So many things are unfair."

Zeus, stretched across her father's feet, raised his head and cocked his ears as if he'd heard a noise. Her father stroked his flank and, after glancing back at his master, Zeus returned chin to paw.

"All right," her father said, "torch the past and start over. I'm sure your generation will do better than mine. Burn all the things I've given you. But be careful, Selva." Something in his tone made her turn to look at him. He was staring at the dying fire as if he was thinking of the saddest thing in the world. "You might need them someday."

"I'll have Together."

"Really? Six far-fetched ideas that some self-org committee

came up with the day before yesterday? Together will crumble under your feet. Then what will you have?"

"What do you have?"

He took a long draw on the cigar and held it in his mouth before exhaling a stream of smoke upward. "Science. Reason. Listening to the other side."

"Oh—your humanism? That tired old thing? Humans aren't so wonderful, Papa."

"When did I say we were?"

"At the bones museum!" He had unsteadied her, but now she saw her line of attack. "We came out here because you thought everyone was exaggerating about Yeomen. *'Don't call them man-eaters!'* Friends today, friends for all days—that's what you thought. Those two guys at the checkpoint—are they what you mean by listening to the other side?"

"Drunken fools. We have them in the city, too."

"You wanted to go back home."

"I have a responsibility to keep you safe."

"I'm the one who kept *you* safe. You lost your nerve."

As soon as Selva said it, a flush of regret washed through her. Somewhere on the lake a waterbird cried out. She shivered. Her father put an arm around her, and she laid her head on his shoulder.

"Why did you want to come with me?" he asked.

"Why did you?"

"I thought it would be another of our adventures," he said. "And I had something to make up to your mother."

"What?"

He shook his head. "It's late. We'll let the fire go out."

When he didn't move she stood up, trying to hold on to a picture of that other girl—not the frightened one behind the goggles or the weak one on the gallows, but the girl in metal and clay with a rifle at her eye.

"Why are we arguing, Sel?" her father said. "In the morning we'll see if the Cronks know where the boy is."

"Are the Cronks still our friends?"

"I hope so."

He stubbed out his cigar on a rock and tossed the last of his whiskey into the hissing embers.

5

Zeus was barking. He was inside the tent on his feet, but Selva had sunk so deep asleep that she couldn't move and only sensed the tautness of his limbs against her leg. "No barking," her father ordered in a wide-awake voice. He climbed out of the tent and Zeus followed, quietly growling, and Selva slipped back into sleep. A few hours later, when the first bars of sunlight over the lake entered the tent flap and struck her eyes, she had no idea where she was.

Her father was already moving around outside the tent, feeding Zeus, getting breakfast together. Last night the Place had been firelight surrounded by darkness. Now Selva saw the blackened remains of the campfire, the needle-strewn ground sloping down to the lake, the low sun over the far ridge glinting silver on the water, and around the lake a wall of thick green gloss speckled yellow and red where the pine trees were smothered in vines with autumn berries.

She reached for her wrist and found the pulse with two fingers and silently counted. Her blood was running calm and ready, the air sharp on her face, the morning sun full of promise. She made a vow to say nothing all day that would hurt her father.

When she came out of the tent he said, "We had visitors last night."

"Who?"

He pointed into the woods. Selva and Zeus followed him

along a rocky path several hundred feet toward the sound of water and a clearing where, a stone's throw from the river that flowed all the way to their city, the hunting cabin stood: a one-room shack of decaying wood siding, abandoned ever since they'd started coming to the Place. Now the open door gave off a smell of smoke and cooked meat and spices. Zeus bolted inside and began madly sniffing. Pieces of clothing lay scattered across the dirt floor, woolen smocks and shawls, flaxen frocks, along with an assortment of tobacco pipes, a toothcomb, a bracelet of woven fibers, a coil of hemp rope, a child's hoop. In one corner sat the remains of a recent meal, dirty bowls and earthen jars.

Selva stepped through the doorway onto a sort of entry rug the color of the vine berries, yellow and red, and felt something hard underfoot. She lifted aside the rug. Beneath it there was a rectangle of wood recessed flush with the floor, like a small trapdoor to a hidden passageway. The panel covered a shallow hole the size of a wash basin dug out of the dirt. She crouched to examine what was inside. A carved, softwood board tightly strung with two lengths of catgut—some kind of musical instrument. A metal bell that farmers attached to the necks of sheep. A handful of imperial silver coins. Half a dozen brass bullets tied together with thread. A small notebook bound in green leather.

"Seems like they left in a hurry," her father said. "Maybe they heard Zeus barking last night."

"Who are they?"

"Strangers. They've been using the cabin."

She showed him one of the coins and the packet of bullets. "Where would Strangers get these?"

"From Yeomen around here. Probably stole them." He examined the bullets. "These are for a small-caliber pistol."

Selva opened the notebook. On the frontispiece, in a pencil whose lead had kept breaking, roughly formed block letters that crowded into the edge of the page announced:

PROPERTIE OF GARD THE STRONG.
DO NOT READ. RETURN TO CRONK FARM.
RETURN THIS BOOK OR DIE!

Squeezed in smaller writing on the bottom of the page like an afterthought: "Rewerd."

Slightly anxious, Selva turned to the first page. It was made of heavyweight paper and lined like a school copybook. Across the top, in the same fiercely gripped pencil, were the words: "The true history of the ~~YEOMEN~~ NATIVE people." A short paragraph filled the rest of the page: "We were here before the Empyre. This Land is our Land. All others are Traspasers and Slayvs. Our Ansesters explained all this in DIRT THOUGHT."

Who was Gard the Strong? None of it made sense to her. She flipped ahead through the notebook. Some pages were empty, others contained isolated sentences and paragraphs in the same large, tormented script. She turned to the last page with writing on it, halfway through the notebook, and found words in an entirely different hand by a different instrument. The letters were spaced like separate pictographs, like the characters on the yellow paper of the boy at the bones museum, in small neat writing composed with a bit of slate or sharpened coal.

> If I die by this stream
> Cover me in dirt and leaves
> You will know me

W h e n t h e y c r y
U n d e r y o u r f e e t

"Find something?" Her father pocketed the bullets in his fishing jacket.

Before she knew why, Selva slipped the notebook inside a front pocket of her jumper. It excited her with something much bigger, heavier, than her own clever ideas and nimble instincts, bearing down hard as iron. "Let's go find the boy, Papa."

"Cronks first," her father said. "Better to let them know we're here than have them find out."

He cooked their porridge in a hurry and left the pot and bowls to clean later. Rather than breaking camp, he stored their gear inside the tent and took only his medical kit in a day pack. Zeus led them along the trail back to the road. Up close at eye level the vines looked almost beautiful, young tendrils wreathing around lower branches with delicate stems and heart-shaped leaves.

On the road, below the derelict water tower, the hauler was gone.

"What the hell," her father said. He pointed to fresh tire tracks in the dirt and stared at them for a long time.

The pig farm was two miles away, up and down country lanes, past orchards and woods and an abandoned cemetery, across the river that flowed out of the lake through the foothills all the way down to their city, and it took them most of an hour to walk. Her father walked at a brisk, purposeful pace, and she struggled to keep up, talking little, feeling the notebook against her hip. Her school shoes weren't meant for hiking, and her left heel began to blister.

The bridge over the river was a high stone arch, and

from its midpoint you could see across rolling fields all the way down to the barns of the Cronk farm, a cluster of red dots half a mile off. At the peak of the bridge Selva suddenly stopped. "We've got nothing to show them. No bone, no pass, no letter."

"They know us. We can explain."

The farm was isolated amid acres of yellowing hay at the bottom of a hill where the grassy lane ended. On one side of the lane there was a sheep pasture and a boarded pigpen and a collection of farm buildings: a small grain silo, a toolshed, and four barns—a hayloft, a henhouse, and two pig stalls, one for sows farrowing, the other for young piglets. (Big Cronk, the farmer, had explained all this to the Rustin children on their first visit.) Across the lane, set back down a dirt path and painted red like the barns, the farmhouse stood in the shelter of an ancient oak. Big Cronk had built it all with his own capable hands, including the chimney from limestone quarried in a nearby pit.

The Cronk farm had always seemed to Selva the prettiest human setting in Yeoman land. It made her think of an enchanted hamlet in one of the folktales from the collection on her bookshelf. Even as a little girl she'd sensed that these were prosperous, successful people, though their rough features and country speech were alien to her. The Cronks were the kind of Yeomen who had more wealth than some Burghers.

The two families had met years ago at an agricultural fair in the district center, where they had happened to share a lunch table. Her father had asked if the Cronks would send their son to one of the new Yeoman schools that the empire was opening around the countryside. Big Cronk had replied that he and Mrs. Cronk could educate him better at home, and then he turned the question around: How would the doctor's city children learn to grow food and make things with their hands? He said that the Rustins were welcome to visit his farm any time they were in the region and promised the kids rides on his tractor.

Big Cronk was the kind of Yeoman who talked easily with Burghers; he had a gentle confidence that commanded respect. Mrs. Cronk was a warm, voluble, very fat woman who always sent the Rustins away with baked goods. The Cronks had only one child, unusual for a Yeoman family—a tall, awkward boy several years older than Selva whom the parents called Little Cronk. He always seemed to be doing chores—chopping wood, scything hay, feeding pigs—and he went about them with a mute obedience that was unsettling to a chatty Burgher child whose parents indulged her every opinion. Selva could never get Little Cronk to open up while he was showing her and Pan how to turn soil for planting or shear a sheep's belly, but she sometimes caught him looking at her with a kind of desperation in his eyes, as if someone else were trapped inside this Yeoman boy, asking her to release him.

Her mother suggested that she could make the time together less excruciating by giving Little Cronk a book on each visit, reciprocating his farm lessons with reading lessons. His ability turned out to be extremely limited, despite instruction from his parents, but she sat with him and patiently listened as he struggled aloud through *A Child's History of the Empire* or a volume of traditional folktales that included the one with the talking bullfrog. Little Cronk showed little aptitude but an ardent desire to learn, and one time, when she complimented him on his progress, a smile flickered on his lips before he killed it. But he remained utterly unable to laugh at, let alone make, a joke, and these sessions turned out to be just as painful as the farm chores. On the Rustins' visit last year, Big Cronk had instructed his son to take Selva and Pan into the barn where a sow had just farrowed a new litter. The boy handed them each a tiny, squirming creature and held Selva's gaze as if the piglet embodied some meaning too deep for words.

A few dozen sheep were grazing in the pasture, hens were pecking at the dirt around the silo, and an immense sow wallowed in a mudhole in the pen. The tractor stood at the bottom of the lane, but there was no sign of human life as Selva and her father, keeping Zeus close, approached the house. She noticed a pile of withered brown vines stacked beside the wood-shingle well and wondered if they'd been cut down from the oak tree or the barns. Otherwise, the property was free of the curse. But a couple of hundred feet back, the shrouded front line of the forest seemed to be massing for an assault.

Morning mist lay over the farm, and with it a strange silence.

"Everything looks the same as always," her father said. "That's a good sign. No vines."

"No people either."

The farmhouse door opened and Big Cronk emerged.

"Doc, Selva, what a surprise!"

He was a giant of a man, powerful from a lifetime of labor, but his muscular frame was sagging, almost collapsing inside his customary overalls and flannel shirt. He shut the door and limped toward them on the path, jamming his broad-brimmed, moth-eaten leather hat low on his shaggy head with one hand while extending the other. He arranged his mouth in a broad smile and at the same time glanced sideways as if someone else might be coming. Selva had an intimation that their appearance wasn't a surprise.

"What brings you here?" Big Cronk reached for their hands and hustled them away from the house as his smile vanished under his bushy mustache. "Let's talk over here, it's more comfortable," and he led them inside the dark farrowing barn where the smell of pig manure was strong and a sow even larger than the one in the mudhole lay breathing in the hay of her stall. Big Cronk pulled the sliding door closed behind them, leaving Zeus outside.

"What can I do for you, doc?"

"How's the family?" her father asked. "Little Cronk must be what, seventeen?"

"We don't call him that anymore. He got too big for that name."

"What do you call him?"

Big Cronk gave an apologetic laugh and cleared his throat. "Gard."

Without thinking Selva asked, "Gard the Strong?"

In a shaft of milky light from the edge of the barn door, under the brim of his leather hat, she saw Big Cronk's suncreased eyes momentarily fill with panic.

"That's a name he likes to use. Got it from some history book. The boy's all about learning new things—must have been your doing, Selva. Mrs. Cronk and I can't keep up with him."

"That's excellent," her father said. "I always knew he was a bright child."

"What can I do for you?" Big Cronk asked again, and this time the question sounded urgent.

"Don't worry, we don't expect you to bring out the good tableware for old friends. Just a quick visit." Her father patted the farmer on the back. "It's good to see you. We've run into some strange things on the way—someone even took our hauler. But everything here is beautiful and peaceful like always."

Big Cronk made no reply but looked at Selva as if one of them should get to the point.

Small talk at an impasse, her father began to explain their mission. She watched him slip into the condescending man-to-man way he always had when speaking to Big Cronk, touching the other man's shoulder to emphasize a point, but the longer he went on with his story the more suspicious Big Cronk looked, mouth half-open, eyes fastened on her father's as if trying to assess his sanity, occasionally glancing at Selva to see if she believed any of it.

"Who's this Stranger boy?" Big Cronk finally asked.

"I don't know him, but he's badly injured."

"Not by us."

"Of course not! But we heard he's somewhere in the area, and we'd be grateful for your help."

"What kind of help do you expect, doc?"

In her stall the sow let out a long, tired grunt.

"Where do you think we could find him?"

"We don't have anything to do with Strangers. We keep to ourselves." Her father nodded to show that he understood. "Not that we have something against them. Just they don't know us and we don't know them."

"Everyone's a little uneasy these days."

"What do you mean?"

Everything her father said seemed to make Big Cronk uneasier. Selva found her father's jacket sleeve and gave a tug, but if he felt it he ignored her. "I mean, since the—" Rather than choose between "Emergency" and "Conspiracy" he left the sentence unfinished. "Since all this nonsense of my side against your side. When here we are, you and me, talking the same as always."

"Why wouldn't we?"

"Exactly. We're not on a side."

"Was there anything else, doc?"

"I don't believe in sides," her father went on as if he hadn't heard the question. "All the years we've known each other don't just disappear because of some new ideas."

"I think we should be leaving, Papa," Selva said. "Mr. Cronk has things to do."

Big Cronk took off his hat and smiled at Selva. "It's a sad day when a farmer doesn't have time for old friends."

The barn door flew open sideways with a squeaky jerk. Flushed and out of breath, her broad bosom straining against her apron, Mrs. Cronk was gesturing to her husband with flailing hands. *They're coming!* she mouthed, before turning a frantic smile to the visitors. "Nice to see you!"

Selva sensed that Mrs. Cronk had known of their presence all along, and that they were a problem.

"Here's my advice, doc." Big Cronk took her father by the upper arm and pointed out of the barn door toward the lane. He began talking quickly. "Head back where you came. When you reach the bridge, get off the road. Take the shortcut along the river upstream toward the lake where you folks do your camping. You might find something in those woods upstream. That's what I'd do if I went looking for Strangers, which I probably wouldn't." Her father started to express his gratitude, but Big Cronk cut him off with a firm pat on the back. "Better get going."

Out in the barnyard Zeus had a hen between his teeth and was furiously shaking her in a riot of feathers and squawks.

Selva's father ran over to free the bird before her neck broke, and the Cronks hurried after him, seeming less interested in saving their hen than seeing their visitor off. Selva, last to leave the barn, began sliding the door closed. She happened to glance across the gloomy stalls to a window opening in back and the misty field outside. In the distance she saw something that made no sense.

The tractor was moving through the field, half-concealed in the hay. It was speeding downhill toward the farm not in a straight line but slaloming around trees and bales of hay, flattening the grass in zigs and zags, and with it came the barking and howling of wolves and the laughter of hyenas. As it drew nearer she saw a figure on the driver's side leaning out, and another on the passenger side, and both of them were waving rifles and making the wild sounds. Two other human figures were standing behind them in the back of the tractor, and these were not howling, not waving rifles, but violently tossed side to side, except they didn't fly out or even fall down because something was holding them up by their arms extended rigidly to the metal rails where they were tied by the wrists as their bodies jerked back and forth, and their gray clothes billowed, and long black hair whipped with the tractor's movements. The last thing Selva saw before she ran from the barn was that the vehicle was not a tractor but their hauler, and that the face of the driver, bearded and somehow grown much older, was Little Cronk's.

6

Zeus kept twisting around and whimpering for his escaped prey as Selva's father pulled him by the collar uphill along the lane. When they were out of view around a bend, he let go and waited for her to catch up, then his long legs began striding ahead, thumbs looped through the straps of his day pack.

"Papa!"

"What is it?"

"Back there—"

"I know, Big Cronk felt bad. They like to entertain their Burgher friends the right way." He took her hand as they walked and gave it a squeeze. "Helpful, though, wasn't he? Maybe I'm not always wrong."

She pulled her hand away. His blindness enraged her, and she decided to spend the rest of the day savoring her chance to show him all that he had missed and she had seen. At the stone bridge they climbed down a steep trail, grasping shrubs and saplings, to the riverbank. It was more like a creek here, flowing much narrower and faster than downstream, where it grew broad and deep enough for boating as it approached the city. The morning mist had cleared and sunlight danced on water running over rocks. The air was sharp and from the deep woods came a smell of tree bark and wet earth. High above a hawk was lazily circling. Zeus splashed into the water up to his belly and lapped with his long tongue. Selva crouched by the stream and cupped her hands for a drink.

They always fished this stream when they came to the Place, but it was now too cold. Zeus leapt out onto the bank, shook himself off, and broke into a canter upstream as if he knew the way, hurdling the trunk of a hardwood tree that had fallen across the trail.

When the family had first started coming out here, the woods became the setting for her endless fantasy. A warrior goddess bathed in the river, garrulous foxes and bears met her on trails, she nursed a broken-winged songbird back to health and left food for forest spirits in the knots of oak trees. What made this world magical was being the only person in it (her parents and brother didn't count), and as she grew up, when their visits began to be peopled by Yeomen—or perhaps when she began to notice that they had been here all along—the woods lost some of their power to transport her. Now, following Zeus and her father along the bank, she had no thought of gods and forest creatures. She was thinking about Little Cronk and the Stranger boy. The world had become entirely human.

They had been hiking no more than fifteen minutes when Zeus stopped in his tracks, cocked his ears forward, and barked. A moment later, over the sound of water, Selva heard voices farther upstream on the other side of the river.

"What's the boy's name?" she asked.

"I don't even know," her father admitted. He put his hands to either side of his mouth and called out: "Monge!"

The voices fell silent.

"Monge!" he called again. He waited. "Is a boy named Monge with you?"

"They don't understand," Selva said.

"Maybe not, but someone's coming."

A hundred feet upstream the someone was moving slowly

out of the trees into sunlight. Moving slowly because he was limping, hobbling, his right foot suspended off the ground, supporting himself on a short branch that he used as a crutch. He was followed by two men. One of them was holding a machete. The other was pointing a pistol at their visitors. Selva knew at once from their long black hair and loose clothing and small wiry stature that they were Strangers. Zeus wouldn't stop barking. The man with the gun lowered it at him, and her father did something she'd never seen him do before: he reached down and pinched Zeus's ear, making him yelp with pain. The barking stopped.

The Strangers approached on the riverbank until they were directly across from Selva and her father, no more than twenty-five feet away, and she was able to see their faces clearly. The two behind looked at least thirty, with wisps of facial hair, closed expressions, and the tattooed dots and dashes on their cheeks that she'd learned from her mother signified manhood. The one in front, leaning on the tree branch, might have been sixteen. His face was unmarked, thin and delicate, his eyes open wide, not in alarm but with an alert curiosity—a sensitive face that nonetheless managed to convey a reserve of toughness.

"I am Monge," he said.

Selva's father whispered, "He's older than Mr. Monge said." Without bothering to ascertain the boy's command of their language, he began explaining himself with a nervous formality—dropping phrases like "Imperial College Hospital" and "Stranger hostel" and "humanitarian mission"—that Selva thought must seem suspicious or absurd but, anyway, incomprehensible.

Here was their journey's goal. And now what?

"You saw my father?" the boy asked.

"Yes, in our city."

"You are not Yeomen?"

"No—Burghers. Can we cross to your side?" After a moment the boy gave a brief nod. Her father gestured to the gunman. "Can he please . . ." The boy turned and said something in his own language that made the man lower the barrel. The boy was half the age of the others, but he appeared to be in command.

The middle of the river was deeper than it looked, and while Zeus paddled across, Selva and her father waded up to their waists in cold, groin-clutching water, slipping on hidden rocks. When they reached the far side, the Strangers turned without a word and proceeded back along the bank. The boy's bad foot was wrapped up to the calf in strips of cloth stained yellow around the heel. Her father kept trying to get his attention, but the boy ignored him.

Around a bend in the river the encampment came into view: canopies of fabric strung between trees, clothes hanging from branches, rugs spread over the ground, firepits in circles of stones, and two dozen Strangers caught in the small moments of people who knew how to make a home where they were not at home. Women were dipping vessels in the stream, families lay on beds of pine needles in the woods, two old men sat on the ground playing a game with slips of wood, children skipped rope with a severed vine. A small, beige-colored goat with yellow eyes was tied to a tree. When Zeus began to bark at it, the children scattered and the adults tensed and edged away. Her father grabbed Zeus's collar to make him stop.

Selva had seen plenty of shanties in alleys of the Rowhouse District, and temporary lodgings in hallways of the hostels that her mother managed, and those lives improvised amid the sturdy structures of the city by the river had become almost normal to her. But this spectacle of busyness and idleness in the woods was unsettling. It made her feel the distance between Strangers and herself as she never had before, and the Together clothing she'd left behind in her room struck her as obscene.

The boy gestured for Selva and her father to sit on the flat surface of a half-buried rock, then lowered himself onto a fallen tree that was hollowing out with dry rot. He turned sideways to support his bad leg on the trunk, while the two guards, as Selva thought of them, stood behind him, one of them holding the pistol at his side like a sentry. The adults nearby continued to go about their tasks while casting sidelong looks at the intruders. A few young children came up close and stared, darting wary glances at Zeus.

"Welcome to our empire," the boy said with a faint smile, precisely enunciating the unfamiliar words, and Selva felt she had permission to smile back.

"We are happy to find you," her father said.

"That one is my smallest sister." Monge pointed at a little girl with a dirty face in a torn frock, who dissolved in hysterics at being singled out.

"I thought you were an only child."

"No. We are five."

"Your father said..."

The boy's face closed up. "Why do you know my father?"

"Mr. Monge is a—a client of my wife. She's helping him get situated." If the boy understood this, he said nothing. "What is your name besides Monge?"

"We have one name. My father gave me his name." The subject seemed to put him in a pensive mood. "What do you think about my father?"

"Mr. Monge? He's going to do fine in our city. He's looking for work, his health is good—except the pain is in his knees."

The boy abruptly laughed. His voice was so soft that some words were almost inaudible, but the laugh came out loud, boisterous. He turned around to say something to the guards, pointing at his own knees, and they laughed together as if his father's knees were a running joke.

"Mr. Monge was very sorry not to come with us," her father said. She knew that this was a lie, but she accepted it as a harmless and possibly useful one. A closer look showed that the boy's whole foot was swollen tight like a block of wood, and she was thinking ahead to how they were going to bring him out to the road and recover their hauler and get past the checkpoints and make it back to the city.

Her father took off his day pack, produced his medical kit, and asked to examine the foot. Monge put him off. "We are not in your city. Trees have no clocks. Tell me about my father."

"We don't have much time," her father said. "That foot looks pretty bad."

"Do you know what happened to me?"

Her father repeated what he'd heard: that the boy somehow injured his foot, Mr. Monge left him by a tree and went to look for help, he came back an hour later to find his son gone, he spent that day and the next looking for him in the woods, before reluctantly giving up the search and resuming his trek with the rest of their group to the city by the river.

The boy looked up with a bitter smile and spoke to the guards. Their eyes widened and they shook their heads. The boy turned back to Selva and her father.

"I will tell you what happened."

7

After years of drought had claimed most of their herd, the Monge family and a few others in their clan were surviving in temporary dwellings—not much more substantial than their encampment by the stream—which they had set up at the base of the mountains, a mile from an imperial border fort. Twice weekly, a group of tradeswomen bearing loads of goods on their heads traveled on foot to the fort. There they haggled with the border guards, bartering dried meat, woven baskets, and carved ornaments for the produce and tobacco they could no longer grow. Monge's father always sent him along with the women, the only male in the group. Without being told, he understood that he was to keep an eye on his mother, for she was still young and considered beautiful despite having borne five children, and the guards were far away from their families and utterly bored at their frontier outpost. While his mother bartered, the boy made a habit of conversing with the guards in order to improve his command of their language, whose fundamentals he'd learned from his father. A friendly guard even loaned him a book of imperial folktales, where he first read about Burghers and Yeomen.

One week, young Monge came down with a stomach illness and was unable to accompany the women. On that week's second trip his mother didn't return. No one knew if she had fallen sick, been abducted by the guards, or—this was the whispered story—chosen to stay behind. When, two days later, Mr. Monge, who said that his knees were bothering him, sent his son to inquire after her, the boy found the parapet unmanned, the fort empty. The guards had disappeared with their weapons and tobacco and Mrs. Monge, leaving behind crates of produce, military logbooks, and their uniforms. That was the first day of the Emergency.

The camps along the border began to empty. Mr. Monge's clan held out for three months, but when they had eaten the last of their seed grain and were down to one month's meat, they gathered to discuss their situation and concluded that, without provisions from the fort, they would all die. According to custom, they voted to choose a leader for their journey over the mountains—someone able to deal with the alien people they were sure to encounter in the empire. Reports had reached their camp of a mostly friendly reception in the city, but the countryside, where people lived off the land and kept to themselves, was another matter.

Mr. Monge was the best educated person among them, the only literate adult, but he had a reputation for complaining and pushing difficult responsibilities onto others. Instead of Mr. Monge, the clan chose his son. The election of a leader who had not even reached manhood was so extraordinary that they held the vote twice, with the same result. An elder argued that they would be foolish to throw away the sacred authority of age just when they would need it most, but one of the tradeswomen replied: "Everything in our life will be new. Let it start now." A boy would lead them.

"I was happy for this chance," young Monge told Selva and her father. "I was thinking always of my mother."

The journey had a surprising effect on the travelers: it turned the order of the clan almost upside down. Male elders, who had been the most reluctant to slaughter the last of their animals and leave behind their grazing land, fell into depression and lagged behind, scarcely saying a word, useless with portage even if they were still physically capable of carrying their own belongings. But clan members of lower status—the tradeswomen and the young—shed their normal deference, chatted in loud voices under their loads, and expressed opinions about everything from the unfamiliar mountain vegetation to the lives they imagined in an imperial city. As for Mr. Monge, he never referred to his humiliation, but from the first day his attitude was sour and mocking. Whenever young Monge had trouble establishing the sun's position, or decided on a path that led them into tangles of brush, his father would say: "You lost your mother—now you'll lose us all."

On the seventh day, their caravan—which included two tethered kid goats as emergency food—descended out of the mountains into the foothills and came to the first Yeoman settlement. Mr. Monge told his son that he would be accountable for every bad thing that was about to happen. But when the boy informed the Yeoman farmer that their destination was the city by the river, they were allowed to pass through his fields unharmed, and even given a jug of fresh cow's milk for the small children.

The trouble came the next day. The vines grew so dense that every tree started to look the same, and young Monge was unable to discern a trail. In the middle of the day they stumbled on an abandoned cabin near a lake in the woods. It was too small to shelter the whole group, but one of the tradeswomen pointed out that it was large enough for nursing mothers, the very old, and storage of valuables. The rest of the group set up camp by a nearby stream, which provided fresh water and fishing for perch. They were running low on food, and the weakest among them needed a day's rest.

Young Monge asked for able-bodied volunteers to scout the nearest Yeoman farm, where they would ask for food and permission to stop in the area for two nights. The party included his father, who seemed to realize that he was losing the others' respect.

The first farm they came upon had pigs and sheep. The six men were walking single file down the lane, hands out and palms up in the way their people showed peaceful intentions, when the first shot rang out. The men scattered as bullets seemed to whiz at them from every direction. A bad instinct drove two of them to hide in the nearest barn, where the squealing of pigs gave them away, and they were cornered and seized. Monge, his father, and the two other men ran into a field and lay down in the high grass, waiting out the pursuers, then escaped separately back to their camp. Mr. Monge was so upset that he openly derided his son in front of the whole assembly.

Their situation was now desperate. The group had lost two of its ablest men and was nearly out of food among enemies in unknown country. The next night young Monge and the two remaining men from the scouting party (Mr. Monge refused to join them) returned to the pig farm in dark cloaks. They broke into a locked toolshed where, to their amazement, they found a pistol, several packets of bullets, and a pair of machetes. They stole away with the weaponry along with a hen under each man's arm. Their luck had been good, and young Monge decided to stage another raid the next night. But someone had laid a wolf trap at the door of the henhouse, and when the boy stepped on the metal plate, its teeth snapped closed over his right heel. He stifled most of his scream and managed to pry the trap's jaws open and free his foot, but the damage was as severe as the pain. Adrenaline and the help of the other two got him back to camp before he collapsed. In the morning he could barely walk.

His father came and stared at the foot for a long time, saying nothing, eyes wide and moist like a kid goat's. He ran his hand through his son's hair. Then he disappeared for the rest of the morning. At midday, Mr. Monge woke the boy where he lay sleeping under a canopy. His supplies were lashed to his back. He placed his arms at his sides and bowed from the waist, something he'd never done in anyone's presence, let alone his son's. He apologized for asking permission to continue the journey by himself. "You are the father," he said.

8

The whole time the boy was speaking, the rest of the group stood at a distance and watched. A few approached and interrupted: a tradeswoman with a wen on her cheek wanted to know if the doctor could remove it; an elderly man made a long speech in which the word "Yeomen" kept appearing, while young Monge listened patiently before sending him away with a joke that made everyone in earshot laugh.

When the boy finished his story, he placed his hands on the thigh he had extended on the tree trunk and bent over until his hair fell forward and his forehead touched his knee, as if talking had left him spent.

After a long silence, Selva's father picked up his medical kit and, in the doctor's voice she remembered from the night of the attack on Zeus, said, "I need to see that foot."

The cloth unwound easily from Monge's toes, but near his heel it stuck to the skin with caked blood and something yellow and sweet-smelling.

"Why have you put honey on it?" her father asked.

"To make my foot healthy."

"But it's already infected."

Her father pinched the strip between his thumb and index finger and tore it free with a quick firm snap that made the boy moan. The bandage released an odor of rotten flesh. On either side of the heel deep punctures, like the twin holes of a snakebite, exposed blackened tissue. The whole foot was swollen and inflamed, reddish through the ball and arch, dark purple around the wounds. Selva told herself that she must not look away.

"Please boil a pot of water," her father said. As she went off to search for firewood, he followed her. "Worse than I expected," he said quietly. "He'll have to lose the dead tissue. If the gangrene goes deeper, I'll need to amputate the foot, and I don't have a bone saw. Or alcohol."

The thought of a saw made her lightheaded. But if she could just pretend to be his nurse, her mind and body might follow. "Alcohol for what?"

"Emergency anesthetic."

"What about giving him your whiskey?"

"None left." He shook his head, chagrined. "I wasn't thinking."

While the instruments were boiling, she laid out the bar of soap and a basin of hot water. She thought she scrubbed more than enough, but he told her to keep going. She longed for a compliment, but now he was Doctor Rustin, a person she didn't know. She pulled on a pair of rubber gloves and eased Monge down onto a wool rug while he stared hard into her eyes and his breathing grew shallower. "Don't worry," she said, "Papa is a great surgeon." On a platter she arranged the instruments—the folding knife, scissors, tweezers, and pliers—alongside the numbing ointment, tourniquet, and gauze, just as she imagined one of her father's nurse assistants would do it. The work made her anxiety tolerable.

"Try not to look," her father said, snapping on his gloves. "It's normal to faint the first time, and I'll need you."

The two guards held the boy down, and Selva placed a leather bit in his mouth. He kept still while her father spread the ointment and tied the tourniquet, but when the knife went to work cutting away infected flesh, the boy began to whimper and grind his pain into the bit. Soon he was screaming. Over and over he cried: "Mama, mama, mama!" The children ran away, the tradeswomen wailed, and the old man who had made the speech about Yeomen was saying something in a rapid monotone like an incantation. Selva's circle of awareness narrowed down to the platter, the instruments, her father's orders, and once when he spoke sharply she was glad because it meant he was not thinking of her as his daughter, had forgotten who she was, and as the metallic smell of fresh blood rose to her nostrils, she thought, *Don't look, don't look, look, look, Brave Selva, look.*

LATER, AFTER HER FATHER SEARED THE SEVERED VESSELS with an ember of firewood and bandaged the wound in gauze, and the guards laid the boy out under a canopy on a bed of pine needles with his foot raised up on a log, and the girl in the torn frock who was his little sister sang him to sleep, Selva sat and watched over him with a sense of quiet satisfaction. She had come through. The boy looked younger—so much younger that she thought of Pan, the way his brows knitted in concentration when they used to share a room and she couldn't sleep and watched him. The memory of Pan brought to mind her mother and home, and suddenly she had to make an effort not to cry. Throughout the journey she'd hardly given them any thought; when she had, she felt a pang of guilt before forgetting again. But now she longed for them, and she tried to imagine what they were doing. It was late afternoon, the sun already sinking behind the treetops, so probably Pan had just come home from school and her mother was making him a snack of brown bread and mulberry jam before dinner.

But that was her old pre-Emergency routine. Maybe she was at the hostel with Mr. Monge. Maybe they were talking about his son, about what Selva and her father were doing this very minute.

When, over family dinners, her mother talked about Mr. Monge and all the other Strangers in her hostels, it reminded Selva of the way her father used to discuss his patients—with a keen but impersonal interest, as a project that required her best effort but would never deeply matter to her. It was the Stranger Committee, not any individual Strangers, that had changed her mother's life. Selva encouraged her work in every possible way, understanding that it had awakened something in her, but she didn't really take it seriously. In fact, she felt a degree of contempt that she tried to conceal, because her mother would always be an amateur in self-org, a woman of the empire, a wife and mother raising two children to be good Burghers, still attached to the family's old life, not for its status like her father, but for the deep comfort of the familiar.

Selva believed that Strangers were to be admired, learned from, aspired to—not helped, not *solved*. The boy's story had done nothing to shake this belief. If Mr. Monge turned out to be a rotten father, maybe it was because he wasn't much of a Stranger, and had never wanted to be. His jealousy, his pride and selfishness, his fragility, his ambition for himself alone, abandoning his family and clan for the city—everything about him reminded Selva of a Burgher. Before the Emergency he would have thrived in the city. But the boy sleeping on the ground beside her, and occasionally uttering a moan, affirmed her deepest feeling about Strangers. They were the better humans.

She wondered what young Monge would think when he saw the city by the river. They would take him to the hospital first, to save his foot and maybe his life. Afterward, she would insist on bringing him home to continue his care, and she was pretty sure that her father wouldn't object, for the boy was now his patient, and anyway, her father was never as rigid and certain as when she was arguing with him in her own head. Then she would introduce Monge to her self-org friends. What would he think of Together? Some things might confuse him, like the elaborate mechanics of We Are One, or the purpose of the Suicide Spot. But she knew that he would welcome Together as much as Together would welcome him, because the ideas, if not always the practice, were alive in every moment of his story. *No one is a Stranger. Listen to the young.*

They had chosen him as leader, chosen him because of his superior education and knowledge. In theory this would have been forbidden by the principles of Together, but Strangers must have their own principles—perhaps even their own word for Together—principles that tied them to the land, the nomadic way of life, and one another, and that had sustained them through the harshest circumstances for hundreds of years. Who was she, a sheltered Burgher girl from the city, to judge whether Strangers met the ideal of Together, when they embodied it, *lived* it?

Something about Together had always troubled Selva. It was a concern so profound that it might invalidate the entire project, and she went to great lengths to hide it from herself. The concern was that she didn't know what Together was for. Other than the experience of it, the freedom and camaraderie of starting over in a new world, what was Together supposed to do? It was easy enough to tick off the deficiencies of the old world, but if anyone asked her to explain how they should be rectified and then list the qualities of the new world that should replace them, to describe what that new world should look like, to draw a picture of its streets and buildings, to write a set of laws to govern it, even imagine a folktale to represent it, she wouldn't have known where to begin. Together was a feeling, not a vision, let alone a plan. At its heart there was a void. On nights when she lay unable to sleep and allowed herself, or was somehow forced, to face this void, it so undid her that she immediately reached for her wrist and told herself never to think about it again, and she fell asleep hoping to dream that her Better Human would have the answers that eluded her.

But as she imagined young Monge in her city, the void disappeared. He would make life *real*, and the meaning of Together would become clear to her through his eyes. The thought of bringing this heroic boy into her world thrilled Selva. She would be a hero next to him. Everyone would sense it, ask her how it happened, hear the story and be amazed. Sheer vanity—but it didn't disgust or depress her or send her pulse racing, because she was proving it every day and hour *out here*, with Gandorig and the farmer judges, the roadblock animals and their hanging dicks, Big Cronk and Gard the Strong, Monge, the excruciating operation they'd just performed. She had overcome terrors she could never have imagined. Her life since the Emergency—her despair after her exams-week triumph, the night with Zeus in the park, the arguments with her parents, her failure of nerve at the Suicide Spot, the *goggles*—all of it seemed dull and petty and horribly embarrassing, like a younger girl's outfit that she'd once thought pretty but that no longer fit and made her look silly, that she could now throw away. As she watched over the boy and the sun sank behind the trees, her body quivered with an excitement that was almost alarming. Something incredible was going to happen to her.

She felt for the notebook in her jumper pocket and took it out. There was the name: GARD THE STRONG. What a strange, violent plunge into the mind of a boy who could never form a complete sentence in her presence. She hadn't gotten a clear view of him as he ran the hauler through the hayfield, so she had to imagine the face of the author, and it looked nothing like Little Cronk's: ragged beard, hard eyes, upper lip curled in a sneer. She turned the notebook's lined pages. Across one he had drawn crude pictures, barely more than stick figures, of animals with exaggerated eyes and teeth and genitalia above name labels: WOLF, BEAR, BUFALO, WILD BORE, FOREST CAT, VIPER. On the facing page, under the heading TRUE HISTORY OF THE YEOMEN PEOPLE, she read: "Before Burghers we ruled this Land. We were not called Yeomen then Yeomen is a Burgher word. We were Natives. There was no Empyre. We did not have laws only the Law of the STRONGEST. We warshiped Animal Spirits. GARD THE GRATE ruled us. Our Bodies were"

The entry ended there, as if the author had run out of time or inspiration; and the next two pages were blank. Then the story resumed:

> After GARD THE GRATE died the Empyre crost the sea and stole our Land. This was a long time ago. Burghers came and lived in Citys. They did not know Animals or farms, they did not love the Land. They loved Words and New Things. Dirt is stronger than Words and Old Things are stronger than New Things but Yeomen forgot our Ansesters. Burgher

Teechers lied us to think this way. But nothing week can stand. Now Young Yeomen are digging for our Ansesters (GARD). We got strong from digging and we found DIRT THOUGHT. This is the entyre Mesage of DIRT THOUGHT.
1. Words lye, Dirt is true.
2. We belong to the Land, the Land belongs to us.
3. Men are Stronger than Womin.
4. Young are Stronger than Old.
5. Yeomen are Stronger than Burghers and Strangers.
6. Gard the Grate is coming back to lead us.

So the War of ~~Yeomen~~ Natives and Burghers is coming.

Other than the strange little poem about being buried under leaves, these were the notebook's last words. Selva closed it with a tingling numbness that she recognized as the onset of fear. On the back cover, embossed in its green leather, were the name of a printer's shop and an address in the Market District. How could she have forgotten? She'd bought this notebook before their camping trip in the last summer of the empire, as a gift for Little Cronk. She'd suggested he use it to record new vocabulary words and summarize the *Child's History of the Empire* that she'd given him. He had run his fingertips over the pebbly surface of the leather cover in solemn silence, as if the notebook was some rare and precious object from another world.

9

Selva had settled her cheek against her knees and was close to falling asleep when Monge groaned and stirred. It was twilight. She became aware of the sounds and smells of food being prepared.

"How do you feel?" she asked.

He was gazing through half-open eyes at something beyond her and didn't answer. She thought of what her father had told her when he came home from the hospital the night of Pan's birth: "Your mother went somewhere I'll never be able to follow."

"Does it hurt?"

He looked down his leg at the bandaged foot as if for the answer and gave his head a brief shake.

"Papa said it went well. I don't think we'll have to cover you in dirt and leaves."

She picked up the notebook where she'd left it on the ground and opened it to the poem at the end.

"You wrote this, right?"

He lifted a weak arm for the notebook and brought it to his chest.

"Where did you find it?" she asked.

"The pig farm. On the seat."

Little Cronk must have left his notebook in the hauler. "I'm glad you stole it," she said. "Write another. I like yours much better than the other guy's."

The boy held the notebook out to her. "Keep for me."

"What I meant," Selva said, putting the notebook back in her jumper, "is at the hospital they'll take care of your infection."

A cloud of confusion drifted across the boy's eyes. "What hospital?"

"Imperial College Hospital. Where my father is chief surgeon."

Monge understood now, and he said, "No."

"No?"

"No."

"But this could still kill you."

"I will not go."

"You *have* to go." This was nothing Selva had expected. "My father and I didn't come out here just to do emergency field surgery. We have to bring you to the city so you can get better. Your father is there, a lot of your people are there. It's too dangerous in the woods."

In the somber light she thought she saw a look of actual dislike cross the boy's face. "Who are my people?"

"I mean—you know, the people who came from across the mountains."

"Strangers?"

"That's what we call them. If it's wrong I apologize. My mother started using 'Friends.' She helps your people settle in our city. They're going to make it a better place."

"What can they do in your city?"

With earnestness befitting a deeply felt truth, Selva said, "I don't mean you can become more like us. I mean we can become more like you."

Monge stared at her and laughed, the same laugh as before, more subdued but still harsh.

"Don't you want to be with your father?" she asked.

"Who is my father?"

His questions were irritating, and her answers filled her with shame because she wanted to bring Monge back home with her like a trophy, saw herself reuniting son and father before the entire hostel, introducing him to her friends in the self-org and to the tall, quiet boy at the Better Humans workshop, presenting him in the main square to the raptures of We Are One.

"He needs you."

"*They* need me."

By now the boy was hardly more than a voice in the gathering dark, and she couldn't tell if he was looking at the children seated under the canopy or at the women singing as they chopped by the fire, but she knew she had lost something. He was receding into the twilight, taking with him the girl made of metal and clay with the rifle at her eye, leaving Selva alone in the unrestful embrace of the past.

"They can come with you," she heard herself plead.

Monge made a sound with his nose, an abrupt snort that signaled the conversation's end.

SELVA AND HER FATHER WERE SERVED CHICKEN STEW AND LEFT to eat by themselves. The two guards, the one with the pistol and the other with the machete, stood watch by the stream whose ripples glittered in moonlight. The women in the encampment were speaking in soft voices while tobacco smoke drifted through the trees. The smell was coarse, much stronger than her father's cigars. He went to check on his patient once more, but the boy was sleeping again.

Back at their campsite, Selva told her father of Monge's refusal.

"Then he'll probably die here."

"That's what I tried to say."

"It's his choice. We can't force him." Her father lit a cigar and drew on the flame. "Maybe he's right."

"How can he be right?"

"You heard his story, Sel. I was looking around the camp, and there's something impressive about these people. Do we want them depending on Burgher generosity for the rest of their lives?"

"If his foot doesn't kill him," she said, "Yeomen will."

"Who, the Cronks? They thought they were shooting at pig rustlers."

Selva told him everything. She told him about the notebook and Gard the Strong and Dirt Thought, about the stolen hauler in the hayfield, armed Yeomen in front, manacled Strangers in back, about the panic of Big Cronk and Mrs. Cronk and everything else her father had missed because he was too intent on salvaging the fragments of a belief that assured his place as a good citizen of a good empire and allowed him to persist in the illusion that he wasn't on a side—that there were no sides. She had woken up promising herself to say nothing to hurt him, but now she threw the day's revelations at him with the accurate fury of her own self-loathing.

Her father was stroking Zeus's head, and when Selva finished he fell into a silence that lasted his entire cigar. Her need to punish him spent, she walked down to the lake to wash her face. The cold, black water reminded her that she hadn't bathed in two days. Tomorrow she would get clean and change her clothes. And then what?

She found him just where she'd left him, propped on an elbow, staring into the fire, still holding the burnt-out cigar. She was used to her father always busy at something, straightening up a room or sharpening a knife when he had nothing else to do, as if idleness was physically painful for him. Now only his eyelid moved, twitching again. This annoying tic alarmed her.

"Aren't you going to bed?"

No answer.

"You're just going to sit here?"

"Possibly."

"What are you thinking?"

Still mesmerized by the fire, he smiled wanly. "The last thing Big Cronk said to me. I completely forgot till now." She waited. "He said, 'It's not personal, doc, but you and the girl should go back to your city.'" He looked up at her with a plea in his eyes. "I'm too old to rethink everything."

Selva wondered what that meant to him—what it would mean to her. Like returning to the Better Humans workshop and finding Hebe an inert and mute dummy. Or saying "Together" again and again the way she and Pan would keep repeating an ordinary word like "kitchen" until it had been reduced to comical absurdity. Or Monge laughing at her vain dream. It occurred to her that she and her father had both come out here under a false pretext, both carrying an assumption too fragile to survive the journey.

She felt something that she had never felt before. It was the pity of a mother knowing how hard the world was and how frail her child. She wanted to hold him and tell him that they were going to be all right, that she would take care of everything. And this feeling brought a sudden sense of her aloneness, the awful responsibility she now had for them both, and she knew that this was what it meant to be a parent—what it had always meant to be him, bearing the weight of her life every day whether she was aware or not. A rush of love came over her, not like last night by the campfire, not as his little girl, but seeing him for the first time as he was, and now she didn't want to burn any of it, she wanted never to forget this moment for the rest of her life.

She laid her hand on his shoulder. "Papa, we did a good thing today. We did what we came to do."

"That's kind of you, Sel, but I've put us in a hell of a fix." He sat up and shook his head as if to get rid of a spell, like Zeus shaking off water after a swim, and he explained with unsparing clarity how his faith in the Cronks, humanity, and himself had placed the two of them in a trap from which he could see no way out.

Selva fell asleep with the sensation of a snake biting deep into her heel.

10

After morning porridge, she splashed cold lake water over her body and then dressed in an old blouse and pair of pants that she'd brought as a change of clothes just in case. The leather notebook was still in her jumper pocket. She left it in the tent and returned with her father to the Stranger encampment, but there was nothing to do except wait until evening for her father to examine the wound. Selva stayed away from the boy. To distract herself from the sky, she gathered the children for games, jumping rope with a vine, climbing pine trees, teaching them to play hopscotch on a board drawn in the dirt with a stone from the stream, and the whole time the sun stared at her as the boy had in the moment before he laughed. She knew from the trembling in her hands that the sky overhead was a void today and the universe drained of meaning, but she kept checking her pulse anyway, hoping to find it was slowing down, until the girl in the torn frock began to copy the gesture, putting her fingertips to her own wrist and moving her lips.

Throughout the day Selva's father kept to himself in their tent, visiting the Stranger encampment only to remove the wen from the tradeswoman's cheek. Just before sunset he returned to examine the boy. When he found Selva his face was grim. The pink tissue exposed by surgery was already turning black. The rot had traveled deep into the foot. In the morning it would have to be cut off.

"With what?"

"My knife, if it's sharp enough. Poor kid."

"And then what do we do?"

He looked at the ground and shrugged. He covered his eyes and shook his head. It was the most abject thing she'd ever seen him do, and again she became aware, now that the last trace was gone, of the immense effort it must take to be her father every moment of her life, the restraint of every weak human impulse—always having to know, manage, get through. And that was when the idea came to her.

She was afraid of falling asleep before her father, but excitement kept her awake long after his breathing slowed. When he was snoring deeply, she took her empty book bag and crept out of the tent and put on her shoes. The paraffin lamp lay on the ground outside the flap, where he kept it for nighttime needs. She found a pencil, tore a blank page from the leather notebook, and wrote: *Gone for med supplies. Your nurse assistant who loves you.* She placed it on the notebook at the foot of his bedding and accidentally shone the lamp near his face. In the half-light she noticed that his beard was growing in, the way it always used to on camping trips. She imagined returning from her mission and pulling aside the tent flap, calling "Papa!," his sleepy confusion, his dawning amazement, and she would feel happiness not for herself but for him as she never had before in her life, and this would be the something incredible that she had known was going to happen, not as it turned out to her alone, but to them both.

Zeus was lying by the remains of the fire, and when she emerged he got to his feet. "Stay, Zeus," she whispered. "I wish you could come with me." He gazed at her with patient resolve, and when she started to walk away he followed. She turned and pointed: "You stay, Zeus. Stay with Papa. He'll need you." Zeus sat in his solemn good-boy posture and whimpered, but this time he didn't follow.

Even with the lamp casting its light eight feet ahead, the distance that had taken forty minutes by daylight in the opposite direction two days ago now took her more than an hour. She tripped once on a root and fell, and during the climb up the riverbank to the stone bridge she kept slipping backward. Once she was on the lane, the going got easier but she felt exposed. By sheer luck the pants and blouse, a hideous outfit she never would have worn in the city except to help her father in the garden, were dark brown.

The smell of manure told her the farm was just around the next bend and down the hill. She turned off the lamp. The only noise was the light tread of her feet through the grass, *shush-shush*. Shadowy barns loomed on either side of the lane. The farmhouse was dark. Animals and humans all seemed to be asleep.

And the toolshed door was hanging loose. For a moment she wondered if this, and not the ready mouth of a sharp-toothed plate, was the trap—if they were waiting for her, just as Big Cronk had somehow known they were coming. The shed was windowless and pitch-dark, so she lit the lamp before taking a step inside and closing the door behind her.

She found herself in one of the secret places that stored the alien knowledge of the Cronks, objects with which they were at ease and for which they had names and uses that she'd begun to learn: plows, spades, harrows, scythes, adzes, and augers propped against the walls, bags of peat and lime stacked on the dirt floor, shelves cluttered with hammers, boxes of nails, chisels, block planes, plumb bobs.

Her father had always preached respect for this world of Yeoman things. He liked to remind Selva that the Rustin guild also required the skilled use of hand tools. Their visits to the farm were entirely his doing: "Good experience for the kids to have." Her mother was impeccably friendly with all three Cronks, but she had little enthusiasm for spending precious vacation time on the farm, and it became obvious to Selva and even Pan that these expeditions caused tension between their parents. After one visit, when their father was rhapsodizing about the beauty of nature and the benefits of physical labor, their mother cut him off with an unusually caustic tone. "Hugo, please. Stop this fantasy. You wouldn't want this life for a minute. These people are isolated and ignorant. The Cronk boy is hopelessly backward. We have nothing in common other than small talk. I sincerely doubt they want us here." Selva, more attuned as usual to her father, had found this judgment harsh and unfair.

Half a dozen saws hung from nails driven into the rough wood of the shed wall. She spotted one that she thought could serve as a bone saw: short, stiff, fine-toothed, sharp to her thumb, without much rust. She took it from its nail and placed it blade down in her book bag. Half her mission was done. She felt a surge of confidence.

Selva had been in the root cellar only once, last summer. Mrs. Cronk had told her son to bring in a sack of yams for the pies she baked and sold at the annual district fair—and since the Rustins happened to be visiting that day, why not show Selva where they stored their winter vegetables? Little Cronk had led her behind the farrowing barn to a structure whose like she'd never seen before—a hump of earth over a set of wooden bulkhead doors in a low stone wall. He had thrown the doors open (she remembered them being unlocked), and she had followed him down a short flight of steps into a tiny underground chamber with barely enough headroom for Little

Cronk to stand up straight. In the light from the bulkhead she saw that the walls were lined with storage cubbies built from logs, containing piles of potatoes, onions, turnips, carrots, and yams. The room was cooler than the summer air outside, and moist. The earthy smell of root was overpowering.

Little Cronk crouched to gather an armload of yams in his canvas sack. When he stood up and looked at Selva with his imploring face, she thought she was going to faint. The room was too small, he was too near, there was nowhere to go. For the first time she noticed that his eyes were unusually close together. For what felt like half a minute his lips formed the first syllable of several different sentences. Her answer for every one of them was no.

"Do you want to see where my father keeps his bottles?"

She didn't say no. Discovering that she did want to see, she held her breath and said nothing. He crouched again and reached deep inside a cubby next to the yams. He pulled out a corked bottle of dark brown glass.

"Come here, look." He gestured for Selva to kneel beside him. At the back of the cubby a dozen identical brown bottles were stacked on their sides. "Most of them are millet beer but some are grain whiskey. The strong stuff."

These last words sounded unlike anything Little Cronk had ever said to her. Until then it had all been simple declarative sentences. Suddenly he had a point of view—had almost cracked a joke. This only seemed to make her claustrophobia worse, but she waited for what he would do next.

Little Cronk bit the cork between his molars, pulled it out with a dull pop, and sniffed. "Whiskey," he pronounced, with a touch of pride in his knowledge. "Don't tell my parents." He raised the bottle to his mouth and took a long, deep gulp, meeting her eyes to be sure she was watching. He wiped his lips with the back of his hand and extended the bottle to Selva. She politely declined. She was not going to take her first drink of alcohol on the verge of fainting in a root cellar with Little Cronk.

He replaced the bottle in the cubby and looked at her. "I'm not as dumb as you think," he said. "I'm not a farm animal. Someday I might visit your city." She didn't answer, but she watched the look on her face kill the little dream that had gathered in his eyes.

Those few minutes underground were by far the most intense experience she had ever had on the Cronk farm, with him. It felt as if he had suddenly broken loose of the constraints that made every moment together excruciating. And yet nothing important had come close to happening—none of the thrilling mysteries that Selva and her school friends speculated about, always ending in hysterical laughter. And when she and Little Cronk came up into the daylight, a sack of yams on his shoulder, and he closed the doors and led her back to the farmhouse, they returned to silence as if nothing had happened at all.

Selva gave one of the bulkhead doors a tug, and it swung open. The lamplight on the steps showed no animal traps. The Cronks wouldn't imagine any Stranger knew about their root cellar. She knelt by the yam cubby and felt for the nearest bottle. She pulled the cork with her teeth the way Little Cronk had done and brought the bottle to her nose. She was pretty sure it was millet beer. That wouldn't do for what the Monge boy was going to endure in the morning. She wanted two bottles of the strong stuff.

The next one had the harsh, medicinal smell of her father's whiskey. She stuffed it in the book bag beside the saw, and as she reached for a second bottle she became aware of a figure standing above her in the bulkhead.

"Don't move, fucking Stranger, or I'll blow your head off."

11

"I'm Selva!"

She held the lamp to her face. Instantly the light blinded her so she could no longer see the figure up in the bulkhead, but she knew it was Little Cronk.

"I'm not a Stranger. I'm Selva."

"Come closer where I can see you."

She stood up and moved to the bottom of the steps with her arms raised, the lamp swinging overhead, throwing her shadow back and forth against the root cellar's walls.

"What the hell are you doing here? I nearly shot you."

Little Cronk was only a dark outline against the night sky, but his body seemed larger than before, almost filling the bulkhead opening, and his voice sounded different. Not deeper—it had broken a few years ago—but stronger, a voice no longer unable to say what it meant, as if a brake that held it down had been released.

"Can I come out?"

"No. Give me that bag."

Little Cronk lowered the rifle's barrel and, ducking under the bulkhead, took two steps down. Selva handed her book bag up to him, and he examined the bone saw and whiskey bottle inside. She set the lamp on the bottom step so that it illuminated him from below. The person she'd imagined at the wheel of the hauler the other day was not quite the one looking at her with intense suspicion. He was wearing nothing but shorts and a sleeveless undershirt, probably what he'd been sleeping in. The scrawny body that had grown longer every year without ever thickening now looked inflated—not just more powerful, but deliberately so: the neck a solid column, the chest pressing through his undershirt, the veins in his upper arm and thigh and calf muscles straining beneath the skin like sculpted clay. His hair, which used to hang uncombed in tangles over his eyes and ears, was now shaved smooth halfway up his head to an oval of short, bristly fur lying on his scalp, making her think of Zeus's flank after the surgery. His face was unevenly bearded, with bald patches on his cheeks and under his mouth and barely a trace of mustache, while a curtain of strands grew so far down from his chin that it covered his Adam's apple. All this wasn't the natural result of farmwork and adolescence but the product of sustained effort. So was the expression on his face, which she had never seen before: chin raised, lips pressed together with the lower one jutted out, glowering. He was Gard the Strong—but his eyes were still the eyes of Little Cronk, hurt, expectant, searching hers for something that only she had the power to give.

She told him exactly what she was doing here, on the farm and in the root cellar. Remembering her father's caution against getting caught in lies, she didn't try to use Kask the Yeoman boy again, but she also left some things out, including how Monge's foot was injured. She tried to gauge whether Gard knew of her earlier visit; she concluded that he didn't and that it was better for him not to know. Her story made him glower harder and also laugh once or twice, sneeringly, with the curled lip she'd pictured before, but she kept talking, slipping into the tone of old acquaintances, for she had always been able to gain advantage over him with words, and she felt that he might be softening, might confiscate her book bag and send her away with a jeer about stupid city girls—until Gard whipped a clenched fist across his chest to cut her off.

"Selva Rustin"—he gestured at her with the gun barrel—"I charge you as a Burgher spy. I charge you with conspiring against my people with the Stranger enemy to steal our land from its rightful owners and poison our Yeoman stock. You will be tried tomorrow at the limestone quarry. Do you have anything to say?"

He had spoken more words than she'd heard in all the summers of visiting. Where had he learned to talk like this? Again she felt like complimenting him, but instead she burst into unexpected and violent tears.

"Papa is going to worry about me. When he wakes up he'll be so worried." She knew that her father would blame himself.

"And he'll come looking for you. Stop your pussy girl moaning, I haven't done anything yet."

Gard waited for her to stop, but the sobs kept heaving through her shoulders. The thought of her father had sprung open a deep well of loneliness.

"I had a feeling that hauler belonged to you," Gard muttered. "No Burghers ever come around here."

Even as Selva wept, she mustered a pretend outrage that instantly turned real. "*You* stole it."

"Looks that way."

"How are we going to get back to the city? We don't want to be here. We want to go home."

"It was on our land. We recognitioned it."

"You mean *requisitioned*."

This was a mistake. Gard narrowed his eyes until, with the shaved head and primitive beard, he resembled some archaic figure from a display case in the bones museum.

"You always were a little Burgher bitch. See how you like sleeping with yams."

He climbed back up the steps and reached with his free hand for the bulkhead door. As he started to swing it shut, Selva caught a glimpse of something on his forearm, an image that had never been there before, like a tattoo. The barrel lock slid closed overhead.

12

All night long she didn't seem able to fall asleep, but she woke up with her head propped against a cubby full of turnips and slivers of light around the edges of the bulkhead and a desperate need to pee. The root cellar was cold. She shivered inside her blouse.

She had slept enough to dream. All she could remember was anxiety, but the dream's residue made her think of her mother—of the time when she was seven and her mother brought her to the Market District to buy Pan a toy. Selva demanded to explore the stores by herself and got hopelessly lost in the crooked old streets for what felt like hours until she ended up wailing in a crowd of shoppers, where her mother found her. She had thought she'd lost her mother to this needy new child, and instead of trying to displace her baby brother she had punished her mother by striking off on her own, only to learn what true need was. Her mother's enfolding arms told her that she was safe because she was loved, would always be loved. All her adventures with her father depended on this anchor. But she never knew it until now, in the Cronks' root cellar, more alone than on that day in the Market District, farther than she'd ever been from the mother she'd abandoned, and she felt the anguish of her own selfishness.

From the first days of the Emergency she had tried to construct a version of herself that would be equal to the new world and every new thing that happened to her. At times she had succeeded, at other times she had miserably failed, but all along there had been a strain of self-creation—like the body and face she'd seen by lamplight, Little Cronk turning himself into Gard the Strong. But the ache in her neck and the moist smell of soil and roots told her that this danger was real in a way nothing else had been. She feared what it might reveal about herself. She could let it destroy her or else try to meet it, not by assembling a Selva of metal and clay, but by being herself every moment of it. If she must cry, then cry. But the tears had receded.

She pounded her fist against the bulkhead doors for a long time. Finally the lock slid open, the doors were lifted, and Gard stood above her, in the same clothes as last night but wearing heavy boots now, and without the gun.

"I need to use the bathroom," she said.

He seemed to consider the request and its possible answers before motioning for her to come out. He led her around the barn toward the farmhouse. As she followed him up the path, she studied his shoulders, his neck, the smooth knobs on the back of his skull, and found the view both intimidating and a little funny, so that her lips were forming a half-smile when he suddenly stopped and turned around.

"How did you sleep?"

She wasn't sure if he was mocking her. The question was ridiculous, but his tone was utterly neutral.

"I've slept better."

He nodded as if to note a semi-important fact and kept walking.

The sun had risen just above the tree line, and long morning shadows were moving across the fields. The bathroom—

she had used it before—stood behind the house under the giant oak, an outdoor stall surrounding a latrine and a hand pump that brought water from the well into a basin. It was somehow reassuring to find everything clean and orderly as always—a trademark of the Cronks. She wondered if his mother and father had been told about the captive on their premises. They'd put an end to this farce as soon as they knew.

When she came out, Gard was leaning against the oak tree, running his fingers through the strands that hung from his chin, watching her. His gaze fell to her chest. Selva's blouse was made of thin cotton, with a drawstring around the neck. It had fit last summer but now pulled tight across her breasts. He looked away from them, then back, and away again, as if he didn't know whether looking was forbidden or his right. She wished that her body was still straight and flat the way it had been until the last two years. She wanted to keep him and herself calm, but the soft lines produced a field of crackling tension all around her.

"You got a tattoo," Selva said to turn attention away from her body to his own.

"It's not a tattoo. Feel."

Gard held out his arm. The image on the back of his forearm was a crude pig's head in profile, with a snout and pointy ears. She could tell without touching that the figure was a ridge of raised pink skin.

"It's a brand," he said.

A vague nausea came over Selva. "You mean you burned it on?"

"We all did. We have a forge at the quarry."

"You all?"

"Me and my unit. Human branding is an ancient custom for Yeomen—Natives. But you kept it from us. It's all written down on the wood slips I found. You'll see at the quarry."

He was obviously enjoying the effect of these revelations. Selva was unable to reply.

"My mother made you something to eat."

Mrs. Cronk was coming around the side of the house with a cloth-covered bowl and a steaming cup. She was as shapeless as her son was finely sculpted, buried alive inside rolls of flesh. Her shift reached just below her knees, exposing veinous calves and ankles crammed like firewood logs into a pair of dainty slippers. She lowered her head as she held out the bowl and cup to Gard, who snatched them away and handed them off to Selva.

"Tell Papa I need the hauler," he said sharply. "Tell him to bring it to the pasture." Mrs. Cronk nodded and waited. "You can go." He waved her away—her presence seemed to embarrass him. As Mrs. Cronk started to leave, Selva caught her eye, unable to believe that she would allow her son to address her as a house servant, and was met by a look of clenched resentment—not of him, she sensed, but of her, the intruder, the captive.

"Look at her," Gard said, watching his mother waddle back to the house. "That's not the way our women are supposed to look. In the Golden Age Yeoman mothers didn't go to hell. You just have to look at her to know something went wrong somewhere back there."

"She's your mother," Selva said.

"She doesn't know she's alive. Most of our women don't. Heads up their pussies." He scrunched his nose in some profound disgust. "Not just women—my father can hardly fuck.

He has to drink boiled goatweed. The Yeoman people have been cursed."

It took her breath away, but she said, "Are you trying to shock me? Because I'm older, too." This was the way: meet his frankness with her own.

He laughed his unpleasant laugh, which she had begun to recognize as a cover for uneasiness, like the tic of stroking his beard. "You live in the city," he said. "Everything in your head is a lie. Eat that and let's go."

The hauler was parked outside the sheep pasture. Big Cronk was standing by the driver's door with the bone saw in his hand. His face was shaded by the brim of his leather hat, but his posture told Selva that he wasn't happy to see her again.

"What's your plan today, son?"

"Going to the quarry. Training with the unit."

Big Cronk nodded at Selva. "What about her?"

"I'll show her the exercises, and the wood slips. Not every day I get a chance to teach one of them the truth."

"But you won't . . . ?"

"Yeah, we will. We have rules."

Gard was talking in a new way—like a man with responsibilities and ambitions, in charge and in a hurry. A rifle lay across his seat, and he moved it to the passenger side before climbing in behind the wheel. He hadn't mentioned a trial; Selva wondered if it had been postponed.

"Lock her in back," he ordered his father.

Big Cronk took Selva by the wrist and helped her into the bed of the hauler. "Give me your hands," he said, and pulled her to the rail where a pair of metal rings hung. He fastened them around her wrists, then gave the key to Gard.

The sound of the metal *click* had the same effect on her as the ache in her neck after a night in the root cellar. She was in trouble and alone.

The hauler engine started with a cough and rattle and an angry roar as Gard gunned it. Under the noise Big Cronk whispered, "Why did you come back?" She looked at the bone saw where he'd set it on the ground. "Did you tell him I saw you before?" She shook her head, and relief swept over his broad face.

"But Papa will—"

Big Cronk glared to silence her. He gave an almost imperceptible nod as the hauler lurched into gear and tore off, spitting dirt in his face.

The drive took just five minutes, but by the time they had flown through the hayfield, swung back and forth around peach and ginkgo trees, bounced across a streambed, and skidded down a rocky hillside to the edge of a steep pit, Selva's wrists were burning, and she thought she was going to throw up.

The quarry was an oval hole in the earth, about the area and height of a typical Yeoman house, walled all the way down in rough stripes of limestone. The bottom of the pit sloped into a pool of algae and green water, but the higher end was dry, and this was where Selva, still tied to the hauler's rail, saw two figures bent over shovels, turning the gray crumbling soil, throwing it aside, turning again. The men were shirtless and barefoot, with lean backs and long hair, and they moved awkwardly, shuffling as they dug. She noticed that their ankles were tied together by a short length of rope, and she knew that they were the two Strangers who had come with young Monge to raid the farm and been captured. Something thick and dark ran across the naked lower back of each man—an identical mark in the shape of an X. The Strangers were branded.

Three Yeoman boys about Gard's age were standing along the lip of the pit, wearing shorts and undershirts and boots like him despite the morning chill. They had been talking as the hauler pulled up, but when Gard got out they shut up and stood at attention, arms at their sides, one of them clutching a rifle with its butt planted in the ground.

From the woods nearby a mourning dove was calling, *hoo-OO-hoo-hoo-hoo*. The only other sound in the still air was the *chug-chug* of shovels hitting dry dirt. The Cronk farm, the Stranger encampment, the Place, the city by the river, the imperial capital, all seemed to have disappeared over the edge of the Earth.

Gard came around to the back of the hauler. "I'm going to free you," he said. "Don't try to run away, you can't."

He had never touched her before. When he unfastened her wrists, her hand jumped and he laughed. He left the key hanging in the metal rings' lock. As she climbed down from the hauler, he was looking at her chest, openly now, with a sort of angry frown, and afterward whenever she caught him staring it was in the same way, as if he were brooding over something that troubled him.

"Why did you bring me here?" she asked.

"I want you to see. I know what you think of Yeomen."

"Don't you call yourselves 'Natives' now?"

"Yeah, because we're the—you know, the first people on this land." Selva stopped herself from helping him with "indigenous."

She followed him away from the quarry, up a footpath into a small meadow where there was a platform built of rough old boards, probably stripped from a barn. The platform was about thirty feet square, and at each corner a flag on a pole hung limp. The still air smelled of fresh sweat from boys engaged in physical exercises: a few doing push-ups against the platform or pull-ups on a crossbar, others lifting big lead balls overhead, one boy shinnying up a rope that was tied to a pine branch next to a large disc of bronze metal, another shooting arrows at a target nailed to a tree fifty feet away. In the middle of the platform, two boys were squaring off with cloth stripping wrapped around their raised fists and blood trickling from noses and lips.

Some of the boys were lavishly muscular, others still bony in the way of young boys growing too fast, and on a few lumpy bodies folds of fat hung from waists. None had honed himself to the deliberate refinement of Gard, who was the tallest of them and the most dominant, not just in strength but in presence. They all had their hair shaved in ways that gave an impression of furred skulls rather than heads, and they all wore the uniform of shorts and undershirts and boots. Selva noticed branding everywhere—on shoulders, thighs, necks, even scalps.

At one end of the platform there was a wooden crate, and when she drew closer she saw that it was full of animal heads, like the wolf's and the bull's—animals of every kind, deer and bison, lizards and wild boar, foxes, birds with long beaks and staring eyes. At the top of the pile lay a pig head with a prominent pink snout. These weren't wood carvings or clay casts; they were made of animal skin and fur.

Gard came up and stood next to her. "We all chose an animal spirit to be like a personal model. There's an ancient Yeoman word for it: Manimal," he said, with pedantic pride, and Selva had to keep an incredulous laugh from exploding in her mouth. "There's a bear burned onto that boy's neck.

The one doing pull-ups has a viper on each shoulder. They're making progress."

The boys took in Selva's arrival the way wild animals become aware of a human intruder: not stopping their activity but suddenly alert, an eye shifting, a muscle twitching.

"These guys are all in my unit," Gard said. "You're the first girl I've allowed here. They know not to talk to you." He folded his arms across his chest and waited for her reaction.

"Who are they?"

"Farm boys from around here, village kids. We've been training since the Conspiracy started. You should have seen what they looked like then—wild turkeys, scrawny chickens."

"Congratulations," she said. It was truly astonishing that stifled, obedient Little Cronk had done all this. Watching the branded boys at their exercises, she wondered if she'd been brought to the quarry not to be tried but to be impressed and shown off, as she'd wanted to display young Monge to her friends.

A breeze kicked up and fluttered the flags on their poles. Before it died, Selva had time to study one: a pair of vertical red stripes on either side of a white stripe, and in the middle the profile of a strutting rooster. Off in the meadow, in the shade of a spreading plane tree, smoke was rising from the chimney of a stone-walled hut.

Gard followed her gaze. "Our forge," he said significantly.

"Where are all the girls?"

"We don't allow them here."

"But you brought me."

"That's different. They don't think of you that way, you're not one of us. Yeoman girls would kill unit morale."

"What do you mean, unit? Like in the military?"

He gave her a dark glance. "Some things I'm not going to discuss with you."

"Will you discuss those two Strangers you've got in the quarry?"

"No. Follow me."

He led her away from the platform, across the meadow to the edge of the woods where there was a small structure, no more than a large shed. It looked newly built, but young vines from the closest trees were already reaching through the air for its roof. The shed was made of the same knotty pine boards as the platform—up three steps to a narrow front porch, window openings with no windows on either side of a doorway with no door. On the doorjamb a long pale snakeskin hung from a nail, and inside, pieces of bone and horn and feathers and fur were mounted on the walls and scattered around the floor. The only furniture was a simple wooden chair at the back wall. On one side of the chair there was a small wooden box closed with a brass hasp, and on the other side, propped against the wall, a piece of black slate was chalked with phrases scrawled in the same brutal handwriting that Selva had seen in the leather notebook: "Citys are full of Human Werms," "Words lye, Dirt is true," "They hate you because you are strong and they are week," "Who is your Manimal?" Along with the same crude drawings of animals there were two human stick figures with terror-stricken balloon faces, connected by arrows to the labels BURGHER and STRANGER.

Behind the chair a banner was nailed to the wall, dyed red and white like the flags around the platform, with an uneven fringe as if it had been sloppily cut from a shawl or nightshirt. The image of a bird skeleton was extending its wings upward to embrace the words DIRT THOUGHT.

"This is our classroom," Gard said. "Sit down."

He took the chair, leaving Selva nowhere to sit except on the floor, cross-legged and looking up at him like the first day of primary school. And yet she had been his teacher. She had given him those books, the *Child's History of the Empire* and the folktales, and read alongside him line by line, encouraging him through every dismal mistake. She'd done it to please her parents, and to feel smart, and maybe because she felt sorry for Little Cronk, but she never believed he would get to the most basic level of comprehension that she had long ago passed. Now he was going to instruct her in ideas half-made from smashed bits of the words she had given him.

13

"Listen to me, because you can't be tried until you understand," Gard began. "Everything you think is true—it's a lie. Two hundred years ago, when Yeomen owned this land, there was a Golden Age. Our women were beautiful, even mothers and grandmothers, not fat sows like today. Our men didn't need to drink boiled goatweed to have children—they stayed hard all day long. We lived off our crops and herds and made everything we needed for ourselves. We had nothing to do with people in other lands. We already had things you think you invented, like engines and—and medicine. We had our own Yeoman writing. You'll see! Our leader was named Gard the Great. We didn't elect him—we *followed* him. Yeomen only had one law—"

"The Law of the Strongest," Selva said.

Gard nodded, but confidence deserted his face, and for a moment he was Little Cronk again. Selva was sorry she had interrupted—a habit from school when she knew the answer.

"Where did you learn all this?" she asked, to keep him talking.

"Not from that lying history book you gave me. Here's how I know."

Gard unlocked the box at his feet and took out a thin wafer of bleached wood about the size of an oak leaf. Selva reached for it, but he shook his head and held the piece up so that its face was visible. She saw faint gray markings, lines and circles and other shapes that, if she stretched her imagination, resembled the characters on the goatskin sheet of the boy in the bones museum.

Gard pointed at the box, which was full of similar fragments. "My unit dug these up in the quarry. That's what our slaves are doing right now."

"What are they?"

"The *Book of Yeomen*," he said with obvious pride. "It tells the whole story of our people. There was an ancient civilization on this farm! If we keep digging, we'll probably find walls and houses and temples. I figured out how these fit together." He retrieved a few more pieces of wood, knelt on the floor, and reaching with his branded arm he arranged them in an order that looked arbitrary to Selva. "I'm learning how to read it," he said defiantly. "See? This means Gard the Great. And look here—they even predict the future. This warns about vines."

He was pointing at a fragment with a pair of lines that rose to meet like the peak of a roof. The markings on most of the other pieces were so faint that they were indistinguishable from flecks of wood grain. She could make out no pattern of symbols and words.

He returned to his chair. "Gard the Great won every war, and he taught us Dirt Thought." He turned around and pointed at the flag on the wall. "That means the people who work with their hands aren't the lowest people—we're the highest. We grow our own food and fight our own wars. We don't make other people do it. We don't learn right and wrong from a book, we know it in our heart and muscles. Did I tell you about Manimals?"

She nodded. "What happened to the Golden Age?"

Gard took a deep breath, and his voice began to quiver.

"After Gard the Great passed on to the world of animal spirits, trespassers invaded here. They said this wasn't Yeoman land, it belonged to their empire, for them to rule. They built cities and colleges and museums and other filthy things that went against the Law of the Strongest and Dirt Thought. Which is *clean*. Understand? Nothing is cleaner than dirt."

Maybe he'd given this speech to his unit a dozen times, but the flashes in his eyes and the cadences of his voice seemed to say that he had personally lived through the joy and pity and horror of his story, and was telling it for the first time now to her.

"In the cities human worms crawled all over each other and ate each other's shit. Burghers could never defeat Yeomen in war, but they found another way to bring us down, with *words*—books and schools—*lies*. Words messed up our minds and turned our boys into girls and our women into fat sows. Our men spent all day drinking grain whiskey and millet beer until their balls dropped off. Yeomen lost our animal spirits, and we had nothing to live for. Every time you came here, I had ashes in my mouth," he almost pleaded. "And you gave me those books."

"But your parents encouraged me!"

"My parents are spoiled meat," Gard said, his lip curling.

"*Listen to the young*," she murmured, more to herself than him. "What happened after the empire fell?"

"The empire didn't fall. That's another Burgher lie—like those folktales you gave me, with talking frogs. The empire is still here. What happened is, our young men figured out what you're doing to us. What happened is we woke up."

"The vines?"

"Not just the vines. Everything. Bringing Strangers across the mountains to do your dirty work, steal our livestock and mate with our girls and poison our stock. We had every right to put those slaves to digging in the quarry. Did you know we had Stranger slaves in the time of Gard the Great? Look."

He held up a small wood fragment with two barely perceptible lines crossed in an X. Outside, a pair of birds in a tree were trading calls.

"And we know what the human worms in your shit city are doing," Gard went on. "We have spies just like you. No one does any work. Girls take off their clothes and fuck in public and then kill themselves. You go to meetings where you talk talk talk in some weird language. You're building word machines and training them to destroy us because we're getting strong again."

"What word machines?"

"Word machines to enslave us without risking your own skin, because Burghers are cowards. But we will never be your slaves again. There's no end to ancient hatred except war. My unit is ready—the whole Yeoman people are."

"Is Leader Gandorig part of your unit?" She told him about the three farmers and the wolf and the bull. Gard scoffed. The farmers were almost as old as his father, he said, and those two Manimals were incapable of being trained. None of them understood Dirt Thought, or had even heard of Gard the Great.

"What we're doing is hard," he said. "I've gone through a lot of lost farm boys here. They couldn't be led—they forgot the discipline. But Yeomen need a leader. We won't survive unless one person takes charge."

"You?"

"No!" The question seemed to offend Gard. Scowling, he gathered several pieces of wood and laid them in a row on the floor. "'Gard—the Great—is coming—back,'" he read, pointing at each wafer in turn. "Understand? I'm just his—his lieutenant. All those boys out there are waiting for him. They're learning to be men so they'll be ready when he comes. They show up before sunrise and stay past sunset. Do you know why?" He waited until she shook her head. "Because they've found a purpose."

"What purpose?"

Gard struggled to reply. He shifted his gaze to the doorway behind her, as if the purpose might be found outside the classroom. "To crush the Burghers and bring back the Golden Age." The answer seemed to energize him, and he continued, "Almost all our Yeomen are awake now. We're more organized than you think. We're just waiting for a sign from Gard the Great to fight. And we will win." He leaned back against the chair, and his shoulders sagged as if the effort of teaching had left him exhausted. "Maybe you're the sign, Selva."

Her body ached from sitting on the pine floor. She stretched her legs flat before her so that her pants slid up around her knees. He was staring again and she let him. She tried to concentrate on something that had flitted through her mind as he was speaking, a glimmer of how to reach through the noise and smoke of his rage and touch him.

"Gard," she said. "Can I call you Gard?"

"That's my name." His calf muscle was doing a nervous jiggle.

"Let me tell you what's happening in my city, Gard. Girls don't do what you said. We haven't stopped working. We're working as hard as you, but not because the empire tells us to. Everyone is doing what their heart commands. We're not building word machines for a war. We don't want you to be our slaves."

She had his full attention.

"I admit I had some ignorant ideas. I thought Yeomen could never be part of Together. I called you *man-eaters*, and that was wrong. But those word machines—you must be talking about Better Humans. They have nothing to do with war and slaves. We're trying to make ourselves and our world more perfect."

He was running his fingers through his beard, unsure, hesitating before the temptation of her vision.

"I had ashes in my mouth like you—I just didn't know it! Comprehensive exams, family guilds, Excess Burghers, generation after generation. For what? Our parents said this was the best world—the *only* world. It was a lie!"

He was nodding. She went on.

"I think I understand you better now. I always wished we could talk like this. I knew there was more to you, but something always got in the way."

"You were nice to me," he murmured.

"I always liked you. Even before you grew up."

His cheeks colored, and he looked down at the hands in his lap. The pig on his forearm seemed to mock his sudden awkwardness.

"Do we have to be enemies?" she asked. "In a weird way we're not that different."

"No?"

"We're both making something new. Better Humans are like our Manimals."

At once she regretted saying it. His face hardened and she saw him close down.

"*That's* a lie. A machine is not an animal. They're the opposite." He sat up in the chair and his voice rose. "You and I aren't the same. We don't want the same thing. I want the Golden Age. You wouldn't like it. Girls didn't get to wear clothes like that and look like that and talk like that. I know what you want. You want everyone to be like you. You hate us, but your perfect world tells you not to, so you try and turn us into Burghers. That's what you've always done. You're doing it right now. *We hate you.*"

From across the meadow came the heavy, muffled sound of a mallet striking metal. Gard stood up, and the body that had filled the root cellar bulkhead loomed over Selva. He watched with hostile hunger as she got to her feet.

"Too many words. We're running out of time."

14

On the platform the boys had stopped their exercises and were crowded in a tight circle. They strained forward, waving their fists, shouting, "Kill him!" "Don't be a pussy!" "Tear his leg off!" Selva couldn't see what was happening inside the circle, but as she approached behind Gard a short boy with broad shoulders caught sight of her and, mid-scream, stared open-mouthed, revealing teeth already going rotten. Gard signaled him to look away.

"What they're doing is in the *Book of Yeomen*," he told her solemnly. "It's how the unit decides promotions. You'll be shocked, but it's our tradition."

Gard pushed aside two smaller boys with cleanly shaved heads and made room in the circle for Selva. One of them—the lizard on the nape of his neck was still fresh, livid and glistening—shrank away as if contact with her might be dangerous.

In the middle of the circle there was a frenzied tangle of muscled backs and shoulders and thighs smeared with blood. A shorter boy in a bear head and a taller boy in a bird head clung and clawed and tore at each other as they bled on the pine boards, so entwined that it was hard to tell where one body ended and the other began. They were fighting for their lives while the other boys pressed in on them and bayed. Then a sudden turn by the bird, a flip of the bear, and she saw that it was true: they were naked, and their bodies had been shaved.

Gard leaned toward her ear and said something that she couldn't hear clearly. It sounded like: "This is why we'll win."

She did not let herself look at the sky. Held like a slave in this loveless place, so far from everyone who knew and cared about her, if she let her tears flow they'd never stop, so she kept her eyes on the fight and set herself the task of giving Gard no pleasure with a sign of weakness. She tried to follow the wrestlers' tactics and began to see that the mayhem followed certain moves that kept them from killing each other or damaging their bodies beyond repair. For example, they kept their hands away from each other's private parts, which she imagined being torn off with a sufficiently violent yank. When fingers dug into a muzzle or beak, they stopped short of gouging eyes. Even with bloodshed, the fighting seemed stylized, and so did the screaming, as if all the boys had been through this ritual many times before.

"How do you decide the winner?" she asked, and turned to Gard, but he was gone.

The bear fell to the platform through several stages of collapse, ending on his side with his knees drawn up to his belly. The bird kneeled over the bear and hammered his beak into the other's shoulder, then stood and planted a foot over the bear branded on the loser's back, and raised his arms above his head, revealing smooth armpits. The whoops and roars around the circle lasted half a minute while the winner kept striking his fist against his chest smeared with his own or his rival's blood, the shaven skin around his groin gleaming. He was transfigured, like an illustrated statue in one of her primary-school textbooks over the caption "Victorious Ancient God." She thought of the moment she'd climbed down the ladder from the Suicide Spot to a round of applause, having chosen neither life nor death, feeling the opposite of victorious. The memory brought an insight that struck her like the rock those Yeoman children had thrown at the hauler.

The problem with Together *was* too many words. Too many ideas, too much thinking, too much straining after perfection and bending her nature into something unnatural until she had no body, until there was nothing left of her at all. She could spend weeks or years in the workshop training her Better Human to think and speak exactly according to the six principles with no mistakes, and she would be farther than ever from knowing how to be herself.

In the classroom she had felt a quiver of closeness to this boy. The note he had struck was still vibrating like a bell in a part of her that had nothing to do with words. Gard—prince of a made-up Golden Age, arranging pieces of wood into his own labyrinth—was no happier than she. Their generation was cursed, coming too late and reaching a point at the end of some road where every future once settled was suddenly closed off, used up, erased, and they had to start all over again, with only the euphoria and despair of youth. How strange that he had entered this struggle with her. These farm boys wanted what she wanted: the power to purify themselves and the world. Or else stand alone under an empty sky.

Perhaps the point was not to rule out anything that made her human, to accept herself all in all. That might mean giving up a lot. It might even mean giving up Together. Her father would probably have something to say about this. She told herself to remember it in case she got to see him again.

Selva stepped out of the circle, away from the platform, and walked over to the trail that led down to the quarry. No one stopped her or even seemed to notice her amid the fervor of celebrating, as if they were so unused to the sight of a girl in their midst that they simply couldn't recognize her.

Standing near the armed guards, looking down into the pit, she saw the Stranger slaves. They were still digging, ankles yoked, backs with the X brand bent over their shovels, *chug-chug*, searching for fragments of a fantasy that kept them toiling in bondage. She didn't want a war between Strangers and Yeomen, but she wanted these two to be as free as she had been until last night, and she wished there was a way to tell young Monge about them. If Monge was still alive. If her father had managed to finish the surgery without the bone saw and grain whiskey and his nurse assistant.

It took Selva a few moments to realize that, on the other side of the quarry, the hauler was no longer where Gard had left it.

Had he driven back to the farm? Selva tried to get the attention of one of the guards, but he refused to meet her eyes. She made her way back up the footpath to the meadow. The flags were flapping open on a breeze, and the boys were at their exercises again—the loser of the fight, in underwear and boots again, without the bear head, was lifting a lead ball—but she didn't see him.

She looked across the meadow toward the classroom. Someone was inside at one of the window openings. Even at a distance she knew from the beard and the outline of scalp fur that it was Gard. Only his upper body was visible, and the motion of his arm made her think he was waving her over, but as she came closer she saw that it was moving with rapid fury at some repeated task, as if he was whittling a recalcitrant stick, or grating a piece of hard cheese. For a moment she imagined he might be slicing up fragments of the *Book of Yeomen*. His face began to materialize, and it was twisted by effort or emotion, perhaps crying or cursing, eyes squeezed shut, mouth hanging ajar. Then the eyes opened and looked across the grass directly into hers, and at last she understood what he was doing, but before she could turn away, he cried out and convulsed with the saddest expression she had ever seen on a human face.

There was nowhere in the meadow to hide. She ran back to the platform and pretended to occupy herself with watching two archers take turns at a target. Then Gard was at her side—but where his face should have been there was a pig's face, with an erect pink two-holed snout, and ears like wings, and slits for eyes, panting.

"Are you spying on us?"

Dumbly she shook her head.

"Manimals!" he roared.

A boy climbed the rope and struck the bell. A metallic chord trembled loud and long across the meadow. At the sound, the other boys stopped exercising and ran to the crate where the heads were kept. There was an excited scramble as the boys shoved one another aside and rummaged through the crate for their rightful head as if this was their reward for all the hard work. With the same hand that had been so busy a few moments ago the pig took Selva by the upper arm and marched her to the center of the platform where she stood inside the circle while heads of all kinds gathered close around her.

"Manimals, soldiers, Yeomen!" Digging fingers into her arm so that it hurt. "What is this girl doing here?"

The heads—there must have been two dozen of them—stared and leered at the girl in their midst.

"Commander, tell us!" It was a boy with a reptile face, the lizard brand still raw on his neck.

"Her name is Selva Rustin. A Burgher girl from the city. I captured her last night on our farm. She was stealing supplies for the Strangers."

Now that they were permitted to look, they devoured Selva through their cutout eyeholes as if she were an extinct creature transported from the first floor of the bones museum and brought to life on the platform.

"Stealing is a crime, but there is a bigger crime. What is it called?"

Another silence as the heads looked at one another for an answer none could offer. The flags fluttered in the wind, a strutting cock, a coiled viper.

"Spying," Selva said.

The pig was surprised enough to drop her arm. If she was going to be put on trial, she would play a part. She would not be led wordless to slaughter like a farm animal.

"Speak when it's your turn," he told her. "We have rules." He raised his voice and addressed the unit: "What's the first rule of Dirt Thought?"

A boy with the long beak and elongated neck of a heron answered, "*Words lie, dirt is true!*"

"*Words lie, dirt is true*," the pig repeated. "That means: don't believe everything a Burgher girl says." Laughter rippled across the Manimals. "What's the third rule of Dirt Thought?"

The answer came from the bear who had lost the fight. "*Men are stronger than women*," he said in a husky voice, and as if on cue the entire assembly followed up with a prolonged roar.

The trial reminded Selva of none she'd ever heard about. If anything, the call-and-response was more like We Are

One, though We Are One had no commander. The point was not to argue but to dissolve in perfect unity. She could sense the eagerness of the boys waiting for the pig to ask the next question so they could all think the same thought and aim it at her.

"*'Men are stronger than women.'* But what does that mean? I know your little brothers could take this girl down in five seconds." More laughter, which he silenced with a raised hand. "It means we have to live by a code. It's called honor."

The pig pulled Selva forward by the arm, and she tripped and caught herself before falling.

"Look at her. She thinks you're a bunch of savage Strangers who can't control themselves. That's why she's scared. She doesn't understand—Manimals submit to the code *because* we're stronger. And it's a harsh code. We follow a strict diet. No alcohol, no tobacco, no girls. Every day we train and perfect our bodies and stand by our brothers and prepare to fight. If we ever break the code, we pay a high price. If a boy gets caught spying on this unit for the enemy, what happens to him?"

"Death!" someone shouted.

"You're right," the pig said. "But not a girl. The code tells us to respect girls. If a girl is guilty, she must be punished, but not with death."

He raised his snout. His narrow eyes were looking in the direction of the stone hut under the plane tree. At that moment a boy came out of the door and began walking across the meadow toward the platform, slowly, almost nonchalantly, a boy with a boy's head preoccupied by something he was holding in his hand.

"Another part of the code is we don't punish without evidence," Gard said. "But we have evidence."

He extended an open hand. A kind of dog head—perhaps it was supposed to be a jackal or wolf—approached and placed in it a pair of white glasses. The pig held them up by the strap for all to see. "Yours?" he asked Selva, and didn't wait for an answer, which he already seemed to know. "These are spyglasses. One of our patrols found them at a checkpoint. They let Burghers see our thoughts."

"No!" one of the heads cried, and was quickly drowned in a wave of indignation that rose to shouts of rage.

Then the unit parted and made way for the boy from the stone hut. He came out onto the center of the platform. He was smaller than the other boys, maybe two or three years older than Pan. His body was still undeveloped, and a bee's fuzz covered his scalp, but his face frightened her as none of the others did, because among all the Manimals it was a human face—the face of a child bored to vacancy, dull-eyed, emotionless, blank, and young enough to be capable of anything. His thin arms were covered with burn scars in shapes that looked nothing like brandings. He was holding the hook grip of an iron rod whose far end glowed orange.

"This is Tee," the pig told Selva. "He doesn't speak but we think he's an orphan. I found him eating grain mash behind our silo. I trained him in smithing." He took the iron rod from Tee and, dangling the goggles in his other hand, held it up by its hook grip for the unit's inspection. "He forged it just this morning. My idea."

Tee nodded, indifferent. Selva saw that the end of the rod was burning with a triangle and, inside it, an open eye. The triangle of femaleness, the eye of espionage.

The pig dispatched Tee into the assembly. "Put them on."

He pushed the goggles into Selva's hand, and she stretched the strap over her head and fastened the eyepieces on her face. "Tell us what you see."

What had once allowed her to flee into a glorious dreamscape gave no help. She was looking into utter darkness. "Nothing."

"What am I thinking?"

"I don't know."

"Selva Rustin, I charge you with spying for the Burgher and Stranger enemy. You are allowed to defend yourself. How do you answer?"

"I'm guilty."

The pig made a sound of surprise. A murmur of confusion and displeasure ran through the unit. She felt the warmth of the rod close to her arm.

"I was spying."

"Selva—"

"No, I want to confess."

She had made her father bring her out here, and now she would have to do this alone, and the sun's eye was merciless, and her family so far away. Whatever Gard had in store for her, she would finish it herself. She began speaking rapidly so that fear couldn't catch up with her.

"Here's my story. I was a vain, naive little Burgher girl. I grew up performing monkey tricks in jumpers and school uniforms. I performed some of my tricks right here on this farm. Gard can tell you."

She felt his free hand on her shoulder—not with the hard command of Gard the Strong but, she imagined in the darkness behind the goggles, with the mute face of Little Cronk, imploring her to stop.

"Then the most wonderful thing happened in our city.

The world ended. Yes, it disappeared—overnight! When the world ended, it was like putting on these goggles for the first time. I could see clearly. I saw through everything. I saw through the world where I'd been performing monkey tricks, the world that had just ended, and it was a foul, stinking, decaying heap of lies. I saw through my good father and nice mother—oh, right through them to the bottom! With these super-powerful glasses my sight was so strong that when I looked at my father, an important and respected man in our city, they shrank him down to the size of my little brother's thumb. I couldn't stand to listen to him because all his favorite words, the eternal truths he raised us on, made a tinny noise like a cowbell, *ting ting ting*."

Someone in the unit laughed, and Selva nodded in his direction. At least they were listening. Maybe she was making sense.

"But the best and worst part was that I saw through myself. It was more than I could bear." A perverse desire was driving her to bring Gard to the verge of doing what she had begun to sense he didn't want to do. "Fortunately, the world started over. We got rid of the stink and the lies in our city and made everything new. It was a lot of work, but we did it with a smile on our faces because we had a purpose. And I'm sure you'll be happy to hear that I made *myself* new. I wanted to be good. You have no idea how good I wanted to be! I wanted to be so good that I could see through myself right down to the bottom and bear it. But no one can be that good without an evil enemy, and it didn't take long to find one. Our enemy had been right there all along. You, of course."

Yes, they were listening, because somewhere a boy howled like a wolf, and another took it up, and soon the whole unit was erupting with barks and roars and shrill cries, and even

Gard's shouted orders couldn't make them stop, for Selva had taken from him the voice of command. On impulse she placed her hands together and bowed her head. This blind supplicant's gesture surprised them into silence.

"Manimals! I'm almost finished, and then you can deliver your verdict, but first you have to let me confess. You were the enemy, and what a pleasure it was to despise you! You made it easy, with your ignorance, your absurd delusions. Just ask your commander how I made him feel back in my monkey days. He must have felt like one of those helpless Cronk pigs, wallowing in the pigpen, waiting for the knife at the butcher's block. Yes, he was always the pig on his head and his arm. Because we can't escape our fate."

She turned away from where Gard was standing and felt that she was facing the place where the meadow ended at the slope down to the quarry.

"To state the Burgher view plainly: you're the past, we're the future. You can keep your Golden Age, because we're making a new world where everyone is perfect except you." She became aware of unhappiness bubbling through the unit and began to hurry. "But something about this view must not have sat right with me, so I had to see for myself. We Burghers have a song about Brave Bella. I wanted to be a brave girl like her, so I came out here to spy on you and see how evil our enemy is. And I've seen—I've seen! You've got those two slaves tied up in your quarry when all they wanted was a meal and a place to sleep. You've got your sisters locked up somewhere, wasting away. You made a branding iron just for me. Oh, I'll have plenty to report back to my city if I ever get out of here."

She felt the heat of the rod near her face. It went away, then came back.

"But I don't want to spy on you anymore. I don't think you want to hurt me, Gard. I think we can be friends."

She took off the goggles and turned to him. The snout was pointed at the sky. The eye slits appeared to be squeezed shut just like at his moment of agony in the classroom. He was shrinking away from her as if she was the one hurting him, though he held the rod so close it singed her hair.

From the direction of the quarry she heard the grind and wheeze of an engine. She looked and saw the front wheels of a vehicle climbing over the slope. She saw the hauler bouncing and skidding across the meadow, she saw a man pointing a gun at her, she saw Gard shuddering and falling into her legs, she saw the little dead-eyed boy coming toward her with the rod, she saw the man running with the gun, and that was the last thing she saw.

PART III

1

As soon as Annabelle stepped outside the air stung her face, and she realized that true fall had come. She should have worn a coat—but after packing Selva's bag, then the difficulty getting Pan off to school, she was already late. The walk to the hostel would have to warm her up. She set off in her black fitted jacket for the riverfront boulevard.

At her back the sun had cleared the park's tallest oaks, throwing a golden spill on the waterway. As she walked along the boulevard with her short, rapid stride, eyes moving around her field of vision for anything unexpected, she was aware of a multilayered unease. At the top was the problem of meals. She had fewer people to feed now, but her cupboards were almost empty, and the markets where she did her shopping were out of everything Pan liked—beef, rice, apples. A black market had emerged somewhere in the city—she'd heard about it from her neighbors and a woman in the Stranger self-org—but she didn't know how to find it, and the notion of getting fleeced by an illegal dealer in some backstreet made her anxious. Hugo would have gone, and probably enjoyed it. For the next day or two she would have to handle such things alone.

Pan had thrown a fit this morning when he couldn't have baked apple for breakfast. Annabelle guessed that the reason for this uncharacteristic tantrum was waking up to no father, sister, or dog in the house, but she was too tired from a bad night to soothe him. Raising her voice, she'd told him not to be a baby, and when he'd shoved his cup of milk aside, spilling it across the table, she'd grabbed his wrist too hard, and now she regretted it.

Regret was one of Annabelle's closest friends; it came around to look in on her almost every day. But the feeling that lay at the bottom of the others was too tangled for simple regret, though that was in the mix.

Last night, after Selva had left their room, Hugo pulled the covers to his chin and turned on his side. An hour earlier they had been sleeping limbs entwined for the first time in weeks, but the insouciance of his gesture enraged Annabelle. She jerked the blanket away and sat over him, saying, "How dare you keep a secret from me, then abandon me?" "I'm not abandon—" he began, but there was no stopping her. "You wanted nothing to do with Together—now you go off to save the world?" and "If something happens to her, am I supposed to just forgive you?" and even "Take her—you always wanted her for yourself." Saying things she could hardly believe in daylight as she passed the old stone footbridge where she used to stroll with Hugo arm in arm when they were courting.

In the morning there had been no time to make up. He went off with their daughter on an adventure that didn't include her, leaving her to Mr. Monge.

In the lilac garden outside the hostel, a circle of Stranger children sat in the sun on the yellowing grass. There were about two dozen boys and girls of all ages, from toddlers in the laps of older siblings to young teenagers, all still and silent, giving full attention to an older Burgher girl who sat at the head of the circle. She was from the self-org committee, homely, with fleshy cheeks that squeezed her eyes narrow. Annabelle couldn't remember the girl's name because she never said a word at meetings but stared without expression in a way Annabelle found unnerving.

But now the girl was speaking, with her head bent over a small chalkboard propped on her crossed legs.

"*No—one—is—a—Stran—ger*," she said—almost sang, in an unnaturally high voice that gave each syllable a different note, while a powdery index finger moved along the words written on the board. She looked up at the children. "Now your turn."

"*No—one—is—a—Stran—ger*," they sang in chorus, exactly mimicking her tone and rhythm.

The girl turned the board around and rubbed her fingers across it with a dry rasp. She picked up a piece of white chalk lying in the grass and wrote something, then revealed it to the Stranger children.

"*I—am—no—bet—ter.*" The girl tapped her chest, and the children echoed her, tapping their own. "*And—nei—ther—are—you.*" She waved her finger around the circle, and they echoed her again, pointing at one another, a few of the younger ones giggling.

"Are you better?" the girl asked, indicating an older boy with the tattooed lines and dots on his cheeks.

"No, I am no better," he said, in the same tune as before.

"Who is better?"

This was addressed to the whole group. The chorus answered: "No one is better."

"Is *she* better?"

"*She* is no better."

"Are *they* better?"

"*They* are no better."

"Very good!"

She led the children through the entire list of Together principles, skipping the one about no Burghers being Excess Burghers, which obviously would have been too complicated. When she came to the last principle and recited, "*You shall be as gods,*" a girl of twelve or thirteen gasped and clapped a hand over her mouth. At least one of the children had begun to learn the language.

Annabelle stood watching by the main doors under the bronze sign IMPERIAL WATER AUTHORITY. She hadn't been to the hostel since Hugo's visit, and whenever she missed a few days something inevitably went wrong: a new family failed to register and didn't receive their meal tickets, a child on the third floor broke a doorknob and no one fixed it. So it was gratifying to see this girl coming into her own—finding a way to combine language and moral instruction while making it fun for the children in the fresh air of an autumn morning. Wasn't this the whole point of self-organization?

Annabelle caught the girl's eye and smiled. In reply, the girl's smile died into blankness, and her eyes seemed to grow narrower. Her expression wasn't actively hostile, but all feeling had drained from her face, as if Annabelle's appearance had pulled a plug. The girl stared long enough for a few of the children to look at the woman standing thirty feet away, and she might have gone on staring if Annabelle hadn't abruptly turned and entered the building.

The hall was emptier than usual, the smell of newly arrived bodies was gone. The HELP tables were no longer set up in the middle of the floor but shoved against the high walls to make room for several dozen Strangers standing in two rows that faced away from the main doors. There were no children here, only adults of both sexes and all ages, including a stooped woman with a whitening braid down her back, all wearing loose, yellowish-gray tunics and drawstring pants—not their own clothes but the costumes Selva and her friends invented as Stranger tributes. Whose idea was that?

It was some kind of adult exercise class: step forward, step back, twist left, twist right, bend knees, arms raised, jump in place, and the echo of feet thundered from the stone floor up to the vaulted ceiling. They moved in precise unison, like a troupe of dance performers or a military squad, as if they'd been training for weeks—except for a small, lean man at the far end of the second line, who was having trouble executing the moves and kept falling out of time. Even without seeing his face Annabelle knew he was Mr. Monge.

They were following the lead of a Burgher girl who stood facing them with her legs apart, hands on hips. She wasn't dressed like the Strangers but in olive-green, close-cut pants and jacket, and a slender cap like the kind imperial mail carriers used to wear. She was unusually tall, and her hair was cropped short like a boy's, a style associated with Excess Burgher girls. Annabelle had never seen her at the hostel or any self-org meeting, and it took her a moment to recognize the girl. Her name was Lynx. Annabelle knew her from before the Emergency.

Under the empire no concept of volunteering had existed. There had been civic offices, guilds, and families, but no middle zone where Burghers acted to benefit neither empire, loved ones, nor themselves, but simply to help people they didn't know. So when a woman in Annabelle's reading circle mentioned a classmate of her daughter who had done poorly on her comprehensive exams (the neighbor didn't say "Excess Burgher" but it was understood), and who seemed to be drifting into the city's underworld of opium smokers and prostitutes, and Annabelle had the bright idea of inviting the wayward girl over for a cooking lesson, she didn't think of herself as a volunteer. She wasn't even sure what purpose it would serve. She just wanted to give the girl something constructive to do.

One bright, cold afternoon a teenager of about sixteen appeared at the Rustins' front door, gangly and fidgety, with bowl-cut hair and eyes that avoided contact. She'd brought a friend, a girl with a prematurely aging face who was so stunted that Annabelle wondered if she might be a dwarf. The first girl was Lynx, and from the way she spoke it was clear that she came from a good family, which made her fate seem all the more poignant. Annabelle was thankful for the uninvited friend, because the baking lesson in her kitchen was so awkward that only the girls' whispered talk and giggles broke whole minutes of silence. But they paid attention, followed instructions, and expressed a kind of self-mocking pride when the result came out recognizably cake-like.

Annabelle had imagined just one meeting, but she found that she liked teaching them and was good at it. On impulse she asked if they wanted to return for a session on meat preparation. The girls looked at each other, shrugged, and agreed.

The lessons continued every Tuesday afternoon, and while the girls were in the Rustin kitchen Annabelle learned something profound about the world they inhabited—something that her own children were too young, and too closely shaped by their parents, to teach her. Their bursts of unfamiliar slang, their jags of feeling and attitude, what they knew and didn't know, revealed that they lived in an entirely different place and time from Annabelle. For example, she once heard Lynx's friend refer to the ceremonial announcement of exam results, which Burghers throughout the empire called the "Day of Joy and Sorrow," as the "Day of Jizz and Barf"—at which Lynx made a face of mock disapproval, causing them both to crack up. *We don't know them*, Annabelle thought, *or care.*

The city where she'd lived all her life—governed by rules that everyone accepted, making slow but inevitable progress, stretching behind and ahead of her to the limits of vision—these two girls experienced as a suffocating place where you had to make your own way by cutting corners and lying, while dreaming of breaking free or fashioning some implausible transformation. None of this was expressed as a coherent thought, let alone a critical idea, but the girls' every knowing look or cynical joke gave Annabelle the feeling that her benign and permanent world might be oppressive and perishable.

Once, she happened to mention the earthquake that had destroyed some of the most important imperial buildings and countless homes in the capital region. This event of seventy years ago, which had seen immense suffering and heroism, came up throughout Annabelle's childhood, and even at dinner with Selva and Pan. It was one of those historical landmarks that continue to shape two or three generations even if they didn't personally experience it. So Annabelle was stunned that the girls had never heard of the Great Quake, nor could they have cared less. It might as well have happened five centuries ago on the other side of the world. Telling the story to Hugo that night, she tried to convey her own disorientation at the chasm that had yawned open, how the city's streets must look entirely different to these girls—the strange mix of alienation and curiosity and sympathy she felt. Hugo commented on the woeful state of history instruction in schools and changed the subject. But that wasn't her point at all.

Annabelle thought the girls might find work as cooks in a boardinghouse or an old people's home—but after two months they stopped showing up. She assumed they'd been claimed by their other life. The cooking lessons had taken place the winter before the Emergency. When it came, her hours with the girls had somehow prepared her for it. Whatever became of those two outcasts, she believed that the change in their world would be better for them, and for her.

2

"Hands together, hands out!"

Lynx pressed her fists into her ribs, then punched straight-armed and hard from her body, and the two rows of Strangers did the same.

"We are Together!"

The Strangers, in heavier accents than the children's, cried: "We are Together!"

"We will defend Together!"

"We will defend Together!"

"From?"

A few Strangers repeated "From?" but others brought the group around to the right answer: "Enemies of Together!"

"Friends!" Lynx exhorted. "Face and fight!"

The Strangers in the front line spun around so that the two rows were squared off, five feet apart. Tentatively at first, then all at once, the Strangers closed in a chorus of incomprehensible yells. A man stumbled and went down, and another leapt on his back. The woman with the gray braid and another woman, no younger than Annabelle and stout from motherhood, grappled and clawed at each other's arms and faces. The combat was furious and yet somehow meticulous, almost balletic, as if they had performed this ritual of violence all their lives. No one seemed to get hurt, though Annabelle noticed Mr. Monge extricating himself from his partner's grip and limping off to the side.

"Lynx!" Annabelle called from the doorway.

Lynx didn't hear. "Friends, separate!" The yells died, the fighting stopped, and the Strangers reassembled. Lynx picked up a metal pail by the handle—Annabelle hadn't noticed it at her side—and, moving along the rows, distributed thin sticks, each about three feet long with something metallic and sharp attached to one end. Then Lynx walked over to a HELP table, picked up an easel that had been lying flat, and carried it to the middle of the hall, where she propped it up on the floor. The easel held a bull's-eye that might have been a dartboard from a city tavern.

Lynx counted off twenty paces. "Okay, listen up! Form a line here where I am! Understand?" It was clear that she had no experience speaking to Strangers. "Line up right here. Try to hit the target." She pointed at the bull's-eye and mimed throwing something hard and fast from behind her ear, which elicited from the Strangers a low hum of understanding and anticipation. "Try your best. This is important. Pretend it's a Yeoman trying to get in here."

Lynx turned to indicate the main doors and stopped mid-gesture as recognition came over her face.

"Line up here. Take turns. I'll be back." The sight of her cooking instructor seemed to have rattled Lynx, and she crossed the hall with a rictus smile. "Mrs. Rustin! What are you doing here?"

"I was just going to ask you."

An ornament was sewn on either side of the crease in Lynx's cap: eyes, a second pair, open wide and watching.

"They told some of us in the Safety Committee to do a training. They want Friends to be ready to help if something happens."

"Who told you?"

"The Wide Awakes," Lynx said in surprise.

Annabelle knew of no Wide Awakes in the Stranger self-org. She didn't really know what Wide Awakes were, other than that Selva had mentioned them approvingly. Annabelle was appalled by the idea of training Strangers who had just arrived here with nothing but small bundles, who didn't know the city or the empire, who had just begun to learn the language in which they were now being given orders. She disliked the drills, too. What made Together lovely was the connections that formed between people. For her it had never been a list of principles, but more like a window thrown open in a stuffy room, a new mood that unlocked minds and hearts and made it possible to listen, empathize, imagine. Together was the opposite of drills and commands and target practice. It was a fragile thing that careless people risked breaking—first Hugo, now these Wide Awakes. They should have at least checked with her before turning her hostel into a military base.

"Why didn't anyone—"

"I didn't know you worked here, Mrs. Rustin. Your name wasn't on the list they gave us."

"What list?"

"Of the Wide Awakes who run the hostel."

None of it made any sense. No one "ran" the hostel, and when she asked for names, the ones Lynx gave were unfamiliar. They stood facing each other in silence, Annabelle confused and irritated, Lynx avoiding her eyes.

"I'm sorry we sort of stopped coming to your house," the girl said. "I wouldn't be where I am today if not for you."

"Where are you today?"

Lynx held out her arms in their olive-green sleeves, then pointed to the eyes on the front of her cap. "I'm a Wide Awake. You taught me to believe in myself."

She was clearly the same girl who giggled to cover her embarrassment when she cracked egg white on the kitchen counter and slapped her friend's hand when she pretended to perform oral sex on a banana. And yet this Lynx was different—no longer slouched in defiance and shame, more grown-up than seemed possible in less than a year, with her uniform, her straight bearing, and her crisp movements. Even the structure of her face looked different. It had lost its hangdog twitchiness; the lineaments were more tight and square. Annabelle thought of Selva on the sofa in the front room, intent on her schoolwork beside a steaming mug of tea, and felt a sudden ache.

From across the hall came muted shouts of *"Yaya! Yaya!"* The bull's-eye was filling up with arrows.

"They're learning civil defense," Lynx said, following Annabelle's gaze. "They want to be with us if the war comes."

Something about these memorized words annoyed Annabelle. "Are you certain you know what they want?"

Lynx cracked her knuckles as she used to when a recipe wasn't going well. "You think they want to be with the Yoemen?"

At the front of the line Mr. Monge was about to take his turn. "I think they might want to be left alone. They just got here." Halfway to the target, Mr. Monge's arrow fell to the floor.

"No one gets to be alone when our city's attacked."

"I keep hearing about this war. Be careful what you wish for."

Lynx straightened her shoulders and adjusted her cap. "Excuse me, I have work to do."

Hugo's voice—critical, undermining—had found its way into Annabelle's head, and she didn't want him there. The hostel didn't belong to her, and neither did Together. All the energy, the relentless forward pressure of life, was with this girl who had come to her house for cooking lessons.

"You're right," Annabelle said quickly. "I'm a bit sheltered, I don't know the dangers. What you're building is precious. It has to be defended."

"That's okay, Mrs. Rustin. Together belongs to all of us. We all have to defend it."

Annabelle didn't want Lynx to go. "How is your friend, the one who came with you to the house? I don't remember her name. Is she a Wide Awake, too?"

"Nati? She's okay." Lynx glanced down at the floor. When she looked up again her face was that of the lost girl at Annabelle's door. "Actually, she's not okay. She died."

"Oh, no! How?"

"You know about the Suicide Spot?" Annabelle's chest went cold. "They're supposed to watch it day and night, but no one was there when Nati went. Maybe a We Are One was happening. Anyway, they found her there. I don't know how she reached the noose!" The girl's gasping laugh moistened into a sob.

"Did you know she was unhappy?"

"I was really busy with the Safety Committee," Lynx choked. "A week before she did it, I saw her at a tavern. I asked if she'd joined a self-org. She said, 'Together's just more jizz and barf.'"

Annabelle fell silent. She was picturing Nati swinging high above the platform, her old woman's face brick red, her eyes open and mocking, her tongue sticking out.

"I'm surprised I never heard about it."

"They covered it up."

Before Annabelle could ask more, the girl turned away. "Friends! Arrows down! Form two rows for firearm safety!"

3

"Mrs. Annabelle! Mrs. Annabelle!"

She was leaving by the garden path, trying to avoid the girl and her circle of children, when Mr. Monge came limping up behind her.

"How are you, Mr. Monge?"

"I am very terrible."

"What's wrong?"

"Too many things!" Out of breath, he pointed at the brick façade of the Imperial Water Authority and fixed Annabelle with bright eyes whose distress alarmed her. "Everything changed when you were not here. New Burghers in green clothes came to us. We do not know them!"

"They're with the Safety Committee," Annabelle said. "That's another part of self-org. It's just training—like sports."

"It is too difficult for me."

"Are your knees hurting?"

"The pain is not in my knees."

Annabelle knew without looking that the girl with narrow eyes was watching them. She led Mr. Monge away from the path to the privacy of a lilac tree.

"The new Burghers are not like Mrs. Annabelle," Mr. Monge went on. "They do not talk to us like you. They are the excess people." He pointed to his scalp. "Their eyes are dangerous for us."

"Wide Awake caps?"

With a short intake of breath Mr. Monge confirmed it. "I do not know their name. But the new Burghers—please excuse me, Mrs. Annabelle—Mr. Camba heard a whisper—they do not want you to come again."

Annabelle had somehow known she would hear this, known it from the moment the girl in the circle answered her smile with a look of blank hostility. "Did they say why?"

Mr. Monge glanced over his shoulder and leaned toward her with the reluctant air of a man about to pass on some painful but urgent news. He had never come this close to her face, and she noticed, along with the tobacco on his breath, a tiny flaw in the iris of his right eye, a stripe of yellow across dark brown. The children in the circle were singing. Annabelle made out the words of "Brave Bella."

"It is the doctor. Your husband."

"My husband? What about him?"

"I do not know. But it is not true! I am telling this to everyone. Even the ones with eyes."

"What did they say about Hugo?"

"I am telling them the doctor is a good man. That it is my fault!" Mr. Monge raised a hand to his forehead and squeezed his eyes shut as if a violent headache had set in.

"What do you mean, your fault?"

"Where he went, they are dangerous pig people. They shoot guns and put traps. The foot of my son was trapped. Why did I leave him? Why did I send your husband? Why?"

Mr. Monge cried out a single word in his own language that made the children in the circle stop singing mid-verse, turn to stare at him, and burst out laughing.

Annabelle walked homeward along the riverfront boulevard with a crowd of thoughts clamoring for her attention. The only one that brought a measure of calm, that gave her some relief from Hugo and Selva and the hostel and anger and fear, was the problem of how to judge the threat of the dangerous pig people. When she was around certain self-org colleagues, especially younger ones, like this girl Lynx, or—she had to admit it—her own daughter, she felt an impulse to scoff. They almost seemed to be ginning something up, to *want* a final showdown with Yeomen, as if the dark scenarios gave their lives a higher meaning. As if Together wasn't enough and they craved more excitement, greater clarity, which only an enemy that wanted to destroy them could provide. If a conflict ever came—the preposterous and fateful word for it was "war"—then they could stop thinking altogether.

Even less did she want to be the type of stolid Burgher—her father was one, and so, in a way, was her husband—who believed that the empire was the best possible world and would go on forever, peaceful, prosperous, united, and that what had never happened would never happen *because* it had never happened. Why wasn't it possible—even likely—for the empire to be torn apart in the kind of conflict that destroyed more famous and powerful empires in other times and places? Hadn't the Emergency itself seemed to most Burghers to come from nowhere? Perhaps an inability to imagine the end made the end more likely.

So she tried to imagine it. A raiding party of Yeomen breaching the city gates with hunting rifles and machetes. A street battle in the Market District, bloodstained cobblestones. A Yeoman leader—overdeveloped biceps and a beard to his waist—standing atop the pedestal in the main square with an armed guard of farmers, facing an assembly of hog-tied Burghers and Strangers, shouting: "Enemies within and enemies without! You are defeated!" A line of people—members of her self-org, the hospital director, Suzana, Lynx, Hugo, finally herself—waiting their turn to climb the gallows. But for some reason these images made her want to laugh. None of it was real.

Instead, an actual memory kept intruding. The incident had happened a year ago—the last summer of the empire. They were on a camping trip to the Place and paying one of their regular visits to the Cronk farm that Hugo insisted on and she tolerated. Poor Selva was, as usual, helping the Cronk boy with some farm chore. Annabelle was stuck in the kitchen with Mrs. Cronk, who was preparing crusts for the yam pies that she would sell at the district fair. She was chatting away about something Annabelle could no longer remember—maybe the unlucky weather that had ruined the previous year's fair. All Annabelle could think about in the farmhouse kitchen, and what she remembered now walking home under the plane trees along the river, was the way Mrs. Cronk's apron cinched the immense girth of her body like butcher paper tied with string around a pork loin. The apron, powdered in flour, was designed with a pattern of pink roses that had been popular when Annabelle was a new mother. In fact, Annabelle owned the very same apron, and this thought gnawed at her, reminding her that, body size and social position apart, she shared a common fate with this pleasant, garrulous, uninteresting woman.

It was in this irritable mood that she became aware of a story Mrs. Cronk had begun to tell—something about bird droppings that had left seeds around the farm, and strangling vines that had grown from the seeds up the sides of their barns and the trunks of their trees, and how much work Big Cronk and Little Cronk had to cut the vines down. Mrs. Cronk insisted that the birds were "working" for some group of people somewhere in the empire who wanted to make life difficult for the Cronks. She didn't say who they were or where, but as she told the story her eyes shifted and her voice fell in a way that suggested she was talking about people in the city by the river.

"That's ridiculous!" Annabelle's face went hot with contempt for the woman's foolish certainty. "Who would believe such a story?"

Mrs. Cronk's fleshy features stiffened, and she returned to kneading pastry dough. "I don't really know, but it could be true."

"Birds trained by Burghers to eat seeds and drop them over your farm?"

"I didn't say Burghers." Mrs. Cronk raised her chin to restore her wounded pride. "We see things that you city people don't, Mrs. Rustin. You think they're fairy tales, but we know the truth."

Annabelle realized that arguing was pointless. She and Mrs. Cronk would never move past this moment, however many more visits the families shared. They nearly hated each other. Neither spoke for a full two minutes, until Little Cronk appeared at the kitchen door with a sack of yams slung over his shoulder. Selva was standing behind him, looking as if she, too, had just had a bad conversation—as if the Rustins had stumbled into a pit that had been hidden on the farm the whole time.

Annabelle never told her family about the incident. She was embarrassed to have lost her self-restraint and offended the woman; later on, the distractions of the Emergency made her forget all about it. But now, as she turned into the street where the Rustin rowhouse stood behind its wooden fence, the memory of her unfortunate exchange in Mrs. Cronk's kitchen disturbed her as her war fantasies did not, and she was filled with dread for her husband and daughter, out there among dangerous pig people.

4

She found Pan at home with the school day only half over and the front room in a state of chaos, games scattered across the floor, a tent of bedsheets strung between the doors. "Do you think you can do this because your father is away?" Annabelle yelled. Her son burst into tears, and she wrapped him in her arms and asked forgiveness.

At dinner, Pan pushed his food around uneaten, then set down his fork. "Why couldn't they leave Zeus with us? They're never coming back."

"Just wait, they'll be back tomorrow," she told him, but a grief beyond her reach was afflicting him as if he'd begun to see a depth beneath the world's bright surfaces, making him seem much older than the boy for whom every new day was a thrilling adventure, and at the same time like her little Pan-Pan again. For the first time in years he asked to sleep in his parents' bed, and she let him, though Hugo would have disapproved.

In the morning Pan complained that he didn't feel well enough to go to school. When she asked what was wrong, he said that his stomach hurt, but at the slightest upset he kept bursting into tears that expanded into uncontrollable sobs. For the next two days Annabelle didn't leave the house, except once to shop at a market in the Warehouse District that was still selling chicken parts and weary-looking vegetables. Her son's mood infected hers, or activated a latent anguish of her own, and during the long days and evenings of card games and reading aloud her stomach kept knotting tighter. Pan slept curled against her, breathing softly while she lay on her back with her eyes open and listened to the tolling of bells, unable to stop her thoughts: *You found a way to take this one thing I have. It's gone and so are you. Why? What's happening?*

By the third morning Annabelle could no longer bear to listen for the sound of her husband and daughter coming in the door. "Let's go see Grandpa."

It was a gray, cold Sunday, and she dug coats out of the closet for them both. This moment in the Earth's journey, when the air sharpened and the sidewalk smelled of crinkled leaves, always reminded her of the final change—the one that waited for her father as he lay sleeping in the old people's home, that would someday find her and the three people she cared for most. Pan clutched a bouquet of flowers while his other hand reached for his mother's and held it tight, just as he used to every morning on the way to nursery school. The touch of his palm, larger now and less soft, awoke an impulse so old that she couldn't recognize herself without it: to hide away so that all the changes that would eventually rob her of everything couldn't find her.

Marriage and children had long ago taught her to embrace the early sunset, for the transformation it promised also brought love. She couldn't flee one without losing the other. And when change had suddenly come to the city, her acquaintance with the urge to hide helped her understand what her husband, who regularly encountered death at work but almost never gave it a thought, who was so much better suited to this life, couldn't understand—that the Emergency was a thing to welcome. It meant their world was still alive, and so was she.

At the corner, two teenagers, a girl and a boy, were leaning against a lamppost, smoking and chatting. They wore the same matching green jackets and trousers as Lynx, and the same peaked caps with eyes sewn on, like mailmen, or soldiers. The girl, her hair pulled back tight over her scalp, was doing the talking, while the boy, shorter and younger, kept glancing around uneasily. As Annabelle and Pan approached on the sidewalk, the girl hit the boy's shoulder. Startled, he stood up straight and glanced in their direction.

Annabelle felt their eyes between her shoulder blades all the way to the tram stop.

Otherwise, the streets were emptier than they'd been since the first days of the Emergency. Had they declared a new holiday while she was indoors with Pan? The distinction between workdays and weekends had disappeared—self-org committees never stopped, because the need for them was endless. But this morning felt like a Sunday of old, when homebound Burghers sat over their paper and coffee for hours with nothing urgent to do. Except this quiet wasn't somnolent like then, but more like a pause that anticipated a very loud noise.

The only other person on the tram was a woman seated at the far end. She looked a few years older than Annabelle, in an out-of-date dress with big shoulders and a lace neckline. Under a hat decorated with artificial roses her face was pinched and unfriendly. She kept glancing out the rear window, then across the car at Annabelle without smiling. Some matriarch with a husband in a high-status guild like banking. You still saw a few women like her in the better neighborhoods—dressed for their ladies' brunch, untouched by the Emergency, making obsolete judgments about everyone else, filling Annabelle with defensive scorn and an infusion of sadness: all life's meaning coming down to the silver serving platter they still brought out on Sunday evenings.

"Heights!" the driver called as the tram came to a stop. When Annabelle and Pan moved to the doors, the woman stood and joined them. Out on the curb she raised her chin and, from under the brim of her hat, gave Annabelle a significant look. Her wide, searching eyes were kinder than those of the arch Burgher wife Annabelle had imagined on the tram.

"You know they said for nonessentials to stay inside this weekend."

Annabelle was startled. She'd never even heard the term. "Who said?"

"The Wide Awakes," the woman replied, just the way Lynx had—as if the source was obvious and the order normal. "I certainly don't consider myself essential," she went on. "I'd be home if not for my aunt's funeral."

"But why are we supposed to stay inside?"

The woman smiled. "Oh, I'm sure there's a good reason. They know more than we do. Something must have started out there."

"What started? Out where?"

The woman waved her gloved hand in the direction of the North Gate. "You know," she whispered confidentially. "*Them.*" She lowered her gaze to Pan. "Are you going to a funeral as well?"

"We're going to visit Grandpa," Pan said. "He's still alive."

The woman found this answer delightful. "Beautiful boy! Beautiful flowers!" She ran a furry finger along Pan's smooth cheek. "Have a safe day."

Annabelle watched her walk away with the brisk step, hips twitching side to side, but not immodestly, of a Burgher woman who was still sure of her place in the world—even a world in which something must have started.

"Who's *them*?" Pan asked.

"The trolls!" his mother said with an effort at silliness. She sang a line from "Brave Bella," and Pan joined her in the rest of the verse, and they would have gone through the entire song if they hadn't reached their destination first.

5

The old people's home was a two-story brick building on a quiet street within sight of the hospital. After her mother's death almost two years ago, Annabelle had secured a room and put her father in it, expecting him to die soon. But his body insisted on continuing to live (as Pan had told the woman from the tram) even while he consumed nothing but salted crackers and red wine and lost the ability to hold any memory less than half a century old. His mind kept dimming like the sky at twilight without ever going dark. She had no idea what he did from day to day, and neither did he. In all the minor ways she was a dutiful daughter, and once a week she forced herself to face his spectral life.

Her husband—who had always gotten along with her father better than she had—once suggested that they bring him to live in their rowhouse. Annabelle had rejected this idea as decisively as Hugo vetoed the Stranger family. She wasn't prepared to take on the care of a fourth person—not one who, even in his diminished state, had a unique power to make her suffer with a single, well-aimed word.

As long as Annabelle could remember, she had been at war with herself. This struggle played out in her head between a voice that sounded like her own and another voice that sounded like her father's, though by now it, too, belonged undeniably to her—a dry voice, not harsh or brutal, at times almost encouraging but in the same instant critical, even mocking, telling her: "You could have done it. Why didn't you?" The nature of *it* changed over the years, but the meaning remained the same: the gifts he'd given her—intelligence, diligence, a place in the empire—were undermined by a fatal tendency to doubt herself, hesitate before the chance, then blame the world for her own failure to follow through.

The crucial instance of *it* occurred when she (always an excellent student) had finished her degree and was about to follow her father into the administration guild. He occupied an important position in the regional department that supervised the collection of land taxes. Under the empire it wasn't just normal but necessary for Burghers to maneuver their children into the family guild. The competition for high-status jobs was so intense that a solid record alone seldom got a young person through the door—an extra push was needed from an established guild member. This nepotism was officially deplored and universally accepted.

Annabelle's father had already laid the groundwork for her to start working as head of an auditing unit, with the promise of swift ascent, when she took her competency boards. Unlike the comprehensive exams she'd sat for at fourteen, this was something of a formality—her position was practically secure. But as she sat in a stuffy room full of aspiring bureaucrats on the grounds of Imperial College, the first question literally made no sense to her. She moved on to the second: same result. She quickly realized that the problem was with her, something had seized up in her brain, neural connections were coming undone, and her father's voice began an ironic commentary on the spectacle of his daughter defeated by a routine exam that held the key to her future. When the proctor called time, she was barely halfway done.

Her father was mortified by her failure—but also, she

sensed, satisfied. He pulled a string to allow her a makeup because of ill-health. Annabelle refused, saying that she would have to face the consequences. He assumed this meant accepting a job as a lowly file clerk in his department. In fact, she had decided to leave the guild path altogether. The reason was a medical student at the Imperial College Hospital with an earnest air and an easy smile. She'd met him through her older brother (who fulfilled their father's every wish but would leave the care of his last years to Annabelle) and found that the war with herself lost some of its intensity when she was with him. He made her feel that the minor-key notes in her character were lovable—that he loved her for them—that they signified a depth of emotion he lacked.

Suddenly the prospect of following her father into the regional department of land-tax collection was less appealing than the adventure of a life with this idealistic young doctor whose guild was a moral calling, not a ladder to status. For once, she grabbed her chance at happiness. Anyway, she told herself, the family guild system was weakening, would soon be outmoded, and then she would be free to join one for which she was better suited, such as education.

So instead of going to work under her father, she married Hugo Rustin.

"You could have done both," her father told her after the wedding. "Why didn't you?"

The guild system was not about to give way. It only grew more calcified as it aged, and no other guilds opened their doors to her. She became a mother, and motherhood turned out to be more interesting than anything she'd ever done. Hugo was content for her to anchor their domestic life while he steadily rose to chief surgeon at the hospital. "Humanist" continued to be a favorite word of his (though she doubted he could define it if she pressed, so she didn't), but over time he seemed to lose interest in his patients and no longer brought home their stories. Instead he became absorbed in the professional side of medicine, especially when his name was mentioned as the hospital's likely next director. He also began to take an intense interest in the education of their daughter. Selva became his project.

The city where Annabelle had no place because she had forfeited it was the ideal setting for her husband's conscience and his ambition. To his mind these were as free of conflict as their marriage, which was smoother than that of anyone she knew. They let earlier friendships wither, and avoided bumping against each other's secret wounds and shaky certainties. Hugo hardly ever said a critical word to Annabelle, and the lack of pressure made it easy to slip into a role that seemed to be laid out for her like a featherbed. She could hardly blame him when the war with herself resumed, but she could always blame herself, and did. She also blamed the empire.

One night, she attended her father's retirement ceremony at the Administrators Social Club, in a historic stone building between the clock tower and the courthouse. His colleagues—mostly old men, a few women closer to her age—drank and chatted and made speeches about his career while Annabelle nervously downed two glasses of wine. When it was her turn to get up and say something as the daughter of the celebrated bureaucrat, a moment she'd been dreading for days, the candlelit room began to swim, the walls hung with portraits of the city's great administrators billowed toward her, and the expectant faces of the guests suddenly appeared to be skulls set on top of elegantly tailored suits and evening dresses, grinning skulls decorated with wigs and eyeglasses and sparkling jewelry. This vision so disturbed her that she forgot all about the piece of paper on which she'd written down some loving remarks, and instead began to improvise at high speed.

"Bravo, Papa! What a career you've had! I'm very proud of you. How many of us can say we devoted our whole life to collecting taxes for the empire? You should all try to imagine what it was like being a little girl with Papa's example right there in front of me like a clock that never stops, every day he went on working, *tick tick tick tick*. I can only say I'm sorry I didn't live up to him. I'm sure you all know I failed his legacy. I just couldn't have done what you did, Papa, keeping your hand on the crank and the gears turning, at some point my arm would have stopped moving like a broken axle and I would have said, 'What's it all for? What if this crank is grinding me to fine powder?'"

Amid uneasy laughter, the eye sockets beneath her father's hairpiece stared at her without expression. Afterward he didn't speak to her for two months, until he finally accepted a written apology and they resumed their relationship on even more fraught terms. Thankfully, Hugo had been home with the children the night of the ceremony—but later on Annabelle wished he'd been there to hear her rave. It might have helped him understand what was coming. The Emergency wouldn't end the war with herself—probably that would never end—but he might have taken more care not to desert her when it came. By then she'd installed her father in the old people's home, where he would finish his days as her last connection to the late empire.

6

In the front parlor an old man in suspenders studied his cards with a puzzled frown, while across the table his opponent dozed, chin buried in his mountainous torso. A tiny white-haired woman in an armchair was gazing into space. When Annabelle and Pan came through the door, she jumped to her feet with surprising agility. "No! No! Get out!" she shouted, waving her arms as if two demons she recognized from an earlier intrusion had come back to do more harm, though Annabelle had never laid eyes on her.

A male attendant in a white apron rushed in from the hall and seized the woman by her upper arms. "Sit down, Minna, we talked about this, you know you're not allowed."

Minna let herself be guided back into her chair while she stared at the newcomers with utter horror.

The attendant apologized to Annabelle. "Go on up. He's sleeping."

She always found her father sleeping. Perhaps, like Zeus, he did nothing else all day until someone offered an alternative. As she led Pan through the dimly lit parlor to a narrow stairway, the smell of the place enveloped her: a mix of dusty carpeting, boiled vegetables, and the sweet and sour odor of old people. It smelled of neglect—not just physical decay but mental abandonment, the airlessness of a home that no one ever thought about. Whenever Annabelle came by for a visit after a frantically busy day at the hostel or in a citywide self-org meeting, she was struck by a feeling of stopped time. The fusty floor lamp beside the card table and the tattered burgundy fabric of the demented woman's armchair returned her to the world before the Emergency. Nothing that had happened since ever penetrated the old people's home. They were given no role in Together; for some reason there wasn't even an Elderly self-org (though a subcommittee of Parks took care of the municipal cemetery). She had immured her father in a museum where a visitor could spend an hour among living figures from the past.

He was at the end of the second-floor hallway. When Annabelle's gentle knock got no answer, she eased the door open. Somewhere in the gloomy half-light a clock was ticking. The room was so small that two steps brought her to the bed. She switched on the bedside lamp. The body of her father lay motionless under a blanket, head tipped back, cheeks sunken, eyes shut, mouth open. His yellowed teeth were broken, and a thin tuft of white hair was plastered against his scalp. This was how she always found him—momentarily dead. She felt a quiver of tenderness.

At her side Pan recoiled. His last visit had been several months ago, and the deterioration was shocking.

"Is he—"

"No, Pan-Pan, he's sleeping."

Her father's chest suddenly rose, and his mouth gaped wider with a long, stuttering breath. Somewhere inside this shrunken form his vital core still throbbed. Annabelle sat on the edge of the bed and laid her hand on the cotton nightshirt that covered his knobby shoulder.

"Papa? Wake up. It's me, Papa."

His lids parted and his eyes, aglow and immense in the

hollow face, met hers. For half a minute she watched as he tried to make sense of this person, mouth noiselessly opening and closing fishlike. Then his smile made her fight down a sob.

"You."

"Yes, me. Your daughter, Annabelle. And I brought Pan."

She nudged Pan forward. He thrust out the bouquet for his grandfather to take, but the old man looked at it without comprehending. Pan laid the flowers on his blanket.

"Who is he?"

"This is Pan," Annabelle said, raising her voice. "Your grandson—my second child. Remember?"

The pale lips formed Pan's name, the balding eyebrows furrowed, the head moved back and forth, *no*, but at the same time a hand emerged from under the blanket—a film of spotted, nearly translucent skin stretched tight over the ray of bones—and grabbed the boy's wrist.

"It's good to see you, Grandpa," Pan said bravely. "How are you feeling?"

"I've been younger."

She saw that her father was already coming back into the world, though exactly what world still wasn't clear.

"Annabelle," he said, looking her over as if recognizing her for the first time, "you've put on weight." And in an instant this ghost had his old power over her.

"No. Same as always."

"You didn't have that belly."

"Papa, I haven't—" She stopped herself. The impulse to take offense was pointless. He saw her as a series of shifting pictures from different phases of her life against the fixed background of the present, and right now she was probably twenty, unmarried, unmarred by childbearing—preparing for the guild boards. And he still knew how to hurt her. "What about you? Are you eating enough?"

He dismissed her concern with an irritable backhand wave. "Did the boy see the thing on the wall?"

"No, Papa, he didn't."

"Show him that paper on the wall."

He meant the Imperial Certificate of Extraordinary Merit that the guild had given him at his retirement ceremony. Annabelle was required to point out the framed document every time she brought Pan, who always nodded appreciatively. It hung next to a picture of Annabelle's mother—an unsmiling woman in a high-necked dress, about the age Annabelle was now—which never seemed to deserve their attention.

"I served the empire for . . ." Groaning, her father struggled to sit up against his pillow and made it about halfway. ". . . forty-seven years. No—fifty-five years." He was addressing Pan, whose identity still wasn't clear to him. "Ask me a question."

"Was the empire good?"

Her father's thin, bloodless lips worked silently to form an answer.

"Ask another."

"But you didn't answer my first one."

"What was your first one?"

"Was the empire good?" Pan said. "Because we don't think so."

"You don't think so?" The old man emitted a short, tart gasp—a weakened version of the sarcastic laugh that Annabelle had known all her life, as if his young questioner had said something so foolish that it revealed an important character flaw. "Who are you not to think so?" His webby eyes shifted to Annabelle's, enlisting her in his derision. "Who the hell is he?"

"I told you. He's your grandson, Pan."

"My grandson . . . Did you get married?"

"Yes, Papa. To Hugo. The doctor."

Overcome with confusion, her father closed his eyes and lay breathing for a time with his mouth ajar. When his eyes reopened there was new clarity in them. "Are you happy?"

"Extremely happy," she replied. Anything short of the superlative would invite him to probe for a weakness in her less-than-complete happiness and gain the upper hand over her.

"Why did you quit the guild?"

"I was never in the guild, Papa."

"What are you doing with your life?"

In an even tone, not pausing to be sure he was able to follow, she ran through the self-org committee and her work at the hostel, then added Selva's triumph on her comprehensive exams, a prize Pan had won at school last year for a model riverboat he'd built, and the hospital directorship that would soon be Hugo's. She knew that her father wouldn't register the overlapping time periods, the contradictions between before and after that she elided. She had once tried to explain the Emergency in its early weeks and left him utterly bewildered—he seemed to think that a foreign army had invaded the city, taken charge of its institutions, and begun executing local notables. "For God's sake," he cried, "why don't we stop them?" Then the whole thing slipped from his mind, and she never mentioned it again.

"Why didn't you bring the doctor?" her father asked.

Pan moved closer to the bed and said, "Papa and Selva

went where the Yeomen live. They're saving a Stranger boy. They'll be home today or tomorrow."

The old man stared at his grandson and tried to make sense of this news, stroking the white stubble on his cheek with crooked fingers whose knuckles were swollen knobs. "Yeomen," he said vaguely. "When I was a boy we had a few in my school. We had boxing matches, Yeoman against Burgher. One of them broke my nose—quick little bastard. Then we all shook hands as sons of the empire. Do you—what's your name? Do you boys still box Yeoman boys?"

"Pan." He shook his head and glanced up at his mother for help.

"Solid people," the old man went on. "Patriotic. Some of them work for me. They collect taxes in farm villages."

"You mean they *worked* for you," Pan said, grinning slyly.

"I most certainly do not mean that. They *work* for me."

"But Grandpa, you're here. That's your retirement certificate up there."

"What do you know about it? Little imp." The old man extended a shaky index finger and poked the tip of Pan's nose. Pan giggled. Annabelle was always careful to avoid provoking her father into inflicting a bruise, but her son was safe, impervious.

"Papa," she said, "you didn't answer his question. Pan would like to hear your opinion about—"

"Of course it's good!" She had assumed Pan's question was long buried beneath ancient memories of boxing boys and Yeoman employees—but nothing cleared the ruins of her father's mind faster than irritation. With a hoarse grunt he leveraged himself up on his elbows. "There's no empire like it. We rebuilt after the Great Quake—my God, the effort! Never lost a war. Venus cheese on every table. Burghers and Yeomen break bread together. Good Development and all that. What's wrong with it?" he demanded, mock-indignant.

Pan fought down another giggle. "But it's gone."

"Where did it go?" The old man held out his arms and turned them over and back, as if the skeletal wrists exposed by the sleeves of his nightshirt proved the empire's permanence. "Under the bed?"

"Papa, things are a little different for Pan's generation and Selva's," Annabelle said. "When you were young, the factions weren't fighting all the time. The empire built roads and bridges. The guilds had plenty of jobs—there were no Excess Burghers. Everything worked the way it was supposed to."

"What's so different now?"

Annabelle remembered an incident that had happened when she was very little. Down the street from her father's office in the Civic District, the clock tower's timepiece had unaccountably stopped with the hands at 3:48. For a week, while a repair crew worked inside the tower, the city by the river was deprived of the hourly chimes that composed its background music. Their silence upset her father a great deal, as if the tolling had always reassured him of his life's reliable purpose. Each night he'd come home from work looking more tired than the night before, complaining more bitterly about some idiot in the department, and then, in the middle of a sentence, he would look up and say: "What time is it? What the hell is wrong?" Throughout the week tension gathered in the house like humidity before a storm, until one night, as it was getting dark and her mother was running her bath, Annabelle suddenly heard the familiar chimes, followed by the bell tolling six times. The next moment her father came through the door with something she had never seen in his face—joy. "Six o'clock and all's well!" he called from the hallway, and for the next few nights he was almost merry.

A few months before the Emergency, the clock tower had stopped again. This time no crew came to repair it. For days Annabelle didn't register the silence of the chimes, and no one around her commented on it. Some mechanism beyond the timepiece itself seemed to have broken, as if the spirit in the civic machine that attuned everyone to its rhythms and kept the regular hours of their lives no longer moved. It was a warning sign, like the two girls in her kitchen, if only she knew to read it. How strange that an empire as old and stable as her father's could disappear, not because flood or drought produced widespread hunger, or monstrous injustice led to rebellion—life remained relatively abundant and secure for families like the Rustins—but just because people no longer believed in it, like a house falling down one day after years of neglect, or a marriage ending for lack of love. No wonder her father couldn't fathom that it was gone.

After the Emergency, a self-org committee called Time got the hands on the clock tower moving again. But the chimes were now set to play a new song that Annabelle found dissonant, that would never mean to her what the old one had meant to her father.

"What's different now?" she echoed him. "It stopped working."

"But why, damn it? Why did it have to stop?"

He was almost shouting, but his eyes had softened in their hollows and shone like Pan's when he needed her help with a hard math problem or a mean friend. She wanted to lean over and stroke her father's remaining hair and gather his wasted body in her arms. But she refrained.

"Because we let it."

7

Outside, Annabelle looked down the empty street and allowed the sadness that had come over her at her father's bedside to have its say. She was unsure where to go. She could take Pan straight home and hope they'd find Hugo and Selva waiting for them—the first sign would be Zeus whining and pawing inside the front door. But something told her they were not back and would not be back soon. She decided to stop by the hostel before going home. She wouldn't let these Wide Awakes keep her away, whatever their reason—wouldn't let *Hugo* keep her away, whatever he'd done. But after three days the place must be unrecognizable.

"I feel sorry for Grandpa," Pan said, and he squinched up his face as he did when something was troubling him. "Sometimes I wish there never was an Emergency."

"Why's that, Pan-Pan?"

"It was fun at first, but not now. Why did they have to go?"

She took his hand in hers and began walking toward the tram stop. The view from the Heights—the brick warehouse walls halfway down the hill, below them the slate rooftops of the administration buildings, the limestone fortress of city hall, the tower rising above it with a clockface on all sides halfway up to the turreted dome, then the emerald expanse of the park's treetops, the shimmer of water where the river curved past the South Gate, and over the city a radiant blue sky that they used to call the imperial heaven—it always filled her with a momentary hope, but not today.

She turned her gaze back to the street and caught sight of a woman in a long white medical coat half a block away. She was Hugo's deputy.

Suzana was walking toward the hospital. Annabelle was sure that she had seen them—seen, looked hard, then snapped her head away and continued with long, purposeful strides. Annabelle broke into a jog, tugging Pan behind. They caught up with her a block from the hospital under a street sign that said THE WAY OF THE YOUNG.

"Hello!"

When Suzana turned around, her face was arranging itself in an expression of pleasant surprise, mouth half-open, eyebrows rising above the rims of her glasses. But her eyes were tense, and she quickly folded her arms across the oversized white coat. A pageboy haircut framed her tight face, and the body behind her crossed arms was small and rigid. She was not the kind of woman to worry her boss's wife, but her cold, dry intelligence intimidated Annabelle the few times they'd met. *You went your way*, her manner said, *and I went mine*.

They exchanged greetings. Annabelle introduced Pan and explained their visit to the Heights while Suzana gazed at the boy with a detached smile. They chatted about the autumn chill, and Annabelle remarked on the city's strange emptiness. Suzana had heard the stay-home order, but she was exempted as an essential.

"We're short-handed right now," she said. The unmentioned subject was suddenly between them.

"Yes, without Hugo," Annabelle said. "He's on a trip."

"So I heard. Where did he go?"

"On vacation, camping with our daughter," she said quickly. "How did you hear?"

"Everyone hears everything these days." It was an odd thing to say, even a little threatening.

"They'll be back today or tomorrow."

Suzana's polite smile faded, and she shook her head as if to clear up some confusion. "Vacation? Is that what Hugo told you?"

Annabelle felt her skin go cold. She had chased Suzana because she could no longer avoid the thing that Hugo had refused to tell her, and now it was coming. "Yes, he's been working hard and the hospital gave him time off."

"I'm sorry." Keeping one arm across her chest, Suzana reached out with the other and touched Annabelle's shoulder. "He should have told you what happened." Annabelle waited while Suzana glanced down at Pan, who was watching her fretfully. "He looks like his father."

"What happened?" Annabelle asked.

Suzana held her with a look of pity and contempt. "It was rather small and could have been made to go away, but Hugo wouldn't let it. Quite unnecessarily, he went to war with the hospital. Then he went to war with Together. I hope he hasn't gone to war with the city."

"What do you mean?"

The clock tower began to chime the jarring notes of its new song.

"I must go." Suzana's face underwent a brightening adjustment suitable for a fortuitous meeting of casual friends. "Lovely to see you, Annabelle. Your Pan is adorable." As she turned away Annabelle saw what her folded arms had been hiding: the words CHIEF SURGEON were stitched in red thread on the white breast of Hugo's coat.

8

"What did Papa do?" Tears were streaming down Pan's cheeks. He wiped his nose on his coat collar, and Annabelle gathered him in her arms and let him cry into her dress. "Is there going to be a war?" his muffled voice asked.

"I don't think so."

"Why did there have to be an Emergency?"

"Oh, Pan-Pan. Does it seem like the grown-ups have lost their minds?"

"Not all of them. You haven't."

She tightened her arms. "You're my best buddy. I'm sticking with you."

"Mama!" He wriggled out of the hug.

"What is it?"

"I have to go pee-pee. You were squeezing too hard."

All around them she saw the manicured gardens and dressed-for-success houses of the Heights District. These were not the kind of Burghers to let in a strange woman who should have followed instructions to stay home, whose child was having an emergency, and whose panic showed in her hot, flushed face. The old people's home was several blocks behind them and had no bathroom on the parlor floor. In the other direction, on the far side of a small park, was the Imperial College Hospital.

Annabelle visited her husband's workplace as little as possible, usually to give him something important he'd left at home. The long white hallways, the sterile smell of the wards, the staff huddled in terse conversations or roaring at some private joke, Hugo apologizing to her as he rushed off to see a patient—she always felt like an intruder with no place here other than as Doctor Rustin's wife. And today a reckoning awaited her.

It had been pursuing her like a persistent catcaller ever since the night Hugo had come home from the hospital looking stricken. He had concealed it from her, and now he had gone off with their daughter, fled in disgrace, leaving Annabelle alone with their son in this deathly quiet city, shunned at her Stranger hostel, still not knowing what he'd done, while anxiety contaminated the purity of her anger. But the reckoning was bigger than this, bigger than her own family's troubles, and she could no longer avoid it. She took Pan's moist hand and hurried uphill toward the hospital's looming façade.

Annabelle didn't know the guard standing outside the glass doors. The usual guard was a hulking man in his fifties, in blue overalls, with a mudslide face and an unstable glare that would collapse at the sight of Annabelle: "Good day to you, Mrs. Doctor Rustin!" That guard had worked at the hospital even longer than Hugo, with almost nothing to do. Like the old people in the parlor, he belonged to the time before the Emergency, a time of school drop-offs and family games and trips to the Place, when no one questioned the meaning behind each remark, everyone's role was known, and she thought herself happy.

That guard was gone. In his place stood a very tall young man, no more than twenty, with a narrow face and eyes set close together on either side of a protuberant nose. Instead of blue overalls, he was wearing the same green uniform and cap that she had seen on Lynx and on the two teenagers outside her house. When she moved toward the doors, he stepped in front of her.

"My son needs to use the bathroom."

"Identification please."

She had no idea where she'd put her certificate of citizenship—anyway, it was no good now, and the notion of issuing new papers went against the spirit of Together. "Well, I don't have any."

"All visitors must show identification."

"Are you expecting trouble?" He didn't answer, but his possum's nose twitched in some discomfort that pleased her, for she had taken an immediate dislike to the old guard's replacement. "I'm Doctor Rustin's wife, and my son needs a bathroom."

"Who's Doctor Rustin?"

"The chief—"

She felt Pan's hand give hers a tug. It pulled something loose in her like a rip cord, freeing all the rage that she habitually turned on herself, releasing a surge of energy with which she pushed past the guard through the glass doors and sailed across the lobby floor and down the bright corridor while Pan kept yanking her hand, saying, "Mama, Mama," until they reached the bathroom and she took off his coat and saw the dark stain spreading between his trouser legs.

Annabelle washed her son's body and clothes. It was cold in the bathroom, and she wrapped him in her coat, which covered him down to his knees. She waited until he stopped crying, then left him and went off in search of a hospital gown to hide his humiliation.

She had been hurrying too much to notice the signs posted

all along the corridor walls. Instead of the handholding cutouts and childlike scrawl of TOGETHER signs, simple block letters stood out on white paper.

> ~~DO NO HARM.~~ DO ONLY GOOD.
> IF YOUR HEALING RECIPIENT IS A YEOMAN, INFORM SELF-ORG.
> THE TRUTH IS ON OUR SIDE.
> WHAT YOU THINK *IS* OUR BUSINESS.
> ARE YOU WIDE AWAKE?

Halfway down the hall a door stood open. Annabelle stopped short and peered inside.

"*You shall be as gods,*" said a young doctor she didn't know. He was holding hands with those seated in chairs on either side of him. He was broad-shouldered, good-looking, with thick-rimmed glasses and a neatly groomed beard, and under his white coat his scrubs were olive green. Then he dropped the hands and leaned forward, elbows on knees, clasping and unclasping his own hands as if working a piece of putty into submission while he listened to a woman Annabelle couldn't see.

"And she believed him?" the young doctor asked.

"I'm not sure. I found her hard to read." It sounded like Hugo's deputy, Suzana.

"What did he tell North Gate Safety?"

"A, quote, humanitarian mission," said a woman seated next to the young doctor. She looked around thirty, with an oval face perched on a tense neck. "Something about saving a Stranger boy."

"Rescuing toasted marshmallows." The flat, charmless

voice sounded like that of Hugo's rival, the chief of personnel. There was muted laughter.

The young doctor (Annabelle thought of him as the leader) clapped twice. "Let's stay focused. When did he leave?"

"Thursday."

"Gone four days in Yeoman country. Lying to North Gate Safety or his wife—or both." The leader sat back and folded his arms across his chest. "What does that tell you?"

"Reckless."

"Unreliable."

"Or conspiring," the leader said.

"He took his daughter," Suzana said. "Maybe they did go camping."

"It isn't even the season. She's in school. And no one is leaving the city."

"But that would be just like Hugo. A grand gesture to show his faith in humanity."

There were scoffs and snorts.

"Wasn't there something anti-Together about his statements in the Restoration Ring? Even pro-Yeoman?" The oval-faced woman was bobbing her head and enunciating to give each word its import. "Does it matter whether he's trying to save the world or join the enemy? He harms us by word and thought. Together lives in the mind. It's woven with gossamer."

"That's beautifully put," the leader said, "but I'd still like to know what he's up to. Your cousin—what's his name?"

"Kask," Suzana said. "Not really my cousin."

"But Hugo wanted to see him. What do we know about him?"

"He does some sort of manual labor in the Warehouse District. We've lost touch."

"He didn't answer the orientation summons, like half the Yeomen in the district," the chief of personnel said.

"And we have no idea who they are," the leader said, "thanks to the terrible recordkeeping of the Imperial Census."

"We'll find them when they need a doctor. They'll come out of the woodwork."

"Isn't it interesting that the summons scares them?" the thin-faced woman said, steepling her fingertips together and tilting her head to demonstrate her fascination. "As if 'orientation' means physical pain to them, not cognitive expansion? Doesn't that tell us something dark about Yeoman culture?"

"I want this Kask brought in," the leader said. "I'll bet he's up to something—maybe with Hugo. And I want to find Hugo."

Annabelle shivered—the hospital seemed to have no heating. And she was looking at someone who deepened her chill. A smooth-faced, ponytailed girl in scrubs, maybe a nurse, with a pair of goggles strapped over her eyes, sat up straight and perfectly still, never shifting her head toward the speaker or changing expression or adjusting the hands in her lap. It was hard to tell where her scrubs ended and her arms began, for there was something shiny and impossibly youthful about her skin, as if age hadn't left a single mark on her. And still she didn't move.

Pan was waiting. Reluctantly, Annabelle turned away from the open door and the obscure talk about herself and Hugo and a man named Kask and orientation—about anything but medicine. Troubled and hurried, she went in search of an extra-small set of scrubs. Nothing was as she remembered it: the floor kept sticking to her shoes, the odor of incontinence pervaded the halls. No orderlies rushed by pushing stretchers, no nurses stood around in loud groups. She seemed to have the place to herself, other than the patients she glimpsed entombed in beds as she passed their rooms, and an old man shuffling along the hall in a gown that bared his wasted hams.

Maybe she *was* the credulous wife they'd been discussing. She still didn't know why Hugo had gone away. Perhaps even he didn't know; perhaps his idea about Mr. Monge's boy was like a dream he'd tried to explain to her and failed, since telling any dream left you more alone. No one ever revealed more than a flicker of the empire within.

For her, that was the real point of Together: to make them all less alone, to dream less private dreams. But a higher command was to be true to herself, and she obeyed it so faithfully that Hugo once said her religion prohibited her from laughing at any joke she didn't find funny. With the Emergency this command had taken her away from him. Now she worried that it was taking her away from Together.

At the end of the hall there was a closet door with two signs: a piece of paper that said DON'T BE A HUMAN. BE A BETTER HUMAN, and above it, in stenciled letters from another time, the word SUPPLIES. Inside, Annabelle found folded stacks of towels and gowns, and a pile of mildewy scrubs that had been in use before the yellow-and-purple of Together and the green of the Wide Awakes. She grabbed the smallest pair she could find and returned to the bathroom, where Pan was boxing with the mirror in her winter coat. She looked away and bundled up his damp trousers while he put on the scrubs.

"We can't stay any longer," she told him. "We'll go straight out the way we came in."

As soon as Annabelle stepped into the hall, a small female voice behind her said, "Mrs. Rustin?" She turned: it was the girl from the meeting. Only she was no longer wearing goggles, and up close her face was neither shiny nor expressionless. Pulled high by the ponytail, her brow was furrowed, her wide mouth pursed in a tense smile, and her eyes peered up at Annabelle's with timorous curiosity. "The director would like to see you."

9

Annabelle didn't care for the hospital director. He was smooth and insincere, and she doubted his loyalty to Hugo if self-interest ever got in the way. He and his wife had once hosted a dinner at the Physicians Social Club, and the director had spent the evening condescending to Annabelle while looking down the front of her dress. But it wasn't hard to rattle a man like that—she called attention to the bit of food at the corner of his mouth and let him know when he was repeating himself. Afterward Hugo reported with pride that Annabelle had impressed his boss. He was the only one of her husband's colleagues who might tell her why Hugo had gone away. This was the reason she had come to the hospital: to see him.

The director's office stood at the end of a narrow hall leading from the admittance desk. But when the girl ushered Annabelle and Pan inside a windowless, wood-paneled room, the person seated behind the mahogany desk wasn't the blandly smiling sixty-year-old she'd expected. The armchair was occupied by the young doctor from the circle. On the front of his white coat, its sleeves pushed up to the elbows, the word DIRECTOR was stitched in red thread.

He reached across his desk to indicate a chair. "Annabelle, please sit down. Lyra, do we have anything to occupy this young man for a few minutes?"

"Do you like building blocks?" the girl asked Pan.

"I'm too old for that."

"What about sketching?"

Pan looked at his mother, who had not yet sat down. "Do I have to go?" When Annabelle hesitated, he added, "What if you need me?"

She told him to let Lyra entertain him—how often did he get to spend time in his father's hospital?

"I'm Saron," the young doctor said when they were alone.

"I expected someone else."

"Ah. My predecessor retired last week. We owe him a great debt—but as he told us, 'Time to listen to the young.' Tea?"

Annabelle didn't want to accept Saron's hospitality, but even with her coat on, she was cold. "Black, please."

Saron smiled to himself as he steeped fresh leaves in a steaming tea service and poured out two cups. By the room's dim light Annabelle recognized that she was in the presence of male vanity. She had known many varieties; Hugo's was among the subtler, largely consisting of affected modesty. Over the course of her life she had learned to tolerate it while occasionally passing inward judgment. But today she did not feel like being quiet.

"Where is everyone?" she asked.

"Who do you mean?"

"The hospital seems empty."

Saron laughed and ran his fingers over a bearded cheek. "I wouldn't call it empty. Some of our patients come from outside the city, and we're no longer seeing them." After a moment he added, "They've stopped coming."

"Yeomen no longer get sick?"

Saron didn't answer but sipped his tea and watched her through the rising steam. "What brought you to the hospital?"

"My son needed a bathroom."

He seemed to weigh whether to accept this explanation

or scoff at its absurdity. "Anyway, Annabelle, I'm glad you're here. Can I call you that?" He set his cup beside a folder on the desk. "Let's speak freely. Where is Hugo now?"

"Camping with our daughter."

"Where?"

She described the Place in vague terms—she honestly wasn't sure of its location and couldn't have found it on a map.

"That sounds like the heart of Yeoman country."

"We go there every year. It's a lovely area."

Saron had begun to flex his jaws, clenching and unclenching. "Why did he tell the North Gate that he was on a, quote, humanitarian mission?"

Annabelle tried to think through the consequences of lying and kept getting lost in thickets where Hugo's behavior only seemed worse. Instead, she told the story of Mr. Monge's son, trying to imagine her husband and daughter searching the woods for this elusive boy, losing faith in her own words as she spoke them, while Saron sat back in his armchair and sipped his tea and slowly nodded as if a problem he'd been parsing was finally solved.

"So not camping—that makes more sense," he said when her story faded into an unresolved end. "But do you really believe he's taking this enormous risk out there just to provide first aid to a Stranger boy?" Annabelle was silent. "Of course, you know him better than I do."

Irritated, she said, "I'm sure I do."

"Hugo was asked to leave the hospital. Did you know that?"

She shook her head. It was a pathetic thing to have to admit.

"It had to do with the woman who's outside with your son."

The steam was fogging up Saron's thick-rimmed glasses, and when he took them off, Annabelle suddenly imagined how he must see her: a nice Burgher wife, still attractive in her forties, an ornament at her husband's side, spoiled by a life of peace and prosperity, titillated by the Emergency, proud to be dabbling in self-org—utterly ignorant of the hard world.

She sat very still, warming her hands around the teacup, avoiding his eyes, and listened. He told her the story as if describing an interesting medical case, and in contrast with Saron's factual tone Hugo's words sounded so extreme that she could hardly believe he would have said such things, or fathom why—they seemed unprompted, unmoored, lunatic. He had once given her a very different account of the same incident, a self-pitying version to win her sympathy. Remembering it now disgusted her. She wanted to rush out and apologize to the girl, but she didn't move. As she listened, she was watching Saron's hands. They were clasped together on the desk, annihilating the piece of putty again, and the effort engorged their veins and rippled through the muscles of his forearms.

When she looked up, his eyes were locked on her.

"I'm very sorry," she said. "Ashamed, honestly."

One of the hands reached across the desk and gave the back of her hand a reassuring rub. The touch made her heart beat a little faster. "You didn't know. He kept it from you."

"Did he apologize to her?"

"Yes—and that might have been the end of it. There's a lot of pressure here, people lose control. But Hugo's pride got the better of him." Saron explained that Hugo had turned his apology into an attack on them all—on the hospital self-org, on Together itself, antagonizing his peers on the committee, demoralizing the younger ones, almost forcing the hospital to send him away for the sake of its own integrity. "He couldn't accept that our city no longer revolves around chief surgeons."

Now she couldn't look away from his eyes. In the gloom they glowed with boyish energy, and with a confident intimacy that belonged to someone older.

"Families are changing, too," Saron went on. "I hate to say this, but in a way he was attacking you, Annabelle. I've heard about your Stranger Committee—you're an essential worker for Together. You're wide awake. You and I want the same thing."

She didn't know if everything he said was true, but the vision of a world she could be part of drew her toward him. At the same time, she felt an urge to close a curtain, to protect herself and her family from this distractingly handsome doctor whom she didn't know.

Seeing her hesitate, Saron leaned back in his armchair. "Let me explain to you where we are. They've cut off our food supply—you know that. They're building a network of spies in the city, boring from within. And right now, while Hugo is on his humanitarian mission in Yeoman country, they're preparing an attack."

"Why would they do that?"

"Because they need us more than we need them. Because we have hospitals, schools, inventions—*brains*."

"They have farms."

"We're already learning to grow our own food. Annabelle, help us. Help us find Hugo."

"You think he—"

"I'm not saying he's joined them. Has he gone that far? I don't know. Maybe he wants to be the man who brings us back together, with reason and compromise and all those nice empire things. But he's in over his head, and he could get himself and other people killed."

"What do you want me to do?"

"If you hear from him, let us know. If he comes home, bring him here."

She was angrier with Hugo than she'd ever been—less for what he'd done to anyone else than for what he'd done to her—lying, concealing, shaming her. Most of all, for leaving her out. But the thought of her husband coming home gave her an image of him at the dinner table, in his weekend flannel shirt (was there ever a greater creature of habit?), after a "project day" of weeding the garden or repairing closet drawers. He would go around the table and have each of them in turn—first Pan, then Selva, then Annabelle—report highlights from their week, unaware that his face was glowing, not at anything they said but at the pleasure of their company. This image was utterly ordinary, and therefore sacred. It didn't matter to anyone else. Compared to the future of the city it was trivial. The four of them were trivial. One by one they would all disappear, while Together would continue indefinitely. She was thinking wrong thoughts and wouldn't repeat them to this young doctor, wouldn't submit fragile sketches of her private life to the scrutiny of the sum of us. She wanted to go home, even if a calamity was waiting.

She shook her head to clear her mind of the hands and eyes. "You don't know my husband."

"We just want Hugo back safe."

"My son is waiting." Annabelle stood up, but she didn't leave. "Can you explain something? The Wide Awakes—these green uniforms, Yeoman orientations, training Strangers. Was Together always about this?"

Not rising, Saron replaced his glasses and sighed through his nose like someone weary of explaining an inescapable truth in the face of stubborn sentimentality. "Together was and is the idea of self-organized movement toward moral, material, and cognitive human perfection. The things you mention are essential to its survival. Any idea this profound will always have enemies."

"It used to seem kinder," she said, and went out.

10

As soon as Annabelle entered the canteen, the girl with the ponytail jumped up from the table where she was sitting with Pan in his winter coat and oversized scrubs amid drawing paper and crayons and rolled-up trousers.

"Mrs. Rustin! Can I talk to you?"

"I already know. I'm sorry."

"No, it's not that."

Annabelle looked out the window. Under a dark bank of clouds the edge of the sky was aflame with sunset. Downhill the city lights were coming on. "What is it then?"

They sat at the table—the canteen was otherwise empty—and Annabelle glanced at Pan's pictures. A black dog with bared teeth and side stitches kept leaping at various human figures brandishing primitive weapons. Her son had never been good at art, but the dog series created a surprising atmosphere of menace.

Lyra spoke softly, in a rush, mostly with her head down, and Annabelle had trouble grasping all of it. The incident with Hugo seemed to be a source of regret to her, the starting point of a spiral. Afterward the hospital self-org committee asked her to take on more responsibility, but she could hardly get through her shift without bursting into tears, and she still needed to learn the fundamentals as a Healing Associate—even inserting needles didn't always come easy. (Just before the Emergency she had barely passed her competency boards and was considered a "contingent inferior guild member.") What kept her going was focusing on a Yeoman boy in aftercare, the one Hugo had operated on. When Saron and the Wide Awakes took over, the hospital decided to send the boy and his parents back to the countryside, and Lyra surprised herself by arguing for more recovery time. Self-org agreed to enroll the family in orientation, and after memorizing the six Together principles and learning to use the vocabulary in appropriate contexts, the boy and his parents were allowed to stay on in the city while he received out-patient care. Lyra found the family temporary rooms above a cabinetmaker's shop in the Warehouse District. But she felt more and more isolated at the hospital. Suzana, her new Healing Technician, hardly ever spoke to her, and she stopped being included in the self-org circle—replaced at meetings like today's by her Better Human.

With her reserve broken the girl seemed to want to say everything, never to stop, and Annabelle experienced a flash of familiarity: Lyra's eyes were like Selva's.

"I don't know why I'm telling you all this, Mrs. Rustin."

"I think you're telling me because you have no one to tell." Annabelle wrote her address in crayon on a sheet of drawing paper and invited the girl to visit if she ever felt like talking again.

No trams were running, and the last markets with food were already closed, and with the spirit of Together fled the streets seemed desolate. Night had fallen by the time Annabelle and Pan reached the Rowhouse District. Two unfamiliar teenagers in green were lounging at the corner. Annabelle ignored them. She had just enough chicken and vegetables in the kitchen for another dinner for two—unless—but behind the front door there was no sound of scratching.

PART IV

1

Rustin slept heavily and woke up at sunrise with a feeling of having important things to do that he was in danger of missing. Zeus lay in the mouth of the tent, watching as if he'd been awake for hours. When Rustin moved to sit up, the dog sprang to his feet, his whole body tensed with energy, his tail gyrating in circles, and yearning filled his eyes.

The smell of lavender soap was gone from the tent, and so was Selva. "Zeus, where is she?" The question prompted wilder tail wagging and a flurry of paws drumming on Rustin's legs. "Selva?" he called in a sleep-strangled croak. Zeus ran out of the tent, and Rustin got up and followed him barefoot onto the frosty ground. The low glare of the sun across the lake blinded him. He pretended to himself that she was kneeling lakeside to collect water for coffee—when he shielded his eyes he would see her. But he knew she wasn't there. Even before he found the note by his pillow he sensed that Selva had slipped out of his hands and gone somewhere he couldn't protect her.

A green leather notebook was lying on his blanket. He picked it up and flipped through its pages. What he read made his heart beat faster. He began to move quickly, clearing out the tent, folding its ribs and pulling up stakes while Zeus devoured his morning meal. Rustin liked to think that, faced with some difficulty or crisis, he was moved to act by conscience when in fact it was fear that usually drove him, and now it was Annabelle's voice crying *How could you lose her?* that made him abandon the tent and most of their gear. Without making coffee he threw together the medical kit, folding knife, canteen, torch, and a few pieces of food in his day pack, put on his fishing jacket, and hurried from the site with Zeus running ahead of him down the trail toward the Stranger encampment. His eyelid had begun to twitch—yet he wasn't truly panicked. Selva had made it clear that the Cronk farm wasn't the place he'd imagined, and the notebook evoked even stranger things, but he couldn't quite believe that she was in danger. The instinctive optimism that growing up under the empire had left in his bloodstream still made him feel that everything would turn out okay in the end.

The Monge boy was awake, sitting up against the same tree as before while his sister, the little girl in the torn frock, spooned broth from a clay bowl into his mouth. A crude stretcher was propped against the other side of the tree—a length of cloth pulled taut and woven around a pair of broken branches. The smell of woodsmoke and cooking spices aroused Rustin's hunger. The boy didn't greet him, or pay attention when Zeus approached and sniffed. He was staring into the bowl with intense interest as if he had never seen broth before and nothing but broth mattered.

Rustin set down his pack, knelt, and removed the bandage. The wound looked about the same as last night—the black tissue hadn't spread. If anything, the rest of the foot was slightly improved, less taut, more pink than purple and red. The infection seemed to have been arrested—but it would certainly return without proper care, even if the Strangers resorted to honey again. In a week or two the boy would be dead, and the intervening period would be excruciating. Rustin caught the little sister's eye and made a gesture of washing his hands. She set down the bowl and, before leaving, said a few words to the boy, who slowly nodded without taking his eyes off the broth.

As Rustin examined the wound, he realized how difficult surgery would be without Selva, without a nurse who spoke his language, with nothing for anesthesia but the numbing ointment, which was just a placebo. He had never amputated a foot before. Even if the operation went well, it would take at least two hours from cleansing and marking to sutures and dressing. His knife might prove inadequate to cutting through tendon, let alone bone. He imagined sawing between the talus and tibia and getting only halfway as the blade dulled, leaving the partly severed foot to hang loose from the ankle in a torrent of blood. He imagined the boy screaming and thrashing and the other Strangers gathering around with increased distress and finally laying hands on the foreigner to stop him from torturing their young leader.

In the old days at the Imperial College Hospital, the decision to amputate would be simple, the procedure relatively straightforward. But these woods were now his operating theater, and surgery would make young Monge his responsibility in a way that yesterday's procedure hadn't. Medical practice would require him to stay with his patient for at least twenty-four hours, observing him in case of heavy bleeding or new infection, no matter where Selva had gone.

Rustin crouched next to the boy. "We have a decision to make," he said, "and we should make it together."

Monge unfastened his attention from the bowl and seemed to become aware of Rustin's presence for the first time. There was something odd about his eyes, the way they gazed into Rustin's with a startled recognition that still didn't fully register him, as if apprehending the gleam of some creature's eyes in a darkness that kept its identity mysterious. He lifted a hand to Rustin's face and ran his fingers over the stubble that was growing on his cheeks.

Rustin explained the situation in the clearest terms possible—the condition of the wound, the risks of amputation and of leaving the foot on—while the boy never stopped staring at him and never blinked, pupils dilating and yet unseeing, until Rustin wondered if carving dead tissue from the boy's heel had delivered some profound shock to his mind.

"You want my foot?" Monge suddenly asked. He was looking down his leg with the same air of discovery that he had focused on the broth and then Rustin's face.

"That's what we need to discuss."

"Forever?" Rustin nodded. "Where will you take it?"

"I—" He couldn't think of an answer that made sense. The boy seemed to be having trouble connecting words to the things at hand.

"You will give my foot to the dog?"

"Zeus? No! Absolutely not."

"To my father?" Rustin started to answer, but the boy interrupted. "I will forbid this. My father has his feet already."

The foot had become something separate from the rest of the boy—a removeable object, a gift, an icon. "Your foot won't be what matters," Rustin said. "What matters will be you, your health. In the city we have false-limb shops. A wooden foot would allow you to walk."

The boy laughed indignantly. "I must trade my foot for wood! Good for you, bad for me."

The girl returned with a steaming basin of water. As she set it down, Rustin saw her reach into the front pouch of her frock and hand something to Monge, who put it in his mouth and began to chew.

Rustin held out an open hand to the girl. "I have to know what he's eating before surgery." Her small hand placed in his a crumble of gray speckled matter that he was able to identify as chopped mushrooms. The girl tapped her temple, then pointed at her brother's foot and giggled. Rustin understood: he was eating the mushrooms for their analgesic effect. How resourceful, Rustin thought, impressed again by the Strangers' ability to make do in extremity. The only problem was that the mushrooms were impeding Monge's ability to think. He didn't seem to understand what might be about to happen to him. He could hardly give informed consent to surgery. His doctor would have to decide.

"My advice is to wait another day or two and see if the wound stabilizes," Rustin said. "But it's up to you." He was fully aware that this advice had little to do with medicine. If he did nothing, the gangrene would almost certainly spread through the foot and into the lower leg. Amputating and then leaving Monge in the woods would probably kill him anyway. *Don't lose me*, the eyes said, but Chief Surgeon Rustin could not save this boy because he didn't matter as much as Selva. So he was going to leave young Monge, for whom he already felt a strangely paternal affection and worry, to die.

They might not think you are who you think you are. Who had said that? But who did he think he was? He had no business being here. The humanitarian mission was a vain gesture. There was no longer a world in which redemption was possible. Had he come all this way to learn that?

"I will keep my foot," Monge said with a defiant pride.

"Is that your decision?"

"I will never let you take it." The boy signaled for the girl to help him stand.

"Careful! Let me dress it before you put weight on it."

As Rustin cleansed the heel with hot water and wrapped it in fresh bandages, he felt the boy watching him, and when he looked up there was a new clarity in Monge's eyes, as if he had come out of his enchantment and now understood who Rustin was. He gave the boy his hand and eased him onto his feet. "You need your crutch, your stick." With Rustin supporting his elbow and Zeus trotting in front, Monge hobbled a few steps, clenching his teeth, his face losing color. Then he jolted to a stop.

"The girl. Your daughter."

"She's gone. I believe she's at the pig farm."

Monge stared. "This is very dangerous. You must find her."

"As soon as I'm done with you."

"No." He cupped his hands around his mouth and called out a single syllable. A moment later a short, broad-shouldered man in a kind of nightdress emerged from a canopy strung between evergreen trunks and hurried over. He was one of the guards, and Monge addressed him with the soft brevity of someone used to giving orders. The guard went back to his tent, and when he returned he was holding the pistol. Monge gestured at Rustin. The guard looked from the boy to the Burgher and shook his head. Monge said something sharp, and the guard, holding the pistol by its barrel, extended the scratched, worn grip to Rustin.

"I can't accept this," Rustin said.

"You will need it."

"I've never fired a gun in my life."

"Take it," Monge said in a tone of command.

Rustin took the gun. It had a surprisingly satisfying weight and balance, and it was small enough to fit in the side pocket of his fishing jacket. Remembering something, he retrieved his pack and dug inside until he found the six brass bullets tied with thread. Monge appeared delighted to see them.

"Not that I'll need them," Rustin said, "but I suppose they're more useful inside."

The guard took the pistol from Rustin and opened its cylinder. Four of the six chambers were empty, and he slid a cartridge into each, then demonstrated how to cock the hammer into the firing position. The weapon's compact power filled Rustin with a sober awe and frightened him enough that he was wary of even touching it, as if the gun might explode in his hand. He tucked it in an outer pocket of the pack where it would be unlikely to fire an accidental round into his leg.

"It's going to stay right there," he told Monge. "You'll get it back when we return."

"If you return," the boy said, "you will not find us." A smile flickered on his mouth, and his eyes glittered with the secret knowledge that Rustin had seen in his father's eyes on their first meeting at the hostel.

"Where will you be?"

"When the soup is finished we will pack everything. The mothers have decided. This is the day we will leave this place. They are already packing."

Rustin turned and saw that the wood fire had burned out. Tradeswomen were stuffing cookware and clothing into sacks and filling jugs with river water while children chased hens around the encampment. A teenage girl was untethering the kid goat.

"Do you know the rest of the way?"

"Your empire is not good for us." Monge gestured to his bandaged heel. "Your empire hurt us. It is—" The boy glanced down, and color rose in his face. "Excuse me, but it is shit."

"You're going back?"

Monge nodded toward the tradeswomen. "The mothers have decided."

"But there's no rain."

"We are hungry here. Better to starve at home."

Rustin didn't argue. He felt the disappointment of becoming acquainted with an interesting young patient whose discharge order had suddenly come. He gave instructions on the care of the wound, and he insisted that Monge take his medical kit. How strange to have a gun in its place—not much of his professional identity was left out here. The prospect of their trek through the mountains led by this doomed boy was unrealistic in the extreme, but maybe no more than his own failed mission in Yeoman country, and certainly more justifiable. If young Monge had only another two weeks to live, wouldn't it be worse to spend them hiding from Yeomen, or among Burghers who would canonize him as a minor saint, than to be home and covered by dirt and leaves that didn't cry when walked on?

"Stay off the foot as much as possible. Use that stretcher. Drink plenty of water. Won't you need your gun?"

Monge laughed as if the gun was already a thing of no consequence, a relic of an empire gone to shit.

2

By the time the man with a pack and the dog came down the lane, it was late morning. The sun had melted the frost from the grass, and Rustin's shoes were damp. He had visited the Cronk farm many times, but today was different. A cloud mass was gathering above the tree line and a pall hung over the barns and fields, as if a brush fire was burning somewhere and he was seeing everything through a filter of baleful light. What had always been so refreshing on arrival—the rich manure smell, the mad clucking in the henhouse, the wave of yellow hay flowing uphill out of sight—was now saying: "Come and find her."

He glanced around the farm. She was nowhere to be seen, and neither was the hauler.

Zeus spotted a hog between the slats of the pigpen and barked. There was movement by the farmhouse—Mrs. Cronk, hanging laundry on a clothesline, had seen the visitors and hurried to the back door. A minute later she appeared on the porch, running her palms up and down the apron over her hips. "Mr. Cronk, Mr. Cronk!" she called across the yard in a voice nearly strangled by distress. "Visitors! Mr. Cronk!"

Her husband came around from behind the house with a saw in one hand and a toolbelt hanging from his hips. "What the hell are you gabbling about?" he said, loud enough for

Rustin to hear. Mrs. Cronk pointed in the direction of the barns and promptly disappeared inside.

Big Cronk wasn't smiling under the wide-brimmed hat as he limped toward Rustin, who placed a hand on Zeus's hackles and murmured, "No barking." He had planned on opening with the bonhomie that was their usual mode—something about a father's difficulty keeping track of a teenager—but the look on the other man's face stopped him. He saw that the years of flimsy goodwill had collapsed. Big Cronk wasn't quite fifty, about the same age as Rustin, but labor and weather and now displeasure made him look at least a decade older, eyes sun-wrinkled and hard, cheeks sliding into his neck, back bent, legs bowed under a torso so big that it was impossible to tell where muscle ended and fat began. The ravages of farmwork seemed to give Big Cronk a moral advantage, as if the truth of life was stamped on his face and body, while Rustin, on his humanitarian mission, with his trim physique and underslung smile, his fishing jacket and leather shoes and day pack, oozed falsehood.

"Is she here?"

"She is. Caught her stealing last night. Didn't I say not to come back?"

Rustin's breathing eased—this was a mistake that could be cleared up. "She wasn't stealing. There's a medical emergency. We'd have returned anything she took." He explained about young Monge's wound, implying that amputation remained a live option.

Big Cronk walked to the open door of the toolshed and hung up the saw. He took off his hat and rubbed a flannel sleeve across his sweating forehead. "First those Strangers come trespassing, next it's your girl, and every time we lose a tool or a gun. But she wasn't stealing?" He fixed Rustin with a narrow-eyed look. "You better hope it was just stealing, doc."

"What do you mean?"

"My boy has her for a Burgher spy—you, too. He's looking into it right this minute. What are you two doing with those intruders up at the lake? What are you trying to start?"

An icy sensation passed through Rustin's body. He remembered the trial with the three farmers, how a kind of paralysis had come over him, and he tried to temper his mind into a hard edge of calculation that would save her and himself.

"Can we sit somewhere? I hope we can still talk to each other."

They sat on a bench outside the farrowing barn. Zeus faced them in his good-boy posture, alert to the tension between the two men. Now and then his ears cocked at the squeals of a piglet, but he didn't bark.

"Those people at the lake have left. They won't trouble you. They're not coming back," Rustin said. "She came out here because of me. It's my fault."

"You never did think much of us," Big Cronk said.

"I'm worried for my daughter. I don't know where Sel is, but she's my flesh and blood and I'm worried everything has gone so haywire that something might happen to her that you and Little Cronk and your whole family would regret. Something in an instant that would last a lifetime. Just like you would worry if it was your son."

Big Cronk hawked and spat in the dirt. There was an odor of sawn wood on him that would have been pleasant at another time. "Nothing's going to happen to her."

"I hope not, but I need to see her."

"I can't do that. She's with my boy and he's in charge."

"Little Cronk is in charge?" Rustin asked with genuine surprise. "This is your farm. Those were your tools Sel was looking for. Since when is he in charge?"

Cronk rummaged under his jowls and scratched the hollow of his throat. "Since all this started," he said, with a vagueness that seemed to conceal shame. "They have a right. I had my time and now it's his."

"We're going through the same thing in the city."

Big Cronk refused to answer Rustin's look. Shaking his head, he pulled a chisel from his toolbelt and with the beveled blade started cleaning the black rims of his bitten-down fingernails. "I don't know where he got all his ideas. Nothing I ever taught him. We take good care of our animals, but we don't make them gods."

Rustin thought it better to say nothing, to let Big Cronk talk himself through his own crisis.

"He thinks he's smarter than me and he probably is. I tried to give him some rope but he keeps taking more. Maybe I should have put my foot down sooner."

Big Cronk seemed to want a reply. "And done what?" Rustin asked.

"Not let those other boys on our farm. Not let him talk to his mother that way, or call himself Gard. Whoever wrote on those wood pieces he likes to collect—they didn't build our house or raise our pigs. Cronks are practical people, but sometimes it seems like he's living in a dream." He was digging under the particularly dirty middle fingernail of his left hand. When he had cleaned it to his satisfaction, he looked straight at Rustin. "I think he got his ideas from you people."

This was not what Rustin had expected to hear. He tried

to answer in a way that was neither defensive nor threatening. "What ideas did he get from us?"

"That girl of yours was always bringing him books. I didn't read them so I don't know what was in them, but I bet they put things in his head."

"Those books had the imperial seal stamped on the cover."

"Stories about animals that can talk."

"Ordinary children's literature."

Big Cronk was gathering energy on the strength of accusation. "Then after it started, the Conspiracy thing, we heard about what you people were getting up to. We all have a cousin or acquaintance in the city. They let us know what was going on."

Rustin thought: *Kask*. Kask had tried to warn him not to come. He'd hardly listened.

"We heard about your girls dancing naked up on some tower you built them, then jumping off. The kids you killed so you could put their brains in a machine. God knows what else—just disgusting. You people lost all respect for human life. Boys like mine hear about these things, it changes them. It disturbs their sleep. Of course they're going to get their own ideas."

He wiped the chisel on his overalls and replaced it in his toolbelt.

"So I lost him." Big Cronk cleared emotion from his throat. "Now tell me why I should help you."

Rustin stood up and began pacing in front of the bench. For some reason he thought of the *Evening Verity*, the newspaper that used to be printed in the capital and distributed to every corner of the empire. Even if no copies ever made it to the Cronk farm, whenever the Rustins paid a visit Big Cronk was always aware of wildfires and floods in distant regions, a notorious murder in a provincial town, even the occasional scandal in the capital. Rustin wasn't sure how news reached Big Cronk, but what struck him now was that it was always the same as the news they had in the city by the river, and that this was completely unremarkable. No one out here would insist that girls were dancing naked and throwing themselves off towers in a city he'd never seen if someone from the city said it wasn't so.

Now it would be impossible to convince Big Cronk otherwise. If Rustin said a story was false, Big Cronk would know it must be true—the wilder the story, the firmer his belief. The demise of the *Evening Verity* made this easier, but it wasn't the real reason. Big Cronk believed because he *wanted* to believe. He felt a need to know things that Rustin didn't know, things that drove a permanent wedge between them so that they no longer inhabited the same world. Maybe a chisel was still a chisel, but everything else was up for grabs.

Rustin found this thought so unsettling that his heart began to pound, as if his windpipe was closing. It frightened him more than Gandorig and the village farmers, more than the wolf and the bull, more than what he had read in the notebook. He looked down at Big Cronk, who was staring in the direction of the hayfield, and under the leather hat Rustin saw unfathomable bloodshot eyes. Some grievance, some hidden wound, sheer perversity—more than he could understand.

He sat down on the bench and said nothing for a long time.

Big Cronk must have had a project going behind the house—like Rustin he was always busy at something—but he didn't move. Utter stillness settled over the farm. It seemed they might sit here until nightfall.

Rustin took off his pack and felt around for two cigars and the flint. He handed a cigar to Big Cronk, who accepted it wordlessly and bit off the end. Rustin tried to keep his hand steady enough to light it and his own. They sat side by side smoking under the empty sky while Zeus watched.

"It's a big world," Rustin said, without knowing what it meant. "And we don't matter."

A while later Big Cronk said, "Nope."

"But they still need us."

Another minute went by. The motionless air filled with smoke. "Seems that way."

When the piglet squealed, it was like a trumpet blast.

"Damn." Rustin had let ash fall on the pocket of his pack with the gun.

Big Cronk drew hard on his cigar and threw the stub in the dirt. "I'm going to try and get her for you. Then you need to leave and never come back."

3

It seemed that the hauler was with Little Cronk, over the hill and a mile away at the limestone quarry Rustin had heard his father mention a few times. Spitting out terse phrases as if they had a bad taste, Big Cronk described a plan that he was obviously making up on the spot. He would hike to the quarry alone and ask to borrow the hauler, then return to pick up Rustin. He didn't want Rustin walking with him because one of the boys at the quarry might see the stranger from a distance and do something stupid. They would drive around the quarry with Rustin keeping his head down, and then up the trail onto the meadow where Gard was training his unit. Rustin would stay in the hauler while Big Cronk got out and talked to his son. Then they would drive Selva back to the farm.

"What will you say to him?"

"The girl's sorry and been punished enough."

"What if he refuses?"

Big Cronk allowed a sad half-smile to crease one of his jowls. "Doc, I raised that boy. I know him better than he knows himself."

"How will we get back to the city?"

"Same way you came."

"You'll give us the hauler?"

"It's your property. Have you got anything of mine?"

Rustin realized that he had something of Big Cronk's in

his pack, but he shook his head. He was trying to picture the plan step by step and kept encountering the same obstacle: Little Cronk would never agree. There was something wrong with the boy, some inaccessible unhappiness that expressed itself in brooding silence. He had always been polite to the Rustin family, but on their last visit Rustin had been a little nervous leaving Selva alone with him. Now he was in charge, with a fourteen-year-old Burgher girl under his power, God knows for what purpose—Rustin didn't let himself take the thought further. Giving her up to his father in front of other boys would be humiliating.

"How has she been punished?"

Big Cronk looked away, toward the hill. "Keeping her overnight, is all."

"What's your son doing right now? You said training his unit—what kind of unit?"

Big Cronk turned to Rustin with a look meant to intimidate a trespasser. "That's enough questions."

Alone, Rustin waited on the bench. An air of violence had come over the farm. He did not do well with men for whom fighting was always an option. It moved a relationship onto terrain where he had little experience or confidence, and the abilities he had would be useless. Like most men he occasionally daydreamed of taking on an antagonist, and he always reduced the other man to a bleeding whimper, but he also knew that the first real punch would change reality in ways he couldn't anticipate.

Rustin pictured a row of Yeoman boys in military uniform marching and drilling with long guns. How comical, here on the Cronk farm where chickens were clucking and hogs snorting. But he had reached this place by failing to imagine the worst, and he made himself pursue the thought.

If it came to this, if the new hatred between groups somehow escaped the realm of words and tales and landed blows, would Burghers be able to defend themselves? They didn't age as fast as Yeomen and stayed healthier longer, but most were physically unimposing and as unused to violence as he was. Far more Yeomen than Burghers had filled the ranks of the Imperial Armed Forces. Under the empire the only firearms in the possession of civilians were for hunting, plus the odd obsolete pistol like the one in his pack. It was hard to say how widely they were distributed, but it seemed likely that most were in the countryside. At We Are One in the main square he'd wanted to tell the woman in the purple raincoat: "Don't you know? They have the guns." What did Burghers have other than the weapon of their righteousness?

In the city it had been easy to feel superior to meetings and slogans and wild tales. Even at his most discouraged and shamed, after the Restoration Ring, when he was wandering the streets like a vagrant, an outcast looking in—even then he had felt brave and pure for standing alone. He had felt the supreme pride of failure. A voice kept saying, "You're irrelevant, old man," and he answered, "Yes, thank God," because he still followed his own creed. What was it? He tried to think of six principles to match Together's but could come up with only three. He would have written them down if he had anything to write on.

> BE TRUE TO YOURSELF.
> SEE THE WORLD TRULY.
> HUMAN BEINGS ARE BROTHERS AND SISTERS.

Fine thoughts! Much sturdier than *"Listen to the young"* or *"You shall be as gods"*! How did they hold up out here?

Without his surgical instruments and gown, without the clock tower's chimes and the tram's bell and the cobblestones underfoot to remind him who he was, his creed turned out to be a hollow thing, and Big Cronk had shattered it with a blow. How could they be brothers with such different worlds inside their skulls?

He looked across the lane toward the house. He guessed that Mrs. Cronk was inside watching.

Annabelle's aversion to visiting the farm had been neither squeamish nor snobbish, but clear-eyed. They'd been apart for four days now—the longest time in their lives. Whenever her face came before him, sometimes smiling, sometimes her rain face, he felt himself fading like a shadow when the sun disappeared. Separation seemed to drain the substance from his own reality, as if all that held him together was the sound of her key in the door, the touch of her hand on his shoulder.

It was shocking to know that he needed her this way. He had always thought the center of mass that kept their lives in motion was his work. When they were courting, he had just started his residency at the hospital, and while they sat in a café or walked along the river he talked obsessively about his patients as if he was the first doctor ever to practice medicine, and instead of drifting away she would ask questions and encourage him to go on, her eyes luminous, listening with a quality of attention that he must have taken for granted, because it had never struck him until now.

Zeus was lying at Rustin's feet, chin on paw, looking up at him with puzzled expectation: *What are we doing here? We should be home in the Rowhouse District.* When Rustin moved, the tail stretching flat from Zeus's body thumped the ground, then stopped when Rustin didn't stand up. He leaned over and rubbed Zeus's head. Its dog warmth was calming.

The wound on the flank had healed; black fur had grown over the scar.

"We're going home," Rustin said. And then he did what he had imagined himself doing the whole time Big Cronk was gone. He took the gun out of his day pack and placed it in his jacket's right pocket.

The thin circle of clouded sun had sunk past its height when the hauler came through the hayfield. Behind the wheel Big Cronk sat grim-faced, but his reappearance increased Rustin's confidence in the plan. Maybe he was still in charge of his farm. Rustin swung his pack onto the passenger seat and then went around to lower the gate for Zeus. In the rear of the hauler he saw unfamiliar objects—metal rings fastened to the rail with a key in their lock, scraps of rag the color of Stranger clothing scattered around the bed, which was smeared with dried blood.

"The dog stays," Big Cronk said from the driver's seat.

"Zeus goes with me everywhere."

"He'll get excited and scare them. I'll need quiet when I talk to my boy."

Wondering what Zeus might see to excite him, Rustin closed the gate. He had no leverage. "Zeus, you stay. I'll be back." Zeus sat with a look of reproachful despair.

Neither man spoke while the hauler bumped up the hill, mowing down hay stubble and jolting over hidden ruts, past an orchard of fruit trees that had shed most of their leaves, across a dry streambed—as if two strangers happened to be sharing this short ride toward their son and daughter. They passed a grove of trees so swallowed up by vines that it was impossible to tell where one tree ended and another began, and Rustin realized they must have left the Cronk farm and entered uncharted Yeoman land. He began thinking about the drive home. Selva would probably be hungry, but he had just a few biscuits and a tin of fish in his pack. They would try to make it back to the city without stopping, but there was a risk of running out of fuel, and if negotiations over her release took too long they might be caught by darkness, and there would likely be obstacles along the way.

Over the rise of a ravine the quarry appeared below them. "Get down." Big Cronk pulled Rustin's arm toward the seat. Crouching, he saw the striped yellow stone of the quarry wall. Three boys were standing on its edge. One of them seemed to be laughing. From beyond the quarry came a cluster of roars that sounded like neither animal noises nor human voices. Big Cronk kept a hand on Rustin's shoulder, applying pressure. The hauler followed a ledge along the rim of the pit and approached within a few feet of the boys. Above the bottom of the windshield Rustin saw that they wore undershorts and boots and one of them was holding a rifle. Big Cronk turned the wheel away from the boys and the quarry and with a burst of speed the hauler scrambled up the rocks of a short, steep hill. With a hard bounce the hauler came out on level ground.

Big Cronk cried, "No, son!"

Rustin sat up. There was a meadow and a platform where a crowd of creatures in undershorts and boots with bear and bison and bird heads were thrusting, hopping, shrieking, saying, *Haarerrrew! Haarerrrew!* The hauler flew toward them and jolted to a dead stop ten yards away. The creatures parted and revealed a pig that held a glowing piece of metal to the head of a girl, who was his daughter, clutching her goggles.

4

Later, much later, remembering for the thousandth time, Rustin tried to move moment by moment through the worst event of their life, but the sequence always blurred and disintegrated because he had experienced it the first time through radical confusion that he could never organize into a story which made sense.

He always remembered the pig head—the phallic snout, the pointed ears, the sinister, grinning line of mouth. The pig head on the boy's body never left him because it shook loose a fixed truth that had been with him all his life and gave him a glimpse of something he wasn't supposed to see, a curtain pulled back on something shameful. He remembered how Selva wouldn't look at the fiery thing in the pig's hand. There was no terror or abjection in her face, but a pained sorrow the way she'd descended from the Suicide Spot, as if she'd come out of an important exam feeling she'd failed, and he wanted to take the feeling away from her. He remembered the heavy, metallic weight of the gun in his hand in his pocket, and he remembered the difficulty of pulling back the hammer, and the pig convulsing as it fell sideways into Selva, and Selva going down with the pig and the goggles falling from her hand, but he did not remember firing the gun or his thought at the moment it was fired. It was as if he hadn't actually done the thing—it happened with his unwitting participation but not his conscious will.

THE EMERGENCY

When the explosion in his ears died, he became aware of a silence filled with distorting light. The pig head had fallen off. The boy—Gard the Strong—Little Cronk—Big Cronk's son—lay on the platform, his undershirt drenching red, but Rustin didn't grasp what this meant. And now there was something else. Selva was kneeling over the boy and crying "Gard!" and she didn't see what was going to happen. Rustin saw before she did, and none of it made sense, but he tried to get out of the hauler, tripped, and fell on the ground, got up, ran toward the platform. He must have been holding the gun because the creatures scattered. He remembered trying to reach Selva before the little boy with the feral face. It wasn't an animal head but something more wicked, a human child's face with the flat eyes of a wildcat stalking prey. The little boy was gliding almost casually across the platform, and Rustin was running but his legs hardly seemed to move. Selva looked up from the blood just as the little boy picked up the rod from the platform where it had fallen beside the goggles and thrust the burning eye into her face.

Rustin screamed as if the hot hard thing had scorched his own skin and shocked his own brain, but Selva fell without a sound. She lay on the platform with her legs tangled, facing the sky. When he knelt beside her, the smell of burned flesh rose to his nostrils. The left side of her face was melting from her hairline across her singed eyebrow and seared eye to her cheekbone, but he was more concerned with what was happening inside her skull. He put two fingers to her throat and found a rapid pulse. A string of drool slipped from the corner of her mouth.

Throughout the three or four minutes between the gunshot and the moment when, her head lying on his lap and her feet squeezed against the passenger door, he put the hauler in gear and gunned it out of the meadow, he was aware of almost nothing but Selva. For a few seconds at a time the rest of the world intruded. Gathering her in his arms he slipped on the platform's bloody wood and noticed the still body of Little Cronk. As he carried her toward the hauler, the boys from the quarry came running over the lip of the hill, and he took the gun out of his pocket. He must have done the same to the creatures and the feral boy because they had stayed clear. And somewhere a voice of ashes kept moaning, "No, son, no, son." Everything else disappeared except for her and an awareness of himself as two people, one on the outside and one inside: the first stabilizing her head and monitoring her breathing and checking for eye movement; the other screaming.

All the way back to the farm he stayed in low gear, gripping the wheel with his left hand while encircling her head in his right arm, trying not to touch her face. Once he failed to anticipate a bounce, and she moaned. She was alive, but the worst lay ahead when she would come out of shock and start to feel the surface agony of the burn and the deeper bruise to her brain. Even if they reached the city, it could be hours or days before he knew if there was swelling inside the skull, if her face could be repaired, would she lose her eye, would her brain function as it had before, would her life be an arduous struggle for six months or damaged forever, would she still be his Selva or someone else, would she live or die. But out here she would die.

Zeus had left the farrowing barn and was dashing back and forth along the fence of the pigpen, barking his deep bark to warn away a threat. Mrs. Cronk stood on the farmhouse porch with her arms folded across her bosom, looking toward the hauler. She was too far away for Rustin to see her face, but her posture suggested exasperation.

He knew, and she didn't know. But she would soon find out.

"Zeus!" he commanded, then murmured, "I'm sorry." The news of what he'd done could quickly spread and overtake them before they reached the city, and then there would be no way for a Burgher to explain to Yeomen. "Zeus!" he called again, for Zeus hadn't heard—the pigs fascinated him.

Rustin thought of the grinning pig head the moment before it fell off. He had not fired at a boy, or anyone human, but at that barbarous thing, like shooting a venomous snake about to strike his daughter. What was the pig head doing there instead of Little Cronk's? And the other heads around Selva, all making unearthly noises? Some terrible collapse had taken place in that meadow, away from parents and farmwork. The discipline of Yeoman life must not have been enough for those boys, and without it their humanity had turned bitter and contemptible. They had answered a call that sounded nothing like the old language of their fathers, or the high phrases of Together. The call promised danger, darkness, battle, and it thrilled their blood. What did the call say? *Haarerrrew!* "So I lost him," Big Cronk said, and it was finally true.

"Zeus!" Rustin shouted a third time. The spell of the pigs finally broken, Zeus sprinted to the hauler, ears back like a rabbit's and eyes seeking absolution. Rustin eased Selva's head down onto the seat, then went around and opened the passenger door, guiding Zeus to lie curled on the floor beside the pack so that he wouldn't move her, though he licked her hand.

The left side of Selva's face had stopped bubbling and was turning bright red. Rustin removed the gun from his pocket and set it beneath his seat. He took the canteen from his pack and dribbled a capful of water over her burned eye. It was already swollen shut and most of the water ran down her cheek, but he tried to bathe her eye with several more capfuls. He took off his jacket and tore a strip from the cotton lining and laid it gently over the burn to protect her eye from dirt. Then he spread the jacket across her upper body. He had given Monge the medical kit, and there was nothing for her burn or pain until they reached the city by the river. But at least he had Big Cronk's gun, with which he'd shot his son. "I'm sorry," he said again, as they drove up the lane and away from the Cronk farm, thinking, *I'm a Burgher.*

5

The road began to straighten as it descended through the foothills, and Rustin accelerated. The low clouds had cleared and the shadows were lengthening. The land felt empty and silent.

He glanced down at Selva's face. Her uncovered right eye remained closed, but from time to time she cried out. Her breathing was regular and the stench of oily fat was mostly gone, but serous fluid was seeping through the cloth. *I'm going to get you home. Oh, my Sel. Those fucking animals did this to you.* He loved animals, he loved Zeus like one of his children, he would never shoot an animal unless he was starving, he had only shot the pig because of what it was about to do to her, but now he wished he'd emptied the cylinder into the rest of them and the feral boy last with one shot between his wildcat eyes. They were not helpless animals, they were not innocent children, they were not ignorant youths, they had made themselves something lower, so low that they could exult in their own lowness. In the folktales he read to Selva and Pan, the animals that could talk were like us, they had human souls, but a half-man, half-goat or a woman with snakes for hair was pure conscienceless appetite. *I'll shoot the whole pack!*

He didn't know if he had thought or said it until he heard himself shout, "Bam! Bam! Bam!"

The voice of ashes kept saying, *No, son, no, son.* Rustin hardened against it. If those creatures were human, he hated human beings, he had no brothers and sisters. He was out here on his own with the broken fences and smothered trees, responsible only to her.

HE IMAGINED CHECKPOINTS ALL ALONG THE ROAD, EACH MANNED by Yeomen fully informed and awaiting them, but not even the wolf and the bull were on duty at the hedgerows. He'd considered the possibility of a different route back but saw only cow paths leading across fields into woods. The worst thing would be to lose the way, and he stayed on the road.

The last sunlight was burning the silhouetted hills in the west when they passed the field with a fallen barn. The village of the three farmers was up ahead. As gloom closed around the hauler, Rustin kept the headlights off and shivered in his shirt.

Selva was still unconscious, but her moans were growing more frequent and louder, and when they entered the village she began to sob. "Oh God," Rustin said. He went faster, getting ready to drive through any roadblock, and the hauler rattled and coughed as if to announce: *Burghers in the village!*

They were coming up to the meeting hall, the building where the trial had been held, when lights appeared on the roadside, casting a warm yellow-orange glow on the sumac stumps. Then the lights became torches in the hands of people, fifteen or twenty of them, moving quickly from the hall toward the road, flames dimming and brightening on their sticks. The villagers were shouting for the hauler to stop. They seemed taken by surprise, and there was no roadblock. The hauler couldn't muster more speed, but the villagers had nothing fast enough to catch it except perhaps their draft horses. They would also have hunting rifles.

More than fear, a lingering need for order, a respect for rules, made Rustin brake to a stop in the middle of the road. The torches seemed to flicker like the lights of some embattled civilization. He wasn't one of them, they were his enemies, they might try to kill him, he had killed one of them, the gun was under his seat—but a lifelong instinct led him toward rather than away from the society of others. At its heart, he knew this now, lay a doubt about his own inner stuff. Not his title or guild or principles or creed, but an elemental strength that he could summon all alone in the big world.

The torchbearers crowded around the hauler and blocked its way. They were not boys but men and women. Lit from above and below against the darkness, their faces took on the exaggerated expressions of theatrical mimes—astonishment, suspicion, curiosity, fear. Zeus began a low growl that Rustin cut short with a snap of his fingers.

"I know him!" a voice said. "He was here before."

Through the passenger window Rustin recognized one of the three farmers—not Gandorig, but the angry one with the flushed face.

"Yes, Brother Baard, it's me again," Rustin said. "I need help."

Brother Baard held out an imperious hand. "Let's see that thing we gave you. The safe conduct."

Rustin had known this was coming, and a sense of hopelessness overwhelmed him. "I don't have it. The wolf threw it away, or the bull, I don't remember. It's gone."

Brother Baard's color deepened and his eyes frogged out, but before he could say anything a man behind him snorted with disgust. "Ah, those useless sons of bitches."

Selva let out a shriek. She was awake, her good eye open and staring at her father in a way that felt at once strange and familiar. She'd never looked at him like this before, yet it reminded him of something. "Sel, Sel," Rustin murmured, and his hand stroked her hair. The villagers, noticing her for the first time, pushed forward for a better view. Brother Baard poked his torch through her window and moved the light around the interior, and the hauler filled with the smell of burning lamp oil.

"Please don't do that. My daughter is badly hurt."

"What happened?"

"They burned her. See?"

With his thumb and forefinger Rustin carefully lifted a corner of the cloth where it wasn't stuck. The skin over her cheekbone was swollen hot and red. A yellow, egg-shaped bubble had risen under her eye. There were gasps and groans, and a woman's voice cried, "Poor thing!"

"Who burned her?" Brother Baard demanded.

Rustin was trying to establish the crowd's mood, what they knew or didn't know, what they would do if they knew—but thinking dissolved in the ruin of Selva's face.

"Now don't do that," said the man behind Brother Baard.

Rustin had begun to weep. It had been years since he'd wept openly, with sobs that rocked his shoulders. He had held down his grief and shame with the doctor's duty of care, but now that she was awake and looking at him, a tear rolling down her undamaged cheek from her one eye telling him *Don't lose me*, now she was his daughter and he was her father who had let this happen to her, and he couldn't stop.

Outside the hauler, voices swarmed over one another.

"That looks bad."

"He said he was going—"

"They used to stop for plum wine. City people."
"Probably lose that eye."
"Going where?"
"And she was a real pistol."
"By the Cronk farm. Said a boy named Kask—"
"The Cronk farm? That boy calls himself Gard?"
"You don't suppose those animals—"
"Goddamn that Dirt Thought."
"I most certainly do."

Rustin struggled to master himself and listen. The villagers seemed to know of the goings-on at the farm, and to regard them with deep concern. Someone mentioned horse thieves—a rumor of a plot to steal the village draft horses. And it was going to happen tonight—that was why they'd brought torches to the meeting hall. Confusion dissipated as the Burgher arrivals, Selva's burned face, the Cronk farm, and the village horses came together in a single narrative with the magnetic force of collective certainty: Gard and his unit were going to raid the village tonight and steal its horses for an attack with a larger Yeoman force against the city by the river, which would result in the destruction of this village because it was the closest major Yeoman settlement. Selva's injury was proof of the plot—its opening blow.

"Maybe he's part of it," said Brother Baard, his eyes still roaming the hauler as if in search of incriminating evidence.

"Now why the hell do you think that?" asked the man behind him.

"He's a Burgher, isn't he?"

"He's going to attack his own people?"

"Not that. Steal our horses, is what. We let him go once, but I said not to. Now he's back."

In the clamor of voices Rustin realized that the man

arguing with Brother Baard was Leader Gandorig. His gesticulating hand was missing part of a finger.

Selva moaned again and reached for her father's hand on her hair.

"Please," Rustin said, to no one in particular since no one was listening. "We need help."

There was a commotion. Torchbearers were moving aside, and a woman who had been standing near Rustin's window was pushing her way around the front of the hauler. She was a small woman of middle age in a plain housedress, with her hair cut short in back and straight across her brow, and in the torch's glare her birdlike face was twisted with fury. "Shame!" she yelled as she shoved through the crowd. "Shame! Shame! Shame!"

By the far window the woman came to a stop directly in front of Brother Baard. With her free hand she began swatting his chest.

"Shame on you, Baard Stope! Do you see that girl or did someone put out *your* eyes?"

Brother Baard stood stunned and mute while the woman kept striking him with the flat of her hand. Rustin decided that she was his wife. From his cramped hideout on the floor Zeus stared at her with fascination.

"Shame on all of you!" She wheeled around and shone her torch in one face after another. "Stop jabbering like a flock of geese. Aren't you Yeomen? The girl needs help." The voices had already fallen silent with the spectacle of her assault. The woman, no taller than the window's height, leaned in and studied Rustin's face with the same indignation that she'd flung at her husband. "I heard you were a doctor—doctors don't blubber. Don't you have something to give her?"

Rustin explained about the medical kit, but his answer only inflamed the woman more.

"You're no more use than him. Shame!"

"I need something for pain. And to get her to the hospital."

With the magnificent authority of her outrage, the woman organized a relief party. Brother Baard had become an irrelevant bystander. In a few minutes another woman appeared with a handful of white pills. Rustin didn't recognize them, but he broke them up with his thumbnail and placed the fragments on Selva's tongue, then held his canteen to her mouth, and by some act of will that lifted his heart for the first time since the day they'd left the city, she swallowed.

"Now *get*," the woman whispered fiercely. "Get on home before they change their minds." She waved her torch at the people gathered in front. "Stand aside! Emergency coming through!"

Slowly, reluctantly, compelled by a superior force, the torchbearers parted, and the hauler moved down the road.

6

Selva slept and woke and slept while Rustin drove through the moonless night. The shock of the blow was wearing off, and from time to time she began to howl in pain, and he had to remind himself that this was a good sign. He tried to think through her course of treatment at the hospital but could never get past the North Gate because he'd forgotten to ask the villagers for the pass that the Wide Awakes had given him. He had the headlights on to see the road, but it made him nervous to be a large illuminated object moving through the switchgrass fields.

"*I'm sailing across the deep blue sea,*" he sang softly, and glanced down for a quiver of recognition in her face. Her eye was closed in a wince, her lips parted as if to articulate a complaint that never came.

He looked out the windshield. A vast field of stars glittered overhead. Without his jacket the night was very cold. He wished for a way—a book, cigar, game of cards, surgery—to rid his overcharged mind of the thoughts colliding like electrons in his skull.

"Sel, do you remember your constellations? I always forget a few. You know them better than me."

He began to say the names. When he came to Ursa Major, he recited the story of Callisto the bear as if Selva were five years old and hearing it for the first time.

"Then Zeus carried Callisto to the sky, and she was safe there." Selva was moaning softly.

Below her legs he made out a pair of dog eyes turned up to his. There was so much sentience in them, such complete understanding, that it seemed as if Zeus was at last about to speak. The words he longed to utter were right behind his eyes. All he needed was the skill to move his muzzle, and they would come.

"For God's sake, say something." Zeus tilted his head, trying to make sense of the unfamiliar command, ready to do anything in his power.

Aren't you Yeomen? Why did that move him? Baard's wife had instantly recalled an earlier time, before the Emergency, before animal heads and hot irons and guns, before the implacable will in Big Cronk's eyes not to know what Rustin knew—when a Yeoman was someone who came to the aid of an injured child. She was still living in that time. There'd been ignorance for sure, and meanness, and plenty of hardship, but no idea like Dirt Thought had been strong enough to snuff out the impulse that made you wince at someone else's pain. Now all that remained of the old world was a woman's torchlit face disfigured by indignation.

He wondered, far from the first time, at how quickly it had all fallen apart. The empire's skin must have been so thin it could hardly hold the body together. Its cohesion turned out to consist of nothing more than names of streets, rooms in a museum, good manners, thoughtless habits—nothing as strong and deep as common feeling, or truth. As if all along there had been something shoddily made, flimsy and fake, about a whole way of life. Yet he had lived as if it would last forever. Even with the Emergency, while he was inside the city walls he continued to believe that any conflict could be averted face to face, with words. Burghers and Yeomen could sit down and establish why the produce trucks had stopped coming, what past injustices needed redress, how to reintegrate the two sides in a new system acceptable to both.

But he had seen the shameful thing at the quarry, and he could never forget it.

When he was a small boy, his father had taught him the names of all the constellations. His father had been a general practitioner and a solemn man of a generation that struggled to find words for their children, but one night on a fishing trip not far outside the city they had stood together on the riverbank and his father had pointed out the lighted figures, human and animal, across the sky. That knowledge had imposed an order on the world as reassuring as the empire itself, had brought the sky near like the painted ceiling of a room in which he was growing up. He used to test himself by picking out the familiar arrangements of stars until he had counted them all. Later, he passed on the secrets of the universe to his children, hoping they would do the same with theirs.

But tonight in the moonless darkness of the switchgrass plains he couldn't find the constellations. There were too many stars, they were too far away, the patterns eluded him. He shivered again. Something cold and random in the night sky was frightening him, and he lowered his eyes to the road. If the tiny, infinitely fragile girl whose head was resting in his lap died, the stars wouldn't care. His loss wouldn't trouble the universe; it would be unutterable, would barely make a sound. And she *would* die, sooner or later, and so would he, and all of them, and everything he cared about would vanish to a cosmic shrug. The stars would go on glittering in their immense indifference. He had never truly known this before.

They weren't human—that was the thing about constellations. They were lucky that way, the stars. What good is it to feel and know and love when it will break you up in the end? No wonder children want to become something else—animals or machines. The Manager at the workshop said something about that—something about a cactus in your brain. "What's wrong with them? What's wrong with *you*?" Because a human being turns out to be the most ridiculous thing in the world. Just asking for it. Asking for a reason and getting a punch in the face. *Human First*? More like *Human Last*.

What a funny little Rustin I am, with my operating theater, my code of ethics and coat of arms and these leather shoes. Articulate sack of shit. Skull full of ideas floating on the deep blue sea. But it's not funny if the universe doesn't laugh.

Again he saw the pig head fall. "I was supposed to take care of you." She was far away and didn't hear.

If the world is going to have a boy with a pig head in it—because we must have given them nothing—who are you to think you can think for yourself? All that matters is taking care of her, and you didn't do it, and you can't do it all alone out here under these stars. Look at what a funny little Rustin you are. You have to join a side, any side, whatever they call it, Together, Dirt Thought, and it doesn't matter if they believe in Stranger Friends and metal gods or birds shitting vines and Gard the Great, because who are you to think for yourself? You have to join a side.

He was on any side that didn't try to kill his daughter.

7

They were on the hard road now, and it was easier to tell that she was breathing, but he held his palm above her face to feel the warmth of her breath. From time to time a howl tore out of her, followed by sobbing that slowly ebbed to dry shudders and then stillness.

Suddenly the hauler sputtered as if it was about to let out its own cry of pain. Her right eye opened. He knew from a glint, a tiny light of recognition, that she was looking at him.

"Sel, can you hear me? It's Papa."

Her lips moved but no sound came.

"You understand me! That's good." He began using his post-op voice, for his own sake more than hers. "I know it hurts. You're being brave. Brave Selva. We're on our way home. We'll be there soon. I'll get you to the hospital and you'll feel better."

The hauler jolted again.

"Damn!" His surgeon's composure disintegrated. Here in the middle of the plains, half an hour from the North Gate, they were going to run out of fuel. And then what? Carry her to the city? "Damn fool Burgher!"

A quarter mile ahead lights were flickering on the right side of the road. The monotony of the plains made it hard to know for sure, but from the semicircle of dwellings he thought this might be the last and the first Yeoman settlement, the one that had greeted them a few days ago with a hurled rock. Quickly he switched off the headlights.

The roadside settlements here survived partly by selling home goods to travelers—garden vegetables, linens woven from flax, jars of linseed oil. Kask had said that the hauler ran on switchgrass fuel. Next to the road, with miles of fields all around, the local Yeomen must have plenty of it stored somewhere.

He brought the hauler to a stop on the dirt shoulder. He was thinking through a plan. It depended on too many guesses and chances, but he saw no other way.

She was still looking at him with her one eye. He kept the engine running, and with almost no fuel left it hardly made a sound. "Sel, I have to get something important. I won't be gone long. If you need me, if it's urgent, just one honk. I'll hear it." He took her hand where it was folded with the other over his jacket and set it on the hauler's horn. "One honk. Zeus will stay with you." Her lips tightened; he couldn't tell if she understood. He eased her head down on the seat and climbed out of the hauler and stuffed the gun inside his pocket. He was about to tell Zeus not to follow, but Zeus hadn't moved.

The lights were a hundred yards away—no farther than the walk from the rowhouse to the tram stop, Rustin told himself, as if this calculus could improve the odds of success. He didn't dare use his torch, but the flint gave him just enough flickering light to see the ground at his feet. He wasn't worried about traps, but he feared stumbling on an uneven patch of dirt and making a noise that would travel across the silence to the settlement. He didn't know these people. He didn't know the people in Gandorig's village either, but a prior contact had made the encounter a little less threatening.

In front of the settlement a produce truck was standing on the roadside. A length of timber ran from the ground up to the lowered gate of the bed. Someone was slowly mounting it with a pail in hand, and someone else stood on the gate, working with a shovel. Rustin stopped short and realized with relief that his own clothes were dark. On the side of the yard closest to the road lamplight shone in the clay-brick house. Three squat structures curved behind it into darkness. He left the road and cut through the field that he thought he remembered, finding his footing on the crumbling dirt with each step, approaching the outbuildings from the back of the settlement. He breathed deeply, trying to locate the warm, baked-bread odor of switchgrass fuel. But what he smelled instead was manure.

The smell was coming from a structure closest to the field. He hadn't known that these Yeomen owned cows or horses. As he drew near, the smell became something so much worse than manure that he had to move away into the field as he passed. It was human excrement—fresh, black, dense shit. The stench was so overpowering that the entire pit must have been full up. Why didn't they douse their latrine with ashes or kerosene? Rustin was professionally familiar with all the juices of life and death—urine, feces, blood, bile, pus, rot—but he had to stifle a retch.

The outbuildings were hardly more than sheds, all in a state of disrepair. He wondered if these people were too poor to have anything to sell. Inside the third shed, separated from the back of the house by just a few yards, he found a wooden barrel that looked like a cask of millet beer. When he removed the lid, the surface on which a ladle was floating gleamed oily. Even here the smell from the latrine was too strong for him to be sure this was switchgrass fuel until he bent over the barrel and inhaled.

He found a canister in a corner of the shed and was about to pick up the ladle when he heard a noise. He ducked under the window and peered out. The back door of the house opened, lamplight fell on the ground, and a figure small enough to be a child came out into the yard. Rustin thought he recognized the boy who had thrown the rock. He was walking toward the latrine, carrying a pail, and for a moment Rustin thought he was going to deposit the family's night soil. Then the boy stopped and turned around to speak to someone inside the doorway.

"Why do I have to?"

"All the men are doing it," a young woman's voice said. "You're almost a man now."

"But I don't want to."

"Shh. Just go on. They need help. It's getting late, they have plenty more stops."

As the boy continued toward the latrine, a man appeared from around the side of the house. He was also carrying a pail, and wearing overalls and boots to his knees. "What's taking your boy so long?" he growled.

"It's not work he's used to," the young woman said apologetically.

"Everyone has to do their part."

"He'll do his part."

From the latrine came the noise of the boy gagging, the pail clanking, a thick splash, then the creak of a heavy chain being pulled to the sound of the boy's grunts. A minute later he came out of the shed. The pail was now so heavy that it turned his body lopsided.

"Go on around to the truck," the man said. "Climb up the ramp and throw it in the bed, you're big enough. If you need help, ask my partner." As the boy struggled through the yard, the man called after him, "Don't fall in!"

"He's just ten," the young woman said. "He's still a boy."

"Other families, I've got six-year-olds carrying pails. Everyone has to do their part."

"We're doing our part," she said. "Been saving it all week, ever since we were told to."

"How many are you?"

"Just me and the four children. That makes five."

"Where's their father?"

The young woman made a noise of spitting out something bitter. "Left me for millet beer."

"Well, that's a shame."

The man disappeared into the shed, followed by the noise of metal rattling and chain clanking. He came back out into the yard with the full pail and paused by the lighted doorway, from which the young woman hadn't moved.

She said, "We appreciate all you're doing for the Yeoman people."

"Being by yourself out here on the front line—you might need help," the man said. "I work at the Tall Pine lumber mill, where the river takes that big bend."

"You think something's going to happen out here?"

"Something's already happened. One of them shot a boy dead in the hills."

There was a sharp intake of breath. "When?"

"Just today. That's why we're collecting tonight. We were going to wait a week, but there's no time. We want to hit them before they do something big."

"But how—" She left the question hanging as if it would be indelicate to finish.

"Built a machine on wheels that can send it clear over the walls. Fire, move, fire, move."

The young woman released an involuntary snort of hilarity. "A shitapult."

The man didn't laugh. "They'll go lower than that if we give them a chance."

"You just can't keep the Yeomen down."

Rustin crouched, holding his nose, straining to hear, waiting for a distress call from the hauler's horn. But the trips to the latrine continued for a quarter hour, until the man came out of the shed dragging the empty pail by the chain and announced, "That's your quota." He went to a pump in the middle of the yard and worked the handle, splashing water over the bucket and chain and his boots. "Good job, son," he told the boy, who was standing by the back door where the figure of the young woman was silhouetted against the light inside the house. The man walked through the yard a final time, carrying the pail with the chain around his neck. "Don't forget," he said. "Tall Pine lumber mill. Ask for Steny."

"I won't forget," the young woman said. "See you around, Steny."

8

Ladling switchgrass fuel into the canister and crossing the field without spilling took another ten minutes. By the time Rustin reached the hauler and filled the tank, the noise of the produce truck had disappeared up the road in the direction of the city, its lights extinguished by the night. Selva's hand still lay on the horn, and her eye was open. There was no relief in it, or anger or fear, or expression of any kind, but he saw that she had been waiting for him. In some way he existed for her.

He was going to tell her what he had just seen and heard, then thought better of it. Too upsetting if she understood. He could hardly believe it himself, and as they drove the last miles to the city, leaving the switchgrass plains behind for the marshy hardwood groves, joining the river and following it past the new Burgher settlements, which were dark and quiet in the midnight hour, he was unable to think of anything else. But thinking yielded no real thoughts, only a kind of horrified stupor. Their project mesmerized him. Maybe that was its genius. There was something so audacious about it, so inventive and barbaric, so *low*, as the man with the pail had said. It would break through the final restraint, and there would be no going back. Nothing could restore the brittle illusion of civilization that had allowed the empire to last so long. They could survive gunfire, but not a shitapult. It was going to smear them all.

He tried to imagine a hatred so deep and hot that it had led to this. His own hatred of the animals who had hurt Selva fell short. It was possible to think of killing them, but not doing this. He saw it as a failing in himself, almost a lack of military preparedness, one that might end up costing him dearly, and he clung to the image of the pig head and the boy with feral eyes.

Rustin was wondering how many trucks were involved in the operation and what time it would start, when up ahead loomed the high arch of the North Gate.

The objects that had been inside the gate before now formed an obstacle course on the other side, forcing Rustin to slow down. Behind the barrier half a dozen guards stood warming themselves around a barrel fire, their uniforms glowing dark green. The first to hear the hauler's engine grabbed the rifle that was slung over her shoulder and raised it to the firing position. Rustin recognized her as the same guard, the Wide Awake, who had asked for his papers when they were leaving the city. She shouted a command—it sounded like "Ready positions!"—and the other guards produced rifles with an efficiency that amazed Rustin.

He came to a stop ten feet in front of the gate. A whole squad of Wide Awakes held the hauler in its sights. The guns were old bolt-action rifles but alarming all the same. From the floor Zeus was barking wildly.

"Cover me, Iver!" the squad commander said. She walked around the barrier, still aiming at Rustin on her approach, while a boy, the same boy who had been at the gate the day of their departure, who had invaded the hospital with the looters, who had sat next to Selva in school, trailed behind with his rifle raised.

When the commander came up to Rustin's window, she

lowered her rifle. "It's you." She looked astonished to see him, and not unhappy. She glanced at the boy standing behind her, who was still pointing his gun while his face twitched in a spasm that he seemed to be trying to master. "It's him, Iver. Humanitarian mission."

This was a better reception than Rustin had expected. Perhaps it wouldn't matter that he'd lost his "Safer Together" pass. He was about to explain about Selva when the commander stepped back from the window.

"Hands on the wheel! Hugo Rustin, you are under arrest on charges of consorting with the Yeoman enemy. Step out of the vehicle."

Her assurance was remarkable. In a few short days she had acquired an air of absolute command. But Rustin didn't move. "How can I step out with my hands on the wheel?"

"Do what I told you."

He sighed. The words "under arrest" were unnerving, but he felt that they had been coming at him for days, for weeks—at the hospital, in Gandorig's village, on the Cronk farm. He was tired of defending himself, and he found that a fine edge of rage on Selva's behalf was giving him courage. "Do you see my daughter here?" He lifted the corner of the fabric from her cheek. She shrieked with pain. "I'm taking her to the hospital."

The commander leaned forward to look through the window and winced. Iver lowered his rifle and stepped toward the hauler, and his face crumpled. "Oh no, Selva!"

"The Yeoman enemy we were consorting with? They did this to her."

"One of us will take her," the commander said.

"You're welcome to come along, but I'm her father and I'm a doctor and I'm taking her."

Rustin saw that he had created a dilemma for them all. He decided to resolve it.

"I'm surrendering myself to your custody. Remand me to the Wide Awake unit at the hospital. I have valuable intelligence for them. But my daughter shouldn't be moved, she has a serious head injury. I'll drive and one of your squad can ride in the bed." He thought of something else, and even prepared the words: *Under my seat you'll find a pistol for confiscation. There are five rounds left in the cylinder.* But he didn't say them.

The conference that followed was into its third minute when Rustin told the commander that he would drive under armed guard or alone but he was continuing to the hospital. She scowled, wrote something down in a notebook, ordered the barrier to be lifted, and appointed Iver to ride in the hauler.

Rustin sped through late-night streets that he knew from countless prolonged surgeries. There were always a few people out—solitary men on their way home from working or drinking, lovers embracing against an alley wall, trash collectors making early rounds, an Excess Burgher asleep on a tram-stop bench. Public life had temporarily withdrawn, but the streets were waiting to be filled again, and you could hear the city breathing even if it didn't speak. But this Sunday night felt as empty as the foothills and the switchgrass plains, or like the first days of the Emergency—abandoned. The houses and shops of the Heights District had lost their human purpose, and without it they'd turned to lifeless stone and brick and glass.

He had counted on being familiar to himself in the city where he belonged. But it was just like out there.

"What's happened?" Rustin said over his shoulder to Iver,

who was squatting at the front of the bed with his rifle across his knees.

"I'm sorry?" He had been staring through the back of the cab at Selva.

"There's no one around."

"Oh—just a precaution. They issued an advisory for people to stay indoors this weekend. In case of unexpected events." Iver seemed to have memorized the phrases.

"What are we unexpecting?"

In the mirror Rustin saw the joke draw a blank, then a look of anxiety, and he remembered that he was under arrest. He recalled Iver's face that day with the looters, the face of a boy who had grown up without ever hearing a word of encouragement, a year or two away from ruin. Now his hair was clean and trimmed short, and the aggrieved look was gone.

"You've done well, Iver."

"Sorry, sir?"

"You were down on your luck when we first met. Now you have a position."

"Together gave me a chance. The city never had any use for me. That's what's different now."

"Did you think you'd be wearing a uniform and carrying a gun?" The question made Iver so uncomfortable that his Adam's apple bobbed and he glanced down at his uniform. "What does Together mean to you now?" Rustin pressed.

"That's—I'm not supposed to talk to you." Around a corner the red and white lights on the hospital's brick façade flashed into view. "Will Selva be all right, sir?"

"Yes," Rustin said immediately. "She's going to be herself again."

It took much too long for anyone to appear at the entrance. At last a security guard in the olive-green uniform of the Wide Awakes came out of the glass doors. Rustin had never seen him, and the guard didn't seem to know the chief surgeon. While they waited for a stretcher, Rustin rummaged in his pack and gave a few biscuits to Zeus, who hadn't eaten since morning, then watered him from the canteen. A few more agonizing minutes passed before an orderly arrived. They lifted Selva out of the hauler and placed her on the stretcher. Zeus climbed up on the seat where she'd been lying as if to hold it until she came back.

In Rustin's twenty years there had never been an hour of the day or night when the hospital wasn't busy. That had always been part of its hold on him—the subdued frenzy, the hive of workers all following separate paths that somehow didn't collide but belonged to a single pattern leading to a common goal. But he encountered no one as they hurried her down the corridor to the examination room and Iver tried to keep up while managing the unfamiliar burden of his rifle. On the wall Rustin noticed signs that hadn't been there before. It had been less than two weeks, but he had the sense of having been away from the hospital for a very long time, months and months.

He was going to have to do it with no nurse or assistant, and that was what he wanted—to be alone with his daughter. He told Iver to stand outside the door. He scrubbed and snapped on a pair of gloves over his flannel shirt cuffs. The hospital felt colder than the night outside, and he asked Iver to find a blanket and pillow, and Iver complied as if the order of things had been reversed and Rustin was in charge.

When he pulled the fabric from the left side of her face, her scream was almost more than he could bear. What a stupid idea to cover it! The dark-red glossy skin around her eyebrow began to weep, but the egg-shaped blister on her cheekbone was still intact. The left eye was swollen shut and leaking serous fluid where the lids were stuck together. He examined her under the dazzle of the lamp while her right eye, swimming in tears, watched him. The pattern of the burn looked like an oval with her eye at its center and a stripe across her forehead. The pig's iron had been wrought with some kind of intricate tip, like a letter on a cattle brand. He wasn't used to treating injuries like this—emergency medicine was far in his professional past—but it was obvious that he should cleanse the burn, apply ointment, and hook her up to fluids. He also gave her pain medication stronger than what Brother Baard's wife had procured.

All the while he was looking for signs of brain activity. It was good that her one eye was open, she responded to pain, and her neck didn't appear stiff, but when he gave verbal cues, nothing came back. "What's our dog's name?" he asked. Her eye filled with an effort to answer, but the only sound she made was a gurgle that buzzed her lips. From the beginning he had feared that a second-degree face burn might not be the worst of it. Selva's keen mind was buried alive, suffocating. He wanted to hear her voice, to hear her say anything, anything—even "I want to burn up the past."

He dreaded taking off his medical gloves, but there was nothing more for him to do. He switched off the lamp and laid his hand on her head. He bent to kiss her hair. "Sleep, Sel. You need sleep."

From the doorway there was a noise of a throat being cleared. Iver was standing at attention, rifle at his side. Next to him was Saron, his hands in the pockets of the director's coat.

"Come with me, Hugo."

9

"Did you know your wife was sitting in that chair just yesterday?" Saron asked when they were facing each other across the director's desk.

"My wife? She was here?"

Saron clearly enjoyed Rustin's surprise. "Annabelle said you'd gone camping with your daughter. When that didn't fly, she came up with a heroic tale about an injured Stranger boy. Okay, Hugo. Why don't you tell me what you've been doing in Yeoman country."

Rustin felt that he must say exactly the right thing. A single slip, a suspicious detail, and he might never see his family again. But everything had gotten confused with the strange atmosphere of the city, Selva's face under the examination lamp, the resident wearing the director's coat, the image of Annabelle in this office, the sound of her name in his mouth, the shock of jealous fear it had sent up Rustin's spine. This young doctor, barely out of the Imperial Medical College, always had the better of him.

"What she told you is true. But things took a turn for the worse, and I couldn't help the boy. Then my daughter—" He saw it all happening again and shut his eyes for a moment. "They hurt her. I saw something out there." Saron was listening with a kind of skeptical reserve, not openly derisive, but without interest in Selva. "And you were right."

"What was I right about?"

"Yeomen. They believe insane things. They hate us. They were going to kill my daughter." Even as he spoke he was thinking: *Not Big Cronk. Or that woman, Brother Baard's wife. I even felt sorry for the switchgrass mother with the four kids. And Little Cronk is dead.* But he snuffed the thought and crushed the softening in his chest.

Saron leaned back in his chair and allowed himself a faint smile. Rustin had never seen Saron smile before; it only intensified the hostility in his eyes.

"I'll tell you what I think happened. You had your little problem here at the hospital. You went out there to be the Great Burgher Savior—whoever needed you, Strangers, Yeomen. Were you actively providing aid and comfort to the enemy? I don't know, but it doesn't matter. You were behaving recklessly—just ask your daughter. You can't be trusted in this city. That's why you were arrested."

"I understand the situation now. And I want to help you."

Saron let out an ostentatious, humorless laugh. "So you've changed your mind about Together?"

"If Together defends my family. I'm a Burgher. I'm on your side."

"Why should I care, Hugo? Do you remember telling me that how you think is none of my business?"

Rustin didn't remember saying this, but he was going to accept whatever humiliations Saron chose to inflict. A few short weeks ago he had been the hospital's chief surgeon and Saron an inexperienced resident, one of many, barely licensed. But Saron had understood the lay of the land and played it beautifully, while he had imagined a role that didn't exist. *Be true to yourself and see the world truly.* He was learning what it really meant.

Instead of answering, he told Saron what he had learned

about Dirt Thought, about the unit training on the Cronk farm, the violence there, the preparations around the countryside for some kind of action, the nighttime collection in the switchgrass plains . . .

Saron was cleaning his glasses in order to remain noncommittal, but at the word "shitapult" he slammed the hand that held his handkerchief down on the desk. "That's impossible."

"This is what they're planning."

"Not even they would do this."

"You saw my daughter. It's exactly what they'd do. It's who they are."

"But why?"

"To demoralize us. To bring us down where they are. To show anything is possible."

Saron began clenching his jaws as Rustin had seen him do at the Restoration Ring. "How far over the walls?"

"I don't know. A lot of the city could be exposed." Rustin realized that both the hospital and the Rowhouse District, at opposite ends of the city, would likely be within range.

Saron returned the glasses to his face, already calculating how to respond to the threat. Together was a lofty and capacious idea, but Saron was practical, narrow, hard. You had to be hard to turn a schoolboy failure into a Wide Awake (Iver was still standing at attention by the office door), and you had to be hard to thrust a hot iron into a girl's face. This must be the type that came to the fore in any emergency. Perhaps Together and Dirt Thought, though philosophical opposites and mortal enemies, had something in common at a level that wasn't easy to see—an uncompromising quality that struck a hidden chord in the young.

"We don't have to like each other, do we, Hugo?" Saron asked.

"Of course not."

"The problem is, I don't know whether to trust you," he said, with what sounded like genuine uncertainty. "I'm going to give you a chance to prove yourself. Till then you're in my custody."

Rustin waited.

"We've asked Burghers to stay off the streets while we summon our Yeomen for orientation. Compliance rates have been pretty good, except for the Warehouse District. Do you know someone there?"

"A Yeoman? Yes, named Kask." Saron nodded—he seemed to be familiar with the name. "But what do you mean, orientation?"

"Obviously, we have to keep an eye on our Yeomen if their cousins are going to start a shitstorm."

"How are they being oriented?" Saron didn't answer. "And I'm to do what?"

"Bring this man Kask here."

"Why? What will happen to him?"

"Bring him here." Saron abruptly stood up.

"Iver's going with me?"

"Better if you go alone."

"I really don't want to leave my daughter."

"She's here with us now."

It took Rustin a moment to pick up the whiff of menace.

10

It was still dark when he came out of the hospital. He hadn't eaten in almost twenty-four hours, and a wave of nauseous hunger dizzied him. The last of the biscuits had gone to Zeus, who was thumping his tail on Selva's seat where Rustin had left him. The only food in the pack was a tin of oily fish. He couldn't face eating it. Then he thought of going home.

For days Annabelle had been hovering on the edge of his awareness. She was rarely a conscious subject but always a presence, inside and around him, like the haze surrounding a lamp on a foggy night, or background music he wasn't quite listening to. He wasn't making an effort not to listen, but whenever the music rose to his ears he felt a quiver of pain and shut it out. He knew that the pain had to do with longing and shame and the unfinished things between them, from the morning of his departure extending back through the whole of the Emergency to all their years together. And now he saw her standing in the front room; he saw her face, not angry or frightened, but with a look of inexpressible, irremediable sadness. Not just for Selva but for what he had let happen to them all.

When she worried, especially when she worried about her family, Annabelle slept badly. Even now, before dawn, she was probably awake. But he wouldn't go home yet. First he wanted to sort things out at the hospital. He wanted to make sure Selva was safe—to show Saron whose side he was on. He drove to the Warehouse District.

At the turnoff into the maze of huddled dwellings and gaping façades, he thought of the gun that he'd left under the seat. It was still there. He was wearing his jacket again, with the lavender fragrance of Selva's soap on the shoulders, and he stowed the gun in its pocket.

The dominant feature of the district—the infernal noise of engines and tools and men—was gone. A ghostly quiet met him as he navigated the dark streets and tried to avoid colliding with junked machinery or falling into watery potholes. He didn't know where Kask had rooms, or whether he was here at all, so he drove deeper in the direction that he thought he remembered would take him to the street of vehicle parts, seeing no landmarks, getting hopelessly lost. All the while he had the sense of being watched from alleys and high windows.

He was jolting along a narrow cobblestone lane that ran between a canal and a row of warehouses. A vague feeling of familiarity came over him. On a brick façade the hauler's lights caught the nearly illegible words ELECTRICAL AND PLUMBING SUPPLY, and Rustin realized where his wandering had brought him. He wasn't surprised. On some level he had known from the moment Saron had mentioned the Warehouse District that he would end up here.

There was nowhere to park except in the middle of the lane. Rustin turned off the engine and cut the lights. Getting out with his pack, he slipped and nearly fell on the slimy stones. He gestured for Zeus to come, and Zeus, confined for hours, bounded out of the hauler as if they were about to go for a long walk in the park, then ran nose to the ground sniffing madly over to the canal and flitted back and forth between new smells, trying to get rid of his pent-up energy.

A corrugated gate was shut over the warehouse bay and padlocked to a metal plate screwed into the cobblestones. To the left of the gate there was a mullioned window. The panes were so filthy that Rustin could make out nothing inside, only a murky stillness.

He was contemplating smashing the nine panes one at a time with a loose stone when he noticed that the warehouse was bordered by an alley. He took the torch from his pack and followed the alley down, led by Zeus, who chased after the scuttling noise of a small creature. A mound of metal scraps and rods and wiring and broken pieces of clay was piled against the warehouse wall. Just past it, before the alley came to a dead end at a fence, there was a low wooden door made of vertical boards held together by a diagonal brace, like a coal door. Perhaps this was where the Manager got rid of unwanted parts. Rustin pressed down on the thumb latch and pushed. The door was loosely bolted on the inside. He had never broken into a building. He stepped back and gave the door a hard kick, and it flew open with a sound of splintering wood.

He was in a cramped, low-ceilinged room. It had a pleasant smell of lubricating oil and melted wax. The light of his torch found a table with scattered papers, clay masks strewn across the floor, and, in a corner, a pile of bronze knobs like the one he'd seen on Selva's throat. It was the office of the Manager. He'd come bustling out of this room to reprimand an intruder: *No, no, no! Absolutely not!* Rustin stood and listened. At this hour the workshop seemed empty.

He went to the table and picked up a sheet of paper

covered with neat scholarly writing in black ink. At the top of the page he read:

> *Wants to stop stuttering. Tangled fingers. Father a city councilor. Hopeless case?*

Farther down:

> *Can't stop being herself. Words words words. Potential learning model for others.*

Was this Selva? Her teachers always used that word, *model*. His eyes scanned the rest of the page and the pages around it for anything that might refer to her. In the middle of an otherwise empty sheet that had been crumpled up and then inadequately smoothed out were lines written in a looser, unsteady hand:

> *They smell like the living—sour secreting things. We are the flaw in the design. Erase these faces, replace them with a perfect world. My lovely gods!*

The words woke a longing in him. Yes, that was it. My Selva, my perfect girl. He had let the animals do it to her and there could be no forgiveness for them or him, but on the other side of that high steel door she lay waiting, calling *Come get me, Papa, don't lose me* in a strong, clear voice that was hers. It had gone silent because the animals had hurt her mind and tried to erase her face, but they couldn't touch this god, and when she spoke again the sound of her voice would repair the world.

He set the paper down. Zeus had gone to the steel door

and was sniffing and whining as if he knew a beloved was on the other side. This door was unlocked and opened easily inward. Rustin confronted a cavernous darkness. The only light was a smear of streetlamp through the mullioned window on the far wall. He looked up into the void of the ceiling for the familiar constellations, but they weren't there, nothing was there. He was afraid to move for fear of stepping on someone. Then he heard a rattle of metal, and his torch found Zeus tentatively pawing at a shoulder. When the boy's face lit up, Zeus leapt away and crouched for a fight and barked until Rustin shushed him: "He's friendly." But Zeus would only compromise with a steady growl, stepping forward, pawing, jumping back.

Rustin ran his torch across the workshop floor. Slowly the darkness gave up a sea of bodies. They seemed far more numerous than last time, and alive, all alive. They lay side by side looking up into space like a gathering of young stargazers in a field on a night when a comet would appear. He had seen nothing up there, but they waited and watched with breathless hope. They were the city's children, its future, dreaming a new world to life. From the moment he'd seen the shameful thing at the quarry he'd been trying to get back to this place, for if humans did such things, became such things, they would need to be better than, other than, human. Here was everything beautiful and good and true.

Gratitude flooded Rustin's heart, and he gave himself to the vision of Together.

It took a long time to find her. He had left her somewhere near the front of the workshop, but the Better Humans must have been rearranged, for Annabelle's dress was nowhere in the rows closest to the corrugated gate. He wondered if Selva had changed clothes—then he was struck by the terrible thought that the Manager had gotten rid of her, thrown her out with the scraps in the alley. Too smart, too difficult, too many words. "Where's Selva, Zeus, where is she?" Rustin called, and he heard panic rising in his own voice. Zeus stared at his master, utterly confused without a scent to know her.

Rustin was beginning to despair when his torch caught a flash of red near the alley wall. *There you are.* "Thank God!" he said aloud. In his hurry he tripped over a young girl in the uniform jumper of primary school. "Sorry," he muttered, but he kept tripping over others, not apologizing, never letting Selva out of his sight. When he came to her side, he knelt and wrapped his arms under her shoulders and hugged her to his chest and pulled her head to his. He kissed her cheek. "Here you are, my Sel, my Sel." He drew away to look at her face. Smooth, untarnished olive skin; mouth with the slight overbite beginning to smile in expectation of something wonderful; almond eyes, both of them open, gazing into his to say *You found me*.

He ran his fingertips along her cheek. "Look at you. You're perfect."

He was aware of running out of time with another urgent thing to do, but he couldn't resist reaching for the knob. He turned it clockwise three times as the Manager had done. There was the whirring sound, and then the voice that seemed to come from far away: "*Father, drink from my golden cup.*"

He had heard this before. "Can you say something else, love?" He gave the knob another quarter turn.

"*Drink and grow young through me.*"

"What do you mean? No, don't worry, we'll have plenty of time. We're together. And Zeus, too. Look who's here, Zeus!" But instead of sniffing her hand or jumping up to lick her face, Zeus was watching Rustin closely, his tail drooping, losing confidence as he waited for some command to make sense.

Rustin gathered Selva in his arms. Trailed by Zeus, he carried her out of the workshop through the office and into the alley just as he'd carried her injured from the platform to the hauler. Only she was lighter now, and he felt lighter, too, free of the churn in his chest, and the sight of her face didn't make him want to cry; he no longer flinched to look at it.

They came out onto the street in front of the warehouse. The sky was beginning to lighten over the rooftops across the canal. Beside the hauler stood two men holding metal rods.

"I thought it was you," one of them said.

Under the watch cap his face was hard to make out in the early dawn gloom, but Rustin knew Kask from the swell of his body as it sank downward through his jumpsuit into the belly and hips. The other man, tall and bony, was familiar as well. From his vacant eyes and the droop of his jaw he was obviously another Yeoman. As Rustin approached, both men looked at Selva and then looked away as if her presence embarrassed them.

"Didn't I tell you?" Kask said to the other man. "I knew from the hauler."

"That was clever of you, Kask," Rustin said.

"You here to return it?"

"Not yet. I would have already, but your people delayed me."

"My people?" Rustin's tone broke through Kask's good nature and put him on alert. "Something go wrong out there? I tried to warn you."

"You did. Even about Dirt Thought." Rustin found himself enraged by the intrusion on his happiness of these two

Yeomen with metal rods—the boys at the quarry reappeared in the city as grown-ups. "Did you know what those animals were up to? Did you mean for me to run out of fuel?"

Kask didn't answer but only shook his head.

"I'm glad to see you, doctor," the other man said. "You might not remember—"

"I remember. I removed two bullets from your son. Not something I'd forget."

The boy's father smiled. "That's right. His mother and I thank you. But our boy's having some problems, which is why—"

"You never told me how he got shot. You just said something about games. What kind of games was he playing with guns?"

The men exchanged a look. Neither of them seemed able to read Rustin, and his illegibility and Selva's presence had them on the defensive, though this was Kask's district and they were armed. Rustin brushed his elbow against the hard shape in his pocket and felt a surge of pleasure at the power it gave him over these Yeomen.

"Target practice," the father said. "Just being stupid boys."

"Training?" Rustin asked. After a moment the other nodded. "What was his animal of choice?" The father shook his head to show ignorance. "Was it a scorpion? I'll bet it was a scorpion."

Kask took off his cap and pretended to study it. Rustin recognized this as his way of dealing with awkwardness. "I think something's got you angry, doc," he said, as mildly as a big man with a metal rod could.

"I don't like being surprised with my daughter by armed Yeomen on a dark street."

"Your dau—?" Kask started to say. Then he laid his rod

down on the cobblestones and gestured for the other man to do the same. "We're with the district watch. Things took a turn while you were gone." He nodded at Selva. "We're protecting our children just like you."

"From what? We don't hurt children here. I saved this idiot's son."

"Like I said, things took a turn."

"The hospital won't see him anymore," the father said. "That's what I wanted to tell you."

"Do you blame them? Born a Yeoman, die a Yeoman, right, Kask? Isn't that what you said? Dirt to dirt." Before he knew what he was saying, Rustin added, "I wish I'd never operated on him. Your son would have been with the animals that killed my daughter. What am I going to tell her mother?"

The father's slack mouth gaped. Kask looked hard into Rustin's eyes as if searching for some truth behind them.

"Come on," Rustin said. "I'll take you to the hospital. Get in back."

When neither man moved, Rustin hoisted Selva over his shoulder with one arm and reached in his pocket with the other hand. He brought out the gun to display rather than aim. A shadow of surprise fell across Kask's face, and then a kind of wounded disappointment that troubled Rustin. But he resolved to be worthy of his perfect girl.

"Get in back, Kask."

11

Selva lay exactly as she had throughout the long night's drive, her head resting on her father's lap, her feet propped against the opposite door. Zeus was in his curled position on the floor beneath her, but now he paid her no attention and instead gazed at Rustin with anxious eyes. Kask was standing in the bed, wrists cuffed to the rail. The boy's father had asked to go, too, but Rustin had refused—it would be hard enough to manage one of them.

The drive to the hospital would have taken no more than ten minutes through empty streets, but outside the Warehouse District the city was beginning to emerge from its withdrawal. An early tram was half full. At street corners Wide Awakes in uniform helped schoolchildren across the main avenue. Burghers came walking and cycling out of the Heights District for exercise or work. A few turned to stare at the hauler.

As Rustin drove he kept fiddling with the knob at her throat to distract himself from the Yeoman prisoner whom he was bringing to Saron, and who wouldn't stop talking.

"My daughter wanted one of those," said Kask's voice behind and above Rustin. "You know how kids are. We live two blocks from the workshop, and she sees all these kids coming and going, and she gets curious. One day she stops a boy her age—she's twelve—and the boy tells her all about these Better Humans. Never heard anything like it. You can imagine how curious she got."

"*Father, your fair-ankled daughter attends you,*" Selva said as she looked into his eyes. "*Eternal unaging, no loss or decay.*"

"Like that!" Kask said. "Amazing. Anything new like that just fascinates kids. My girl came home and kept after me until I had to surrender. Next day I took her to the workshop and saw the fellow there."

"The Manager," Rustin said, turning the knob back and forth. He was growing frustrated with the lack of new words.

"Is that what he's called? Well, the Manager sure threw cold water on my girl's little dream. First, she was supposed to come by herself. I wasn't supposed to know about it, even though I live around the corner. Second—"

"It won't work with Yeomen."

Kask sighed. "I guess it isn't news to anybody else, but try explaining that to a twelve-year-old girl. I took her home and she cried and cried. She's been moping around to this day. And to be honest, I never could give her a good reason."

Rustin wanted Kask to be quiet. He wanted to focus on Selva, for he seemed to have broken the knob with his fiddling since no sound was coming out at all. And he was bothered by a question that wouldn't leave him alone, though it offered no words either.

"I guess you're taking me in for orientation." When Rustin didn't answer, Kask went on: "I didn't like the sound of it, that's why I didn't report. I never did do well with orders. My teacher used to call me mule head."

Rustin pictured a boy at his school desk, in uniform shorts and high-collared shirt to a chinless neck, topped by the head of a donkey with Kask's sad, benign look. The image took him straight back to the quarry.

"I've got nothing against Together," Kask said. "It sounded

fine as long as it left my family alone. But when you start separating people out after twenty years here, bringing them in to be *oriented—*"

"Stop talking, Kask," Rustin said.

"And then they don't come back."

"Just stop talking."

"Okay, doc," Kask said. "I'll stop."

At the rear of the hospital, facing the hill that led to the North Gate, there was a freight entrance for deliveries of equipment and supplies, which the public never used. The door was kept locked, but Rustin knew the combination. He followed the narrow streets behind the hospital to the freight entrance because his inability to operate Selva's Better Human and the pressure of a question that wouldn't take verbal form gave him a sense of acute vulnerability, maybe incipient madness, that he did not want to expose to Wide Awake guards, hospital staff, or Saron himself.

He parked the hauler along the hospital wall in back of a large metal trash container. Zeus sat up, ready to jump out, but Rustin didn't move from his seat. Selva was still looking at him. The steadiness of her gaze, her frozen, embryonic smile, mocked him. She was suppressing a cruel laugh that was about to animate her whole face. *Keep trying, Papa, you'll get it before you die.* He took the serrated circumference of the knob between his thumb and fingers and wound it three, four, five times. From somewhere inside her the scratchy, whirring sound started up.

"Thank God," he said, "talk to me," and he listened for her voice.

"*In fields of flowers blooming bright and fair, the nymphs dance gracefully beneath the sun. Their laughter fills the fragrant summer air, a symphony of joy that's never done.*"

He shook his head. "Where are you?" When nothing else came he turned the knob again.

"In fields of flowers blooming bright"

"No, Sel, come on. The way we talked at the campfire. 'Burn the past'—like you really feel."

"nymphs dance gracefully beneath the sun"

"No! You call this better? *That* was better."

"Inspire my words with wisdom from above"

He gripped the knob and turned it with such force that it tore loose from her neck with a snap of metal and broke off in his hand, trailed by a thin, copper wire. He pulled the wire fist over fist, and it kept coming out of her body until the coils wrapped around his arm. He seized the wire at the jagged hole in the base of her throat and tried to rip it free, but there was no end to it. He opened his door and lifted up her body and threw her out of the hauler.

Rustin got out and ran to where she had landed on her back with her legs twisted in a copper tangle. He knelt and caressed her left cheek, but its smoothness enraged him. He raised his fist to smash it.

"Go easy, doc," Kask said, wrists together, arms extended from the rail. "You did your best."

Rustin looked up and nodded, though he didn't know if it was true or what it even meant. Something in the man's doughy, mournful face calmed him and recalled him to himself, as if he were coming out of a long and vivid dream. He found that he was breathing hard, his eyes were wet, and he was pushing pieces of metal around on the pavement. And suddenly he was struck by the wrongness of the sight of a man bound to the rail like a head of cattle on a livestock truck. The man was not a head of cattle—the head was human—it was Kask's head. Rustin felt a current pass through him, the pity in the other man's eyes stirring pity in himself. He thought, *I always liked Kask. I don't know why he's here or how it all happened, but he is my brother. That's the answer, and now I can't even remember the question, so don't forget.* But within a moment he had already forgotten all of it.

"I'll be right back," Rustin said.

"I'll be here," Kask said, with a sad grin.

He must have had a plan but it seemed to come to him step by step, each one showing the way to the next. He took his pack from the hauler and strapped it on his back, then tied up the Better Human's loose wiring and swung the machine over his shoulder so that his hands were free to open the lock on the freight door. Even at an early hour this part of the hospital was normally a hive of deliverymen and staff, but the corridors were as empty as last night, until an aged orderly came out of a storeroom and seemed to recognize him. They exchanged nods, and Rustin was aware of the old man's stare at his back as he continued down the hall. Near the heart of the hospital nurses and nurse assistants appeared in and out of patient rooms, but he knew every alcove and washroom and escaped notice.

Through the examination room's window he saw that she was alone. As he approached the bed, her breathing told him she was in a deep sleep. Her red, blistered face and seared eye shocked him, but at the same time a silent voice said *Here you are*. He laid the machine beside her on the bed and tucked it in so that the blanket concealed the hole in the neck where the wires spilled out. He went around the room stuffing instruments, gloves, gauze, ointments, and medication in his pack. Then he lifted Selva from the bed, careful not to disturb her sleep or touch her wound. With a last look at the Better Human lying under the blanket, its two eyes open and staring at nothing, he carried his daughter in his arms out of the room, down the warren of halls, through the freight door to the street.

Kask and Zeus were waiting where Rustin had left them. His reappearance drew opposite reactions. Zeus began thumping his tail on the seat and then, unable to hold back, leapt out of the hauler and rose on his hind legs to lick Selva's dangling hand, while Kask's face lost its color and he uttered a groaning noise that sounded like *Yeeaawoh*.

"What happened to her?"

"I'm not going to tell you," Rustin said.

"But she's alive, thank God."

Rustin remembered what Kask was referring to. It was part of the long and vivid dream, which must contain thousands of pictures and words that would occasionally surface to haunt him for the rest of his life. But for now there was the next step.

He had learned how to pick her up and lay her down without difficulty, even in the cramped space of the hauler. He took the key from the outside pocket of his pack where he'd first stored the gun and went around to the gate, but his body was too sore and hungry and simply old to climb easily onto the bed. Kask made an instinctive move toward him, but the cuffs jerked him back. With an unashamed moan Rustin swung a leg as high as he could and hoisted himself up onto his knees. Kask watched with puzzled detachment as the metal restraints were unlocked and removed.

A missile fell out of the sky into the hauler's bed.

It landed at the back, away from the two men, but its mass and velocity were sufficient to spatter the tips of their shoes.

"What the—" Kask started to say.

Rustin understood at once and cut him off. "Get inside!"

he shouted, flashing on the sack of food that had sailed out of an upper window in an alley and hit these shoes in the same way. The mess in the bed was large and runny, but he managed to climb out without touching it. He reached up for Kask's hand, but Kask was rubbing his wrist and staring at his feet.

"Is it—"

"Yes."

"But how—"

"Hurry up, step around it. Once it's on you—like skunk spray, you'll never get clean."

"My God."

As soon as they were inside the cab with the doors closed, Selva's legs resting on Kask's thighs, another round struck the nearby pavement. Rustin shifted into the wrong gear and jolted forward into the trash container, shattering the hauler's lights. "Sorry," he muttered, but Kask hardly seemed to notice. As they backed out and sped away, the hospital wall began to take one hit after another. Rustin wondered if the Yeomen had found their true target.

It was strange to come through a zone of flying horror and find his fellow Burghers a block away patiently waiting for the tram, walking hand in hand with their children, stopping to read a sign on a lamppost as if there was no danger anywhere in the world, while an enemy army gathered outside the walls.

"Where are we going?" Kask asked.

"It'll be safer in the middle of the city."

As he drove, Rustin briefly explained what was happening. Kask listened without saying a word. Finally, he murmured, "I don't get it."

The simplicity of this remark touched Rustin. "I don't get

a lot of things about the Emergency," he said. "Maybe some historian will explain it all someday."

There was a crowd at the main entrance to the Warehouse District. Rustin couldn't tell if they were Burghers or Yeomen, but Kask said, "You'd better stop here, doc. These guys aren't in a mood to talk."

"You know them?"

"I told you. The district watch."

Rustin pulled over by the tram tracks. Kask eased himself from under Selva's legs and stepped outside. He leaned in the window. "Will she be all right?"

"I don't know, but I'm taking her home. I'll get the hauler fixed and cleaned and return it to you when I can." Kask shook his head to say that the hauler didn't matter. "What's your plan, Kask?"

He shrugged. "Some of those people want to go back to the country."

"And you?"

"Me? This is where I live." He reached with a big calloused hand for Rustin's, and they shook. Then Rustin thought of something. He took the gun from his pocket and laid the grip in Kask's palm.

"It's going to get worse before it gets better."

12

The streets to the Rowhouse District were so familiar that Rustin could have driven them blind. At last there was nothing left between him and his home and family. He had made a mostly successful effort not to imagine the moment when he would open the door with the small nail hole just above eye level and meet the faces of his wife and son. He had let them get so far away that at times it seemed his daughter was his family. He had taken her from them only to let this thing happen, and every sentence he started collapsed halfway and died of inadequacy. And yet he felt a kind of possessiveness about all that the two of them had been through together. He remembered the expression he'd put on the night he came home from the hospital in disgrace—his normal look of contentment. Pan called it his "sunrise face." It was the look of a man who would say, "That's just the way it has to be." Now the thought of it revolted him.

He turned onto the riverfront boulevard and glanced down to prepare for what Annabelle and Pan would see. Selva's eye was watching him, and her mouth was open.

"Papa," she said with a dry, clotted mouth. His heart leapt, then froze when she added: "Gard?"

He didn't have time to think of an answer, because someone screamed. Up ahead a woman at the tram stop was flailing at something around her hair. She ran blindly one way and then another, waving her arms, shaking her hands, and her screams rose to a frantic pitch. She appeared to be under attack by a swarm of wasps. Then something came flying over the tram shelter and exploded on the sidewalk, and Rustin understood that they had the city surrounded.

On the riverfront men and women were looking up at the sky. It was crowded with crisscrossing flight paths. By the stone footbridge a small child was pointing and laughing while its mother stood motionless. Two schoolgirls sprinted toward the hauler with book bags on their heads. A man with a cane fell to the ground.

Rustin accelerated around the schoolgirls, then turned so hard into the narrow street of rowhouses that the hauler went up on two wheels. He misjudged its width and scraped against their wooden fence. Before he had Selva out of the hauler, the front door flew open, and Annabelle was there in her nightdress and robe.

"No, go back!" he called. "We're coming."

Annabelle ignored him. She ran down the steps through the gate and around to his door and stopped short. Her hand flew to her mouth.

She insisted on helping him carry Selva into the house, though it was more awkward this way. He had forgotten how beautiful distress made her. He tried to meet her eyes, to learn from them who he now was or could be, but as Annabelle prepared the sofa in the front room with pillows and blankets, and knelt to hold Selva's hand, and soothed Pan's sobbing, and put on a pot of carrot soup, she avoided looking at him. In her face there was a kind of resolve, a clarity that said: *whatever comes, this is what matters*. It seemed to indict his ambitions and creeds, and he wanted to tell her, "They didn't survive out there," but she allowed no chance for intimacies. She moved about the house with practical energy, feeding Zeus, serving early lunch at the walnut table where one chair stood empty, and when she looked at him there was neither the judgment nor the forgiveness that he craved in her eyes.

"She'll stay downstairs," she told him. "Make the front room a treatment room."

"Annabelle—"

"Wash up and eat some soup. You can tell me later."

When the moment came, they were standing in the kitchen where Selva couldn't hear them. He began an account of her injury, and Annabelle listened for a minute before putting her face in her hands and turning away. The urge to tell her about Selva's courage and his own foolishness, the village trial, young Monge and the Strangers, the mysterious change at Big Cronk's farm, the animals at the quarry, the Yeoman wife and the switchgrass mother and the shitapult, the indifferent stars, the Better Human, Kask, the whole long and vivid dream, was so strong that her refusal to let him felt like a punishment.

He returned alone to the front room. "Selva! Oh God!"

His daughter was lying on the sofa as before, her open eye watching him. This was where she always used to study, and at last he saw what he had done to her. He made an effort to compose his face as he unpacked his stolen medical supplies, and cleansed the burn, and reapplied ointment.

The most immediate danger was infection. The egg-shaped blister was going down, but she would probably lose her left eye and suffer some disfigurement. He began to think through the skin graft that would be necessary to repair her face. It was impossible to know the long-term cognitive damage, but his hopes clung to the two words she'd uttered. Different shades of expression showed her awareness of each family member. She even managed a faint smile at Pan's self-aggrandizing, self-mocking tale about his day at Grandpa's and the hospital. She hadn't spoken again, but he believed, without saying so or allowing himself to be consoled, that she would come back to them.

There was plenty for him to do, yet he felt superfluous in his own home, as if he had never lived here. A small matter like how to work the tricky latch on the pantry door confused him, and he had trouble making simple decisions, such as whether to take the nap that Annabelle suggested. He kept waiting for instructions from her.

Late in the morning, he found her weeping by the sofa where Selva was asleep. When he came near, she looked up at him with unutterable reproach.

AROUND NOON THERE WAS A KNOCK AT THE FRONT DOOR. Zeus, as comfortable being home as Rustin was uneasy, sat up and barked. Rustin's first thought was that Saron had sent a Wide Awake to bring him in. He stood up from the armchair, then looked at Annabelle, who was reading aloud to Selva from her favorite collection of folktales. "Should I see who it is?" he asked.

At the door stood a pair of teenagers, a girl and a boy. The girl, who wore a set of hospital scrubs, with her ponytail coming loose and a look of apologetic fright on her round face, was his former nurse assistant, Lyra. The boy, a few years younger, a foot taller, and skeletally thin, was his former patient, the son of Kask's Yeoman friend, shot during "games." He had an arm draped over the girl's shoulder and was gasping for breath. His forehead and chin were covered in outbreaks of dry red skin.

"I'm sorry to bother you, Doctor Rustin," Lyra said. "Hello, Mrs. Rustin."

Rustin looked over his shoulder. Annabelle set the book down and said, "It's you," as if she knew the girl and might have been expecting her.

"Yes, because you said to visit if I needed anything. I'm sorry to bother, but I didn't know where to bring him because his parents are worried that he's getting weaker, his lungs are filling up, and the hospital wouldn't take him, so this morning I went to the Warehouse District and we walked here with everything going on outside—"

Rustin had never heard Lyra say so much, neither in his operating theater, in the Restoration Ring, nor at We Are One. Her acquaintance with Annabelle alarmed him, because Lyra was one of the unfinished things between him and his wife; he didn't know what might have been said, and now it was too late. But Annabelle caught his eye, raised her eyebrows, and shrugged in her way of acknowledging something slightly absurd, as if to say: *I guess we've both seen new things.* "Show them in, Hugo."

"We'll take off our shoes first," Lyra said. Rustin looked down and saw that her hospital shoes and the boy's laceless, shredding boots were stained. He closed the door behind the visitors before the house became a target. "It's really bad out there, Doctor Rustin," she said.

"What's going on?" Annabelle asked.

"It's like a war." Lyra described the terror of the air assault, the rush of armed Burgher and Stranger units to the North and South Gates, the roundup of Yeomen at orientation sites, the conscription of cleanup brigades. The most dangerous part of the city was the Warehouse District, which was why they had such trouble getting to the Rustin rowhouse.

"Did you know about this?" Annabelle asked her husband. She had turned pale.

Rustin briefly explained what he had heard at the switchgrass settlement, but no one seemed able to grasp what he was saying. "Is it happening on our street?" he asked Lyra.

"Stopped," the boy wheezed. His open mouth stank, revealing bloody gums and black gaps between his loose teeth.

"Sit down," Rustin said. "Take off your jacket. Let me look at you."

The boy's long, wasted frame sank into the armchair. The eyes that had pleaded with Rustin on the operating table now watched him nervously. With a pilfered stethoscope he listened to the liquid chest, and by the light of the torch he examined the rotting mouth and the face rash. He gave the boy Selva's book. "Can you lift this above your head?" The boy raised the book a few inches before his arm collapsed into his lap. Rustin looked under his shirt and studied the surgery scars. At least those were healing as they should.

"I don't know what's wrong with him," Lyra said.

"Scurvy," Rustin said. "Vitamin deficiency. We don't see it often here. What are you eating?"

The family was subsisting on potatoes and turnips. Everything else in Warehouse District markets cost too much with the blockade of produce trucks. Yeomen were starving Yeomen.

The boy was looking at Selva, and her eye was looking back at him. "Who in the world did that to you?"

Rustin almost said, "Your friends," but he stopped himself. The boy was his patient again, and this gave him something to do—this was what he would do. "He should stay here a few days, don't you think?" Rustin said to Annabelle, who was returning from the kitchen with a bowl of carrot soup for the boy.

She nodded. "We can put him upstairs with Pan."

Lyra was lingering by her former chief surgeon. He understood that she wanted to be helpful, and he asked her to sterilize his instruments in hot water.

In the middle of the afternoon Rustin announced that he was going to take a quick walk around the neighborhood and see if anyone needed first aid. Pan, who was showing Lyra his collection of dead caterpillars, jumped to his feet. "I'm going, too." Rustin looked at Annabelle, and she looked at Pan, who looked at Lyra and said, "I've gotten older since Papa went away." With Annabelle's permission father and son went out together carrying umbrellas.

The hauler was gone, again. In his hurry Rustin had left the key inside. He felt a twinge of regret, but Kask would have more serious things on his hands. The street and the sky were empty. The Rowhouse District had no obvious strategic value—it just happened to be close to the city walls—but the Yeomen had done their work. The sidewalk was hit especially hard, and he took Pan's hand to lead him out onto the street, but Pan pulled away. At first Rustin thought it was done in anger, but he saw how his son walked on ahead with a deliberate stride, looking right and left like a young soldier inspecting the ruins of a battlefield, and he realized that Pan was letting his father know he was no longer the little boy he'd left behind four days ago.

From the riverfront boulevard came a rasping noise of metal on pavement or stone. At the corner half a dozen men in blue jumpsuits were standing around smoking while two others scraped the street with shovels. When Rustin and Pan appeared, the smokers threw away their cigarettes and went back to work, which was shoveling shit and dumping it in a trash barrel. Rustin looked around for a Wide Awake guard. Then he noticed that the Yeomen shovelers, like the Strangers in the quarry, were chained by the ankles.

A well-dressed woman was sitting on a nearby bench, and for some reason she was sobbing.

The scene on the riverfront was far worse than the Rustins' street. A few pedestrians were walking in the middle of the boulevard, too dazed to notice where they stepped. The windows of the bakery where he used to pick up pastries on weekend mornings were coated in filth, and so was the wall of the shop where he bought his cigars. Across from the footbridge a few feet of tram tracks looked impassable. Zeus's favorite sniffing ground around a plane tree was humanly bespattered. These places to which Rustin had never given thought because they were the little things of ordinary life—all marked for desecration. It would take a platoon of shovelers a day and a night to dig out the Rowhouse District, and even that wouldn't be enough. It would never be the same. The city by the river was no longer his city.

He was overcome with sadness. This wasn't a divine plague like an earthquake, or a remote event like an empire's collapse. It was done by human hands, by people he knew, and the ruin was so total that neither Burgher nor Yeoman hands were clean. He, too, must have played a part. He had killed a boy, and failed to save another boy, and put his daughter in harm's way. He had lost the hospital forever.

He would have to start over again, without a guild or title or creed, with only this human stuff—water, protein, and love. He would still be Annabelle's husband, Selva and Pan's father. But what was left for him to give his children? This ground, this sky.

The woman on the bench kept sobbing.

Pan moved next to his father, and Rustin felt a hand reach for his. "What's happened, Papa?"

He pretended to scan the riverfront, but in fact he was thinking, *I must get to know him better.*

"It seems we've lost our minds, Pan."

"That's what Mama said."

"When did she say that?"

"When you were away, after we saw Grandpa. Grandpa said Yeomen are solid people, but Selva said they're man-eaters. Is that boy with bad breath a Yeoman?"

"I think so, but we should try not to think about him that way."

"They're the ones that hurt Selva!"

Rustin saw the animals at the quarry and had to push away the urge to shoot them all. "He didn't do it."

"Aren't we having a war?"

He squeezed Pan's hand. "I'm afraid so."

"What are we going to do?"

Because Rustin did not have an answer, he approached the bench where the well-dressed woman was wiping her cheeks with a lace handkerchief. He asked if she wanted a cup of tea.

She turned up her raw, swollen-lipped face. "What?" She didn't seem to understand the question. "Please leave me alone." She went back to the comfort and anonymity of her handkerchief.

"Do you know her?" Pan asked as they carefully made their way along the riverfront boulevard. Rustin shook his head. "Why did you talk to her?"

"Because she's unhappy."

Yeoman crews were shoveling and wiping down the tram stop. A man walking his dog paused to hurl the vilest curses at them. Pan could no longer stand to breathe and asked to go home. That was when a pair of vehicles blew past in the direction of the South Gate.

Both were haulers, and Rustin knew from the broken headlights that the one trailing was Kask's. At the wheel of each was a Wide Awake in uniform, and in the beds, crammed together so that there was hardly room to move, were men and women with weapons of various types—nail-studded clubs, metal rods, even crudely sharpened sticks. Those in the first hauler looked like city Burghers. The ones in the second were clearly Strangers, and all the way in back, holding his stick in a death grip and staring at the fouled street, was Mr. Monge. When his eyes met Rustin's, their terror vanished for an instant, and he waved.

THROUGHOUT THE AFTERNOON THERE WERE KNOCKS ON THE door, each one greeted by Zeus. Rustin and Selva's arrival, and then Lyra and the boy's, seemed to summon the city. First came Iver and his Wide Awake commander. At the door they told Annabelle that they were doing house checks, making sure district residents had what they needed. "Yes, I've seen you watching our street," Annabelle said. Over her shoulder the commander was examining the front room in a way that suggested investigation more than assistance. "Please come in." Annabelle opened the door wide, and the commander stepped inside, followed by Iver, who stopped short when he saw the room before him.

It smelled of rubbing alcohol and soup. The doctor, who was still technically under arrest, was using a cotton ball to clean the gums of a sick boy in an armchair. A small collection of bloody cotton lay on a plate at the doctor's feet.

A girl in hospital scrubs was standing next to the armchair, holding a bowl of steaming water. Another girl, Iver's former classmate, was lying on a sofa, head propped on a pillow, the wound he had seen on her face last night now glistening with some ointment, and a patch of gauze covering her left eye. A young boy was sitting cross-legged on the floor beside the sofa, pausing for a moment at the visitors' arrival before continuing to read aloud from a book. The dog who came to the door to bark had returned to lie down by the boy.

"You never went back to the hospital," the commander told Rustin.

"I thought I'd be more useful here."

"Where's the man you were sent to bring in?"

He held out his hands to show that he didn't know. She seemed uncertain what to do next, and perhaps her hesitation emboldened Iver to take initiative for the first time in his life. He told Annabelle, who was still by the door, to let them know if the family needed anything, since the fighting was getting worse near their neighborhood. Then he thanked her and turned to leave, and with a last look around the room his commander followed him out.

At sunset a tall, gangly girl with a boy's haircut appeared at the door. The upper arm of her Wide Awake blouse was slashed, its sleeve soaked and dark with blood. When Rustin cut away the material, he found a deep wound, almost to bone, that must have been made by an ax or machete. The girl was too woozy to say much, except that she had been defending the South Gate, and there was no way to get to the hospital, and someone had pointed to this house as a place where they were still opening the door. Annabelle seemed to know this girl, too. Rustin let her in.

By now the front room was getting crowded. The Yeoman

boy with scurvy was led upstairs to Pan's bedroom, and the Wide Awake girl took his place in the armchair. Her cut would have to be closed. After scrubbing at the kitchen sink, Lyra held the instruments on a dinner plate while Rustin cleansed and sutured the wound. He found that the circle of his concern had shrunk from humanity, the empire, and the city to the people in this room.

It was a long night. At one point the shouting outside grew so close to the house that everyone stopped what they were doing and fell silent. Then came a gunshot. The only conceivable weapons were Rustin's garden tools in the backyard shed. He was kneeling by the armchair, holding a hemostat. Annabelle had just come in from the kitchen, where she was boiling water for tea. Their eyes met and they waited for more shots. None came; the shouting died away. There was another knock at the door. They went on looking at each other, and his long acquaintance with her face allowed him to imagine her thoughts. Something was ending, and they were too old to understand. What came after would belong to their children. But they would go on opening the door, and in this way they would live.

Acknowledgments

My thanks to Mitzi Angel and Sarah Chalfant for giving this novel the wisdom and support it needed. Thanks to Ayad Akhtar, Emma Chuck, Bryan Garsten, Morten Jensen, Rob and Heather Kitchen, Mark Lilla, Dr. Panagiotis Manolas, Brian Morton, Rebecca Nagel, Alex Star, and Thomas Williams for their generous help. My gratitude and love to Nancy Packer (1925–2025), who set the example; to Charlie and Julia Packer, now old enough to be my collaborators; and to Laura Secor, my compass in writing and in life.

A NOTE ABOUT THE AUTHOR

George Packer is an award-winning author and a staff writer at *The Atlantic*. He has written many books, including *The Unwinding: An Inner History of the New America* (winner of the National Book Award) and, most recently, *Last Best Hope: America in Crisis and Renewal*. He is also the author of two previous novels and a play, and is the editor of a two-volume edition of the essays of George Orwell.